"*The Last Collection* is a skillful weave of compelling characters grappling for both fortune and affirmation, and is set against a vivid backdrop— first the glittering cosmos of Paris fashion, then the hardships of World War II, and then the remains of beauty after war. Beautiful prose and imagery enrich every page. Mackin is an insightful, engaging story- teller."　　　　　　　　　　—Susan Meissner, author of *The Last Year of the War*

"Jeanne Mackin takes the reader on an enthralling journey, complete with such vivid descriptions of the clothing, you can practically see them on the page. Beautifully rendered and meticulously researched, *The Last Collection* is a must-read."

　　　　　　　　　　—Renée Rosen, author of *Park Avenue Summer*

"Chanel is all pearls and clean lines; Schiaparelli is bold color and invention. . . . By turns fascinating and tense, *The Last Collection* is a colorful and evocative novel about the price of loyalty."

　　　　　　　　　　—Heather Webb, international bestselling coauthor of
　　　　　　　　　　Meet Me in Monaco

"An exceedingly well-dressed historical catfight."　　　　—Bookstr

"*The Last Collection* is more than a good story. It is a consideration of love, work, and art; war, freedom, and memory."　　　　—BookTrib

"An in-depth tale of an enchanting, dangerous, and fascinating time period in Paris. Mackin's attention to detail and lyrical prose bring Chanel and Schiaparelli to life in a gorgeous and riveting manner."

　　　　　　　　　　—She Reads

ALSO BY JEANNE MACKIN

THE
LAST COLLECTION

• • •

JEANNE MACKIN

BERKLEY
NEW YORK

BERKLEY
An imprint of Penguin Random House LLC
penguinrandomhouse.com

Copyright © 2019 by Jeanne Mackin
Readers Guide copyright © 2019 by Jeanne Mackin
Penguin Random House supports copyright. Copyright fuels creativity, encourages
diverse voices, promotes free speech, and creates a vibrant culture. Thank you for buying
an authorized edition of this book and for complying with copyright laws by not
reproducing, scanning, or distributing any part of it in any form without permission.
You are supporting writers and allowing Penguin Random House to continue to publish
books for every reader.

BERKLEY and the BERKLEY & B colophon are registered trademarks of
Penguin Random House LLC.

ISBN: 9780399585906

The Library of Congress has catalogued the Berkley hardcover edition of this book as follows:

Names: Mackin, Jeanne, author.
Title: The last collection: a novel of Elsa Schiaparelli and Coco Chanel / Jeanne Mackin.
Description: First edition. | New York, NY: Berkley, 2019.
Identifiers: LCCN 2018043153 | ISBN 9781101990544 (hardback) |
ISBN 9781101990551 (ebook)
Subjects: LCSH: Chanel, Coco, 1883–1971—Fiction. | Schiaparelli, Elsa,
1890–1973—Fiction. | BISAC: FICTION / Biographical. | FICTION /
Contemporary Women. | GSAFD: Biographical fiction.
Classification: LCC PS3563.A3169 L37 2019 | DDC 813/.54—dc23
LC record available at https://lccn.loc.gov/2018043153

Berkley hardcover edition / June 2019
Berkley trade paperback edition / August 2020

Printed in the United States of America
1   3   5   7   9   10   8   6   4   2

Cover art: image of Eiffel Tower by f11photo/Shutterstock;
image of woman walking by Ildiko Neer / Arcangel
Cover design by Rita Frangie
Book design by Kristin del Rosario
Interior art: art nouveau pattern by Curly Pat / Shutterstock.com

For Steve

The fashion world is no place for timid dedicated souls; it is a field for strong, determined egotists who have an innate desire to impose their wills on the world—wills of iron disguised in rustling silks and beautiful colors.

—BETTINA BALLARD

I am not a heroine. But I have chosen the person I wanted to be and am. Too bad if I am disliked and unpleasant.

—COCO CHANEL

Fantasy is a flower that does not flourish on passivity. Determination is what it needs.

—ELSA SCHIAPARELLI

THE LAST COLLECTION

PART ONE

BLUE

. . .

Of the three primary colors, blue is most suggestive of paradox: it is the color of longing and sadness, and yet it is also the color of joy and fulfillment. On a ship, at night, blue water merges into blue sky, so blue is the color of places with no borders, no edges.

If you throw salt into a fire, the flames will burn blue. Salt rubbed into a wound renews the pain, intensifies it. Seeing others kiss and embrace was salt in my wound, a blue flame burning the length of me.

Blue best represents the contradictions of the heart, the need to be loved and cherished at the same time that we wish for freedom.

Blue, the color of the Worth gown that the little girl Elsa Schiaparelli found in her Roman piazza attic, the color of the covers of the penny romances Coco Chanel found in the orphanage attic.

Blue is what made Elsa Schiaparelli's daring color, shocking pink, so special: it is pink infused with blue, turning a demure blush into an electric surge. Schiaparelli turned girlish pink into the color of seduction by adding that touch of blue.

And always, there is the blue of the Paris sky on a June day.

Listen. I'm going to tell you a story about fashion, and politics. And, of course, about love. The three primaries, like the primary colors.

· ONE ·

"For you." Liz, the gallery assistant, handed me the telegram. Pale blue paper, bold blue lettering. I turned it over and over in my hands. During the war we had learned to dread telegrams. The war was over and whoever was coming home was already there, but dread remained, the fear of again reading those words, "We regret to inform you . . ."

"Aren't you going to open it?" she asked.

"Of course." I hesitated. The only people I loved, those still left to me, were just a few blocks away, downtown. No telegram would be needed if something had happened to them; they were a local telephone call away. *Open it*, I ordered myself.

I sat on a packing crate and tore at the paper with my chipped fingernails, reminding myself that sometimes telegrams carried good news. It was possible.

The message was brief. *Come to Paris. Need to see you.* Signed, *Schiap.*

Elsa Schiaparelli. Of course she would send a telegram instead of making a transatlantic phone call. It wasn't the expense of the call but one of her many phobias and superstitions: she hated telephones. All the noise of the Madison Avenue gallery, the hammering, the whir of measuring tapes, the scraping of ladders being pushed across the floor, fell away. New York dissolved, and I was in Paris again.

I closed my eyes and remembered the accordion player on the corner of rue Saint-Honoré playing "Parlez-moi d'Amour," the throaty laugh of Schiap as she shared a bit of gossip with her assistant, Bettina. Usually, it had been gossip about Coco Chanel, her archrival. Charlie, handsome in his tuxedo, blond bombshell Ania turning heads in the Ritz bar. The taste of strong *café*, the smell of yeasty bread, the colors, the gleam of the Eiffel Tower, the medieval miracles of rose windows in the churches.

How long had it been? I'd been twenty-five when I met Schiap in Paris. She'd been forty-eight, only nine years older than I was now. And I had thought of her as old, though she never had. "Women don't age if their clothes stay new," she had told me once. "Grown women must never dress childishly, but neither should they accept age as inevitable. It is not, not in fashion."

After the war Schiap and I had gone separate ways, eager to get on with our lives, to return to what had been interrupted, to try to find what had been lost. Of course, there is no going back. Time is an arrow that flies forward, not back. I'd learned that particular lesson well. Too much looking over the shoulder turns you to salt, like Lot's wife, salt which burns blue.

Even so, why did Schiap "need" to see me? Why not just "want" or even demand, as she was known to do? There had usually been a bit of drama in her messages, a bit of the self-importance and self-absorption often found in the personalities of the very driven, the very successful. She'd earned that drama, the very famous, some would say infamous, Elsa Schiaparelli, designer of the most beautiful, and sometimes most bizarre, women's clothing ever worn.

"Bad news?" The assistant put down the wooden frame she was carrying.

"No. I don't know what it's about," I said, folding up the telegram and putting it in my pocket. "Just from an old friend. In Paris."

She gave an exaggerated sigh of relief. Mr. Rosenberg's gallery employee was a caring person, likely to give you a hug for no reason, to hold your hand if she suspected you'd had bad news. I liked that quality in her, and I liked how her hands, pale and slender, reminded me of Ania.

"Paris. I'd love to go there some day. You've been, haven't you?"

"Yes. I've been." Oh, how I had been. "We're just about done. Can we call it quits for today?" I needed to think about that telegram, to decide.

"But the show has to be hung by Monday." She looked more worried than ever. It was my first show in the famous Rosenberg gallery and was not to be taken lightly. I had been in several group exhibits, and even sold some paintings, but if this show was well received . . . well. I'd be successfully on my way.

Liz looked at the telegram I was still holding. "Okay," she agreed.

"We can finish tomorrow. Go. Go home." And that was what Schiap had said to me once, years ago. Life was breaking into repetitive refrains, pulling me back.

The echo of her words didn't startle me, though. It was the echoed action of opening a telegram and reading those words that had. *Come to Paris. Need to see you.* Exactly what my brother, Charlie, had written sixteen years ago.

Of course I would go. Impossible not to, in both cases. As Liz began to clean up, I found a scrap of paper and began the list-making needed for any complicated journey made during a busy time. I'd stay for my opening reception, and then I'd take an airplane to Paris. An airplane! Before the war, the ocean had been busy with steamers to-ing and fro-ing; now, people traveled by air. It was cheaper. It was faster. Schiap had been one of the first to fly transatlantic, had loved the possibility of being in Paris for breakfast on Monday and New York for breakfast on Tuesday.

Liz folded the stepladder and gave me another concerned look over her spectacles, always worn low on her nose, the way Coco Chanel wore hers when she thought no one was looking. Outside the gallery window, Madison Avenue throbbed with life. New York had recovered from the war. The shelves in the neighborhood delis were full; the window displays at Bonwit Teller, Macy's, and Henri Bendel were opulent. The city was stronger than ever, like a flu patient who wakes up to find himself healthier for having spent a few days in bed.

The children out walking with their mothers or nannies that day were well-fed, rosy-cheeked in their winter hats and mittens; the women were dressed in their new postwar coats and dresses, mostly Dior and Dior knockoffs; the New Look, the yards of fabric in the full skirts speaking of wealth and prosperity, the pinched-in waists making women ultrafeminine once again.

The Madison Avenue women looked so gay in their new clothes, the fashions meant to restore the world to glory, or at least to normalcy. Schiap had taught me that. Clothes aren't just clothes. They are moods, desires, the quality of our souls and our dreams made visible. The female shape morphs into the dreams and hopes of a generation. Clothes are alchemy, the philosopher's stone, my friend Schiap would have said. The second skin, the chosen skin, the transforming art we wear on our backs.

During the war women were filling shells in ammunitions factories, spending lonely nights on top of skyscrapers listening for the angry growl of Messerschmitts. Perhaps they nursed the wounded at Normandy or the Ardennes. But that was over. Women were staying home, making families. New York was full of babies and strollers, and thanks to the new bras, women's bosoms were as full and pointed as weaponry.

Every once in a while a different kind of woman would pass by the window with an expression in her eyes that made me wince: loss, the kind that paints permanent blue shadows around the eyes. My face had looked like that, during the war, after I'd opened my *We regret to inform you . . .* telegram.

I watched out the gallery window until Liz came out from the back room, jangling the door keys. The next time I stood and stared out a window the view would be of Place Vendôme, not Madison Avenue, the view outside Schiap's boutique, that elegant, glorious circle of Paris where Napoleon stood guard on top of his tall colonnade. Napoleon and all his little soldiers. Except Charlie wouldn't be there. And Ania . . . so many wouldn't be there.

Okay, Schiap. Let's hear what you have to say. Maybe she had some gossip about Coco Chanel, her old enemy? The thought made me smile. It would be like the old days, full of malice and fun. No. It wouldn't be. Nothing would ever again be like the old days. And then I thought of even older days, the long sad days before I had met Schiap, when, young as I was, I thought my life was already over.

England, 1938

There are moments of convergence in life when the stars align just so. Every mundane detail, from the burnt morning toast to the ladder in your new stockings, when the universe itself becomes a question demanding an answer. The answer will decide the rest of your life. Stay. Or go.

That moment, for me, occurred on June 6, 1938.

"Telegram for you," said Gerald, the school physician, my supervisor, once my brother-in-law. By then, we had both said farewell to any family relationship, to anything other than stiff greetings, cold nods of the chin as we passed each other in the school halls or met to discuss work.

The telegram on his desk was from France, and it had already been

opened. Since I worked for the school, Gerald assumed any correspon-
dence sent to me would be about a work matter and he could read it.
He was wrong this time.

"From your brother," he added. He didn't hand it to me. I had to
reach over, pick it up from his desk.

> *Come to Paris. I need to see you. Arrived from Boston,*
> *here for the summer. Meet me at Café les Deux Magots.*
> *June 9. Two pm. Charlie.*

I read it twice, then folded it and put it into my pocket.

"You won't go, of course," Gerald said, looking up from his folder
of medical charts. "To see your brother." His glance was icy. I didn't
blame him for this, nor was I surprised. If the situation were reversed,
if I thought Gerald was responsible for the death of my brother, I'd give
him the same look, even worse, a dragon look, a dragon breath to incin-
erate.

"I won't?" I said.

"Classes aren't finished. The term hasn't ended."

"Of course," I said. "Here are the notes for the week." I kept notes
on the girls who took my art classes, especially those who had been ill,
and Gerald, as school physician, read them dutifully. The boarding
school had a reputation, an excellent one, of educating and caring for
exceptional girls, especially those with serious and long-term health
problems. There were several recovering polio victims, young girls
with uncertain steps who needed daily therapy and exercise, and a girl
with a stutter so severe she could barely speak. At the school, they were
able to receive treatment while also living a social life with other girls
their age.

Keeping the notes on the students was part of my contract with the
school. Free room and board and a decent if not generous salary in
exchange. It had seemed a suitable arrangement two years ago, after

Allen's funeral, when I had no idea of where and how I was to live. The school's offer of employment had seemed an answer of sorts. And it meant I could stay where I had been happy with Allen.

Passing on those notes had come to feel like a betrayal to my students, a breaking of confidence. Art begins as a private exploration of dreams and desires and should be kept private till the artist deems it is ready to be shown. My notes to Gerald betrayed those secrets I discerned in the paintings and in our classroom conversations. What about those dark places that we need to keep for ourselves, those mysterious shadows where others couldn't intrude with their *should*s and *should not*s, their Freudian theories and respectable dictates?

Florrie, a quiet girl with red braids, had confessed yesterday to sketching a nude male but had torn it up before anyone could see it. *Next time*, I told her, *let me see it first.* Hands and feet are difficult, all the bones, tendons. The other parts are actually rather easy. Look at Michelangelo's statues. Simple geometry. Florrie, intelligent girl that she was, had the sense not to giggle. She'd be married in a few years. A mother soon after, a busy, responsible woman with a trunk in the attic full of her unused art materials.

"The notes seem a little brief this week," Gerald said, still not looking at me.

"There wasn't much to write." I certainly wasn't about to reveal Florrie's growing curiosity about the male physique. "Miserable weather, isn't it?" Rain pelted at the windows, running down in sad rivulets. *Not go to Paris? When Charlie has asked me to come see him?*

"Good for the gardens." Gerald studied the neatly arranged papers on his desk, pushing and sorting in a way that indicated this meeting was over.

"So much green," I said.

Green is a secondary color made by mixing yellow and blue. Blue for sky, yellow for sun; *chloros*, or green, in nature. And that's the problem: only the true greens of nature look believable. All other greens look what they are: imitation. Green is unreliable. There are so many wrong greens, greens where the yellow is too dominant, making a sickly tint like a fading bruise, or greens where the blue is too dark, making the green look like a storm cloud over an angry ocean. To me, only when green is accented with black does it look authentic in a painting, black pigment made from burnt bones. Fire. So much of life is about fire and destruction.

"Travel is very difficult these days," Gerald said. "All those Austrian refugees clamoring at the embassies."

The sad clock ticked. Footsteps rushed down the hall, one of the girls late for her class. I studied the pattern in the worn carpet, torn between obeying Gerald and my duty to the school, and a growing desire to see Charlie. It had been a long time.

Gerald looked up, and I could see in his face that awful puzzlement: *Why is she alive, when my brother is dead?* It was my fault, and it was unforgivable. I agreed.

I ate boiled beef and greens with the students and other faculty in the dining hall that night, and then went to my studio. I hadn't painted since the accident, since Allen's death. Colors defied me, wouldn't come true. I would try a study in blue, but when it dried it would be gray, only gray, and I didn't know if it was my vision that had changed or the paints themselves. It was like a singer losing her voice, knowing what the notes are but not being able to replicate them. Death can do that, make reality as hard to hold on to as water dripping through your fingers.

That night I tried to size a canvas, just to see if I could still do it. It felt important not to lose the craft of painting, even if the art of it eluded me. The schoolgirls were at a dance in the great hall, drinking pineapple punch and pretending, as Allen and I had, that they were somewhere else, somewhere festive and gay. I could hear the gramophone, a Freddy Martin song, "April in Paris."

One of Allen's favorite songs. I was so distracted I applied the glue too thickly and ruined the linen. I decided not to try a second one. Why waste school supplies? I turned off the lights, locked up the room, and crossed the graveled courtyard to my little bedroom over the school garages. It smelled of gasoline, but I had my own entrance, a modicum of privacy. An owl hooted. Somewhere in the fields beyond the manicured lawns a fox barked, a rabbit screamed. Life and death in the peaceful English countryside.

I listened to creeping darkness, a light patter of rain on the roof. What if I did go to Paris and see Charlie? I dared a brief moment of happiness. And there it was, a pale blue rising in me out of the gray, not quite joy, but something close to it. Anticipation.

I hadn't seen my brother since my husband's funeral. Charlie had wanted to visit, but I always said no. I did not want consolation or reminiscing about earlier times. I wanted to be alone with the heartbreak.

My father had been a physician famous for his treatments of skin grafting during World War I. After he and my mother died of the Spanish flu, Charlie and I were taken in by my father's sister. I was five, Charlie only three. He barely remembered them, so during our childhood I would make little sketches of Momma and Poppa from my own memories to share with Charlie, so that he would know them, at least through my own memories. Art can do that, save the best of the past for us.

Aunt Irene had married a man who owned the northeast franchise of the Fuller Brush Company, but they were childless. Their parenting style required that we be fed, housed, and educated but never coddled, so Charlie and I grew completely dependent on each other, two primary colors not needing a third to be complete.

After I finished high school my aunt and uncle supported me through a year of studies at the Art Students League. I exhibited one small oil, a portrait, in a minor exhibition in a small downtown gallery, and thought I was on my way to a career—but when I was nineteen Aunt Irene said, "Enough! You can't be a student forever!" She offered to "finish" me with a trip to Paris for a month. I wouldn't go unless Charlie came with me.

That was in August of 1933, when, after the crash, a Hooverville appeared behind the Metropolitan Museum on Fifth Avenue, tin and cardboard shanties in straggling rows of the newly homeless. In Paris money stretched further—whenever my aunt said that, I imagined bills and coins of rubber, stretching like broken hairbands. We shopped, dined, walked in the parks. When my aunt was resting in the hot afternoons, Charlie and I went to the Louvre.

And one day, when I went to revisit the *Mona Lisa*, a young Englishman, tweedy and polite, was sitting there, on what I thought of by then as my bench. He looked straight ahead at the *Mona Lisa* in front of him, and the ginger color of his hair and mustache, the sharp line of his nose, reminded me of one of Renoir's early self-portraits. Say what you will of the cloying sweetness of some of his subject matter, Renoir knew how to use color.

The Englishman rose gallantly and offered to share the bench. "Allen Sutter," he said, taking my hand. That single touch, a warm grasp, and I felt I had been jolted awake from a deep sleep.

"Lily Cooper, and my brother, Charlie."

The three of us sat down and pretended to study the *Mona Lisa*, but all the while I was giving Allen sideways glances and he was returning them. He was thin and tall, and his eyes were very dark brown, not the pale gray that often goes with red hair. Unusual coloring that made me want to try a portrait of him. And then I wondered what it would be like to kiss him, to hold him.

Why him? It was the time, the place, and there was a sparkle in his dark eyes that made me want to make him laugh. *Coup de foudre*, the French call it, the lightning strike. Love is partly what we feel about the other person and partly how that other person makes us feel about ourselves. With Allen, from our first meeting, I felt confident and as pretty as a girl in one of Watteau's paintings of country courtships.

THE LAST COLLECTION   13 •

After that initial encounter, for the next two weeks, we met at the Louvre every afternoon, when my aunt was napping.

When Aunt Irene did finally return to New York in September, I didn't go with her, insisting that I was going to stay in Paris and study art there.

She peered hard at me when I told her. "If I hear so much as a whisper of misbehaving, your allowance will be cut off and you will return immediately to New York," she said. "Do you understand?" Charlie studied the ceiling and gave me a little poke in the ribs.

When Charlie hugged me good-bye at the pier, just before he boarded, I had my first and only moment of doubt. We had never been separated before. "Don't behave," he whispered. "Have fun."

Three months later, Allen and I were married in a civil ceremony at the Mairie de Paris. *Well, I suppose you are "finished" now*, my aunt wrote, when I sent her a telegram announcing my marriage. *Try and be happy. You'll find it's not as easy as it seems. Good luck, and love. Fingers crossed.*

Allen and I spent our honeymoon in a Left Bank one-room studio, eating bread and cheese and rarely rising from the mattress we had put on the floor. We were young and so delighted with each other we couldn't imagine needing anything else. In that first year I didn't even miss my brother, who had begun medical studies in Boston. Allen was lighthearted and full of practical jokes, a perfect antidote to my somber childhood, his sunny yellow next to my gray-blue. He once taught children in our apartment building how to fill water balloons and drop them from the roof, a morning's work that did not endear us to others in the neighborhood. He was playful, and passionate in our lovemaking, teaching me the delights the flesh could provide, the way colors burst upon closed eyelids in ecstasy.

Allen was a math tutor who helped students prepare for the difficult *baccalauréat* exam, and I received my allowance—it was to continue until my twenty-first birthday—so we made do for an entire year in Paris, with the mattress on the floor and a single cooking ring smuggled into the room. But one morning the silly jokes were gone and he was serious. When I asked what was wrong, he said that it was time to plan for the future. "I have to provide for you," he said. "And there may be children, you know."

Children. Believe it or not, I hadn't even thought of that, hadn't realized that there could be even more love in the world than I already had. "Children," I repeated. "Lovely. Let's practice."

His brother, Gerald, got him a job as math teacher at the girls' boarding school outside London, where Gerald was resident physician. Newly serious, somewhat reluctantly, we left Paris and went to damp, cold England. As much as I had grown to love Paris, I didn't mind, because I was with Allen. We were a universe of two. A quiet universe of two, still waiting for my first pregnancy to happen, when two years later I, still waiting for motherhood and bored of so much countryside, begged Allen to go to a dance in town with me.

He was tired and wanted to stay in. He already had his slippers on, his pipe lighted, a pile of algebra tests on the table, waiting for grading. "Come with me," I pleaded. And he did.

If I had known then how easily, how quickly, total destruction could arrive around the next bend in the road, I would have locked him in his room, like a treasure, and me there, locked in with him.

Instead, I killed him. I was driving, and I hit ice on the road and barreled into a tree. A brief memory of screams, and when I woke up, in the hospital, Charlie was there, trying to comfort me, to calm me, to rouse me back to life, but not even Charlie could do that. My universe had collapsed, because Allen had died in the crash.

After the funeral, I sent Charlie back to Boston, to his medical studies. Gerald, my brother-in-law, told me to stay at the school as long as I needed; he would move me to a smaller room, a room for one person, a widow's room. My punishment, and I accepted it, wanted it. Gerald never looked me in the eyes again.

———————

B ut now Paris, the city where I had fallen in love with Allen, was calling me again. Paris, and Charlie—I wanted to see them. Both of them. I wanted to take a deep breath, to walk on city streets, to have even a small vacation from misery, from the constant ache for Allen.

I found a scrap of paper and began making a list of what I would need to pack.

T wo days after receiving Charlie's telegram, Gerald drove me to the train station. I had given the girls a final evaluation, turned in my paperwork, and ended the semester early. Gerald was furious, and I could see in his face that he wished I would lose my passport in Paris, that I would never return, never stand before him again, reminding him. I was alive. His brother wasn't.

When I arrived at the Gare du Nord the next day, it was a sunny June afternoon, and the cavernous station was busy with girls in summer frocks, *les hommes d'affaires* with their briefcases and rolled-up shirtsleeves, younger men sitting at the buffet tables drinking coffee and watching the crowd, looking for a specific face or perhaps any pretty face. I found a cab on rue de Dunkerque and went to meet Charlie, my little brother.

He wasn't at Café les Deux Magots when I arrived, still a little sick from the Channel crossing and train ride. I checked the telegram— correct time, correct place. Charlie was late. This was unlike him, good, responsible Charlie, but it was spring and Paris and I decided not to worry, to take in my surroundings, to observe how the Parisian women sat in their chairs, how they tilted their heads to the side, lifted their coffee cups with their hands wrapped possessively around them, women with the colorful frocks and dark eyes that Matisse painted.

Saint-Germain-des-Prés was busy and the café crowded. All the tables huddled under the faded awning or sprawled into the street were occupied and the air was thick with the hum of conversation, the chink of coffee spoons against china, and occasional bursts of laughter. When the café door swung wide I could see the two brightly painted Chinese figurines posed atop pillars that gave the café its name. The mandarins looked very contented, those two, subdued and self-possessed, as if nothing could startle them.

Sunlight gilded the pavement and the gray façades of the buildings across the street. A ginger cat strutted past, his back arched high, sniffing his way toward the fishmonger's shop. Schoolchildren in blues and plaids, a fruit seller with trays of oranges and apples and grapes—a rainbow, all in one place.

The sky was the shade of blue that Rossetti had used for the sky in *Dantis Amor*. I wasn't a fan of the ethereal pre-Raphaelites, but when their colors appear in a real sky the effect is fabulous.

"Another coffee?" The waiter hovered over me, formal in black trousers, with a white towel tied around his waist. I tapped the paperback spread-eagled on my table, pretending I was preoccupied, though I hadn't read a single word since I had sat down a half hour earlier.

"Yes, please."

He squinted and leaned a little toward me. "Perhaps an aperitif as well? A Pernod?"

I shook my head. "Just coffee, please."

A group of boys wearing new khaki-green French army uniforms took the table next to me. Two and a half million young Frenchmen had been put into uniform that year, according to the BBC. Yet we all hoped, still believed, there would be no war. Roosevelt said so, over and over in his fireside chats.

It was a warm day, so the newly conscripted young soldiers had taken off their berets and neatly folded them into their front pockets, making sure the golden anchor, the army symbol, glinted visibly and brightly.

I could tell from the loudness of their comments about the menu and their field training that they were trying to impress me. One of them, the tallest, most handsome one, winked at me. I frowned and looked away.

Opposite me, a table with four young German soldiers, dashing in their tall black boots and fitted uniforms, made sideways glances at the passing girls and whispered together the way boys do, ignoring the curious, sometimes hostile glances of the older people at the café, some of whom would remember Verdun, the Somme, the other bloody battles of World War I.

In March, Germany had annexed Austria, but many people thought they had been within their rights to take back territory that had once been theirs. And if Hitler was running amok in Germany, that was their problem, not ours. So we thought. That was the time, the brief time, when French and German soldiers could still sit peacefully opposite each other in a café.

At the table on my other side a young couple sat, staring into each other's eyes, oblivious to everything and everyone around them. Birds sang. An occasional breeze stirred the scalloped awning, making it snap like a sail. Happiness lapped at me like waves at the shore, but I was separate from it, the way water and sand are separate, even when they touch.

A half hour later I was ordering my third coffee. Where was Charlie? Had he forgotten? That wasn't like him, but then maybe he had changed. I certainly had.

Just when I was beginning to worry, a blue Isotta roadster with a convertible top pulled up to the curb in front of the café. The car was the color of a package of Gauloises cigarettes, the blue that Gaugin used to paint Tahitian lagoons. The driver, his face obscured by a silk scarf and sunglasses, maneuvered closely to the wooden cart in front of him, and the vegetable seller, startled, skipped up to the curb.

"Hey! Good-looking!" the driver called.

I stared down at my unread book and pretended not to hear.

"Lily," the voice said more softly.

"Charlie? Charlie!" All the colors of the street glowed a little brighter when I recognized his voice.

"Wherever did you get that car?" I shouted back. It was the kind of car that movie stars like Gary Cooper or Fred Astaire drove, not exactly what medical students from Harvard could afford.

"Borrowed from a friend," Charlie said.

He took off his sunglasses and studied me. There was so much in his eyes . . . love and worry, and something else I couldn't name. Anticipation, an announcement. He looked like someone hiding a gift behind his back.

"Get in!" he said. His hand was resting on the car door and I took it and grasped it, hard, and it was like being pulled back from a dangerous place.

"It's been too long," he said.

We stayed like that for a long while, just enjoying being together again. He laughed when that moment passed. "What are you wearing?"

I looked down and brushed some lint from my dress. The waist began just under my bosom and the skirt fell almost to my ankles. "What's wrong with it?"

"Nothing except that it is hideous."

"Clothes don't matter."

"Sure they do. Believe me."

"So this friend of yours who owns the car. A woman?"

"As a matter of fact, yes, a woman."

"If you have so little to say about her, I'd guess she's a married woman."

Charlie stopped smiling.

"Oh, Charlie, does her husband know you've borrowed both his wife and his automobile?" My brother had a reputation, and one for which he wasn't completely to blame. Women found him irresistible, and when he left New York for Harvard Medical, he'd left behind several brokenhearted debutantes, according to Aunt Irene.

"No, he doesn't know, and we won't tell him, will we?"

"Does that mean we'll be meeting him?"

"I hope not, but it is always a possibility. How long are you here for? Did you book at the Hotel Regina?"

The Regina, a respectable hotel just steps away from the Louvre, was the hotel our aunt had chosen years before. "Bye Bye Blackbird," she sang, when she first saw it.

"No. I decided to stay at L'Hotel Paris. It's cheaper."

"And it's on the Left Bank, with the artists," he said. "You can't fool me. Did you get Oscar Wilde's room? I wonder if it has the same wallpaper. 'Either the wallpaper goes . . .'" Charlie gave me a gentle poke in the ribs.

"'Or I go,'" I finished. Those supposedly had been poor Oscar Wilde's last words before he died. He left; the wallpaper stayed.

Charlie turned the steering wheel, and the automobile pulled away from the curb. I flinched as soon as he put his foot on the accelerator pedal. "It's safe, Lily," he said.

Two years had passed since the accident, but I still felt dizzy with fear whenever I got into an automobile, still felt the sudden lurch off the road, into the stand of trees.

"Where are we going?"

"To buy you a birthday present. Something to wear to a party."

"A party. How nice of you, Charlie." I tried to sound enthusiastic, but he heard the reluctance in my voice. I forced my hands to relax in my lap, fingers unclenched, palm up.

"How long since you've had some fun, Lily? A while, I'd guess. We're going to change that. I do have my motives. If all goes well and we get the thumbs-up, I'll be invited to an even bigger party later. One with lots of rich potential donors. I need you to look your best, so we'll get you a dress. Have any cash on you? I may not have enough."

"A little. And my birthday isn't for another two months."

"Who's counting? So, on to Chanel!"

"Coco Chanel? Couture? Shouldn't we go to a department store?"

"Not off the rack this time. You need to look swell. Better than swell. Magnificent."

"It doesn't work like that, Charlie. Even if we did find a swell—a magnificent dress that didn't cost every penny we both don't have, it takes weeks for the fittings." Besides, *magnificent*, even *swell*, weren't adjectives for a woman in mourning, a woman who, when she bothered to look in her mirror, saw a tragedy of her own making.

"Please, Lily," said my little brother, just the way he'd said when we were small and I wouldn't let him play with my pick-up sticks, even though now he was twenty-one and I twenty-three.

I pulled off his driving cap and ruffled his hair. "You win. But not Chanel." I wanted to go somewhere else for that party dress. Allen had sometimes looked over my shoulder at the fashion magazines I read and hadn't liked Chanel, thought the clothes too severe, almost masculine.

"You're kidding. What woman doesn't want a Chanel evening frock?"

"This woman, at this moment, wants Schiaparelli. Let's go there. Her daughter was a student at the school. I'm curious to see if she remembers me."

The student, Marie Schiaparelli—she used her mother's name, not her father's—had been a girl with the kind of accent acquired only by belonging nowhere and everywhere, a girl born in New York, educated in France and Germany and England. She'd had polio, and Allen and his brother, Gerald, had been fascinated by her medical history, the long list of therapies and surgeries that had transformed the polio-crooked, thin legs into those of a beautiful young woman who swam and skied.

Her mother came up from Paris sometimes on Sunday afternoons, draped in furs and heavy jewelry and impossibly stylish frocks and suits, to take her daughter out for a Sunday lunch. "And to see her London lover," Marie had told me straightforwardly. "Actually, both of them. Brothers."

One dreary November Sunday when the sky was littered with gray clouds, Madame Schiaparelli had invited Allen and me to join them.

"Gogo tells me that she loves your art classes," she had said, standing in the school's reception room, her tiny head peeking out of a huge sable coat. "So, come. Roast beef and a salad. No bread or puddings. This school is making my daughter fat!" Even in the dim room, Madame glittered with jewels and gold embroidery, a bird of paradise who had wandered into a pigeon coop.

We drove into London, Madame's chauffeur maneuvering around bicyclists and strolling parsons, and at a hotel dining room lavish with gleaming silver and white cloths we stuffed ourselves on roast beef, more meat than we'd normally eat in a fortnight at the school.

Marie—I couldn't yet call her by that strange nickname, Gogo, that her mother used—was shy and did not look up often from her plate. Madame Schiaparelli was full of jokes and gossip. Even the stiff waiter smiled when Madame told the story of how, as a young woman, she'd traveled to Cuba with the singer Ganna Walska. She'd had to smuggle Walska out a back entrance between acts because the Havana audience had begun to riot, Walska's voice was so bad.

"In Havana, people on the street mistook me for Anna Pavlova. We looked much alike," Madame said. "Too bad. I'm not particularly fond of dancers."

Marie tilted her head up and raised her one eyebrow knowingly. "They tend to steal other women's husbands," she said. Her mother ignored her.

Elsa Schiaparelli, as she revealed in a streaming monologue punctuated by jokes, had been born in Rome; escaped—the word she used—a strict family by fleeing to New York with, I assumed, the husband who had later left; and then, solo again, went to where all artists and city adventurers went: Paris.

"I go back to Rome only to see my mother, as little as possible. Rome is filled with brown shirts." She shivered. "Oh, that awful man, Mussolini. What he is doing to my country. When I saw his photo in the paper with Hitler next to him, I sat on the curb and wept."

"Mussolini and the Italian fashion board have forbidden Mummy's designs to be shown there," Gogo added. "She refused a luncheon invitation with Il Duce."

"Let it be said, now and forever, I have nothing to do with fascists, and I certainly don't want them wearing my clothes. God forbid. Coffee? Then we must start back."

"Wasn't she charming?" I asked Allen later, when Madame's limousine was pulling away down the school drive. "So confident and worldly. Sophisticated. That beautiful fur coat."

"Not bad for an old lady. I like them younger." He kissed my neck, just where the itchy wool collar of my dress ambushed the skin.

"And now," Charlie said, taking back his cap and tilting it over his forehead, "Schiaparelli it is. Your choice. But I have to make a quick phone call. We were supposed to meet someone at the Chanel salon." He went into the café and was out again a minute later, smiling sheepishly.

Charlie aimed the blue roadster into the thick traffic of Saint-Germain-des-Prés. We prowled down lanes and avenues, dodging around fruit and vegetable carts, policemen on horse, jaywalking pedestrians, and other automobiles. We crossed over the Seine. "Pont Royal!" Charlie shouted. "Tuileries," he shouted as we whizzed by pastel gardens. "Remember?" We had played there as children. Charlie saw me gripping the door, white-knuckled, and slowed down.

A silver Seine, trees in full leaf, pots of red geraniums on every stoop, under windows, rows of schoolchildren in uniform following black-and-white nuns, handsome gendarmes, and over it all, hanging like an invisible presence, the sense that this was the best place to be. Even I, indifferent to so much, felt it. June in Paris.

"Place Vendôme." Charlie pulled over to the curb.

The huge open square shimmered white with sun on pavement and stone façades.

"That's Napoleon up there," he said, pointing to the top of the tall central column, a bronze shaft made from the melted cannons from the battle of Austerlitz. "They keep pulling him down, melting the bronze, and redesigning his outfit."

"I don't imagine the emperor would appreciate the pigeons sitting on his shoulders."

"And this, it seems"—he waved his arm—"is the Schiaparelli boutique. You're sure about this? I mean, look at the crackpot window!"

Gilded bamboo stalks made a grid over the panes so that the window was like a museum display, or a shuttered palace, or . . . a jail? Inside the window, behind the gilded bamboo, straw figures stooped over trays of earth, watering jars in hand, as if they were tending a summer garden. But instead of flowers, out of the earth poked lobsters, some still half-buried, their red claws jutting against the painted backdrop of the sky. The figures wore dresses that hung straight down from the shoulders and past the knees, brightly colored, adorned with buttons of different colors and shapes. Some of the buttons were fish-shaped; others were large squares or flowerpots.

"Very strange," I agreed. The colors of the dresses were beautiful, though, deeply saturated shades of orange, blue, red. "Schiaparelli made the trousseau for the Duchess of Windsor. There was a photo layout of it in *Vogue*."

"I bet she didn't wear that necklace of gilt pine cones." He pointed at it.

"Probably not," I agreed.

The ground floor of the boutique was full of ready-to-wear: hats, scarves, handbags, sweaters, gloves, those things that could be worn without the many fittings bespoke clothes required. *Vendeuses* dressed in elegant black-and-white suits glided through the room, opening cases, answering questions. I tried on a large-brimmed summer hat.

"That's the hat that Marlene Dietrich bought," a *vendeuse* said. "It suits you."

"Not today." Charlie pulled it off my head and whispered, "No accessories. We're not at Macy's, and there's a reason why there's no price tag on these things."

"Right," I said, amused by a pair of gloves I spied. They were the color of poached salmon and had a frill stitched up the center that looked like fish fins.

Women turned in our direction and coolly assessed me and my clothes; they found me wanting, judging by the disdain in their faces. These women, rich and stylish, wouldn't be caught dead in off-the-rack and hand-me-downs. But when their eyes went to Charlie, they fixed on him the way children fix on cake and candy displays. Tall and slender, he looked a little like the aviator Lucky Lindy. Charlie had to be the handsomest man in Paris, with his thick, white-blond hair and sapphire eyes, the way he shuffled his feet shyly and held his hat in front of his chest as if in need of protection. Something about the suggestion of vulnerability in a man brings out the flirtatiousness of women.

Charlie ignored them, which made them stare even harder, and we walked up the stairs, to the showing room. We sat on little gilded chairs. Charlie placed the automobile keys on the tea table between us.

"Can I help you, monsieur?" asked a young woman, her eyes narrowed with pleasure.

"Yes, please. A frock for my sister. Something . . ." He struggled for the word. "Something swirly, if you know what I mean."

"Sister?" She gave me a sly, sideways glance. While Charlie is fair in that Nordic white-blond kind of way, I'm dark. Brown hair, brown eyes, olive skin, a throwback to my grandfather from Italy. "Certainly," she said in that knowing way of salespeople.

"Is blue still your favorite color?" he asked me.

"I suppose. Haven't thought about it. It was Allen's."

"A blue frock," he told the salesgirl. "For evening."

A few minutes later a mannequin with eyes ringed with black glided past us in a midnight-blue floor-length gown, tight to the knees, then swirling out to the ankles. The pink jacket that went over it was embroidered with elephants.

"No," Charlie said. He was right. I, unused to evening wear, would trip in such a thing, although I thought the elephants added a pleasant touch, something unusual.

"Something shorter," Charlie said. The next dress had a neckline that plunged almost to the waist. Charlie winced. The third gown was worn with a violet matador's bolero embroidered with plumed dancing horses.

When the mannequin reappeared in the fourth selection, her pasted-down spit curls no longer as precisely arranged and a glint of impatience in her eyes, Charlie and I both leaned forward with interest. This dress was white chiffon printed with blue lines of sheet music, with red roses dotted here and there as notes. The neckline was scalloped, the waist tight.

"That's the one, isn't it, Lily? How much is it?" Charlie asked, another testament to his charm, because no one else could have asked that crass question in a couture salon and gotten away with it. The salesgirl bent toward him and whispered something in his ear. The dress whispered as she moved, the red roses fluttered.

His fingers drummed on the wooden arm of his chair. "It's three months' salary for an intern," he whispered to me. My heart sank, and the drowning of desire for that frock was like an *I told you so. How dare you want. Anything.*

There was a commotion in the arched doorway. Everyone turned to look at the woman who had just come in, tall, majestic, her pale summer dress billowing about her knees as if she carried her own personal breeze with her, a woman with the kind of looks and style that made heads turn. Her hair was blond without the brass that peroxide gives; her eyes were copper, long and narrow so that she seemed to be smiling even when she wasn't.

"Charlie. How good to see you!" She came to us and bent to give him a kiss on the cheek. Was I the only one who noticed that she discreetly picked up the keys he had placed on the table? She slipped them into her purse.

"I got here as soon as I could. What a to-do! Charlie, whatever did you say to that woman? Coco is having a tantrum because I left without making an order."

"Only that we were meeting at the Schiaparelli salon instead," Charlie protested.

"My God. No wonder. Coco and Schiap detest each other. She is, what do you say, fit to be tied?"

"They are in the same business. You'd think they'd be colleagues," Charlie said, blushing.

"That is how a doctor thinks, not a dress designer." She laughed, showing a misaligned tooth, an imperfection that made her even more charming. "But why are we here? You know I love Chanel."

"My sister's choice. Ania, this is my sister, Lily."

"How do you do?" she asked formally. "I think I am a little afraid of you. Charlie talks about his older sister so much."

The salesgirl pulled a third chair to our table, and Ania sat between Charlie and me. I could see their fingers touch under the table, then twine together so tightly their knuckles whitened. I looked away, overwhelmed by the intimacy.

"Very strange, this place," Ania whispered. "That window! Have they shown you something you like?"

"Yes, but the cost is . . ."

"Formidable, of course. Which costume is it?" Charlie described it, and one of her long eyebrows, pale as a moth wing, shot up. "I have seen that dress. It is from the collection Schiaparelli showed the season before the Circus Collection."

The way she said "Circus Collection" indicated we should know it. I, an art teacher in a girls' school, and Charlie, a medical student, did not. Ania read our ignorance in our faces.

"The Circus Collection," she repeated. "Buttons shaped like leaping horses, gowns embroidered with elephants and drums. She showed the collection in February when Hitler took over the German army, when they began to call him the ringmaster."

"That madman," Charlie muttered. "Why don't the Germans get rid of him?"

"He promises them work," Ania said quietly. "He promises that he will make Germany great. And they believe him."

"He's already gotten the communists working. In labor camps," Charlie said.

There was a long moment of silence. Talk about Hitler did that to conversations, truncated them and turned words into meaningless sounds. No one knew what to make of him, of what was happening in Germany and Austria, and what would happen next. We'd already begun hearing about the camps, how Hitler had exempted them from all German laws and left the prisoners at the mercy of the guards and administrators.

We sat, making small talk about the weather, the latest Hollywood films, whether or not Mae West would make a comeback. Her latest film had bombed, and the *Hollywood Reporter* had put her name on the box office poison list, along with those of Greta Garbo and Fred Astaire and Katharine Hepburn, names, they assured us, we'd never be hearing from again.

Ania leaned over Charlie to speak directly to me, and I caught him inhaling her perfume, eyes briefly closed and head tilted as if the sun had suddenly caught his face. "Did you have a pleasant trip?" she asked me. "The Channel crossing was not too bad? I get, what is the word, Charlie, *mal de mer*? Seasick?"

"If you look straight ahead and not down, the motion sickness is not as bad," he said, opening his eyes.

"Your brother is so smart."

"Yes," I agreed. "He is." Head of his class at Harvard Medical, but Charlie didn't like to boast about that.

End of that conversation. The ormolu clock ticked away on a marble mantelpiece.

The salesgirls whispered in corners, worked lethargically at straightening displays and folding sweaters . . . the strangest sweaters, with bows knitted into the pattern, like a surrealist joke.

"Madame would like to see something?" The salesgirl who had sniffed at me like I had come in through the wrong entrance all but groveled before the beautiful Ania.

"No, I think not. Too strange!" She laughed.

"Go ahead, Ania," I said. "As long as we're here." Why did I say that? Was I making small talk, encouraging this beautiful Ania to try on a dress that was humorous and not necessarily beautiful?

"We have a little time," Ania agreed.

The parade began again, the model strutting out in dress after dress as Ania tilted her head, put a scarlet-tipped finger to her dimpled chin, and contemplated. Her wedding ring was set with a huge diamond that glittered each time she moved her hand.

"That!" Ania exclaimed when the model had come out in a long, clinging gown of black satin worn with a white organza blouse tied at the waist, peasant style. A half hour later she had also ordered a brown-and-yellow morning suit with oversized buttons, a sequined cocktail dress that glistened like mermaid scales, and extravagantly wide silk beach trousers in four different colors.

"So playful!" she said. "From Coco I get the beautiful suits and dresses, but I think she maybe lacks humor? So serious, her clothes."

I looked at Charlie, who was beginning to fidget like a child being held after school. His girl was rich. Or at least her husband was. I felt that thud in the bottom of my stomach that was foreboding.

Ania was just rising to go into the fitting room when the atmosphere in the room charged with electricity.

"She's here," someone murmured, and even the straw and wire forms the clothes hung on seemed to stand straighter.

Elsa Schiaparelli, small and slender, and her face, with its olive complexion and heavy-lidded eyes, was striking rather than pretty, exactly as I had remembered her. With that solemn, Roman face she could have been a saint preparing for martyrdom, so stern was her expression. She wore a simple black suit, belted at the waist, and a huge bangle on her wrist, a golden snake entwining it three times, and a little cap with a curling black feather that almost encircled one eye.

She strode into the room and gave the lingering salesgirls an evil glance. They scattered in different directions, back to their counter stations and fitting rooms. Then she headed straight for us, her hand extended, all smiles. Rather, she was heading for Ania.

"Madame Bouchard? Yes, I think it is. How marvelous to finally have you in my salon. Have you been treated well? Have they shown you anything you liked?"

"I've been meaning to come so many times," Ania lied. "Yes, the most marvelous dress and jacket and a suit. The beachwear . . ."

"I will supervise the fitting myself," Madame Schiaparelli announced.

"My friend has found a dress as well. But . . ." Ania, eight inches taller than Schiap, leaned over and whispered something into the designer's ear. Schiaparelli frowned, then whispered something back. This went on, back and forth, for several minutes.

"Lily Sutter," I said, interrupting them, extending my hand. I waited to see if she would remember our lunch together in London with Allen and her daughter, how Allen had amused her by trying to explain Zeno's arrow paradox about change and time. "Then they can't exist?" she had shouted at Allen. "Nothing ever changes? That's very bad for fashion."

But she didn't remember, and it would have been rude to mention it, to make a claim of acquaintance with her daughter when we were haggling over the price of a dress.

Schiaparelli and Ania continued their whispering for a few minutes, and then Ania smiled at me. "You can have the frock at half price. It is from an order that was not picked up. Will that do?"

"Yes!" I lifted the dress from the chair it had been draped over and walked to the mirror, holding it against my shoulders. Behind me, Madame Schiaparelli was also reflected in the mirrors. Her business-like expression changed to one of curiosity.

"I know you," she said. "Gogo's art teacher at that awful school! They made her so fat!"

"Yes," I said, relieved that she had brought it up, not me. "You took me out to lunch once. Roast beef and salad, no bread or pudding."

"And your husband, who told me change is impossible, that nonsense about Zeno. How is he?"

I put down the dress and felt the brightness of the day grow dim. Charlie put his arm across my shoulders and hugged me closely.

"He died," Charlie said softly. "Two years ago."

"Oh, my dear. I'm so sorry. You two, so in love. I saw it." She turned in a little circle, thinking, then went to a glass case. She took out a hat of blue satin formed like a sailor's cap. "You should have this, to go with the dress. A gift." She gave my battered straw hat, resting on the table next to Ania's coffee cup, a malignant glare.

"I couldn't . . ." I protested, no longer interested in dresses or hats.

"It is nothing," she insisted. "Once, when I was a child in Rome, I gave away all of my mother's fur coats and evening gowns. Threw them out the window to the people in the street, just like Catherine of Siena did. No sweets for a week after, but it was worth it. It's good to sometimes let things go. And people, too," she added.

I threw my arms around her, and it was like hugging a child, she was so tiny. A very well-dressed child, of course. "How can I thank you, Madame Schiaparelli!"

"I'll think of a way," she said. "But you must call me Schiap. All my friends do, and we will be friends." She looked at Ania. "We will all be friends, yes? Try on the dress, and if little needs to be altered, I'll send it to your hotel later today. You are going to Elsie's soirée tonight? You will wear this."

"Make the alterations this afternoon? You are crazy!" a salesgirl complained.

Schiap clapped her hands. A fitter came running through the arched doorway, the rose pincushion on her wrist bobbing, several tape measures around her neck swaying. With astoundingly swift and precise movements, she measured me from shoulders to waist, from waist to knee, around the bust, around the shoulders, her hands moving in gestures as precise and ritualized as a Java dancer.

Ania pushed me into a dressing room and had me out of my faded cotton dress and into the Schiaparelli gown before I could say a word. The fitter came in, and I was measured a second time with the dress on me. The fabric was so light it billowed and swirled with the slightest movement.

"Good shoulders," Schiap declared. "Small waist. You measured accurately?" she asked the fitter, who was still on her knees, her mouth porcupined with pins. "Good. It must fit perfectly."

Then, Ania's turn. The green sequined dress was lifted over her and smoothed down over bust, hips, thighs. It already fit perfectly, even the length. Ania was a perfect model's size.

"I would love to wear this tonight," Ania said.

"Then you will. This very dress." There was a glint in Schiap's eye, a giveaway of victory to come that I wouldn't understand until later.

When we were leaving the shop, Schiap gave me another hug. She turned away and stared out the window at the column where Napoleon posed on top, presiding over the Place Vendôme.

"You are maybe four years older than Gogo? You remind me of when my daughter was a schoolgirl and needed her Mummy. They grow up so quickly," she said. "And then, they are gone. All his little soldiers," she murmured. "It's something between Gogo and me. She says, 'Napoleon,' and I say, 'And all his little soldiers.' It is how we tell each other 'I love you.'"

Just as we were going out, another group was coming in, speaking in Italian, and Charlie and I both had enough school Latin to understand them. They were talking about the parades in Rome a few weeks before, when Hitler had visited, the jubilant glory with which Mussolini had shown off his city.

"Not all of the city," Elsa Schiaparelli said in a low voice. "The pope locked the doors of the Vatican Museums and turned off the lights."

The Italians hadn't heard her, and weren't meant to. They were customers, after all. The comment was for Charlie and me.

"From what I've heard of Herr Hitler's artistic ambitions, it was a wise move," Charlie said.

When I stumbled a little going out the door, Schiap said, "Quick. Touch iron, for luck." She guided my hand to a metal hat form on a table.

· TWO ·

COCO

Coco Chanel sat at her desk, fuming. Her black-rimmed spectacles had fallen down her nose, giving her an owlish look, and her left hand twirled a strand of huge, obviously fake pearls. Underneath the layers of fake pearls were the real ones, the ones that Duke Dmitri had given her. She liked to do that, mix real with the fake. *Just like life*, she told herself. *Just like men.*

There was a knock on the closed door. "Yes?" Coco quickly removed her glasses. She avoided, as much as possible, being seen in them. The very thick lenses magnified the lines under her eyes. She sat up straighter, stiffening her spine. Like all children who had grown up cowed by too much adult authority, who had spent as much time as possible huddled over a book to escape into other worlds, her spine rounded when she was relaxed. "Come in."

The salon manager, a tall, stern woman not easily frightened, hence her ability to work with the famously difficult Coco Chanel, came in.

"Telephone call in the other office," she said. "Lady Mendl wants to make sure you received your invitation."

"Elsie knows I did. She's just nagging. Let her worry a bit. It's good for business. Tell her I can't come to the phone, I'm in a fitting with . . ."

Coco paused. Better make this one good. "Just say 'the princess.' Make her guess."

"Very well, Mademoiselle." The door closed again.

In fact, the princess she had in mind, but hadn't named, hadn't been in this week, or even this month. She'd been to that Italian woman's salon, though. She'd defected, just like some of the other customers. Business was still excellent. Mademoiselle was one of the richest women in the world, a household name, a purveyor not just of clothes but of lifestyles, of dreams, the modern woman, slender, free, athletic, independent. Coco Chanel had brought women into the twentieth century, liberating them from corsets and double standards. *Me*, she thought. *I did that. And more.*

But now that Italian *arrivista* was turning women into clowns. Dresses with silly buttons as big as tennis balls, flopping feathers all over the place, trains three yards long, animal embroideries and sequins like circus performer costumes. A coat made of braided copper. Must weigh a hundred pounds. Who could wear it? A hat shaped like a shoe . . . just a joke, of course. But that other hat, that frightful thing she called the madcap that sold in the thousands . . . a knit tube pulled over the head with the points sticking up. Even the heiress Daisy Fellowes had the nerve to wear one into the Chanel salon!

It will not do, Coco told herself. *Not at all.* Lately, she had just begun to recover her equilibrium, had managed to convince herself that Schiaparelli was a fad good only for a few seasons, and then Ania had pulled that stunt.

"Must go," she had said, standing so quickly she had dropped the note that had been brought to her a moment before, the message from a telephone call placed through to the boutique downstairs. Ania had raced out without looking at a single dress, without placing a single order. When no one was looking, Coco had bent to retrieve the note. *Meeting at Schiaparelli, not Chanel*, it had said.

The Italian woman, again.

One or two dresses didn't matter. Coco could have retired and still earned more money from her perfume, Chanel No. 5, than most people earned in several lifetimes. But Ania mattered. She was a certain type of customer, one of those beauties who turned heads everywhere she went, and she went everywhere. All men wanted her. All women wished they could look like her. If she began wearing Schiaparelli, then others would as well. It was a question of reputation, of fame. And this would not do.

The knock on the door, again. This time Coco did not bother to remove her glasses. It wasn't as if her assistant hadn't seen her in them thousands of times. "Yes? Now what?"

"Lady Mendl insists on speaking with you."

"Tell her I'll ring her later. I'm busy."

Alone again, Coco fidgeted with the statuette on her desk, a little male figure by Arno Breker, Hitler's favorite sculptor. The figure was Apollonian in its neoclassical homage to the male form. Her friend Salvador Dalí, when he had seen it, had fallen to the floor in a faked fit. He had wanted to paint it lime green and pound nails into it, not because he had strong opinions about German politics but because he hated, absolutely hated, neoclassicism.

Dalí was good-looking in that darkly Spanish way but too strange to be considered as a bedfellow. Besides, did he even bed women? He was married, but that meant little.

Coco's heavy, straight eyebrows moved closer together in a frown. How long since she'd been in love, really in love? Yes, there were lovers. Playthings, really. And former lovers, now old friends, who still shared her bed occasionally.

The day felt sad, and when she thought of her bedroom, all those nights alone, it felt sadder yet. None of her lovers had measured up to Boy Capel, the first of the great ones. He'd been the most handsome, most generous, most understanding. He'd gotten her started in business, and his beautiful English blazers had helped her create the Chanel

Look. How she'd loved rummaging through his wardrobe, the crisp shirts and pleated trousers, silk ties by the dozen, the riding coats and boots, all bespoke, all perfect down to the last detail.

She'd never really recovered from his death, twenty years ago. Two decades? Not possible. It felt like yesterday; there was still that knife twisting in her gut whenever she thought of it. He'd died in a motor-cycle accident, on his way to rendezvous with her for a Christmas holiday.

And then Paul Iribe, the artist who had used her face for so many beautiful illustrations, the second of her great loves, had died three years ago. Again, suddenly, playing tennis at her house in the south, La Pausa. She loved exercise, riding and swimming and tennis, but every time she held a tennis racket she saw him again, crumpling to the ground. So much death. It stalked her, had done since she was eleven and her mother had died, poor and abandoned by her husband. One night, in the tiny rented attic room where she had slept with her mother and sister, Coco—she was still Gabrielle then—had listened to her mother's rasping, asth-matic breath grow slower, lighter, then cease completely.

Too long ago, Coco told herself now, going to her mirror to apply fresh lipstick. Why think about that now? She saw herself looking back at her, lips red and glistening, eyes large, dark.

She hadn't been in love since Iribe's death. Plenty of sex, plenty of parties. But she'd always felt alone, not just after but during, as well, when the silk sheets were still being tousled and twisted, when the champagne corks were still popping, she'd been alone. And it made her feel old.

No, this will not do. She stood and straightened her skirt, pulled back her shoulders, and went to the door.

"Charlotte!" she shouted for one of her assistants. "Get Lady Mendl on the phone. Tell her I'm free to speak now. I want to ask her some-thing."

Would Baron Hans Günther von Dincklage be there tonight?

They'd met at several dinner parties but talked only briefly. Like Boy Capel, he was a man of extraordinary male beauty and culture. At the races at Longchamp she'd felt his eyes on her and grown warm, sensing his desire. She hadn't encouraged him. Hadn't let their eyes meet and linger, hadn't touched his hand when accepting a cigarette from him, hadn't stood a fraction of an inch closer to him than other people at the cocktail party.

She knew instinctively he was not a man to toy with, not a lover who'd expect only a weekend with her. If she took him on, it would mean something. If he took her on. What if . . . She could still have her choice of lovers, boys and men, and women as well, when the mood struck. But she had arrived at an age when she no longer took her power to attract, to hold, for granted.

He was younger. He was powerful and important in the Abwehr, German intelligence. Could she still hold a man like that, a man who could have his pick of the beauties of Paris?

She'd find out. She felt the old energy flowing through her, the electricity of desire for both the trophy and the fight leading to it. Today, she'd leave her office a little earlier than usual, go to her Hotel Ritz suite and take a long bath, dress carefully, make sure her maquillage was perfect.

Tonight.

"No dinners out for me next semester," Charlie pretended to grumble when we were back on the street. "Though I admit the dress suits you. Schiaparelli, hey? A good designer, I think."

"And what do you know about designers and clothes?" Ania teased.

"Only how you look in them." His eyes devoured her. "I like those new things."

"And you don't like my old things?" Ania pretended to pout, forcing her mouth into a sulk, but her eyes sparkled with amusement.

"I think I like these better. You look happier in them."

"Then tonight I will wear the new sequined satin. For you. I will buy all Elsa Schiaparelli."

"How did an Italian woman come to be named Elsa?" I asked, reminding them I was there.

"Her parents wanted a son so much that when she was born they let the nurse name her." Ania stared into Charlie's baby blues and leaned toward him. "Or that's the story she tells. Who knows?"

Her uniformed chauffeur appeared from around the corner, checking his watch and throwing a half-smoked cigarette to the curb. He walked with authority, not subservience. *He works for the husband, not the wife*, I thought. Charlie and Ania jumped a guilty arm's length away from each other. The chauffeur opened the passenger door of the roadster. "See you tonight?" Ania asked Charlie, her voice light, almost cold.

"Why not." He gave her a quick kiss on the cheek, and I understood that this aloofness, this public nonchalance, was a performance. After Ania had gotten into the automobile and the chauffeur had pulled away from the curb and into traffic, Charlie took my arm and we went to the corner to hail a cab.

"Where did you meet her?" I asked.

"Here, in Paris. After your accident, when you were in the hospital . . ."

"And Allen was dead," I said.

". . . and Allen was dead, when you didn't want to see anybody, I thought I'd spend some time here, closer to you than if I'd been in New York. Just in case. I spent the summer studying at the Sorbonne Medical College. Brushing up on my French and anatomy at the same time. And one day I saw Ania in the park, this beautiful woman who just took my breath away. We talked. One thing led to another. And when I went back to New York, she just stayed on my mind. So I came back this summer, looking for her. And I found her. Same park."

"Thank you for staying close, even though I didn't know it. And for the dress, Charlie."

"So I don't eat for weeks and can't afford books next semester. Think nothing of it. Schiaparelli did give us an awfully good discount, though. Ania has that effect on people." A cab pulled up, and we climbed in.

"Schiaparelli's daughter was a student at the school," I said.

"That explains the hat she gave you." He gave the driver my hotel address.

In the taxi, he put his arm around my shoulder again. "You've had a tough time of it," he said. "I'm glad you came. Let's see if we can get you smiling again. I've really missed you, Lily. Life has missed you. You disappeared. Come back. It's time."

My room was the cheapest the hotel had, with a cot-sized bed, a straight-backed chair, a three-drawer dresser, and a torn silk screen with a washing basin behind it. It was on the fourth floor under the eaves, and I could barely stand up straight in it. But the window faced east. I would see the sun rising over the red rooftops of the Left Bank.

I unpacked, hanging up the few clothes I had brought, placing my hairbrush on the washstand and Allen's photo on the little table next to the bed.

On the rue des Beaux Arts, below me, women swept their stoops, the Latin Quarter students rushed by, and children in their blue school uniforms bounced balls, played tag. If I leaned out the window, I could see Notre Dame and its stained-glass rose window sparkling with all the colors of the saints.

There was so much color. The red striped awning of the patisserie, the window boxes of pink geraniums and green ferns, the pinks and yellows of women's summer frocks, the dusty charcoal of men's berets.

I fell asleep to the rusty rhythm of the creaking bedsprings, drifting in and out of all the colors like a bee sipping nectar.

I woke up once, startled by a clattering in the street, the sound of a screaming child, a mother shushing him. Only half-awake, I thought I was in the hospital again, screaming for Allen, that the scream had been my own; I imagined I felt the plaster cast on my broken leg, the bandages on my burnt left hand.

The environment of illness, those austere white rooms, is like a colorless desert, barren and overheated, a place where people tiptoe through the drying concrete of guilt and grief, where voices are never raised. In the hospital, to negate all that whiteness, I dreamed in vivid colors, all the shades of blue and red and yellow, swirling in and out and around one another, turning into every other color and then separating again.

Blue. The color of sickness, of doom, the color of both air and water, day and night. When I was bed-bound, if I concentrated hard enough, I could stare at the white nurses' uniforms, and they would turn blue and I would feel alive with that simple act of creation and then memory would turn everything white once again. I would force myself to remember the secret of the primary colors, that they cannot be obtained by admixtures.

Blue, red, and yellow cannot be faked or forced. They are for themselves, of themselves. Variable, like moods, yet always themselves. Perfect. Allen had been the human equivalent of a primary color.

When I woke up hours later in my hotel room I reached across the bed, to Allen, my hand seeking the familiar comfort of his shoulder, his back. Panic seized me when I remembered where I was and that I was alone. Death is a fact that is only slowly assimilated. There were still three or four moments of every day when I forgot, and therefore had to realize all over again, that Allen was dead. Waking up was one of them.

A moment later there was a knocking at the door and the porter called through the keyhole.

"Box for you, Madame."

Schiaparelli had kept her word. I opened the box reluctantly and folded back layers of tissue. Even in the box, the dress looked beautiful. What a waste. I'd probably wear it only once. I splashed water from the basin on my face and hands, dropped the gown over my head, and combed back my hair, all without glancing in the cracked mirror over the washstand.

Then I turned and looked at myself. The dress fit perfectly, the white chiffon hem fluttering around my calves, the red printed roses enclosing my shoulders and throat like a picture frame. The roses on the white chiffon gave a hint of pink to my olive skin. The neckline showed off my shoulders, my throat. I wished Allen were there, to see me.

"Swell," Charlie said when I met him later in the hotel lobby.

"I thought it needed to be magnificent," I teased him.

"Close enough.

"How long are you staying, by the way? I may have to go into training to fight off the wolves." Charlie put up his fists and made a jab at an invisible opponent.

"Not funny," I said. "I'm not interested in wolves, or even nice men."

"Eventually, Lily, you have to let yourself recover. You have to start again."

"I'm staying a week."

"Is that all? I'll be here till the end of the month. I was hoping you might stay longer. I would like you to stay longer. Please?"

"I get it. You want me to pose as a chaperone for you and your girl."

"It would help. We could spend more time together and there'd be less talk. And I'd like you to get to know her. Think about it. I mean, what are you going back to?"

Charlie pulled my arm through his and out we went, into the pale June twilight. He was dressed in *le smoking*, all black and white with a red carnation in his buttonhole, his top hat tilted at a stylish angle, and passersby stared at him, that beautiful young man in evening dress.

"You look like you need time away from that school," he said. "I'll never understand why you decided to stay there after Allen's death, rather than going back to New York."

"I'm closer to Allen there." How could I leave the place where I had been so happy with Allen, where every table, every room and garden path, reminded me of him?

Charlie read my thoughts. "He isn't there, Lily. He's gone. I know your heart broke, I know you loved him. But this is a kind of emotional suttee, and I won't allow it. Be heartbroken, but live. Don't lock out anything and anyone that might bring some happiness. And in all honesty, the future isn't looking that great in Europe right now. France may end up at war, and if France does, England probably will, too. Who knows where Hitler will stop, and when."

"Now you're being alarmist. No one really believes that, certainly not Gerald." The few conversations I'd had with Allen's brother in the last two years had been as impersonal as a newspaper.

"Yes, well, I wonder if Gerald might be a little admiring of Hitler and his law and order and trains on time. Quite a few in England, including the Duke of Windsor and his wife, seem frankly sympathetic. But you, Lily. You're too thin, your hair needs a good styling. I bet you've even stopped painting."

"I try. Once in a while."

We paused at the river, Charlie leaning on the balustrade, me leaning on Charlie. There was a washing barge somewhere beneath us in the darkness, and we could hear the women chattering at each other, smell the bleach from the day's work. There was a clank and clatter, and a bottle was thrown into the river.

"I think they are relaxing with a little wine. Could use some myself," Charlie said. "Lily, it saddens me to see you so sad."

"You are the only thing I love in this world, little brother. And right now, I'm more than a little worried about you."

We turned away from the river and continued our walk to the Place Vendôme, both of us a little shy for having confessed that mutual adoration. Love can be an easy thing to take for granted, but when it's voiced it fills you, the street, the city; it becomes its own destination, something always followed by small talk because the most important thing has already been said.

"How come we had to walk, Charlie? Where's the automobile?"

"Spoken for, at this hour."

So is Ania, I didn't say.

"Chin up. You look great," Charlie said when we were in front of the Ritz. The Place Vendôme was already lit with dozens of streetlamps, round circles of light dancing through the darkening evening. There had been a gentle rain in the afternoon, and the pavement shimmered. The floodlight directed at the statue of Napoleon, standing on his tall column, was turned on and made a streak of white through the night, as if a fallen star had left a permanent record of its descent.

The huge hotel, with its façade of columns and arched windows, was large enough to house an entire village. You couldn't see it all in one glance; you had to turn your head, left and right, to see it from end to end. Ania later told me that five hundred people worked there.

I looked up at one of the second-floor balconies and saw a woman standing there, twirling a strand of pearls and leaning lightly on the railing. She was alone, and I don't simply mean there was no one standing beside her; she was alone in every sense of the word. Solitude could be seen in her posture, in the way she stared into the distance. That was my first glimpse of Coco Chanel, that solitary woman who seemed as alone as I was.

She must have sensed my looking at her. She looked down at me, then, with a shrug, disappeared indoors.

"Ready?" Charlie danced a quick little shuffle and cocked his arm for me to put mine through.

Arm in arm, we climbed the steps of the Ritz. The future is always just two or three steps ahead of us. We stepped into the future, with its joy, its danger, its crowding memories. I felt Allen there with us, the light pressure of his hand on my neck, rubbing where it got stiff after a day of painting. *Two years since you've been gone*, I told him. Two minutes, two seconds. All the same.

SCHIAP

It was already evening when Elsa Schiaparelli kicked off her heels, rubbed her pinched toes, and put her feet up on her cluttered desk. She should be dressed by now, but she wanted to savor the victory of the afternoon.

A coup. That was what the afternoon with Madame Bouchard had been. Nothing less. One of Chanel's most famous, most admired clients had just ordered a season of Schiaparelli outfits. One of the last holdouts in Paris had crossed the couture border, and tonight she would be wearing one that hadn't needed to be altered because Madame Bouchard was a perfect model's size, as perfect in shape as that American goddess, Bettina Ballard, for whom the gown had originally been cut. Bettina hadn't grumbled much about having her bespoke gown sold out from under her, not when she learned who had bought it.

"And she's wearing it tonight," Schiap had told her.

"This will drive Chanel insane! Her best customer, now wearing

Schiaparelli!" She and Bettina had danced around the room a bit, and then Bettina had gone off to meet her husband for dinner.

In the narrow hall outside her studio, Schiap—that was how she referred to herself, that was how she instructed her friends to call her—could hear the *grisettes* bustling back and forth with bolts of fabric, putting away the afternoon's working materials, getting ready for the evening, for the various cafés and dance halls and beds in which they would end their long day.

She paid them as well as she could; there was a solid foundation for the rumors of her Bolshevik tendencies. But there was a tradition in Parisian sewing rooms that the *grisettes* added to their income with paying evening customers, and who was to judge? Coco had started out as a *grisette*; she'd probably had paying customers after her long hours in the sewing room.

Schiap, she had married. And what a disaster that had been, in every way except one: it had given her Gogo, the daughter she loved above all things.

She had worked compulsively, to acquire wealth for her daughter. She had courted some of the most famous, most important people of Europe to make the right connections for her daughter. And now she would make certain that no matter what happened, she would be able to get Gogo out of Europe before disaster struck.

The sun slipped low behind the roofs and steeples of the city, making the dark studio even darker. There were larger, brighter rooms at 21 Place Vendôme, but Schiap preferred this one, where she could see and hear everything that went on in the square outside.

A few hours before, the handsome American boy and his sister had stood there with Madame Bouchard, waiting for Madame's driver to appear. "Beautiful!" Madame Bouchard had said of her new dresses. "Why hadn't I come here before? I'll buy the whole collection!" Schiap had heard every word. Heard, and rejoiced.

S he knew, though, why Madame Bouchard hadn't come in before:
her lover . . . not that American boy, the other one, the German . . .
didn't approve of Schiaparelli. Schiaparelli, who during the General
Strike two years ago had negotiated with her workers rather than try
to throw them into the street, the way Chanel had. Well, better Bol-
shevism than fascism. That was how the world, how France, was divid-
ing: fascist or communist. At some point, everyone would have to
choose a side. And she had made hers clear. Thumbs down to the fascists and Nazis.

That will show them, she thought. *Madame Bouchard will be wearing Schiaparelli tonight at Elsie's party. Let Mussolini put that in his pipe
and smoke it.* Mussolini, who thought he could frighten her by sending
his thugs and spies around to her mother's apartments in Rome.

The American woman, the schoolteacher, had brought in Madame
Bouchard, so she would have to do something nice for her. A favor
repaid, when she could, something more than a reduced price on a
gown. There were a few women she dressed for free because they went
everywhere and looked so good in her clothes. You couldn't really say
that about the American girl. She carried sadness with her like Atlas
balancing the world on his shoulders, and sadness is not attractive.

Schiap stood, stretched, lit a cigarette, and danced a little jig of
delight around the studio. She rang a bell. Her assistant came in, already dressed in her street clothes, a red skirt and jacket, and threw up
her hands in alarm.

"Madame! Really!" Schiap's pagan dance had ended in the middle
of her studio in a pile of discarded ideas and experiments, a tidal wave
of color and texture—red satin, woven gold braid, brown flannel, orange
twill silk, things that had looked right on paper but wouldn't fold
or hang or pleat the way she wanted once attempted in fabric. The huge
pile of discarded fabrics made her look even smaller than usual, like a

misbehaving child, an illusion strengthened by the mischievous grin on her face.

The assistant wagged her finger and took away Schiap's cigarette, moving slowly so that the ash wouldn't fall before she found an ashtray.

"What should I wear tonight?" Schiap asked the walls, knowing her assistant would never answer such a complicated question. "It must be something special and eye-catching but not too outré. You know how conservative these people can be." Schiap knew. She knew that many people found her garments to be more appropriate for costume parties than sensible wardrobes, that they were often described as bizarre. Surreal. And so? Fashion is art, not just craft. Why not surreal? It worked for Dalí, Man Ray, and Magritte. Of course, they were men and therefore artists. Because she was a woman, she was merely a dressmaker, not an artist? No and no!

"Something waterproof, in case it rains tonight," her assistant said.

"You think my dresses are jokes?"

"The world always needs a good laugh, doesn't it?"

Schiap picked up a book from the table near her and made as if to throw it at her. The assistant, knowing better, didn't duck or put up her arms. "Put it down, or I won't have your coffee ready for you tomorrow morning."

"Tonight," Schiap said, dropping the book. "Tonight, once and for all and forever, I will show the world who is the number one designer. Tonight, there will be more women wearing Schiaparelli than Chanel. Oh, if only Gogo were here."

"Where is Gogo?" The assistant pulled the curtain shut, getting ready to lock up for the evening.

"London, I think." Schiap tilted her hat over one eye, glaring at herself in the mirror. "Or maybe that was last week. Cannes? You know Gogo. Doesn't like to stay in one place too long." That was how she'd gotten her nickname as a baby; even before she could walk she was always on the move, scuttling over floors, clambering on chairs and sofas.

And then, when it had been time to walk, then, when Schiap, visiting her toddler, who had been sent to a country nurse, outside noisy, unhealthy New York, then Schiap had seen that her daughter wasn't walking or even crawling as well as she should have been.

Polio. Her husband had broken her heart when he abandoned her, but it had been nothing like this. The guilt, the fear, the despair. Oh, the despair.

Her daughter's illness didn't break her, not the way foolish love for a man can. Instead, it turned her core to steel, to a determinism that bordered on the miraculous in her belief that she would make Gogo well again. And she had. At a price. The doctors, the surgeries, the therapies, the special schools, more surgeries. There had been a time, in her childhood, when she saw her daughter's face cloud over with fear when she saw her mother approaching, because it meant some new therapy, a new doctor, a new exercise, maybe even another surgery.

That was the mother's price she had paid, the cost of the love she had given.

"Well?" Schiap straightened her jacket. "I'll wear the new mustard-yellow dress tonight. You don't think it makes me look too olive, a little on the green side?"

"No. It is a good color for dark brunettes. You will glow, like a candle, like fire."

Elsa pretended to spit three times. *Ptu, ptu, ptu.* "Don't mention fire when you're wearing red. Bad luck. Go call a cab. And if Gogo calls . . ."

"I'll get the number and tell her you'll call later."

When the office door was locked behind her, Schiap gave it a little pat for luck, for love.

"Don't forget to lock all the doors and windows in the rooms," she said.

"I have never forgotten, Madame."

"I know. But I have a feeling."

"Madame often has feelings. All will be locked."

Schiap touched the door three more times to make four, her lucky number.

· THREE ·

When César Ritz built his great hotel, he had two things in mind: luxury and privacy. The Paris Ritz, unlike other hotels, doesn't really have a lobby. There's a thickly carpeted entrance, several officious clerks keeping guard, and then passages into the private rooms. Loiterers and photographers and gossip columnists were personae non gratae. Without a large lobby, there was nowhere for them to lurk.

Charlie and I, pretending not to be impressed, followed the bellhop who led us to the Lady Mendl private affair, passing the famous bar where F. Scott Fitzgerald once ate an entire bouquet, petal by petal, trying to seduce a young woman. I glanced in, and Charlie did, too. There, gleaming through the blue smoke, sat Ania, chatting with the bartender. I raised my hand and started to call to her, but Charlie stopped me.

"Keep walking," he said under his breath. "Ania and I can't walk in together."

The private room, up the grand staircase where Charlie led me, was filled with the scent of gardenias, hundreds of them in vases placed on tables, in corners. On the buffet, platters of chilled lobsters and roast beef, cut glass bowls of caviar nestled into larger silver bowls filled with ice, candied tangerines arranged as beautifully as a Dutch still life, reds and pinks, charcoal blacks, blues, the white gleam of light reflecting on polished metals.

I took a plate and helped myself to the lobster salad.

"These are Lady Mendl's two hundred closest friends," Charlie whispered, grinning, and it was like being a child again, Charlie and me dressed in our best, mixing with the grown-ups. Our aunt's friends had never dressed like this, though, in couture and with jewels dangling from wrists, necks, and earlobes. "Smile," Charlie whispered, guiding me through the doorway. "Pretend we do this every night. Act rich." He gave me a little pinch on the arm.

"You mean I shouldn't tuck my napkin under my chin?" I whispered back.

We passed the orchestra dais, where a jazz band was playing "Georgia on My Mind." The dark-haired, mustached guitarist was using only two fingers on his left hand to fret the chords; the last two fingers were curled, frozen, into his palm. His hand danced over the neck of the guitar at dizzying speed.

"Django Reinhardt," Charlie said. "The gypsy jazz musician. He was in a caravan fire when he was eighteen. He retaught himself to play guitar with his injured hand." Reinhardt looked up just then and scowled as if he knew we were talking about him.

Ania came in a minute after we did and sat at a table with a group of women who looked as if, between themselves, they owned most of the rubies mined in India, the diamonds of South Africa. She was wearing her new Schiaparelli dress, the pale green sequined dress with a deeper green turban wrapped around her head, and a heavy necklace of turquoise and golden topaz. When she rose to greet us, all heads turned to stare. Ania, I would learn, always had that effect.

"Don't be nervous," she whispered to me after she had given Charlie *la bise*, the double kiss on the cheeks that, in France, you would give to just about anyone except the dentist about to pull your tooth. In my mind's eye I saw their hands entwined under the table in the Schiapa-relli salon, that "never let me go" grip.

"I'm not nervous," I said. To be nervous, you have to care about the place, the people, their opinion. To care, you have to be awake inside, under the skin. It had been two years since I had cared, since I had been fully awake.

Ania took my arm and guided me through the candlelit room, Charlie following. She found a little table at the edge of the room and installed me there.

"Smile for the camera. That's Cecil Beaton, the photographer." Ania nodded in the direction of a slender, balding man hungrily eye-ing the crowd, looking for shots. "Next to him, Daisy Fellowes, the sewing machine heiress, with Duchess d'Ayen. That man who looks like a homeless bum, that's Christian Bérard, the artist. The actor Douglas Fairbanks, his wife, Sylvia. Darryl Zanuck, the movie pro-ducer. Maurice de Rothschild, the banker. The Duke and Duchess of Windsor . . .

"And that," she said in a softer voice, as Charlie came to the table with a plate of foie gras and biscuits, "that is the handsomest, sweetest man in the world. Not a penny to his name."

We sat and listened to the music, hot jazz with the saxophone sobbing out blue notes. A troop of waiters moved through the crowded room with buckets of champagne and trays of gem-colored cocktails: amethyst, ruby, quartz, pearl. Ania took one of the amethyst cocktails, an "aviator" made with gin and crème de violette. Purple is a combination of blue and red, cold and hot, the color of royalty and mourning, the color of early evening on a cloudy day.

Charlie handed me a cocktail and whispered, "Try to enjoy your-self, Lily."

The room shimmered with crystal, candlelight, sequined gowns. I silently compared the evening with my nights in England, most of them spent alone in the studio, pretending I was going to begin painting any moment, listening to the ticking clock, the static on the radio, the sense that nothing was ever again going to change.

Charlie moved from table to table to chat—he had a mission that evening; it was never too soon to begin thinking about rich patrons, and the room was full of rich Americans as well as French and English. I saw how many faces turned his way, female and male, to watch him, that charming, ambitious young man. Ania also fluttered away to various people once she realized I was content to sit and watch.

I took a pencil from my handbag and began to draw on a cocktail napkin, just lines, no modeling, no hint of light and shadow, only black graphite on white paper.

"You're a quiet one," said a man, leaning close to speak into my ear. "And I wouldn't let Bérard see that caricature of him you've drawn." It was the black-eyed guitarist. Up close, I could see the beading sweat on his high forehead, the threads of gray beginning in his narrow black mustache. His black jacket and shirt smelled of smoky campfires.

"Bérard would find it insulting, I suppose."

"No. He'd be jealous. It's good." Django sat in the chair opposite me and drank the cocktail Ania had left.

"I like your music," I said. "Especially that version of 'Dark Eyes.' Usually it's played so slow, so sad."

"I play it the jazz way. Life's already sad. Music should move the passion down into your feet. But oh, sister, you don't dance. Why?"

"Not in the mood. Your name, Django. What is it?" I asked.

"A gypsy word. It means 'I awake.' Unlike most of this crowd. It is a circus, isn't it? That woman over there . . ." He nodded toward the table on our left. "She's wearing enough gold to buy her own country. Maybe she already has." He laughed and lit a cigarette.

"That's the Duchess of Windsor," I said, and hoped she hadn't heard.

"Duchess!" Django called out, and waved. Wallis Simpson smiled stiffly and looked in the other direction. It occurred to me that the band members weren't supposed to sit with the guests. Screw that. I pulled my chair closer to Django's and smiled at him, looking conspiratorially into those dark Roma eyes.

"Damn the duchess," I said.

"That's the spirit, sister. Her and her Nazi-loving husband. I can't wait to finish this job. Too many snobs, too much gold here. I miss my people, and believe me, they aren't in the Ritz eating caviar."

He leaned back and squinted through the smoke from his cigarette. "You are American? First time in Paris?"

"Second. I was here when I was younger."

"You picked a strange time to return." He nodded toward a corner of the room, at a table where a group of men in uniform were sitting together, laughing loudly. German uniforms.

"You know, they hate the Roma," Django said, lighting a cigarette. "Maybe even more than they hate the Jews." One of them must have heard Django. He turned and stared at us, his eyes moving from Django's face to mine, back and forth. Django stared him down, though, and it was the officer's turn to blush and look away.

Django muttered something I couldn't understand, words in a language that seemed as old as time and just as incomprehensible.

Charlie and Ania were leaning against a column in the shadows. "You know the last line of the opening verse of 'Dark Eyes'? 'I met you in an unlucky hour.' That blonde sister has bad luck, and she'll pass it on. You came in with him?"

"He's my little brother."

A loud commotion at the other end of the room interrupted the buzz of conversation, and all attention tilted in that direction, as if we were on a listing ship.

"Elsie is here," Django said. "Elsie de Wolfe. Lady Mendl."

A slender woman of indeterminate age entered the room and surveyed it in a queenly fashion. She was backlit, and the lights in the hall behind her made her look like an angel for the top of a Christmas tree.

Her red gown was cut in Oriental style, with sleeves that draped over the skirt and a high collar on the overcoat.

Definitely a Schiaparelli gown, I noted.

Lady Mendl made a stately beeline for the table to our right, and when she spoke to the Duchess of Windsor, we all heard it.

"Wally! Dearest. Why didn't 'cha tell me you were gonna be here! I woulda been on time for a change!" Elsie de Wolfe had the broadest, loudest New York accent I had ever heard, and it was so at odds with her stylish appearance, the regal way she had entered, and the reverence with which the others in the room obviously admired her, I couldn't help but laugh.

Django took a long drag on his cigarette and blew the smoke over my shoulder. "Don't let the accent fool you," he said. "She's the smartest person here, male or female. Get in her good graces and stay there if you want to be a success." He stubbed out his cigarette in a bronze ashtray and pushed back his chair. "Back to work," he said.

The other musicians had already gathered on their platform and were through the first measures of a song.

"They started without you," I said.

He grinned. "If this crowd doesn't stop acting like a room of corpses they'll finish without me, too. Thanks for the drink."

Elsa Schiaparelli made her appearance halfway through the second set. She was draped in purple jersey embroidered with silver flowers. Her quick, black eyes scanned the room, and she waved when she saw me.

From the corner of my eye I could see my brother and his girl in the middle of the dance floor, swaying together, his blond head leaning against her even blonder one. I wondered if her husband was somewhere in this crowd, watching. Schiap saw Charlie and Ania, too, and stopped briefly to talk with them. She said something that reminded them they weren't alone, I thought, because after that they put some distance between themselves when they danced.

Schiap came over and sat with me. "I just told Madame Bouchard that some sequins might loosen if she danced quite that closely with your brother," she said. "And people do talk. I see your dress fits. Good." Schiap beamed so that her little saint's face lit up. One of the waiters working the room immediately brought her a glass of champagne, but she did not touch it. This was work, her posture said, and Schiap didn't drink when she was working.

"You should get up, move around, let people see you in that dress," she said.

"I will. In a few minutes."

The music ended and Charlie and Ania came back to the table. Ania was flushed and lovely; Charlie looked worried. Schiap, narrowing her eyes, taking in all the implications of the scene, toasted the couple with her untasted champagne.

"See that woman over there? The one in the backless black velvet?" Schiap leaned her head close to mine, and her eyes blazed in the direction of the woman. "It's one of mine, and she's removed the white satin bow that's supposed to be just above the derriere. I've warned her that if she keeps altering my gowns she'll be barred from the salon. I'm an artist. You don't meddle with my creations."

"Why would you?" Ania agreed.

I thought Schiap's response was a little strong for a tiff with a client till I saw where her gaze had stopped: the woman in the altered gown was sitting at the table of German officers.

She rose. "Well, time to mingle. And oh, a word. Baron von Dincklage's automobile was just pulling up a minute ago." There was acid in her voice when she said "baron." Schiap, it was apparent, had no great fondness for titles. She smiled at Ania and left.

"I thought he was still in Sanary-sur-Mer," Ania whispered. She had turned ashen.

She dropped Charlie's hand. They looked like two guilty adolescents who had been caught out. *Who is Baron von Dincklage?* I wondered. *And what is he to Madame Bouchard?* Certainly not her husband, unless she used a different name for some reason. I had a sudden urge to flee, to pull Charlie away with me, like we did when we were children being chased by a snarling dog, pulling my brother away from danger.

What if I had left then and pulled Charlie along with me? Would things have turned out any differently?

Django and his band started playing a quick fox-trot just as the woman I'd seen standing on the balcony entered. I recognized the long string of pearls, the slim black jersey sheath. Now, in the stronger light, I could see the details of her face, the heavy black brows over black eyes, the long scarlet mouth. She was as thin as an exclamation point and leaned slightly back as she walked.

She was accompanied by a man in military uniform, a German uniform. He was a head taller than she was, broadly built, stern, good-looking in the same blond way that Charlie was.

"Coco Chanel. She's wearing the pearls from the Grand Duke Dmitri," a woman behind me whispered.

"And the diamond bracelet from the Duke of Westminster," said a second woman, her voice full of both awe and disapproval.

Coco, unsmiling, surveyed the room. It seemed to me that she and the German with her had met by accident rather than appointment because they were both hesitant about what to do next. Von Dincklage made a little bow as if he would go to a different table, but Coco put her hand on his arm and her diamond bracelet glinted its thousands of facets. He nodded yes. They sat together at an empty table, two tables over from us.

Ania drained the fresh cocktail Charlie had brought and turned slightly away from him so that she was facing me. There was panic in her eyes. I had never hunted, but I imagined this was what the fox looked like when the dogs had found its trail.

I smiled, laughed a little, said something fatuous, the kind of comment made in the middle of a silly conversation, pretending we had been talking about her hairdresser for hours. Ania caught on. "Too much pomade," she agreed. Charlie discreetly rose and made his way to the buffet table.

Von Dincklage helped Coco out of her neat little bolero jacket and handed it to an aide who had followed closely behind them. The other man, young and deferential, made a heel-clicking half bow and went off in search of the hat-check room.

Ania by now had also left our table. Her initial panic had resolved into confidence of what she knew must happen next: she went to the baron, gave him her hand, and offered her cheek for a kiss to this formidable man who eyed the room as if he expected applause simply for arriving.

Charlie, who had returned with a plate of strawberries, leaned close and spoke as quietly as possible. "That's Hans Günther von Dincklage. Head of the German press and propaganda department in Paris. Ania is his mistress."

"Are he and Coco Chanel also lovers?" I asked. There was intimacy in the way she looked at him, the way she took his hand as he pulled out her chair for her. The air felt thick with danger and secrets.

"I don't know. I hope so. Maybe that would keep him away from Ania. Is that Coco Chanel?" Charlie and I watched, our attention as fiercely caught as if we were at a play, complete with costumes and lighting effects: the famous designer, the German officer, Ania standing there, her arms hanging at her sides like a child about to be reprimanded.

Charlie looked absolutely miserable.

"Oh, Charlie. What have you gotten yourself into?"

"Love," he said.

Coco looked up from where she had put her evening bag on the table. "Good evening," she said to Ania, finally acknowledging her. "A new frock, I see. What a sense of humor Schiaparelli has. This is the reason you left my salon so quickly?"

Say something, I silently ordered Ania, *something witty and light,* but she could not, and the look in Coco's black eyes, dilated from the dim light, was frightening.

"Really?" Von Dincklage tilted his head back for a better look. "I rather like the frock." He corrected himself hurriedly. "Not as lovely as one of your gowns, of course, Mademoiselle Chanel."

Mademoiselle. He hadn't called her Coco. They weren't lovers. Not yet. But judging by the look in Coco's eyes, if she had her way, they soon would be.

The aide standing stiffly behind von Dincklage saw us watching. He blushed when our eyes met, and then he frowned. Coco and von Dincklage rose to dance, and the aide came over, stood in front of me, and clicked his heels. He looked about my age. There were the beginnings of fine lines at the corners of his eyes, that first sign that announces the midtwenties, but he had that very fair complexion that Charlie and Ania had, the kind of coloring that looks almost childish well into middle age.

"No, thank you. I don't dance," I said.

"May I sit?" He sat without waiting for my response.

Ania and Charlie were dancing again, but with a good foot of space between them, acting the way men and women act when they are mere acquaintances, not lovers, avoiding looking into each other's eyes even as they whispered together, studying the room and the other people, all that had not existed for them until a few moments ago. I wondered what she was saying to him, what he was saying to her. There was fear in her face, worry in his.

"Your brother knows Madame Bouchard?" the aide asked, tapping his fingers on the table.

"I believe so," I said, feigning disinterest. "Not certain, though. She's very pretty, isn't she?"

"If you like the type." He drummed his fingertips on the table.

Let the games begin, and oh, how they did. My first day in Paris, and the stage was already set, the actors in place, and I had only a vague prickling of the scalp to announce it, that excitement you feel at the theater just before the curtain goes up. Of course, it's the same prickle you feel when you go for a walk down an unknown street and discover yourself in a graveyard.

Much of that evening is a blur, because the one cocktail I'd allowed myself became two and three and there was a familiar numbness of my mouth and nose that said I'd had too much and should stop. I did, unlike that other night, two years before.

Django Reinhardt's music, that blue jazz of the saxophone, the heart-pluck of guitar strings, the demand of drums, made even me get up and dance with the aide, who had stayed at my table. He was surprisingly awkward, so much so that I felt a little pity for him.

"I have not danced much," he admitted.

"Only marches, I guess." He heard the note of unfriendliness in my voice and reacted with another blush. "Yes, we have war marches. Teufelslieder. But also Mendelssohn, Handel, Schumann."

At one point I caught Coco Chanel staring in my direction, her eyes wide with curiosity and more than a little hostility.

The aide, whose name I still didn't know, hummed as he danced, a gentle bumblebee of vibration tickling my ear. I managed to keep my eye on Charlie and Ania and von Dincklage, off and on during the evening. Once in a while I would glimpse Ania dancing by with someone, her expression a mask of forced gaiety, with a tight-lipped smile that never reached her eyes.

Lady Mendl made sure the champagne kept flowing, made sure the wallflowers all had someone to laugh with. This was her party, and she stage-managed it like a professional, steering some people away from each other, leading others together. I sensed a purpose behind the laughter, the meetings, and it felt as if I had walked into a situation already far in progress. The room was alive with secrets and infidelities, with competition and animosity and an overriding need to simply enjoy what there was to enjoy, that "eat, drink, and be merry" desperation of people who sense there is much too much to lose, who fear a war on the horizon.

At midnight, the witching hour, Coco Chanel came to the table. I stupidly rose to greet her, as if I were going to bow to the queen or something. Coco smiled, delighted by my deference. She studied me the way I'd seen art students trying to find their visual way through a model's pose, the emotion of the crooked elbow, the significance of one slightly lower eyebrow.

"So young," she said under her breath. Coco, that year, was fifty-five years old, still beautiful but with the kind of beauty one begins to describe as "well preserved." Fifty-five, for a woman, especially for a woman who bases her fame and fortune on appeal, is a dangerous age. And von Dincklage, only at the party for an hour, was already bored.

"Interesting dress," she said, her tone making it clear she found it not at all interesting. "One of Elsa Schiaparelli's? It doesn't suit you. Wrong color. You should wear ivory, not white, and it doesn't hang well. Too bad for Lady Mendl her party turned out to be so boring, so silly. It must be all the Schiaparelli gowns. Even Madame Bouchard, who looks so beautiful in my clothes . . . Never a good thing, all these laughable dresses with their feathers and peasant embroideries."

She dismissed me with a shrug and said to the aide, "The baron is ready to leave. Come."

Across the room, I felt Schiap's eyes blazing on us. She gave me a thumbs-up, and I knew this night had been her victory. Coco passed Schiap on her way out, and they eyed each other like hungry lionesses looking for prey. The air between them was so bristling they could have impaled themselves on it.

With von Dincklage gone, the room seemed to relax. Ania and Charlie danced cheek to cheek again, their eyes closed.

Sometime around two in the morning, Lady Mendl came and sat at my table. "Call me Elsie," she said, assessing me with a gimlet eye. Elsie was one of the few in the room who was stone sober. "So. You are Charlie's big sister."

"I am," I admitted.

With her pointed, ageless face resting in the palm of her hand, she leaned closer. "You know, we all like Charlie very much. He is a fine boy."

"I love him like a brother," I said.

Elsie laughed. "Talk to him. He is in a dangerous situation, I think."

I imitated her posture, leaning an elbow on the table and my face into the palm of my hand. The room whirled a bit around me. "He never listens to me," I said. "Oh, how I have tried to warn him of the dangers of womanizing. You should have seen him during the New York debutante balls. A string of broken hearts."

"This time, it will be his."

"I like Ania, and she certainly seems smitten with him." *Husband,* a voice in the back of my head reminded me. *She has a husband.*

"I like Ania, too. Never said I didn't. Well." Elsie sat up straight again. Our little tête-à-tête was over. "Never complain, never explain," she said, standing. "Are you here for a while? Yes? I hope I see you again. We can talk about New York."

"We could, but I haven't been there in a long while," I said.

"And to think being an expat used to be a sign of rebellion. Times have changed." She gave my hand a gentle shake and moved off into the throng, her red brocade gown disappearing into the melee of colors.

"Elsie liked you," Charlie said later, as he put my wrap over my shoulders, sometime around three in the morning. "We'll be invited to the Durst ball." His bow tie had come undone, his evening jacket was rumpled, and there was a bit of the lost boy in his eye, an expression I would learn to associate with Ania's absence. She had left earlier, alone, as if separate exits would erase the open intimacy of their dancing, observed by so many.

"The Durst ball. It's just a party," I said.

"No, it's not. It's going to be the biggest ball of the season, with the best people. And some of the richest. They'll come in handy someday." Charlie was ambitious. When he finished his studies he planned to open a clinic, and clinics cost money. A lot of money. Without at least a few wealthy patrons he wouldn't be able to make it work.

"Well, even so. I won't be here for the ball, will I?"

"You could always come back, you know. For a day or two. I'm sure Gerald and the school wouldn't mind."

"Probably not," I agreed.

When Charlie and I left the Ritz, the party was still in progress, though the decorations and guests looked worse for wear. Couples clung wearily together on the dance floor, barely moving. A woman had passed out in a corner, her legs sticking straight out from her sleeping body so that people had to step over her. Men argued drunkenly and waved ash-tipped cigarettes at each other.

Django was leaning against the doorway at the hotel exit, a cigarette poised between his lips. He was speaking with another man, and I heard the slow burn of disagreement in his tone, saw it in the angle of his heavy black eyebrows.

"'Night," I called to him.

He waved without looking at me.

"Did you notice that when von Dincklage left, everyone started talking about the possibility of war? Too many Germans in the city right now. Everyone wonders why." Charlie kicked at a handkerchief someone had dropped on the street, and the Ritz doorman glowered, then came and picked it up, gingerly, between his thumb and index finger.

"Roosevelt says we'll stay out of it, even if there is war," I said.

Charlie sucked in his breath, the way he used to do as a little boy, just before he began teasing me. "Roosevelt is an America Firster. A lot of people disagree with him, think that if Europe goes to war, we must as well."

"Would you, Charlie?"

"If it comes to that."

"What does Ania say about it? What does her husband think?"

Charlie grew very still and quiet. When he lit a cigarette, his hands were trembling.

"Sorry," I said.

"Think nothing of it. You think I'm having the time of my life, being in love with another fellow's wife, trying to make some sense of all this? I've tried to get over her, but she's . . ." He paused and took a long drag. "She's the one for me. Can't help it, Lily. Any more than you could help it with Allen. It kind of takes over, doesn't it?"

"Yes," I agreed. "It takes over so much that nothing else matters."

A taxi pulled up, and Charlie opened the door for me. We were too tired to walk any farther.

"So tell me about the other one. The baron," I said, leaning into Charlie for warmth.

"A friend of the family. More like a business associate. And yes, they are, or have been, lovers. From the little that Ania says about it, I suspect the husband actually approves. The baron is very well connected and high up in the German government, which could be useful if there is a war. Don't make that face, Lily. It's not such an uncommon arrangement here."

Out the cab window, the Seine glowed like tarnished pewter in the predawn light.

Charlie stared gloomily at the river. Night was lifting, and Paris emerged from grayness into the lavender shades of early morning.

"She loves me, too. I'm certain of it," he said.

"Then why doesn't Ania just divorce her husband and run off with you? It's not a great beginning, but at least it is a beginning."

"There's a child. Ania has a young daughter. And her husband won't let her take the child with us."

I sank back into the upholstered cushions, stunned by this revelation.

"Oh, Charlie," I sighed. "You are in trouble."

· FOUR ·

When I woke up the next day—the same day, actually—the birds in the chestnut trees had already finished their morning song-fest and the housewives of the neighborhood were shouting their children in for lunch. As soon as my eyes opened, anxiety and guilt made the room spin even more than the hangover did. I had missed my first class of the day and Gerald would be angry.

Slowly, my pulse throbbing in my head like a hammer, I sat up and remembered where I was. Paris. No classes. No Gerald. Freedom washed over me. I wouldn't have to dread the first glance of hate from Gerald or the whispers of the schoolgirls who had turned the story of Allen and Lily into the kind of tragedy they whispered to one another late at night, in the dark.

There was a note under the door. *See you later*, Charlie had written. *I'll pick you up at six. I have lectures to attend at the Salpêtrière. The day, what is left of it, is yours.*

A whole day, and no one to account to, no chores, no classes, no boring sherry hour with the school faculty. The day was a blank canvas for me to fill in with color. Trailing immediately behind the pleasure, though, was guilt, like a stray dog that wouldn't go away. I was alone.

I dressed in my old frock and walked to the corner, aware of the strange glances I received from the very chic Parisians who knew an out-of-date dress when they saw it. At the café, I had a coffee and a roll with butter. I dawdled at the bookstalls crouching under the plane trees, then stopped at another café opposite the river for another cup of coffee, knowing all along what my destination was but wanting to postpone, to anticipate it the way Christmas gifts are anticipated, and embraces in dark rooms.

The Seine was a hard, brilliant silver in the strong afternoon light. The gardens of the Esplanade des Tuileries were busy with nannies pushing prams, young lovers walking with their arms around each other's waists. The garden beds under the canopy of trees were filled with impatiens the exact color of one of the gowns I had seen at Elsa Schiaparelli's salon. Shocking pink. I didn't want to see pink, though, but blue: Leonardo's *Mona Lisa*, with multihued sky and river in the background.

When I had spent that summer in Paris, this had been the painting that most captured my imagination, with its golds and reds and blues, blues made of precious azurite and lapis from the mountains of Afghanistan. On the bench in front of it was where I had fallen in love with Allen, who loved the painting for its mysterious geometry. "There are no straight lines," he would point out with delight. "No suggestion of beginning or ending, or journey. No strife."

I entered the crowded Louvre at the Denon wing, making my way up the grand staircase, loving all over again the mosaic floors, the grand vaulted ceilings, the crowds.

Mona Lisa's smile represents Leonardo's concept for the painting: happiness. Lisa was the wife of Francesco del Giocondo, and the name itself means *smiling, happy, carefree*—all those things that are the opposite of *unhappy, sad, desperate*. When you are first in love, Mona Lisa smiles with you, agrees with your joy. When you are widowed, her smile is a reminder of all you have lost.

And what many viewers of the *Mona Lisa* don't recognize is that the colors, those subdued browns, russets, golds, and blues, have been changed by time. The varnish has added a layer of yellow to the painting. Originally, the sky and the lake behind Lisa would have been the bluest of blues, her sleeves a more definite red. To see the *Mona Lisa* is to see two paintings: what had been, and what is now. It had become a painting about what is stolen by time.

I sat on the burnished wooden bench, absorbing those shifting blues, the red of the road behind Lisa, the darkness of her garments that, when da Vinci painted her, would have been very stylish. Even the eternal Mona Lisa wanted to be fashionable.

It's just a painting, Gerald would have said. But the calmness of the blue and the muted red besieged me with memories. I was crying, silently, with tears streaming down my cheeks, crying like I hadn't since the funeral. People tiptoed past me, and I remembered what my father had told me once after a day of ice-skating in Central Park, the year before the Spanish flu invaded the city: that when the toes are frostbitten they are numb, but as the blood begins to flow through them again, as life begins to return to them, there is pain, a terrible burning. I sat in front of Allen's favorite painting and burned with the loss of him.

Charlie and Ania took me out for supper at Café Dome, where we could eat cheaply and sit for as long as we wanted. Ania had purple circles under her eyes and had lost the easy vivacity of the day before. She wore a Chanel suit with a fitted jacket and epaulettes, military style, and a five-strand bracelet of perfectly matched pearls. Charlie had his arms folded over his chest. They seemed to be in the middle of a quarrel, so I talked for all three of us, asking questions and answering them. *How was your day? Great. And yours? Get any sleep last night? Not much.*

Gossip, maybe? "Interesting, meeting Coco Chanel last night," I said. That woke up Ania, at least.

"Interesting," Ania said. "Such a mild word for her. She was born poor, you know. Very poor. Somewhere in the south. Her mother died; her father abandoned her and her sisters and her brothers. She learned how to sew in an orphanage, though she tells people she was raised by aunts. Childhood," Ania sighed. "How many stories we invent for ourselves."

"Charlie and I were raised by our aunt," I said, remembering how losing our parents had bonded Charlie and me even more fiercely together. Who was Coco Chanel close to?

"A sister, somewhere," Ania said. "Gossip says that there might be a child that she calls her nephew, but I don't think so. She doesn't have much of the mother about her." Her voice grew quiet, a sign, I would learn, that she was thinking of her own child.

"What stories did you invent?" Charlie asked, his hands now spread wide over the tabletop, good strong hands. But perhaps Ania didn't know this yet, about him, that he stared at his hands like this when he was unhappy.

"About a Prince Charming who would come for me. He had blond hair and blue eyes. Let me see. He looked like you!"

"And here I am." Unable to resist her, unable to continue whatever the quarrel had been, he picked up her hand, the one without the wedding ring, and kissed it.

"Coco knew how to use her looks," Ania said. "She knows how to please men. Do I please you, Charlie?"

"You already know the answer, don't you?"

An accordionist took up his place on the corner and began playing the bittersweet musette music of the Parisian streets. There at our little table at Café Dome, as I crumbled pieces of baguette as waiters in black suits and white aprons bustled around us, Ania began to cry, two large crystal tears sliding down her cheeks.

"Oh God," said Charlie. "I can't take this." He rose, his chair scraping over the floor like a grinding gear in a badly shifted car. He skulked in the direction of the bar. I sat with Ania and put my hand over hers. Her shoulders shook, and she hid her face behind a lace handkerchief. We sat like that for a long while, till the handkerchief fell onto the table. Ania grimaced and sat up straight, pulling at the emerald-green bolero jacket she wore over her dress.

"Want to talk?" I offered.

"It is all so bad," she sighed in her deep, beautiful voice. "So very bad and so difficult. Charlie doesn't understand." She would not explain what it was Charlie would not understand, but given that she had a husband and a child and a lover and seemed to be also in love with my brother, I thought the situation was pretty self-explanatory.

The long summer day disappeared, and the evening stole all the colors. Ania and I sat in gray twilight punctuated with flickers of candles, glowing tips of cigarettes, and the headlights of passing cars. We were sitting outside, and I could hear Charlie inside, arguing with someone at the bar. He did not come back out to join us, and when a car came for Ania at ten, she gave me a quick embrace and walked out alone, to where the driver held the door for her. There was a defeated slump to her shoulders.

Someone was waiting for her in the backseat, a man who kept his face turned away from the café. Von Dincklage.

"Ania!" Charlie shouted, running into the street as the car pulled away.

"Too late," I told him. "Sit down with me. Have another drink. Charlie, what do you know about her?"

"She's from Warsaw. She married young, an arranged marriage. I think it helped to pay some debts her father had. Her husband is an antiques dealer, too. Furniture. Other things."

"Antiques?" She wore jewels that a duchess would have coveted and seemed to wear only couture. Her husband would have to sell a lot of

Louis XVI chairs to pay those bills. I wondered if Ania, like Coco, embroidered her own story.

Charlie turned away and with a long, steady finger traced the ornate molding on the black iron café chair. "Who we were yesterday doesn't matter."

That was a physician talking. The past could be cut away like damaged tissue, like a crushed limb.

Charlie and I spent the next day together, from breakfast till bedtime, and by his devotion to me I understood the depth of his quarrel with Ania. They were staying away from each other.

"Oh, just call her," I said. "We've gone to the Eiffel Tower, Versailles, too many gardens with too many roses. I'm tired of being a tourist, and you're not really here with me, you know."

"Sorry," he said. "But I can't just phone her, can I?"

No, of course not. Who might answer the phone?

We were sitting in the dappled shade of plane trees in the Place Dauphine, watching old men play *boules*. Charlie, next to me on the bench, leaned forward so I couldn't see his face.

"I want her to leave her husband. To come with me, back to Boston. She may not be the perfect doctor's wife. Marrying a divorced woman . . ."

"If she can get a divorce . . ."

"A divorcée wouldn't have been my first choice. But I love her, Lily. The kid's okay, too. I met her once. She's about seven, looks just like Ania, sweet as honey."

Charlie, the boy who earned straight As and excelled in collegiate sport; who had dated girls whose fathers owned banks and whose mothers organized charity balls, who queened it in the society pages; Charlie, who planned to open a private clinic, would risk it all for Ania.

"She is lovely," I agreed, "but—"

"Stop," he said. "No lectures."

We sat in silence and watched the old men playing *boules* with a ferocity and competitiveness that made me wonder what they, in earlier years, had done for their various loves.

"I'm sorry about Allen," Charlie said. "I can't imagine how difficult this has been for you. Well, maybe I can now, after this thing with Ania. If I lose her . . ."

"I know. Missing Allen is all I have left of him."

"You need someone to take care of you, someone who is actually here, with you."

"Do I? You know, I've never really been on my own for more than a month or two. My brother-in-law wasn't exactly sympathetic after Allen died, but at least he made sure I had a roof over me. Now, I have no idea what I'm capable of."

He didn't look convinced. "Is this the best time to find out? There may be a war, you know."

"Even if there is . . ." War was something that happened to other people, wasn't it? For two years I'd carried a sense of immunity, the feeling that the worst had already happened to me. In Paris, if anything, it felt even stronger. Nothing could touch me. Nothing, except my brother's unhappiness.

· FIVE ·

COCO AND SCHIAP

The fifth act was heavy weather. Storms and murders and tears and, finally, victory. Coco sat in her private box at the opera, trying to ignore the empty seat next to her. Alone, again. But not for much longer, she promised herself.

Hamlet was von Dincklage's favorite French opera, he had told her. The others—*Beatrice et Benedict, Carmen, La Vie Parisienne*—had a certain frivolity that was fine for dance halls but not the grand stage. Opera should elevate and inspire the soul, not fill it with private ephemeral romance that fizzed away as quickly as an opened bottle of champagne. *Hamlet*, though. Wagner would have approved of Ambroise Thomas's score and Barbier's libretto. They had taken liberties with the play: no more the final crowded scene in which everyone dies, including Hamlet. In this version, ending in a graveyard, Hamlet kills the false king and hears his father's ghost proclaim, "Live for your people! God has made you king!"

That was a fine moment, Coco agreed, a glorious moment, but oh, the journey getting there! Well, the next time she saw von Dincklage she could mention this performance, the fine voice of Ophelia—who was she? Coco surreptitiously put on her glasses and checked the program, memorized the name.

Her backside ached, her feet had gone to sleep, and she wished, more than anything, to be in her somber little bedroom in her dear little suite at the Ritz, feeling sleep finally creep up on her, take her more gently, more sweetly, than any lover. That was the problem with insomnia, and she'd had insomnia since Iribe's death. No matter how physically tired she was, she never grew sleepy. Not without a little help.

Soon, she promised herself. Soon, her bed, her little helpers, the little pills, or maybe even a syringe, to help her sleep. And sometime after that, in a day, a week, a month, von Dincklage would come to her. Madame Bouchard's hold on him couldn't last much longer, and she, Coco, could wait because she knew he would come. He must. She willed it!

But first, she must leave the theater. And that would be a contest, because Schiaparelli, that Italian woman, was there that night as well, seated not in a box but in the orchestra, fourth row center, so that it seemed the entire audience had been arranged around her. Such a skill for theatrics, such a need to be the center of attention. She'd heard that when the woman was in New York with her husband, the fake Polish count who had abandoned her, they'd appeared onstage in a cheap mind-reading and hypnotism act and been asked to leave town rather hurriedly by the New York police, or be charged with fraud. Hah! At least the New York police knew a talentless cheat when they saw her.

Coco calculated the best moment to leave her box, to make her way down the left arm of the grand marble staircase. Too soon, and no one would be there to see her. Too late, and they would have left or, worse, already crowded around the Schiaparelli woman.

Count to one hundred. Slowly rise, let the maid arrange her wrap around her shoulders. Slowly glide to the grand staircase, pose a minute at the top, and then . . .

They swarmed her. Photographers, journalists, fans, clients, nobody-women who wanted to be clients, who wanted private showings, who didn't know better than to wear heavy furs on a warm night, men who wanted advice about wardrobes for their mistresses, husbands who needed an exceptional gift to make up for an exceptional "mistake" discovered by their wives.

It was the opera, not the *bal musette*, so they were polite, they did not jostle her or shout at her, but it was adoration all the same.

She pretended indifference, pretended fatigue, even a little humility, said *yes, no, yes, yes, no. Maybe.*

And there was von Dincklage, standing far outside her circle of admirers, watching, and on his arm that blond tart, Madame Bouchard. She was wearing a Schiaparelli gown. A different one. How many had she purchased?

Coco froze her face into a smile. Waved. Von Dincklage, from the great distance, made her a little clicking bow, his eyes on her face, running down her figure. He liked what he saw. She saw it in his eyes. His politeness and attention at Elsie's party hadn't been forced or faked. Her smile became authentic. She felt the frisson of shared passion flow between them. Soon.

There was a burst of loud laughter. And there, coming up behind von Dincklage and Madame Bouchard, there she was, Elsa Schiaparelli, looking ridiculous in white crepe with gray stripes painted on it, and a fluttering cape of goose feathers. A drowning duck, that was what Bendor, the Duke of Westminster, would have called her. He detested her and her Bolshevik leanings.

Schiaparelli was with the Spanish artist Salvador Dalí, who had dressed even more outrageously, in emerald-green satin, his black mustache too long, too waxed.

Dalí bowed for von Dincklage, wrapping his cape around his arm with a flourish, giving Madame Bouchard an exaggerated kiss on the hand. The three of them began an earnest conversation, probably about the little soprano's voice, her heartbreaking version of Ophelia. But the Italian woman stood a little to the side, looking up at Coco.

Neither of them waved or nodded. Yet the huge foyer was reduced at that moment to just two people, Elsa Schiaparelli and Coco Chanel, and the energy flowing between them was ready to catch on fire.

Boring, Schiap thought. *Does she never wear anything but black, has she no humor or wit whatsoever?* But that was a good trick, coming down the grand staircase alone, even her maid hanging far behind. An entrance. Schiap had observed it all, watched carefully and done her best to distract Madame Bouchard and her German as long as she could, so that they did not look up at that white marble staircase landing, that woman in black and pearls, an overthought study in black and white, hypocritically prim.

It had worked. Chanel had already been on the last stair when von Dincklage finally looked up, finally noticed her. But he had noticed, his eyes had lingered, and Schiap couldn't read the look in her new client's eyes. Was Madame Bouchard frightened of the competition or relieved by it? Not every mistress wanted to keep her lover always close by her side, and Madame Bouchard seemed quite taken with that American boy. A husband rich as Croesus, though no one knew exactly where the money came from, a handsome protector who was one of the most influential men in the German government, and Madame had fallen for a boy who had to haggle over the cost of a dress.

Well, wasn't that the way of the world. *L'amore domina senza regole.* Love has no rules. Or sense, for that matter. *Good for Ania*, Schiap thought. *Touch iron for luck, she's going to need it.*

Tableau: Coco and von Dincklage staring at each other, Madame Bouchard staring into the distance, Schiap taking it all in. The moment passed. Coco looked away, talked to a man who had just tapped her shoulder, and now Dalí was pulling at Schiap's arm; he wanted to leave, now, to go down to the river, to one of the sailors' drinking places where there was supposed to be a man who could swallow two-foot-long knives.

People who had seemed as frozen as a photograph the moment before began moving, talking, heading toward the multiple arched doorways of the opera house, to rue Scribe where their taxis and limousines were waiting.

"The Krauts will move into Czechoslovakia next, mark my words," Schiap heard a man behind her say, heated words from the middle of an argument she had only just noticed, so focused on Coco had she been. "That Nazi-lover Henlein will gift-wrap it for Hitler's birthday."

"Even so," his female companion said, "Czechoslovakia is far from France. What difference does it make?" She shrugged, and her fur stole slipped a little down her shoulders.

What difference? Schiap felt a flutter of panic. *Am I the only one who sees? Who understands? I need an escape route. I must know I can get my daughter out of France, when the time comes. I need connections. More connections. Good connections. Ania could help with that.* Impulsively, Schiap gave Ania a tight hug, her little dark head barely reaching Ania's shoulders.

Von Dincklage, unsmiling, took Ania's hand and led her away. He hadn't even looked at Schiap, and she knew why. Two years ago he had come into her salon with one of his mistresses and Schiap had refused to greet him, the embodiment of Nazi propaganda. Suave and as cold as a Moscow winter, he was the kind of man who changed the subject if the Jewish problem was brought up, who refused to acknowledge the labor camps Hitler had begun building as soon as he'd become chancellor. Because of what he stood for, she had refused to greet von Dincklage, and that had been a mistake. Keep your friends close and your enemies closer.

And of course Coco saw all that, the snub from von Dincklage, and was satisfied to see that the Schiaparelli woman had become as discomfited as she had been. Their eyes met, flared, looked away.

"To the sword swallower, then!" Schiap said brightly to a glowering Dalí, who was angry that so little attention of the past minutes had been directed at him. "Quickly, because once my daughter is here I won't want her to know I go to see such monstrosities."

Schiap and Coco turned their backs on each other and left by separate entrances.

For the next several days Charlie and Ania and I spent almost all our time together. There was a forced quality to our gaiety, and the little furrow between Charlie's eyebrows became a constant. Allen and I had been so happy together, unlike Charlie and Ania, who veered between quarrels and desperation. But then Allen and I hadn't had to hide and lie and pretend.

One afternoon, when Charlie had to attend another surgery demonstration, I took Ania with me to the Louvre and we sat in meditative silence before the *Mona Lisa*, Ania studying it with her hands folded childlike in her lap, her painted red nails echoing the reds of the road in the landscape, her blue dress matching the blue of the river.

"Your eyes are the same coppery brown as hers," I told her.

"You must tell that to Charlie. It will make him laugh. Not much else does these days, I'm afraid." She rose, and her heels clicked over the parquet floor. Heads turned in her direction; the guard at the door shook his hand loosely from the wrist, that very Parisian gesture that is the equivalent of a wolf whistle. She was oblivious to it all, lost in thought.

We walked outside, between the green of the Tuileries Gardens and the pewter Seine.

"I'm supposed to return to England in a few days," I said.

Ania stopped cold, her eyes flashing with panic. She took both my hands and pressed them to the base of her throat. We could have been a tableau of murder about to happen, so dramatic was the look on her face.

"Don't go," she said. "Please, Lily. Charlie is so much happier when you are here." She remembered herself and dropped my hands, smiled with one side of her mouth slightly turned down. "Anyway, what is there back in England? Paris is better, isn't it?"

I thought of my room over the garage, the way I met a memory of Allen at every turn, twist, and staircase of the school, in the gardens and wooded paths. I thought of the way Gerald looked at me, and of my studio there, where I hadn't begun a painting in two years, the purgatory of my existence there. Orpheus and Eurydice. Live in the underworld with your beloved, or leave him behind, travel back into the light.

"I'll run out of money soon." My allowance had ended when I turned twenty-one, and I had been living off the small amount of money Allen and I had saved to put down for a house.

"Something will come up. I feel it. Please, please." Ania took my hands again, this time with joy, shaking them and pulling me in the direction of the American Express office near the Hotel de Ville.

Staying longer in Paris, I telegrammed to Gerald. *Hope you are well.* Gerald responded the very next day. *Well enough. Will put your things in storage.* Not a single friendly word, nor a suggestion that my job would still be there when I returned.

A door slammed in my imagination, and I stood in the American Express office cold with doubt, already missing the memories waiting there for me at the school. How many ways can you lose a beloved? Every day seemed to offer a new one.

"You look pale," Charlie said the next morning.

"I'm fine. I'm staying longer in Paris, you know. Until this big party you've been telling me about."

"Ball," Charlie said. "The biggest high-society ball of the season. Thank you, Lily."

"I never knew you were so taken with costume parties. I understand potential patrons will be there, but there's something else going on, isn't there?"

We were drinking coffee and eating ham sandwiches in one of the nameless corner cafés that are all over Paris; this one was across from Cador André, the tea shop. The windows were filled with pink, green, blue, and yellow pastries arranged in artistic mimicry of stained-glass rose windows.

"Ania has promised to decide by that night. At least, her husband has promised to let her know if she can have a divorce or not."

"You mean she's actually considering it? Leaving her husband and . . ."

"Yes. She's actually considering it."

"And the child?"

"She won't come with me if she can't take her daughter with her. God, Lily, what have I got to offer her? I'm still in medical school, no money, nothing."

"You have everything a woman in love could want," I said. "That's all."

"I love her so much. God, I couldn't even afford to pay for her clothes."

"I don't think that's a deciding factor, Charlie. Besides, she'd look good in anything, even a paper bag."

Beautiful Ania wore couture from morning to night and probably even in bed. Clothing can be worn as a kind of armor, a good-luck charm. *I'm wearing Chanel*, the woman says. *Who can harm me in a Chanel suit? I'm wearing Schiaparelli. Who can abuse me?* If only it were that easy. But maybe it's enough to feel safe because, in fact, no one is safe. Not always; sometimes not ever.

"Where are we going this afternoon? Where's Ania?" I asked Charlie. It was eleven in the morning. The trees made shortened, dappled shadows over the pavement, and the colors were the colors of summer, of girls in bright dresses, window boxes full of flowers, blue sky fading to silver directly overhead.

"We're meeting Ania at the Coco Chanel salon."

"I thought she'd decided she preferred Schiaparelli?"

"Me, too. Apparently one must appease both sides. It's more complicated than politics." Charlie pushed his hands deep into his pockets and hunched his shoulders. A hot wind was blowing that day, stirring the dust and ashes of the streets and whipping my hair into my eyes as we crossed the busy rue Saint-Honoré. *I need a haircut*, I thought, tired of the old gesture of pushing my hair behind my ears.

The Chanel salon was on rue Cambon, just around the corner from the Place Vendôme. They were steps away from each other, Coco and Schiap. The Place Vendôme was the most elegant shopping section of Paris, so of course they would need to be there, to be close. But it must have galled, that possibility of always running into each other.

From the street entrance, a mirrored stairway led up to the famed Chanel showroom. Clever, I thought. What woman looks into a mirror and thinks, *I look wonderful! I need no new clothes at all!* No. She looks, she frowns, she tugs at her jacket, pulls at her skirt, adjusts her hat, and thinks, *Time for a new look, a new wardrobe.* All the way up that long stairwell to Coco Chanel, waiting to douse dissatisfaction with one's appearance with a new dress, new sweater, new jewelry.

Coco's salon didn't have the friendly atmosphere of Schiap's; the *vendeuses*, all dressed in black and white, stood at attention, their hands folded in front of their waists like schoolgirls ready to recite a lesson. The rooms were intimidatingly magnificent, all gleaming mirrors and gilt furniture and thick carpeting. It was busy that day. The society ladies were being fitted for their summer resort wear, the sporty yachting outfits daring, and swimsuits, all in the famous jersey that Chanel had made so popular.

Charlie and I sat on the beige sofas and waited for Ania to finish in the fitting room, and as we waited I watched the models pacing the room, shrugging in and out of light coats and sweaters, twirling ropes of fake pearls. The clothes were elegant and almost all in black, white, and beige. I remembered what Ania had told me, how Chanel had grown up in an orphanage ruled by nuns in their black-and-white habits.

We carry our childhoods with us all our lives, no matter how tall, how old we become. Inside me was a little girl who would always remember the red scarves of the skaters in Central Park that last day I spent with my father, before the Spanish flu took him and my mother.

Elsa Schiaparelli's Roman, upper-class childhood was there in her collections, those wild colors as vivid as the boldly striped orange-and-blue uniforms of the Swiss guards of the Vatican, the ultrafeminine shapes of the bustles and corsets found in the trunk in her attic. Chanel's childhood was in her work as well: the jersey she made chic had been the workday fabric of laborers, the subdued colors of austere orphanage life.

Charlie grew uncomfortable, sitting on the beige sofa waiting amid all this feminine flurry, fidgeting and checking his watch.

"How many fittings can one dress require?" he muttered. "What a waste of time."

"You have no idea," Ania said, creeping up behind him and putting her hands over his eyes. "And why a waste? Think of how beautiful Ania looks in her outfits."

"Ania would look beautiful in a flour sack," Charlie said, pulling her hands away and looking up at her. *Don't kiss*, I thought. *Not here, not with all these people.*

"You've never seen her in a flour sack, or probably in anything less glamorous than couture. It is part of her charm." Ania laughed.

"Madame!" The fitter called to Ania as if she were a misbehaving schoolgirl. "Come here! I am not finished!" Ania threw up her arms in mock terror and disappeared again.

A door opened on the other side of the room, and Coco Chanel, dressed in beige jersey, came through the doorway. She eyed the room, taking inventory of who was there.

"Ah. The girl from Elsie's party," she said when she saw me sitting there with Charlie. "And her very handsome brother."

Charlie blushed a bright red.

Coco smiled at us, standing in the pose that had been photographed over and over again: one leg slightly ahead of the other tilting the hips forward, one hand in a pocket, the other on her hips, opening space between her arms and body the way men of power do in Renaissance portraits.

Small head with short black hair, sharp nose with nostrils permanently flared, as if a fit of temper was coming, going, or already upon her. That Coco was famous for her fierce temper I already knew from Ania's gossip, but her lean body had the fragile, sinuous curve of an ivory figurine.

Ania was beautiful. Schiap had verve and confidence. But Coco was the epitome of style.

She gave us her bright, metallic smile, her face turned slightly sideways, just short of coy and flirtatious. She may have started out as a half-nude singer in a cheap revue in the South—Ania's gossip—but she had acquired grace and class, had learned the hard lessons that turn a peasant child into one of the richest women in the world, with the beauty and social skills to match.

"You need a new wardrobe," she said, giving me a hard look.

"I do, but my stock portfolio is a little low at the moment, and I'd hate to sell the family jewels," I said. "I'm only a schoolteacher, Mademoiselle."

My impertinence took her by surprise. People did not talk back to Coco Chanel.

She laughed, then raised her hand, and I saw she was holding a small scissors, not a cigarette. "May I?" she asked, and, not waiting for a reply, grasped the faded silk rose corsage that had been stitched onto my old cardigan. Deftly, she cut it away and smoothed the cardigan flat over my collarbone.

"Better," she said. "No need for frippery. The sweater is a good color, once it can be seen."

I looked in the mirror. It was better without the old cloth corsage. Simpler, cleaner, classier.

"Ania will be out in a minute," she told Charlie. "We're almost done. Such a lovely woman. I wish all my clients wore my clothes as well as she does. Too bad about that Schiaparelli dress. Not right for her, not at all. And you . . ." She turned back to me. "Come to me sometime. Let's see what we can do." She smiled again and disappeared back through the doorway. When she was gone, the *vendeuses* sighed with relief.

"I can't afford vanity," I said to Charlie.

"Dressing well is not vanity. Even if the fittings do take too long." Ania was out of the dressing room again, lipstick freshly applied, white-blond hair smoothed back from her forehead. Charlie jumped to his feet when he saw her. I wished he could hide his emotion just a little, make her guess just a little, but then I saw the light in her eyes and knew she felt the same about him.

"You have been honored," Ania said to me. "Mademoiselle Chanel usually does not come out to speak with her customers. You have sparked her interest, I think. She likes Americans."

"You've made a conquest," Charlie joked.

We spent the rest of the day together, walking, eating when hungry, sightseeing. On Boulevard Saint-Germain we passed a long line outside a pharmacy, mostly men, a few women, avoiding eye contact with those around them.

"They're saying that France is going to ban contraception," Ania said. "They want us all to have more babies. Lots of babies."

"Countries want lots of babies when they know a war is coming," Charlie said. "Of course, all of the would-be fathers will be off in the trenches, so it's not even logical."

"There won't be a war," Ania argued. "France does not want one. That's what everyone says. That's why they let Hitler take Czecho-slovakia."

"But Hitler does want one. Condoms won't be the only thing disappearing soon. If I were you, I'd buy a good warm fur coat. There are some cold winters coming." Charlie jammed his hands deeper into his pockets.

"Charlie, you're frightening me," Ania said.

"I want to frighten you. I want you to leave with me, when I leave Paris."

"You must see the Pont Alexandre III," she said. "We must go to Saint-Roch, where Corneille is buried. The puppet show in the Parc Monceau, the catacombs in Montparnasse," she said. And we went, Charlie pretending to huff and puff, Ania's face radiant with joy, racing through the sights of Paris as if we had this day, this one day, to enjoy it. I should have paid better attention, I realized years later.

By nightfall we were exhausted and ended up in a Montmartre poetry café, slumped on rickety ancient chairs, drinking beer and eating cheese sandwiches. The poetry at the café that evening had a rough quality of anger. My schoolroom French couldn't accommodate all of it, but what I understood had a knife-edge quality of danger combined with sour bitterness. It made me think of what my aunt had said one night about the bread lines and shantytowns that had mushroomed after the market crash, that people had grown a layer of scar tissue over their emotions. After Charlie and I had finished high school in New York, she and my now-retired uncle had left the city and moved to Los Angeles, looking for more sun, for an easier life.

Two loud people at a table next to us began arguing, shouting. It was political, one man agreeing with Chamberlain that Hitler would stop in Austria, the other shouting, "Never!"

"This is dreary," Ania said, forcing a smile. "Let's go to the Casino and see the new Maurice Chevalier revue."

"Can't afford it," Charlie mumbled.

"But I can. Oh, Charlie, please. To make me happy."

So we ended up at the Casino, surrounded by men in tuxedos, women in feather boas, and waiters who tried to seat us as far from the center of the room as possible, till Ania pressed a wad of bills into their palms.

The revue, *The Loves of Paris*, featured, as they usually did, many naked girls and some exotic dance troupes—it was "The Sixteen Red and Blond Greasely Girls" that season, but Maurice Chevalier was the star. He sang all of his biggest hits, tipping his hat, tapping his cane, and winking his way through "Valentine" and "Prosper." But it was when he sang "Lili Marleen" that the audience rose to its feet, howling with pleasure and clapping.

He sang it in a strong German accent, mocking the voice of Adolf Hitler, making the love song comic and ridiculous.

Ania laughed so hard she coughed up champagne, and Charlie had to thump her back.

Not everyone was laughing, though. Coco Chanel sat six tables away from us and the look on her face was a combination of hostility and wistfulness. Only someone with those very large black eyes, those heavy brows, could manage such an expression. She was at a table with von Dincklage. Oh God. Did Ania know he was there?

"Time to leave," I said, and both Charlie and Ania understood instantly. Ania left twenty more francs on the table, and we ducked out a side entrance, laughing like truant schoolchildren.

By then Paris had grown quiet and dark and shuttered, and we were sitting exhausted on a bench alongside the Seine.

"Maybe that is enough for today," Ania agreed. "But we must not waste any time, you know. You can buy anything but time."

"Right," Charlie agreed, looking up. Black clouds shuttled overhead in the midnight sky. A brisk wind whipped Ania's skirt around her knees and knocked off Charlie's hat. "I think a storm is coming. We're going to get soaked," he shouted, chasing his pale gray Stetson down the street.

· SIX ·

SCHIAP

Rain fell down the windowpane, making trails like the veins in an old person's hands.

You can temporarily erase wrinkles with cream, add false eyelashes to those grown skimpy, pinch in a widened waist with a corset, even find a surgeon to lift up the fallen face. But hands . . . there is no remedy for aged hands. Schiap put her own small hand flat on the windowpane. It was still pretty, she decided. Plump and long-fingered. But she thought of her mother's hands, how their veins mimicked blue rain rivulets over glass. Time. So little.

The house was absolutely still, all its inhabitants, the cook, the maid, the chauffeur, wrapped in sleep, all except for Schiap, who could not sleep. She leaned her head against the window, staring out into the dark, glistening night. Three o'clock in the morning. The hour of regrets.

So many. Well, of course there were. She had lived without limits, without caution, always with passion and a certain selfishness. That is how ambitious people achieve success. If you want to be always good, always kind, always self-effacing, then marry a hardworking man and spend the rest of your life bearing and raising his children.

She'd never marry again; she'd decided that long ago. Not even to her best beau, Henry Horne, the very handsome Englishman who had helped set up her London shop and little pied-à-terre in Mayfield, or his older brother, Allan, dull, correct Allan who could be so sweet when they were alone. She had shocked even herself a little by taking both brothers as lovers. But they did get along so well, no jealousy, no quarrels, that friendly comradery during hunting weekends in Scotland, civilized dinners in London.

London. Poor London. It would not be spared. She sensed it, that loud roaring overhead like hungry lions, bomb doors whirring open.

Thunder rumbled in the distance. Schiap, afraid of lightning, jumped away from the window. She was wide awake now because of fear, her drowsy insomnia kidnapped by uncompromising alertness. She counted to two hundred by fours, her lucky number, as she wrapped her magenta silk robe around her shoulders and stepped into mules made huge and fluffy with downy feathers. She slapped down the dark hall, the staircase, past the dining room, her study, all the rooms of her glorious house filled with decades of acquiring—art, curiosities, useful things, silly things.

She listed them in her head as she passed through the dark rooms and laughed to herself when she passed the dining table and its chairs all neatly tucked into a straight row. The chairs were covered in heavy brocade now. They hadn't always been. When she had first come to Paris, years ago, she had given a dinner party for the people who could help or hurt her new couture business. Her father, the medieval scholar, had taught her that: pay as much attention to potential enemies as to friends, or the battle is already lost.

Because she was very broke those first years and very inexperienced—*admit it*, she told herself, *you knew nothing about fabrics*—she'd had her dining room chairs covered with a cheap white rubbery material. The evening of her debut dinner party fifteen years before had been warm. Too warm. As the people sat and chattered and drank the champagne—

you may skimp on many things, but not on the wine, it must always be the best—the heat of the evening had begun to melt the rubber fabric.

When her guests rose to leave, they all had white skeletal imprints emblazoned on the backs of their dresses and trousers, rubbery imprints on their thighs and buttocks. Schiap had rather liked the effect and used it, years later, in her famous, her infamous, skeleton dress. The bones under the flesh.

Chanel had been there that night. It was their first meeting and Schiap understood immediately that Chanel would be foe, not friend. When the guests rose after the long meal and discovered their ruined evening clothes, everyone had laughed, except Chanel. Her eyes had become dark beads of disapproval; the chill emanating from her had frozen the others. They all left rather hurriedly after that.

Another rumble of thunder, closer like a premonition of something huge and vicious stalking the land. Quick, into the cellar. Schiap always felt safe in the basement. Hers was very large, a series of vaulted rooms leading in and out of one another like a medieval cloister, and it reminded her of an illustration she had found in one of her father's books, monks lined up at a long table in a vaulted room, quills in hands, heaven on their faces as they worked on their illuminated pages.

She'd had a similar table made for her cellar and had kept the room as bare as modern living allowed: there was no electricity, only oil lamps and candles, and everything was wood or stone, smelling of a pleasantly familiar damp.

She sat at the head of the table and listened. Good. Down here, you couldn't hear the thunder. She was shivering and pulled her wrap closer. Was it also raining in Nice? Was Gogo safe asleep in her bed at whatever house she had been invited to? Hard to keep track, though she knew a mother was supposed to.

Gogo. Her beautiful daughter. She hadn't known what love was till she held that mewling red newborn in her arms. Everything she had done—the sixteen-hour workdays, the constant search for new ideas, the courting of wealthy and influential customers—everything had been for Gogo. To keep Gogo safe, to make sure there was enough money.

Gogo, of course, hadn't seen it that way. Gogo had known only that her mother was often away, often distracted, distant. Perhaps even a little cold, as her own mother had been. But someday, when she had children of her own, Gogo might understand that a mother's sacrifice can be to serve love by serving her own ambition. Someday she would understand that the surgeries, the therapies that Gogo had hated, had been part of that love. She had vanquished the damage from the polio, and Gogo was perfect again, straight. Just the slightest suggestion of a limp still lingered, and, the doctors had told her, there was nothing to be done for that.

She would do anything for her daughter. But how stupid she had been, refusing to greet von Dincklage the one time he came into her Boutique Fantastique. Even her beau, Henry, that good-natured man, had been angry when she'd told him about it.

"Don't you know who he is, who he's likely to become, under Hitler?" he'd muttered, his words forming around the huge cigar jammed in his mouth so that the dangerous sentence chugged like a train leaving the station in a cloud of smoke. "Bloody hell, Elsa, just bloody hell." They were still in bed in his apartment on Upper Grosvenor Street, and he'd turned his naked back to her.

She'd never make that mistake again. She didn't know, not then, that von Dincklage would be the German officer carrying the life-and-death knowledge of when the Wehrmacht would begin its march on France, when it would approach Paris and turn the city into a prison.

No excuses, though, she told herself. *You have to protect your daughter, and you can't afford mistakes.*

For months she'd been thinking of how to get an ear, a good set of eyes, inside the Chanel salon, how to get the information that would not be whispered in her own salon because she'd made her own loyalties too well known. Schiap, the Bolshevik lover; Schiap, who had refused to have lunch with Mussolini, who was a little too obvious in her hatred of Hitler, even though so many of her very wealthy customers supported him. The Duchess of Windsor still came in and bought new seasonal outfits, but when she ordered clothes for a visit to Germany she ordered only from Chanel. Hitler approved of sensible Chanel, though it was said he thought women looked best in traditional German costumes.

God, how ugly those Fraus must look in that Berchtesgaden eyrie, in their aprons and dirndls and braids coiled over their ears like huge snails. The blouses, though, the puffed sleeves and embroidery . . . those could be interesting. Things were getting complicated in Paris, and a bit of nostalgia might suit the new mood.

Schiap reached for a piece of paper and pencil—there were piles of them placed in every room. Artists never knew when inspiration would strike, and an idea could be easily lost between first thought and a finally discovered pencil.

In the darkness, keeping her hand moving within the small halo of light given off by a single candle, she sketched a dress: a long, pinched-in waist, a kind of apron that pulled back to form the beginning of a bustle. It was like something she'd found in her mother's attic, an evening gown worn long ago by one of the women in her family, perhaps her mother's sister, a woman said to be so beautiful priests fled in terror for their souls when they saw her.

Gogo looked a little like her, with those huge soulful eyes. Gogo was eighteen, too young to understand what was happening in the world, too young to be concerned with anything but boys and yachting parties.

Schiap, further from sleep than before, pushed away the drawing of the gown and started a list. A leaving-Paris list. Number one. Close the store in London. Thirty-six Grosvenor Street had been useful—it had spread her name and reputation, allowed her to spend time in

London when Gogo was still in school. *But let's face it*, she thought. The English aristocracy had a habit of not paying their bills, and the London store had lost money since its beginnings. She couldn't afford that anymore, not with a war coming, and soon it would be impossible to shuttle back and forth between London and Paris, impossible to get the supplies she would need even for her Parisian clientele. No. Close it. Concentrate on Paris. On Gogo. Henry would understand.

Number two. Where to get information. Timing would be everything. She wouldn't leave a day before it was absolutely necessary, but to delay even a day too late would be disastrous. Always, it came back to that: information.

Madame Bouchard. Ania, von Dincklage's mistress. Thank God that American girl had brought her into the Boutique Fantastique.

Color is a response to the way light hits the retina, so light, and color, are time made visible. Color speaks of our mortality, and time didn't care that Ania and Charlie were in love, or that I was still in mourning. It moved relentlessly forward at the pace of a marching army.

The morning light was blue a few days later, when Charlie sent Ania up to my room to fetch me. It was the kind of blue that brings on nostalgia, a realization that every day was not going to be as beautiful as that light promised.

Ania wore a yellow silk dress that cast gold shadows under her chin. Her face was somber.

"Is something wrong, Ania?"

She sat on my unmade bed and twirled a fringe from the covers around her finger.

"You mean more than usual? Yes. News from home. I haven't told Charlie; it would make him, I don't know, too quiet, and I need to be gay today. A friend of mine has been attacked. By the friends of Hitler.

Her family has been driven out of their home. I don't know where they will go, where they will live."

Ania turned her back to me, and I understood that I was to respect that space she had created between us, that some things we must put into words go far beyond simpler commonplace reactions, a hug, a pat on the shoulder. Poland had seemed far away, until that moment. Now the threat was in the room, with us.

"I only wish . . ."

"What, Ania?"

"That my father would come here, leave Poland. But now, we talk of something pleasant. Put on your hat, and we will not talk about this in front of Charlie. No worries." She paused in front of my dressing table, where I had stacked books bought over the past few days from the bookstalls along the river, all biographies of artists, books of color theory.

"What do you want? From life, I mean," she asked, running her finger over the book spines.

I had wanted Allen. Allen, and a little house, and Allen's children. Had there been anything before that?

"If you use the word generously enough, I am an artist, or at least used to be." I ran a comb through my hair. I'd had it cut the day before, above my chin, all the way up to my earlobes so that it clung closely to my head. A single curl on each cheek made russet brown commas around my mouth. I didn't recognize myself in the mirror, and it was a pleasant sensation. "I wanted to paint and to show my work."

"What kind of painting? What kind of work?"

"At first, portraits. I like to study people's faces. Yours, for instance. Did you know there is a shadow at just one corner of your mouth? In low light it looks blue, like the blue around the mother's throat in Klimt's *Death and Life*."

Ania put her hand up to her mouth, as if she might touch the color she hadn't known was there.

"I was working on Allen's portrait when he died," I said. "But I couldn't finish it. After that, I tried landscapes. But there was too much green. And then, I couldn't paint at all."

"Lily, did you love your husband so much when you married?"

The question weakened my knees, made me sit on the bed. "More than anything or anyone."

"For me, it is different."

"How?"

"I married when my father decided I should, to a man my father chose."

"You could have refused."

She laughed. "You Americans are so funny. You believe so much in freedom, in deciding your own way. Here, it is different. We marry to suit our families and then we . . ."

"Then you take a lover. I don't think I've met a single married couple out together all week."

"And is that so terrible? If it works, and everyone is happy?"

Happy? She was going to break my brother's heart. Charlie was American, like me; Charlie wanted love and marriage, not marriage and then love elsewhere. He wanted Ania.

She touched the wedding ring on my left hand. "It wasn't your fault, the automobile accident. Charlie said it wasn't."

"Yes, it was. Allen was tired and hadn't wanted to go out in the first place."

"I'm sorry. But it was an accident, Lily."

"Perhaps. But it happened to me. To him."

André Durst's Bal de la Forêt was to be held in the forest of Morte-fontaine. Its theme was taken from Fournier's popular novel *Les Grand Meaulnes*, about a mystical chateau in the forest that comes to life, and then disappears again, driving a young man to wandering distraction as he tries, endlessly, to find that forest paradise once more. Later, I realized his choice of theme had all the splendor of prophecy. Paris, during that last year before the war, would become a lost paradise.

"What shall I be? Little Red Riding Hood?" Ania asked. "You know, in the original version it does not go well for the grandmother and the little girl. The wolf eats them both." She gnawed at a broken nail. That broken nail bothered me. Ania was so perfectly manicured, so careful in her appearance. A misaligned tooth added to her appeal; that nail spoke of some part of Ania that neither I nor Charles knew. She had been late meeting us, but Charlie knew better than to ask.

We were standing in the street outside my hotel, still deciding how to spend the evening. The weather had changed, moved from light spring to a heavier heat, and the air, thick with damp and street grit, was almost visible, graying the colors of the city. To make the background of a painting look distant from the foreground, a thin layer of gray needs to be applied over it, to suggest remoteness.

England and the school seemed far away, and the distance felt good and right. I had realized that I didn't need the sight of the actual oak tree outside the gate of the walled garden to remember Allen sitting under it. In fact, the memory seemed clearer from this new distance.

"I think you should go as Snow White," I said. "She fled to the forest to escape her wicked stepmother, and you look so beautiful, all in white."

"I like that. Snow White," Ania agreed. "Pure, virginal. No one will recognize me."

Charlie made a kind of growl in the back of his throat and crushed his cigarette under his heel. He didn't like it when Ania made comments like that, self-deprecating poisoned arrows. "If Durst expects virgins, he'd better invite some gals from out of town. I doubt there are any in Paris," he said.

"We should ask Elsa Schiaparelli to do your costume, shouldn't we? It will need a touch of humor, a kind of slyness, to make it work," I said.

"Coco has asked to do my costume. Maybe I'll order one from each, then choose that day." Ania grinned with mischief. "Keep them both guessing."

"You keep too many people guessing," Charlie grumbled. "Make up your mind!" Ania's mouth began to tremble. "I meant about where we're going tonight," Charlie said more gently, and put his arm around her shoulders.

"You." Ania pointed at me. "You must go in something pretty, something diaphanous. I know. You must be a woodland fairy, all pink and green gauze and wings. I will make up your eyes, blue shadow and lashes longer than Joan Crawford's, and put beauty marks on your cheek."

"Sounds good," Charlie agreed.

"To Bricktop's," she said. "I want music. I want to dance. Come on, the night is wasting away."

"Bricktop's," Charlie agreed, forging down the street like a man on an important errand.

How could a young man convey such a sense of urgency when the night was so heavy, so enervating? All the time I'd been in Paris, three weeks now, he'd been full of the kind of energy you feel when you are already late for an appointment and the bus just isn't coming; when the doctor looks at you with pity and can't find the words.

"Charlie, not so fast!" Ania, laughing, pursued him, her white-blond hair shining silver in the dim light of evening.

"Come away with me, you fast woman," he said, slowing down and hugging her again in a tight embrace. "Come away, come away."

They kissed, standing in the street, a long, slow kiss that burned me with the salty blue flame of what had been and, for me, was no more.

Bricktop's on rue Pigalle was packed. The denseness of the crowd, the smell of alcohol and sweat and smoke combined with the sultriness of the summer evening, made the air even heavier. You could almost see the notes from the trumpet suspend in the air before they fell onto the heads of the dancers.

Bricktop herself, with her flaming red hair, came to welcome us. She greeted Ania with three kisses on the cheek, right, left, right. Was there anyone Ania did not know? Or maybe the connection was not with Ania but with her husband. Maybe he was a financier, one of the behind-the-scenes people who kept so many businesses afloat during the bad times? I tried not to think about the husband, just as Charlie tried not to think about him, nor about the lover, but they were there, invisible authorities watching over us.

"Looking swell!" Bricktop shouted at us in her West Virginia accent. She was famous for the cigars she smoked, and the blazing hair and freckles inherited from her Irish father, while her soft African features and tight curls had been inherited from her mother. Bricktop had started out as a revue dancer, had taught Cole Porter how to dance the Black Bottom, and now she owned nightclubs in several countries. That was Paris, before the war. You could come from nowhere, be a nobody, and end up a society queen and rich as hell.

Red-tipped cigar leading the way, Bricktop guided us to a table in the far right corner, the table with, I saw, the best vantage point in the club. We could see almost every other table, but we were in the shadows and they could not see us. Django Reinhardt and his band were onstage. He smiled when he saw me. I waved back.

"I thought Josephine Baker would be performing tonight," a peeved woman's voice said behind us. "Instead, it's just that gypsy guitar player."

"Josephine's gotten uppity," her companion said. "Gone and married a French Jew. Won't they just have a future." His laugh was guttural and cruel.

Ania froze, one bare arm escaped from the light sweater she wore, the other arm crooked into a stiff angle. "What a shame, darling," she said to Charlie in a voice meant to be overheard. "More dreadful tourists. Do you see that rag she's wearing! They ruin the place."

The woman turned white. "Jeesh. What's her problem?" her companion muttered.

We danced for hours, the three of us, arms around one another's shoulders, a little tipsy, a little desperate, each for our own reasons.

Ania and Charlie kissed again when we were walking home later, oblivious to me, to the stares of passersby, to everything they were trying to lock outside of that embrace.

"Snow White? Yes!" Elsa Schiaparelli could barely contain her enthusiasm. "It must be the correct shade of white, more cream than gray," she said to Ania. "You don't want to look washed out. And a red vest over it, a red vest sewn with sequins to flash and shine."

She was almost dancing, she was so excited. She knew Coco was to have done Ania's ball costume. Of course. These Parisian women seemed to know everything about everyone, who was sleeping with whom, whose father or husband or lover was dangerously close to bankruptcy, whose teenage daughter had gone away for half a year to visit an "aunt" and left behind an illegitimate child, who had bruises hidden under the silk dress, who was using morphine a little too frequently to sleep through the night. That last one, I'd heard, was Coco herself.

Where a woman bought her clothes was almost a matter for public record, compared to the other whispered rumors that buzzed through the salons and cafés and dinner parties of the city.

"I will have the white skirt embroidered with sequins making the constellation of the bear," Schiaparelli said.

Ursa Major. Her own symbol, known all over the world. Elsa Schiaparelli had a cluster of moles on her face in the exact shape of the Great Bear, or what Charlie and I, as Americans, called the Big Dipper.

She designed jewelry and embroidery to match that constellation, and it was as effective as writing *Designed by Elsa Schiaparelli* on the garments and jewelry. Coco Chanel would be furious.

"And you?" She looked at me with more than a little skepticism. "What will you be?"

"A woodland fairy," Ania answered for me. "All pink and glittery, with wings."

"Hmm." Schiap leaned her little pointed chin into her fist and considered me with as much concentration as the housewives at the fish market considered the catch of the day. "Yes," she said. "Yes, it can work. I have some leftover tulle. All it will need is a gathered waist and ribbons holding it at the shoulders. An hour's work."

"What about you?" Ania asked. Of course Schiap was going. Everyone but the dairy maids of the Auvergne seemed to have been invited to the Durst ball.

"Me. I will be a tree," Schiap said, lifting her arms and waving her fingers as if they were leaves shivering on a branch. "Secret. Don't tell anyone!"

The salon was full that day. There must have been forty women in various stages of shopping and ordering and fitting. One of them listened closely; one of them took notes and had a little conversation with Mademoiselle Chanel. The next day a box was delivered to Ania from Coco's salon: a Snow White dress of simple beige jersey with a rust-colored vest. She brought it to my hotel room and tried it on for me.

"It's beautiful," I agreed. "Elegant. But . . ."

"But not fun," Ania agreed. "And Charlie likes the Schiaparelli dress. How will I tell Mademoiselle I can't wear this?"

"Maybe she won't notice. Maybe it doesn't matter," I suggested, but Ania looked at me as if I had just said the world was flat.

"And I think maybe I won't tell Elsa about this. It would be war." Ania folded the dress back into its box.

Ania wasn't with us the next day. "She's gone to see her husband,"

Charlie said. "To try and sort things out with him. About the child."
He was in the most serious mood I'd ever seen him in. But I understood what was at stake.

Two days later my Schiaparelli gown for the Durst ball came in a huge cardboard case filled with so much tissue paper I had to rustle through many layers before my hands touched the silk. It wasn't the simple tulle frock she had promised. It was a magnificent white column of draped silk, decorated with a dozen small painted metal brooches of insects. A beetle sat on the right shoulder; a butterfly fluttered over the left hip. Because of its simple, loose lines and because the salon already knew my measurements, it needed no fitting.

It was a thank-you, I realized. I had delivered Ania to her, and Ania was wearing Schiaparelli to the ball. I wondered how Coco would react. I had an impulse to fold the gown back into the box, return it to the salon, and take the next boat train to England. I paused the way you do when a ladder is in your path. *I'm not superstitious*, you tell yourself. But you walk around the ladder, not under it, anyway.

There was a card in the box as well, a little note from Schiap reminding me to remove all my jewelry before putting on the dress. As if I had jewels. It was one of her jokes.

When I stepped into the dress it was as if I could suddenly exist outside my own skin, wear a new layer that was me but not me. Me, transformed.

"Lovely," Ania said. "So lighthearted. Stop frowning, Lily! We're going to have so much fun tonight." Charlie was waiting downstairs, in the Isotta, and she had come up to fetch me. "And it's perfect for the Durst ball. Another bespoke order that wasn't picked up?"

"Probably. I could never afford this. How did things go with your husband, Ania?" She knew what I was asking. What was Charlie's future?

"We will talk of it later," she said. "So many details." She strapped on the wings she had made for me, wire hangers bent into demi-heart shapes and covered with silk. I wore slippers instead of high heels, and Ania twisted glass pearls into my hair and around my wrists, then tipped a jar of small sequins over me. It was past nine by then, a Parisian summer twilight, and I glittered like a Christmas tree in the dusky light.

She was in her Snow White costume, with the red bodice and yellow skirt designed by the Walt Disney studio but made seductive, sinuous by Schiaparelli, with long, tight sleeves and clinging fabrics. Schiap had added crystal embroidery along the hem so Ania glittered with every movement. And there was the Ursa Major, embroidered on the front of the skirt, the Schiaparelli brand.

Charlie had decided against the wolf costume and instead came as Charlie, handsome as a movie star, but with silk leaves basted onto his sleeves and lapels. They rustled in the breeze of the open windows as we motored out of Paris, to the ball.

Ania's chauffeur drove that night, and I was sardined in the backseat with Charlie and Ania, those silly wings of my costume backdropping all three of us, like overlarge angel wings in badly painted medieval altar pieces. Charlie and Ania, sitting next to each other, pretended, for the chauffeur's benefit, to make conversation for all three of us. I recognized the lovers' codes, the *remember when*s and *do you think*s that pass for conversation but are instead lovemaking with words.

I could sense the chauffeur's suspicion and disapproval. He hadn't fallen for my little act with Ania: me, the inseparable friend who happened to have a brother always tagging along. He knew what was going on; he knew what the conversation really was. And I couldn't help thinking that this chauffeur, in the employ of Ania's husband, wasn't as attractive as von Dincklage's driver, that serious, unsmiling boy with the blond hair.

The evening shone with blue—the sheen of Charlie's lapels, the blue crystals on Ania's dress, the sky overhead, deep-blue velvet with glittering stars. I wasn't happy—Allen wasn't with me—but I was beginning to remember what happiness had felt like. Even the automobile drive, which I had dreaded, wasn't too bad. Every once in a while the road would curve and my hands would curl into white-knuckled fists, and then the road would straighten and I would be okay again. Even so, I had a sense of foreboding, as I always did in an automobile, after the accident. Ania was in a gay mood, refusing to be serious about anything, to answer any questions.

The air was almost too soft, the temperature too perfect. The oppressive daytime heat had tempered itself into something milder, sweeter, closer to a welcome embrace than a suffocating blanket. Charlie and Ania spoke in soft murmurs. Under cover of the wrap thrown over her knees, they were holding hands again, like they had that first day, under the tea table in the Schiaparelli showroom.

"What a night," Ania sighed. "I'll never forget it."

Charlie whispered something to her, and I saw the driver's eyes dart into the rearview mirror, checking.

"Ania, are my wings okay? They're not getting crushed, are they?" I asked, reminding them they weren't alone.

It was my first, my only, full-dress costume party. They were events planned for, and attended by, the very rich and sometimes, I suspected, the very bored or at least those who feared boredom more than any other condition. People with more money than I could imagine, dressed to kill in disguises that sometimes defied description. The worse the economy grew—and in Europe and the United States it was growing worse by the day—the fancier the balls became. It was fairy-tale time, as if truth could be ignored.

. . . as if the reality that was Hitler could be ignored.

When reality threatens to become unbearable, we make believe. Children do, and adults, too, except their make-believe is more expensive, in terms of either dollars or emotional cost, because reality is there, waiting for you around the next corner.

Paris that year had already concocted a silver ball, where everyone dressed in silver and the rooms were plated in silver. A golden ball had followed; a Racine ball with everyone dressed as characters from a Racine play, the ancient regime risen from its own, moldy grave.

It was mad, this ignoring of reality just as reality was about to turn horrific. There were so many things we should have been paying attention to, newspaper headlines, a look of fear in some people's eyes, a restlessness like that in a herd before lightning strikes. We were the passengers on the *Titanic*, still hoping that the thud and shudder of the ship was just a large wave, not an iceberg.

· SEVEN ·

Outside Paris, the city lights dimmed behind us so that the stars were even brighter overhead. Ania and Charlie began singing Cole Porter love songs to each other, Charlie in his deep but tuneless baritone, Ania's voice wandering in and out of the English lyrics like a child lost in a toy store. "You're the top!" Charlie boomed at her, and she came back with "You're my hat on Gandhi," instead of "Mahatma Gandhi."

When we laughed, there was an edge to it. Tonight, Ania decided Charlie's future. And hers. I almost wished she would send him home alone. It would, in the long run, be so much easier. But then I remembered Allen, and what the word *alone* meant after you had been in love with someone, and I hoped with all my heart she would leave her husband for Charlie. But what if the husband wouldn't let her take the child with her?

When the car pulled over in the long gravel drive, we put on our masks before getting out. Mine was white, to match the dress, with crystals circling the eyeholes and feathers at the corners. As soon as I put on that mask, I stopped thinking and entered the dream.

André Durst had created a perfect replica of an enchanted chateau in the forest of Mortefontaine, with rooms of mirrors and greenery, gauzy screens instead of walls . . . the inside was the outside. We couldn't tell which was chateau, which was surrounding forest. People costumed as birds, druids, satyrs roamed the rooms and the gardens. A woman costumed as a leopard glided through the fields with a man costumed as a lion. A group of people arrived together as a flock of doves; a rabbit danced with a flower.

And it was all illuminated by thousands of candles on branching candelabras.

Ania and Charlie danced away together almost as soon as we arrived, leaving me alone in rooms glittering with so many candles, so much crystal, the rooms looked like they were on fire. In the midst of darkness, there was light everywhere, prisms of it casting rainbows on walls, mirrors throwing out reflections, windows with their darker light, still shimmering. It was like walking through flames without being burned.

In a costume, I discovered, you don't mind being unpartnered. Perhaps that is the nature of solitude: it requires a sense of self and separateness. When you are not yourself, when you are costumed, you are no one and everyone; there are no borders, no separateness, perhaps not even between life and death. A breeze tickled my neck, and it felt like a memory come back to life, Allen's breath tickling my neck.

I started to feel like a creature of the forest, solitary, wary, visible only to those who have the patience and the eyes to see the truth of you, to catch the movement of a life in camouflage, in disguise. If someone took my hand, a red-caped Richelieu or Harlequin, I danced, coupled in a waltz that made my dress flare at the hem, or in a line of dancers, each one with a hand on the shoulder in front of her, snaking in and out of the crystal rooms.

When a waiter passed with a tray of champagne, I took a glass. Many glasses. A couple of hours later someone put his hand on my waist for a fox-trot.

It was von Dincklage's aide, that solemn German boy.

"You should at least be wearing a mask," I told him. "It is a costume party, after all."

"I think we won't be here very long," he said. So von Dincklage was here. Of course. I hoped that Charlie and Ania were keeping to the shadows.

He pressed slightly on the small of my back, bringing us closer together. I could feel his warm breath on my cheek and closed my eyes for a second, enjoying his scent of cloves and aftershave. For a moment, his face brushed against my hair. Then we both took a half step back and we were again two almost strangers.

"You dance well," he said stiffly, trying, and failing, to make small talk.

"Where is the baron?"

"Somewhere nearby, I've no doubt. He won't object if I dance, I think. It is a costume party, after all."

So we danced.

That night there were people whose faces I recognized, a blur of memory from my first night in Paris, at the Ritz, and many more people whom I didn't recognize at all, men with military posture, women covered with jewels, men in dresses, women in tuxedos, ingénues in pastel gowns. And Charlie and Ania, beautiful Charlie and Ania, so immersed in each other's gaze they could have been alone rather than dancing through crowded rooms.

Ania saw me over Charlie's shoulder, saw my dancing partner, and her eyes opened wider. They were on the other side of the room, near a doorway draped in a garland of flowers, and Ania steered Charlie through it, out of the room. Von Dincklage's aide had seen them before they disappeared, though. He said nothing.

Coco arrived around eleven, in a diaphanous green gown that looked like fern fronds moving in a breeze when she moved. It was Coco, blending into nature, but still Coco.

Schiap arrived soon after, dressed, as she had promised, as a tree, covered in a rough brown cloth that looked like tree bark, with branches extending from her arms and the crown of her head. Several cloth and feather birds perched on her shoulders. Whimsical, humorous, always-make-it-look-easy Schiap. Schiap got the louder applause when she made her entrance, and I saw Coco's smile fade.

Schiap came to me and gave me a tight hug, and I felt the rough-edged sackcloth of her tree bark bite into my bare arms. "Look," she said, "there's Elsie in the spangled orange tulle. I designed her gown. And that one, and that one . . ." She surreptitiously pointed at all the women in the room wearing costumes by Schiaparelli, her brown-bark little hands covered with green felt leaves dancing right and left.

"I see so far only three gowns by Coco. Yes," she said. "It is a night for victory. Even so, I have a bad feeling. No, keep smiling. Maybe it is nothing, maybe it is just the stars lining up strangely. My horoscope indicates this is a complicated time for Virgos."

I knew by then that Schiap was superstitious, but that evening her words brought gooseflesh on my arms. There was so much at stake, and Charlie, born in September, was also a Virgo.

Coco, in her diaphanous green gown, came over to us to greet Schiap: the runner-up admitting the prize goes elsewhere. Her face was frozen into a smile, her red lips stretched so taut her teeth flashed.

The partygoers danced around us, a dangerous tableau of Schiap and Coco, and me, with the music, a boisterous rendition of "Pennies from Heaven," sounding too loud, too fast.

Ania danced by with someone I didn't know, and he gave her a twirl under his arm as she waved to me. The twirl made Ania's Snow White skirt flare into flower-shaped fullness, and there, bright and unmissable, was the embroidery in the outline of Ursa Major, Schiap's insignia.

Something dangerous flickered in Coco's flinty eyes.

"She's not wearing the costume I made her," Coco said, to everyone and no one.

Von Dincklage was at her side, then, carrying two martinis. He offered one to her, and when Coco took it her hand was shaking so much it spilled.

"Easy!" Von Dincklage laughed.

"She's not wearing the costume I made," Coco said again, this time specifically to von Dincklage.

"So! It is just a dress. Don't be so mercenary."

The word *mercenary* made her visibly cringe. Well, of course she was. She was a businesswoman. She was the kind of woman who would have been shown the servant's entrance at his baronial estate.

He would have been kinder if he had thrown his drink at her. Of course a baron like von Dincklage, old family, old money, centuries of wealth, would think that her motives were merely mercenary, not realizing that nothing less than honor and reputation were at stake.

Coco turned white. Her face froze into a mask of hatred.

Schiap was dancing across the room by herself, surrounded by a clapping group of drunken admirers. She waved her branch-arms, leaned her head side to side so that the treetop looked like it was swaying in a strong wind. People laughed and applauded even more loudly.

The music changed to a soft, sweet "The Way You Look Tonight," with the band singer giving a credible imitation of Fred Astaire's quavering voice.

Coco began to sway, her head and shoulders moving in subtle willowy circles. Von Dincklage took her in his arms for the dance, but she broke away from him. Instead, she danced toward Schiap, her billowing green skirt making the forest floor for Schiap's brown tree. They danced together, two women no longer young but still deeply needing admiration, two businesswomen locked in fierce competition, two women who couldn't be more different in their aesthetics, their way of being in the world.

Time slowed like it does when you see a car slide out of control, heading for a tree. Time slows, but all you can do is watch because you, too, have slowed, you are in the same altered time as the approaching disaster.

Who knew what else was going through Coco's mind that evening? Perhaps she had dreamed the night before of those cold white walls and black doors in the orphanage, the father who had abandoned her and the mother who had died, the many wounds of childhood that still haunt the adult. Perhaps, all those wounds of childhood, the fear and rejection, had reawakened when she saw Ania in the Schiaparelli costume.

Perhaps she wasn't thinking at all but only reacting, the way dry wood reacts when a match is put to it.

Coco danced forward, her hips and arms swaying, and Schiap, laughing, kept dancing back, until Coco finally caught her and pulled her into her arms the way a man would have. Their faces were just inches away from each other, both women grinning, laughing, dancing. Coco, leading, danced Schiap back, back, back until she was against one of Durst's floor-standing candelabras. Coco released her and stepped away.

For a moment, Schiap stood there, not realizing what had happened, what was about to happen. Then her halter of branches, her costume of tree bark, caught fire. An azure shimmer appeared over her shoulders, rising up from her back, where she'd danced into the candelabra.

We watched, frozen in horror like moviegoers waiting for the train to fall over the tracks into the gorge.

Blue phosphorus flames danced down the branches extending from Schiap's arms and her head, the flames dangerously close to her face, her fingers. Schiap, no longer laughing, turned in confused, panicked circles, the way wounded beasts do when danger is near but they are too terrified even to run. She turned in circles of blue flame tinted red at their tips, as the partygoers moved into concentric circles around her, pointing and laughing.

I'm dreaming, I thought. *This is a nightmare.* The flames shimmered, opalescent, blue. The glittering wood of Schiap's costume welcomed the flames so that soon, in seconds that felt like hours, the flames were licking her hands, singeing her hair, and I stood there, still frozen, staring in horror and guilt.

Leopards, tigers, clowns, several Cleopatras removed their masks the better to laugh, believing this was an illusion, part of the festivities. Hadn't Elsie de Wolfe, at her Circus Ball, hired acrobats and dancing elephants? They thought Coco and Schiap had planned this, though how they could have believed that, knowing as they did—we all knew—how Coco and Schiap felt about each other, was beyond comprehension.

Finally the horror that had frozen me in place—how long? Three seconds? Four?—turned to panic and I ran to Schiap.

Charlie was beside me, urging me forward, thrusting a seltzer bottle into my hands. "The hands," he instructed, as he himself threw water over Schiap's head, dousing the flames moving closer, closer to her eyes, her ears. With a hiss and sparks, the branches on her head accepted the water, and with resignation, the flames died.

People began throwing their drinks at Schiap. "More water!" they shouted. "Where's the fire brigade?"

They kept throwing their drinks at her long after the flames had been extinguished.

Schiap, safe but looking like a drowned rat tumbled in debris, began to laugh, but the sound was high and strained. I had never before seen such pleading in someone's eyes. I knew what she wanted, needed.

I laughed, too, put my arm around her wet, trembling shoulders, laughed *ha ha, wasn't that funny!* Because if Schiap didn't laugh, if I didn't laugh with her, then all those others would be laughing at Schiap, not with her. And once Parisian society laughs at you, your career is over. No one likes a victim.

Coco had disappeared by then, and no one went looking for her. Von Dincklage had disappeared as well, and I hoped he had taken Coco home. I didn't want her to be alone.

That may sound strange, considering what she had just done to Schiap, but the look on Coco's face when Schiap burst into flames had frightened me as much as the flames on Schiap's bark costume. Her face had been cold with satisfaction, certainly, and also with horror at what she had done, and a certain resignation. As if it had to be done, there was no other way to win, to conquer her rival once and for all. But every victory has a price, and Coco was already wondering what the price of this would be for her.

"Hello, again," Schiap said to Charlie, when he took off his jacket and put it around Schiap's trembling, sodden shoulders. She smiled brightly at him, but I saw the lingering terror in her eyes.

"Hi," Charlie said. "Good to see you again." That was what a good doctor did. Reassure. Pretend all is well, normal. "Are you feeling dizzy? Let's get you dried off and warm."

Charlie was alone. Where was Ania? Gone, I realized.

Schiap refused to admit that she was in a state of mild shock, that her fingertips and nose were pink from too-close flames. When Charlie tried to dry her face she pushed his hands away.

"I'll see to it," I said.

"Right," Charlie agreed.

I helped Schiap upstairs, into a powder room and out of the still-smoldering costume.

"Look at me," she said, sitting on a pink boudoir chair and staring into the mirror. "A disaster."

"Shall I find your driver?"

"No. Of course. I'm staying. Leaving now would be the worst thing I could do. My horoscope was right," she said. "A bad evening."

"For Charlie, too, I'm afraid."

"No one set him on fire," she protested.

"Just the opposite."

"No, don't hug me. You'll get stains on your dress. My makeup is a mess."

"We'll just clean up a bit and you'll be more beautiful than ever."

"Beautiful. Hah!" Schiap's voice was gravelly. "Not even my own mother thought I was pretty. I had an Aunt Zia who was so beautiful her town declared a festival when she married and went to live elsewhere. Me? The priests are safe, aren't they?"

"No one looks their best after they've been set on fire," I pointed out.

She laughed once, a sound like something breaking. "I'll show her," Schiap said. "I'll get even for this."

"Maybe it was an accident."

Schiap snorted in fury. "And maybe two plus two makes four is an accident. God, I miss Gogo. Why is she staying away so long? I want my daughter."

She dabbed at her nose, her little saint's face raw and pink from flame, then crumpled up the handkerchief and threw it to the ground.

Schiap had been wearing a sequined sheath under the tree costume, and the smoke and water stains were somewhat masked by the glint of the metallic embroidery. She stood, checked her stocking seams to see if they were straight, then went back down to the ball.

I found Charlie again. We shouldered our way through the laughing crowd and went outside to find a quiet bench to sit on, far from the noise.

"Hard to believe that's the same moon I was happy under a few hours ago," he said.

"Ania isn't going back with you, is she?"

"No. She is staying here, with the child. Her husband won't let her have custody if they divorce."

"I'm sorry." I took his hand and held it. His face was stony, the way boys' faces get when they are trying hard not to cry.

We sat for a long while staring up at the traitor moon, a big round moon fit for a fairy tale, but now it looked like painted cardboard. The costume ball swirled and clattered, butterflies with gauze wings, kings in gilt crowns, but there was no more illusion; it was just people in strange clothes trying too hard to have a good time, a ragtag group of disheveled, dispirited strangers who seemed to barely know one another. It was a place where tragedy had occurred.

The ball ended sometime after dawn, when people look their worst: makeup smeared, shadows under the eyes and in the hollows of the cheeks, costumes rumpled, some even torn. Chauffeurs lined up in their Bentleys and Mercedes to pick up their patrons, and the chauffeurs, neat in black-and-white uniforms, better rested, mindful, looked better than the partygoers.

All the glitter had been extinguished. Diamonds need light to give back light, and the morning sky was leaden. The women's jewels looked like cheap paste imitations; the candles and torches in the ballroom had burned themselves into nonexistence hours before.

Charlie and I found a cab at the end of the long queue of chauffeured and gleaming automobiles and returned to Paris, alone.

PART TWO

RED

. . .

Goethe's favorite red was a pure carmine painted over white porcelain, passion and purity mixed together. Unlike blue, there is little paradox in red. It is a color that separates and defines and cannot be contradicted. Carmine, that brilliant shade of red, comes from death itself, from the bodies of insects boiled to release an acid that is a color both beautiful and fugitive, in that carmine red does not last. Many artists use it to paint scenes of intense emotion, only to discover that like passion itself, carmine fades.

Hitler reversed Goethe's theory when he had his uniform designers place a white circle inside a red background, and in the center of the white circle, the black swastika.

Flame often appears carmine red, and paintings of battle scenes are full of carmine. Battles are full of carmine.

Red is the color of love and of death.

And of course, always, it is the color of passion.

· EIGHT ·

Just as there are moments of convergence, there are also moments of coming apart. Departure.

Four hours after arriving at Charlie's hotel, hours of thrashing, uneasy dreams, and waking regrets, we were back in a cab, rushing to the Gare du Nord. I stood on the platform with Charlie, waiting for his train, indifferent to the looks of the other waiting passengers. I was still in my evening gown, that marvelous Schiaparelli creation not quite intended for a train station, now stained with smoke and gin and Schiap's smeared makeup.

The image of Schiap in flames—well, her costume at least—was haunting me. It seemed a culmination of what had been, and a prophecy of what was to come. It had shaken me fully awake from the emotional semisleep I had been in for two years. Allen hadn't been the first thing I had thought of when I woke up that morning. It had been Schiap, and Coco.

The train station was crowded, and people jostled us. Charlie bit his lip and kept looking over his shoulder to see if Ania might be coming through a doorway, suitcase in hand. She didn't. Such hope, bound to end in disappointment, is a terrible thing to witness. A coming apart.

"He changed his mind at the last minute. The husband," Charlie said. "Bastard. Won't give her a divorce, won't let her take the child. At the very last minute. He's been playing us all along. Ania was supposed to leave with me this morning."

His hands were trembling with anger and disappointment, so he gripped his suitcase harder, to stop the shaking.

"What now, then? What about you? What will you do?" he asked. "Are you going back to the school?"

"I think I will stay on in Paris a bit longer. I'm not ready to go back." To go back seemed just that, a backward step, when Schiap had already begun pulling me into the future. I wanted to see her again, to see how she was doing. She had left the ball before I had, quietly and without saying good-bye. Slipped away. Well, being set afire will do that to a person.

"Good idea," Charlie said. "And as long as you're here, you can keep an eye on Ania. I'm worried about her."

Charlie's train pulled into the station, and the platform bustled with people disembarking, calling for porters and trunks, rushing into embraces. I leaned into Charlie, put my head on his shoulder. *Good-bye, good-bye again, my lovely brother.* Since Allen's death I had held myself apart, even from Charlie, for fear of exactly what was happening now. I would be alone again.

"Things are going to heat up over here soon," he said. "It won't be safe, Lily."

"If there is a war, America won't join it."

He tried a different tactic. "You know, you could come to Boston with me. We could set up housekeeping together."

"Oh God, Charlie," I joked. "The brilliant young doctor with his widowed sister keeping house for him?"

"You wouldn't be expected to iron the linen and write menus," he grumbled.

"Even so, no thanks. Don't worry about me, Charlie."

Charlie looked absolutely destroyed. His blue eyes seemed pale to the point of colorlessness; his white-blond hair lay limply on his head, revealing the shape of his skull.

Charlie would travel to England, and from there to New York. "The same route the *Titanic* took," he pointed out.

"That's not funny."

The crowd on the platform was thinning again. People were getting on the train.

"Sure it is." He forced his mouth into a rictus of a smile, made a noise somewhere between a chuckle and a sigh, and it magically turned into a real laugh.

"I'll miss you." He put his arms around me and hugged hard. "Be good."

"As good as you."

"Then we are in trouble." The old jokes, only this time they had significance.

Hiss. Steam. A grinding of metal on metal, women around me crying and waving handkerchiefs, children demanding sweets from the one-legged man who sat at the newspaper kiosk, cooing beady-eyed pigeons, a shrill whistle from the conductor, a last-minute wave out the window, a blown kiss. My brother was gone. I stood there till the train was out of sight and the gray puffs of steam and smoke had melted into the hot, sooty morning.

I went back to my hotel, ignoring the puzzled glance of the concierge, and climbed the dusty, creaky steps to my attic room. I changed into a plain skirt and blouse, splashed water on my face, and looked back at my reflection in the cracked mirror that turned my face into separated cubist planes.

Look at you, I thought. Wide-eyed as a frightened rabbit. I felt hollowed out, like a well that has gone dry and is waiting for the answer to fall into it.

And I was hungry. Very hungry. I checked my purse, the dog-eared copy of Goethe's *Theory of Color*, where I had tucked what remained of my savings. I was going to have to find work.

COCO

Coco put on her warmest, most charming smile, the one that required her to tip her head down ever so slightly, the way children do when they are being both shy and mischievous.

"And the problem with the dress?" she asked. The salon was almost empty, so she kept her voice very low, almost a whisper, so that she wouldn't be heard by the few people who were there.

"Madame says the color no longer suits her." The maid spoke loudly, and heads turned in their direction.

Coco felt her face flare into a warning red blush. Madame had sent a maid for this errand. Madame wouldn't face Coco Chanel.

"It's not been worn," the maid lied, as she had been instructed.

Madame had worn the dress last night, at the Durst ball.

The morning after, Coco called this event, when the "angels" of society began returning worn garments, demanding a full return or a new dress in exchange. She knew by name at least three other Madames who would be returning their gowns, now that the Durst ball was over, all with unabashed lies.

How was a hardworking woman supposed to earn a living?

Or perhaps this time would be different. Maybe the angels would decide to keep their gowns as souvenirs of the night Mademoiselle Chanel made a fool of herself. Coco shivered and forced the memory back into the shadows of her imagination: those flames, Schiaparelli's evident terror, the laughter of the others, too drunken to see what was actually happening. How had she done such a thing?

"If she wants to return it, of course I'll take it back," Coco said. "Vera, take the dress away and mark it for the discount rack . . . since, yes, it has been worn. There's a stain. Egg, I believe, from the hors d'oeuvres. But we will list a credit on Madame's account." Her sales assistant took the dress from the maid with a snort of disdain that would certainly be reported back to Madame, but that was just as well. Mademoiselle was gracious. Her assistant, well. Someone had to be the store watchdog, didn't she?

The maid turned on her heel and left without a thank-you. They always did, leaving Coco to fume over the angels who rarely paid cash, returned worn clothing, and used her sales assistants as confessor priests and analysts, taking up their time and keeping them from other customers.

Oh, she was tired, and not just from lack of sleep. That stupid stunt last night was going to cost her plenty. Just to keep angels from talking, she'd have to put up with all sorts of rudeness and being taken advantage of.

She hadn't planned it. Of course she hadn't. Had she? She knew the different levels at which the mind worked, one layer singing a silly cabaret song, another layer feeling the pinch of the cheap high-heeled shoes that made her toes bleed, the top layer scanning the crowd, looking for a good face, a generous and well-bred face, the kind of face that belonged to the kind of man who could show a girl a good time while also helping her out of that cabaret, out of that cheap costume. Layers upon layers, all working at once.

So had she planned it, without even knowing?

Merde. Of course not. An accident. She hadn't even seen the candelabra. And that was the lie that made even Coco Chanel blush. Who couldn't see a flaming candelabra just inches away?

I didn't. I didn't see it.

The shop was quiet today, and just as well. There would be the inevitable returns and little else, perhaps a little tourist traffic, out-of-towners wanting to buy a touch of glamour, a souvenir of what their own lives lacked, the sophistication and leisure of a Paris society angel. Perfume. They'd come in and buy the smallest bottle of Chanel No. 5

because that was all they could afford and even then their husbands, bank clerks from London, dairy farmers from the Auvergne, would stand and scowl as they paid out the money. *For perfume? For a bottle that small?* they'd complain.

"I'll be in my office. No interruptions," Coco told the sales assistant.

"Certainly, Mademoiselle."

Merde again. Was her own clerk smirking at her? Was there anyone in Paris who did not know?

Coco shut the door a little more loudly than she had intended. Behind that closed door, she put on her glasses and leaned back into the desk chair, slouching the way she would not allow herself when someone else, anyone else, was around.

The Durst ball hadn't been a total failure, though. The baron had put Ania in a taxi and sent her home. And he himself had seen Coco back to Paris in his chauffeured automobile. At the door to her Ritz suite he had kissed her hand and smiled in a way that meant, *Soon, soon. But not tonight.*

God, he was good-looking. And rich. Money itself did not matter, but oh, what one could do with it, and there was never enough to completely bury those early memories, the breakfast bowl of stale bread and milk, sleeping with all your sisters in the same bed, the wooden clogs always bought several sizes too big so that one could grow into them, and meanwhile your feet spread and spread into things that looked like broken spatulas.

Never enough to make her forget those early years, the dark and hungry years.

And meanwhile, there were the society angels, looking to cheat her, often getting away with it, and her own workers demanding, always demanding, a better salary, a shorter day, a better lunch with meat every day.

As in all the couture houses, Coco ate a communal lunch with her staff, served in a room reserved for the meal and for breaks. They'd had roast chicken today, and a soup made with the last of the season's asparagus, and they'd complained. The dessert biscuits had been stale; there was no fresh fruit.

She'd show them. Maybe tomorrow she'd let them eat a half-empty bowl of stale bread and milk. See how they liked that. She couldn't, of course. It would be all over Paris before the bowls had even been washed out. The Bolsheviks would march with protest signs in front of her shop.

Let those complainers put in the hours she had worked, the risks she had taken to get ahead! She'd pulled herself out of nowhere, worse than nowhere, and now they envied her the wealth she had earned. The Germans were all that stood between hard workers like herself and the Bolsheviks.

She picked up a sketch pad and studied the drawing she had been working on, an evening gown of white satin with a striped bodice of red, blue, and white. Like a gypsy dress, she thought. With more than a touch of patriotism adorning it. It wasn't as subtle as she liked. The sleeves needed to be a little narrower, the striped border on the hem less extravagant. She pushed her glasses higher up her nose, picked up a pencil, and started making corrections.

Work was the answer. Work was always the answer.

Three days after the ball, after Charlie had left, I woke up with both my arms tucked under my head. I hadn't reached for Allen in my sleep. That made me cry, because it seemed another kind of forgetting, so after I dressed and had a café crème at the corner I went to the Louvre. *Mona Lisa* was there, waiting for me, it seemed, and I sat for a long while admiring the color and geometry, trying to remember everything Allen had ever said about the painting.

I hadn't spoken to anyone except café waiters for those three days.

Solitude had formed around me like a glass wall, and I missed everyone and everything, even Gerald's scowls and cutting remarks, the chatter of the little girls in the hall at school, Charlie's teasing, Ania's laughter.

When someone stood next to my bench I was so eager for conversation, even with a total stranger, that I had to will myself to keep staring straight ahead, at the painting.

"Beautiful, isn't it?" asked my new neighbor, his German accent clipping his words short.

"Very," I agreed, and allowed myself a slight turn of the head in his direction. It was von Dincklage's driver.

"Day off?" I asked, hiding my surprise.

"Just so. The baron has gone out of town. I like to come here, to the museum, when I can."

"This is my favorite painting. Mine, and my husband's."

"I admit to a preference for Botticelli. I am Otto Werner." He tucked his head in a little bow.

"Lily. Lily Sutter."

"May I?" he asked.

"You may." He sat next to me.

He seemed shy, and I had lost the habit of small talk, so we were silent after that. We sat side by side, staring straight ahead, till I had absorbed as much of the color of the painting as I could that day. When I rose to leave, he did, too.

When we were standing, face-to-face, he did something so unexpected it took me off balance, the way a strong wind will do. He picked up my hand and kissed it.

"Why did you do that?" I asked, pulling my hand back.

"You looked so alone. I am sorry about your husband." He answered the question before I could ask it. "Madame Bouchard has told me this."

So he and Ania had talked about me? Why? "You are displeased. Please, I am sorry," he said, looking now at the museum floor. "It was not gossip, I just . . ." He didn't finish the sentence. "Your friend. Madame Schiaparelli. Is she well? Not harmed?"

"I believe so, though no one would have enjoyed that little prank. What did the baron think of it?"

"What he always thinks when women act crazy. That it was weakminded, a sign of the less-strong sex, and not important." Otto blushed a fierce pink. "I am sorry," he said. "I should not speak of the baron in that manner. It is disloyal and base. He is most respectful to Mademoiselle Chanel. She is strong and hardworking, and she has good politics. And she is very lovely."

"Is loyalty important?"

"It is everything. Please, tell your friend I asked after her." A slight bow, a frown to disguise what might have been a smile, and he was gone.

It was hot that day, the first real heat of the summer announcing its arrival like a furnace blast. The sun glittered so brightly that the beams seemed sharp-edged, metallic. People moved in slow motion, sweat dripping into their eyes.

At Place Vendôme, outside Schiap's boutique, I looked up at the statue of Napoleon atop his column, admiring his swagger, captured for eternity in stone. He was supposed to have been indefatigable; that was why exile to an island had been especially punishing. Better than a cell, certainly, but he circled that island, round and round, trying to spend all that unused energy, searching for the way off he knew he would never find.

That was what grief had felt like to me, a constant circling round and round, all the paths of life twisting into a circle of blame and loss I couldn't break free of. Why had I been so angry when that young man, Otto, offered sympathy for the death of my husband? Because my grief had changed into something different, into a private wound rather than a public one, something I confronted by myself in those dark hours before dawn. It was mine alone, not to be shared with strangers.

Schiap was upstairs in her office, shouting into the telephone about a bolt of fabric than hadn't arrived. She looked fine, no remnant pink on her ears or fingertips, nothing to suggest she had been set alight just a few days ago.

"Oh, how I hate having to talk on the telephone!" she complained after she hung up. "He should have come here in person instead of making me shout into an instrument. How are you, Lily? And your brother? He was very kind to me. He will make a fine doctor, I think."

"He's gone back to Boston."

"And you?"

"In a bit of a jam."

"Like most of the world, I think."

Maybe this isn't the right time, I thought. Elsa Schiaparelli wasn't in a particularly good mood.

"I was just at the Louvre," I said, thinking some chatter might smooth the tense atmosphere of that crowded, cluttered treasure cave of an office, with its shimmering bolts of fabric leaning against the red-papered walls, the samples of embroidery lying here and there like jewels. "Von Dincklage's driver was there," I said. "He asked about you."

Partially, I was making small talk, to delay the moment of having to ask a favor. But it also seemed significant, that the driver of Coco Chanel's new lover would ask about her.

She stood and stared out the window, turning her back to me. "Did he? And you and he . . . are you friends?" Her voice had changed from shrill anger to a low, friendly purr. "This jam you are in? Is it marmalade or strawberry?"

"Nothing so tasty. I'm broke, and I need work."

She sat back down, folded her hands on her desk, and smiled. She wore a black suit that day with a demure white blouse peeking out at the neck, and the costume made her red lipstick seem even redder. The desk ashtray was full of half-smoked cigarettes, their tips tinged with that red.

"And what can you do?" She looked me up and down, assessing, always assessing. It became one of the things I loved about Paris, how everyone looked long and hard at everything, and not just the artists. All of us, assessing, noticing, remarking. Memorizing. As if we anticipated that much we saw, much we enjoyed and admired, would soon disappear.

"Paint," I said. "Maybe help with the window displays?"

"Perhaps. Bettina does most of it, and of course you must answer to her, but I think she will be glad for an assistant. She will tell me if your work is good or bad, she is in charge of that, and if she accepts you, then I will give you a little cash and a good discount on your clothes. You need new clothes. Let your friend, Madame Bouchard, help you choose them. Bring her often. I will give you both good discounts. Samples, if they don't require too much alteration."

I remembered the glint of satisfaction in Schiap's eyes at the Durst ball as she had counted the women wearing Schiaparelli, not Chanel.

And so, I entered the world of *la couture* at the invitation of Elsa Schiaparelli herself. Bettina, whom I met the next day, was not particularly pleased to be presented with an assistant.

"Another *arpette*?" she asked. *Arpettes*, in the great *maisons de couture*, were the lowest of the low, girls whose main job was simply to pick up pins from the floor, sweep up scraps.

"She says she is an artist. She can help dress the windows and the fitting rooms," Schiap said. "If you like her work." She had been staring fixedly out the window at Napoleon's column in the middle of the square. Sometime in the evening before, sandbags had been piled around its base. Newspaper headlines that day had glared in large bold type that Mussolini had signed a military covenant with Berlin.

"Schiap," Bettina said, her voice turning down in a note of complaint. She eyed me the way my aunt once eyed a stray puppy I'd brought home, without sympathy for child or puppy.

Schiap smiled at Bettina. When Schiap smiled, she won every argument. "It will mean less work for you," she pointed out. "And you will have someone you can boss and yell at. Wouldn't you like that?"

Bettina lit a cigarette and studied me through the blue smoke.

A tall, slender New Yorker with a cool gaze, Bettina had the face of a Renaissance Madonna but a fierce temper always emphasized by the speed with which she walked and the angry clicking of her heels. Bettina, the *vendeuses* joked, walked as if the devil were after her. And then a second *vendeuse* would pipe up: *No, she's after him! Look! He runs for his life in the other direction!* This exchange never occurred when Bettina was actually in the boutique or anywhere in hearing range, and she had excellent hearing. It matched the sharpness of her temper.

"What can you do?" Bettina asked me that first day of my employment with Elsa Schiaparelli. "Certainly, you don't know how to dress." This was said matter-of-factly, without animosity. The *vendeuses*, some folding sweaters, others dusting shelves, all tilted in our direction, eavesdropping.

"I can paint the backdrops and scenery for your displays."

Bettina took a long drag on her cigarette and studied me some more. I met her gaze without flinching, even lowered my chin in a bull-about-to-charge pose to add some ferocity to my face.

This amused her. "Okay." She laughed. "Paint me a sunrise. A very big sunrise, big enough to fill the window."

"Seen from which vantage?" I asked.

Bettina dragged again on her cigarette. "It only rises in the east, I thought."

"But the sunrise is to be seen from which part of Paris?"

"Take your pick. No one will know the difference. It's only a sky."

Only a sky? I thought of the illustration for April in de Berry's *Book of Hours*, how the sky changes from pearly pale blue to the deepest marine and the blue garments of the lovers in the foreground echo the drama overhead. "The embroidery of the sun," Allen had quoted the poet d'Orleans to me once; I'd had to look it up.

That was what a sunrise was about. The embroidery of the sun adding coral and gold to a gray skyline. And because beauty requires opposition, the fire of the sunrise would be offset by a cool undertone of blue and green lingering in the west.

That afternoon, I went to Sennelier's on Quai Voltaire, across from the Louvre, the store where Cézanne and most other artists after him had obtained their art supplies. I stood transfixed in front of the trays of pastels and tubes and brushes, and something moved in me that had been slumbering for two years. Color. So much color. I bought paper and a box of pastel crayons and an extra handful of indigo, cerulean blue, and carmine crayons.

But how, in my tiny hotel room, was I going to paint a sunrise big enough to fill the shop window?

The next morning, at first light, I began painting the sunrise on small pieces of paper that would have to be collaged together. If I was allowed to hang it as I wished, the lines wouldn't register; the one large sunrise would be a series of smaller ones. A month of sunrises, all seen at once, some stormy, some serene, some all pastel, some gray.

"It works," Bettina agreed two days later, after I had pieced it together with straight pins instead of tacks. I had made a sunrise that looked somewhat like a dress in progress, pinned together, not yet stitched.

Schiap came in later that morning and stood on the street a long time, staring pensively at the boutique window.

"It is very strange," she said. "I think it works. Come with me, Lily. We will now select the gown that will be in the window with your many sunrises."

I thought Bettina would be angry that I had been given this honor, but when I looked over my shoulder she was smiling, a little catlike smile as if she had let the mouse get away so she could play with it again later. Men who persist in the belief that women are soft, sentimental creatures have never worked in the fashion industry.

"When I was a child," Schiap told me that afternoon as we searched through a rack of gowns for one in particular she wanted to show me, "I used to climb up alone to the attic high atop our villa in Rome—so many stairs!—and play with the clothes in the trunks put away up there. I dressed up in them, Spanish lace mantillas and Chinese brocades, bustles and corsets, boots with two dozen buttons on each. There was one dress that looked like something a medieval princess would wear, like something worn by ladies in the Duc de Berry's *Book of Hours.*"

"I was thinking of de Berry's *Book of Hours* when I painted the sunrise," I said, surprised.

"Then you have painted well, because I saw it there, in your collage. My father had a seventeenth-century copy of it in his library, in Rome. He was a scholar, you know. Oh, the books we had. Like this," she said, pulling a purple gown from a rack that held models of her most recent collection. "This is for a medieval princess." The gown's waist dipped low in front and was decorated with a garland of orange and gold musical instruments, trumpets and horns and piano keyboards.

"And these." Short gloves in the same purple silk crepe, with a cello embroidered on one hand and a tambourine on the other, in gold and silver thread.

"Lesage embroidery," Schiap said. "The best. Always the best. What do you think?"

"Magnificent. Like walking music," I said.

"Good. Yes, walking music. A miracle. You know, once I jumped into a vat of quicksilver, when I was very little. I thought it was water and I wanted to walk on the water, like Jesus did. That was how strong my faith was."

"Your faith in God?" I asked.

She laughed. "No. My faith in myself. I thought I would walk over cool water, the tops of my feet not even getting wet, only the bottom. But quicksilver burns like fire. Instead of walking on water I sank in silver flame. I would have died if a servant hadn't been following me and saw what had happened and saved me. My mother always had a servant following me. But I've been afraid of fire, since then."

Her black eyes narrowed, and I knew we were both thinking of the Durst ball.

Bettina carefully arranged the dress on the shop dummy, Pascaline, a tall wooden female form with short, classically carved curls and a sphinxlike gaze. I was to be trusted with paper and pencils and ink, but not the clothes themselves. Bettina turned Pascaline sideways, so that she was looking into the distance with those always-calm wood-and-glass eyes. Next to her, on the floor, Bettina placed a child's drum and pipe and splashed confetti and pastel streamers in drifts of even more color. It looked like the end of a party, and there was a quality of sadness mixed with the gaiety.

"It will do," Bettina said, and that was the highest praise she ever gave.

Later that day, when I returned to the boutique to again admire my work, a handful of women had gathered in front of the display. I mixed in with them and got my comedown when I heard that the talk and oohing was all about the dress and gloves, not about my sunrise. *But that is how it should be*, I reprimanded myself. *You painted the background. That is all.* That was why Schiap's boutique modeled the clothes on simple straw figures; fashion is about the clothes.

Schiap and Bettina were skulking in a fitting room doorway, staring out at the women in the store, when I went into the boutique.

"Yes. She's here," Bettina muttered darkly.

"I see her," Schiap agreed.

"Who?" I whispered, joining them.

"Mademoiselle Yvette. She works for Chanel," Schiap said.

"She always comes to inspect the new displays," Bettina added. "And then she goes back and tells Chanel."

Bettina hissed a few words in French whose meaning I could only guess, but they definitely were not schoolroom vocabulary. "Chanel hates it when others copy her." Bettina pulled a silver cigarette case from her pocket. "And here she is, sending a spy to see what we are up to."

Mademoiselle Coco, I would learn, like the other couturiers, liked to keep a close eye on the competition.

Chanel's spy, Mademoiselle Yvette, gave the salon floor one last turn before going to a shelf of sweaters, white with blue bows knitted into them. These, she probably had seen before since they were not the most recent items, yet she felt she must carry on her charade of being a woman in for a little casual shopping.

A minute later she waved cheekily in our direction and left. Bettina lit her cigarette. The *vendeuses*, who had been standing straight and silent during this performance, clicked their tongues in annoyance and went back to their tasks.

"Do you think she was the one in your office last week?" Bettina asked Schiap. "Did she sneak upstairs?" Papers had been gone through, drawers left open, Bettina explained. Such a to-do, but nothing stolen. Even so . . . She and Schiap exchanged covert glances.

"No," Schiap said. "She would have tried to cover her tracks. Whoever was in the office wanted me to know they had been there. Ah, my dear," she said, taking my arm. "You look a little frightened. Didn't you know I'm a wanted woman?"

"Don't joke," Bettina said. "This is not a safe time for jokes like that. Yesterday they arrested one of Gaston's comrades. The police are on the lookout for communists; all they need is a little information."

"They are ridiculous, these people," Schiap insisted.

"Who? Who is ridiculous?" I asked.

"Let me count." Schiap sat on one of her shocking pink chairs and held up her hand. "One. The Americans. I was a communist in my youth, you know, when I lived in New York with . . ." She paused. Schiap never mentioned her ex-husband's name. "The Americans never forget that. Two. The French communists, because they think I am not communist enough." Bettina grimaced. Her husband was one of the leading communists in Paris. "The Italians, because I live in France, and the French because I was born in Italy. Five. Coco Chanel and her people, because *Time* magazine said I was more important than she was."

"Don't forget von Dincklage," Bettina muttered.

"What about von Dincklage?" I asked.

"He came into the salon once with one of his women and Schiap snubbed him."

"He's a Nazi. Why should I pretend to be his friend?" Schiap waved her manicured hands as if bothered by a plague of flies.

"Sometimes one must be diplomatic," Bettina said.

"Sometimes one must stick to one's beliefs," Schiap countered. "Don't you have something you should be doing? Go check the sewing room, make sure those girls are sewing and not just chatting. You, come with me." Schiap beckoned with her forefinger. There was a determined look on her face, a slight vertical line appearing between her dark brows. "We are going to have a talk. You work for me now."

· NINE ·

"Me? Spy?" I protested when Schiap and I were behind her closed office door.

She was standing at her window, looking at the colonnade and the statue of Napoleon on top.

"Not spy, actually," she said, turning and giving me the full intensity of her dark gaze, a look that sent shopgirls scurrying and customers bobbing in obedience. "Just listen. Look. Pay attention. Visit that Chanel woman once in a while. It is for Madame Bouchard as well as me. And Gogo. She must come back to Paris soon; she can't stay away forever. And I need to keep her safe."

There was hurt in Schiap's voice, the mother's pain of knowing her daughter preferred to be elsewhere, not with her. From what I could remember of Gogo when she'd been at the English school where Allen and I had been, she was shy, very self-contained, easily overwhelmed. And Schiap could be very overwhelming.

"How does my keeping tabs on Coco and von Dincklage help you and Gogo?"

Schiap looked at me as if I were a little slow-witted. "Von Dincklage is head of propaganda. He knows everything the German army is going to do almost as soon as Hitler has planned it. It would be good to know what Germany plans for Paris, don't you think? They say that von Dincklage will be Chanel's next lover. And you are already friends with his driver."

"Not really," I protested.

"Yes, really, I think."

Schiap studied a ragged fingernail she'd torn that afternoon and hadn't had time to repair. "You . . ." She gave me that appraising glance once again. "You, I will dress in my sportswear. Culottes, a long split skirt with a tight jacket. And a hat. You must always wear a hat, with a brooch or feather pinned to it. It will add some sparkle. One of these." She rifled through a basket of samples next to the ebony screen and brought out a deep-scarlet knitted cap, the kind of grandmother-knitted whimsy you'd put on a child for a day playing out in the snow, but this was knitted of cotton string, for warm weather, with a tawny pheasant feather tucked into it. When she pulled it onto my head, very low over one eye, it became chic, whimsical, and a little mysterious. What is it about a woman's face when only one eye is showing?

"I will have one made for you in forest green, with navy sequins and a little corsage of feathers on one side. For evening. But this one"—she gave the scarlet cap a little tap—"this one you must wear every time you go to Coco Chanel. She will know it's mine, and it will drive her mad."

Schiap laughed gleefully. "So?" she asked.

I was still studying my reflection in the mirror. Short hair, a frisky little hat, the red lipstick Ania had convinced me to use. I didn't know what Gerald and the schoolgirls would have made of their art teacher. Or Allen. This was another step away from him in the long, eternal parting.

"Okay," I agreed.

"And maybe you should thin your eyebrows a little. Arch them," Schiap said. "Open your eyes."

That same day I climbed the glamorous and intimidating mirrored staircase to Chanel's salon. It was a sun-high early afternoon, and the streets felt like all the ovens of Paris had been opened, it was so hot. July hot, with shimmering sidewalks and the leaves of the chestnut trees curling at the edges in self-defense. My steps dragged with lethargy and second thoughts.

When a woman went to Chanel she had no choice but to glimpse herself all the way up that stairwell and notice everything. Perhaps Coco had taken the Delphic oracle's advice—"know thyself"—as a business motto, thereby forcing her clients to have a long look at themselves before entering her salon.

"An evening frock," I told the *vendeuse*, who eyed me warily when I was upstairs in the gleaming crystal-and-gilt salon. "Something in satin, low neck. Then maybe a cocktail dress?"

"Certainly."

Champagne was offered. I declined. Coffee was brought instead. Feeling more than a little foolish, I eyed every corner of the salon, taking mental notes of the glamorous, expensive furnishings, the displays, the people.

"Is this the gown you wanted to see?" A mannequin strutted out and turned in a circle, showing how the bias-cut gown swirled with movement. "The Duchess of Windsor recently purchased one very like this."

The dress was of black satin, shiny as lacquer, liquid as water, completely formfitting except for a low cowl neck that draped over the bustline, adding dimension.

"Very nice." I sipped my coffee so that she wouldn't see the envy in my face. Schiap's clothes were beautiful and whimsical and suggestive of Oriental luxury, with their embroideries in gold and silver threads, and feathers from rare birds. Chanel designed clothes for women who preferred reality to fantasy, women who believed so strongly in their own beauty that embellishment was not needed, just a good cut and the right fabric. I already had a preference for Schiap's designs, her insistence that clothing was art, not just fashion.

"No, that won't do. Bring out the black jersey smocked gown," a smoky rasped voice said from behind me. I looked over my shoulder, and there was Coco Chanel. "No. Something . . . the gown Diana Vreeland ordered. Show her that model."

Coco sat next to me on the sofa and stared hard into my face, keeping silent until the mannequin returned in a different gown. It had a huge skirt of silver lamé quilted with faux pearls, topped with a lace bolero also embroidered with pearls. It had to weigh at least thirty pounds, but it was beautiful.

"Gorgeous," I agreed.

"I thought you might prefer something a little outré, rather than subtle," she said. "But what a silly hat you are wearing. Doesn't suit you at all. In fact, doesn't suit anybody." She was wearing one of her jersey dresses, short and close to the body, cinched at the waist with a wide belt. "How is my dear friend Schiap?"

"No lingering sunburn," I said, and Coco flinched.

Recovering immediately, she leaned into the sofa, one arm resting on the back of it. "You don't look like him at all. Your brother. Pity." She patted my knee. "You enjoy yourself, my dear. Jeannette, show her as many gowns as she wishes. But not the new collection, of course. Only what is already being worn. And no discounts, no credit. She is getting those elsewhere, I think."

Coco rose and gave me a cool smile over her shoulder. She walked away, slightly turned, showing to best advantage her narrow, elegant figure.

"On second thought," she said over her shoulder, "come with me. Let's have lunch together. I can't have you distracting my salesgirls like this."

We left the salon on rue Cambon, the mannequin sighing heavily with relief, and crossed the street to the Ritz, Coco leading the way. A side entrance led to her apartment, suite 302.

"I keep an apartment here. So convenient," she said over her shoulder as we went down a hall, up a stairway, and down another hall, our steps making no noise on the heavily carpeted floor.

"Convenient to your salon?" I asked.

"That, of course. But also, when the Germans come into Paris, a good hotel will be safer than a private home or apartment. They will stay here, don't you think? The German officers? There is no finer hotel in Paris, or in France."

"They may not come," I said. "It is not certain there will be war."

"Of course. I misspoke." But there was a tone in her voice, that of an adult reassuring a child.

I had already seen some of Coco's suite at the Ritz two years before, in *Harper's Bazaar*, in an advertisement for her perfume, Chanel No. 5. Coco had posed for the ad herself rather than use a model. It hadn't been her fabulous black evening gown and jewels that caught the eye, but her gaze. She looked away from the camera off to the side, slightly bored, a little challenging, her long, lean arm resting of the mantelpiece of her fireplace. A queen would have posed in this fashion, except for that sideways gaze.

It gave Coco great satisfaction, I think, when the maid opened the door and I stood there, in the hall, gaping. Here, in this hotel suite, was all the fantasy that Coco would not allow in her clothing. The walls were covered with carved Chinese lacquer screens, except for the walls lined with bookcases. Aubussons covered the floor. Pictures hung over marble fireplaces, and the tabletops were covered with precious objets d'art. It was like a jewel box, that suite.

No one had ever accused Coco Chanel of being a simple, uncomplicated person. Here in these rooms were two of her most dominant aspects: her origins in austerity, the peasant poverty followed by the hard years in a convent school, made visible by Coco herself in her simple black jersey sheath. And here, too, was her love for luxury, the costume jewelry that mocked real jewels, the glitter of make-believe.

"Nice, yes?" she said, waving her beringed hand at the marble fireplace, the gilded screens.

"Very," I agreed, thinking of my attic hotel room with its washbasin behind a torn linen curtain.

"Sit, please." And we sat on a comfortingly soft velvet sofa.

"Poor Schiap!" She lit a cigarette and drew on it. "She will never forgive me for ruining her costume. She wasn't injured, was she? God, how clumsy I was." Coco sat there, surrounded by her velvet furniture and expensive carpets, the gleaming antique screens and Louis XVI side tables, acting as if she'd merely spilled cigarette ash on Schiap.

I understood what Coco wanted from me, needed to hear, that had been buried under her false sympathy for Schiap. Were people gossiping about her? What was being said? Ego. Both Coco and Schiap were larger than life; they both had the egos of Olympian deities.

"No, she was not injured. The flames were put out before any real damage was done. Except to the dress, of course. It was scorched."

"I will pay her for the damages." A peasant's thoughts. Make everything right by the exchange of coins.

"She won't expect it. It was an accident, after all," I goaded.

Coco had the sense to blush because we both knew it had not been an accident.

The maid, her head bowed, announced lunch, and Coco led the way to her dining room. We sat, the two of us, as the maid served a chilled cucumber soup followed by roasted lamb with salad. Coco ate very little, mostly pushing the food around her plate with the heavy silver cutlery.

"That night . . ." she began, and I put down my knife and fork to focus better on what she was about to say. The lamb was delicious, and I'd had nothing but bread and coffee for the past two days, trying to stretch my money.

Coco dabbed her handkerchief at the corners of her mouth. Stains of red lipstick came off on the white cloth, and she frowned at them in disapproval. She twisted her rope of pearls, and her black eyes flickered over the ornate, luxurious dining room as she worried over the words to say.

"It was an accident," she said finally.

"I don't believe you."

"Is that what people are saying? Is that what Schiap thinks?" She couldn't leave it alone, wouldn't admit that the more we talked about it, the less able we would be to pretend it had been an accident.

Coco began twisting her pearls again, this time with such force I thought the string might break. She thought better of it and placed both hands flat on the table, next to her crumpled, lipstick-stained napkin and crystal water glass with its own red imprint of her rouged lips.

"You know," she said, not looking at me, "when I was very young and living with Étienne Balsan—you have heard of him . . . my first love, my great love?—in his chateau, I had to eat with the servants. No one knows that. He picked me up out of the revue I was appearing in—God, the costumes, the cheap, disgusting costumes. He taught me how to use the right forks." Coco, one of the richest women in the world, picked up her fork and flung it across the room like a petulant child. Her maid, waiting in a corner, wordlessly picked it up, put it on a side table. She disappeared through a doorway and came back out with fresh plates and a bowl of grapes and oranges.

"That Ania," Coco said, peeling an orange. "Do you know her well?"

"We've just only met," I said, not wanting to discuss Ania or my brother.

"Baron von Dincklage knows her. Very well. In fact, she is his mistress?" She was still uncertain. Of course, she couldn't ask him such a question. Couldn't ask anyone that question, without giving herself away. Except for me, who was a nobody in Paris. For a second I let the sense of power I had in that moment thrill me the way a brushstroke of aquamarine thrills. I didn't answer. I withheld. And I peeled my orange.

"She is attractive in a predictable sort of way, I suppose," Coco said. "Her family in Warsaw keeps a junkyard, I hear."

It was an antiques shop, and they specialized in Louis XVI furniture, according to Charlie.

"Such a lot of books," I remarked, changing the subject. There was one on the table, and I picked it up. *Mouchette*, by Bernanos, a bestseller in France that year, a misery tale about a young peasant girl.

"Have you read it?" Coco asked.

"Not yet. Are you enjoying it?"

"Bernanos sentences are like Christmas trees, full of decoration. One should know when to stop. Schiaparelli, like Bernanos, never knows when to stop. But the story is good. I've read all of these." Coco gestured at the bookshelves, the piles of titles not yet shelved. "Once I start a book I have to finish it, have to get to the end. Books saved me, when I was a girl. In the orphanage I used to steal up to the attic, at night. There were trunks of books there, mostly cheap romances, but I devoured them. I learned about life from those books, about the life I wanted to live."

The revelation, that intimacy of what she had said, seemed to surprise her. She stopped in midsentence and smiled her public smile, the Coco Chanel smile, head tilted, lips barely turned up, eyes wide open as if a flash had just gone off.

"Let me guess," she said. "Your family . . . New York, is it? . . . has a large house and a library filled with leather-bound books that nobody reads anymore. Correct?"

"I've read quite a few of them. A little privilege doesn't guarantee illiteracy."

She laughed. "Very good! I think we will be friends, you and I.

Well, I learned mostly from books, but not all. Étienne taught me how to ride, how to have polite conversation, how to leave behind my childhood of swiping my soup bowl with a piece of bread, sleeping four or five to a bed, bathing once or twice a month in water already used by others. And then he made me eat in the kitchen with his servants."

"I'm not going to feel sorry for you," I said. "We've all, most of us at least, lived through things that still give us nightmares."

Coco stared down at her plate in confusion. When she looked back up at me, she was smiling.

"Your husband. Yes, I know. We have that in common. Motor accidents. That is how Boy Capel died. My first great love."

I rose to leave and my napkin tumbled to the floor. The maid again approached and picked it up for me.

"I'm simply saying, don't judge. Please sit," Coco said. "I know Elsa Schiaparelli laughs at me. She laughs at everybody. Enough. I'm getting bored. It's too warm today, don't you think?" She rose. The maid began to clear the table with the unnaturally quiet, precise gestures of a servant trained to be invisible. Coco knew that kind of training.

We went back to her drawing room and sat on the beige sofa. How elegantly Coco moved, so full of charm and confidence and style, yet underneath it all was a little girl abandoned by her father, raised too strictly in a colorless orphanage of bare walls and grim silences.

"Baron von Dincklage wonders how well you actually know Elsa Schiaparelli. She is a communist, you know."

"That was a long time ago, in New York."

"She still has sympathies. She's backing the wrong side. Russia won't be able to save France when the war comes."

"Isn't Hitler about to sign an agreement with Chamberlain and Daladier? That's what the BBC says." Like most Parisians, I'd begun listening to the radio, to the nightly news, as well as reading the newspapers.

Coco looked at me with exasperation. "As if that will stop anything. Go now," she said. "I need to get back to my office.

"Wait!" At the door she stopped me, pulling me back inside and grabbing at the hat I'd been wearing, the strange little scarlet cloche that Schiap had given me.

"That ridiculous thing," she said. "Wear this. Much more flattering." She took one of her own hats from the antique carved credenza, a straw hat with a tiny brim that turned up just over the eyebrows.

"Young women don't need mystery, that is for older women who have lost their freshness. You are what, about twenty-five? Believe me, age comes soon enough. Don't rush it."

She stood back, admiring her hat and that precise angle she had achieved.

"Lovely," I agreed. "But . . ."

"A gift," Coco said. "I insist." She took Schiap's little scarlet cap and tossed it in a wastepaper basket near the door, and then she emptied an ashtray over it. "And this." She pulled at my dress, a short-sleeved linen print. "It must fit at the shoulders. If it doesn't fit properly at the shoulders, it won't fit well anywhere. Have it tailored."

Coco started to shut the door behind me, then opened it again. "Thank you for coming," she said. "I don't have many friends, you know. People are either afraid of me or dislike me. You seem different."

After the door clicked behind me, I sleepwalked down the hall of the Ritz, away from Coco's rooms, over the plush carpets, past the gleaming, curtained windows and little gilt side tables of the grand hotel. The sun blazed red over the curved glass dome of the Grand Palais, hues as bright as a Matisse interior. Crimson, scarlet, Chinese red, sienna, madder, formless shapes of pure color. Who needed line and representation? Color was enough.

I crossed the vast granite expanse of the Place Vendôme, avoiding stepping in the shadow of Napoleon's column, no longer interested in the emperor's swagger. What a huge, empty space, so exposed. "When the Germans come into Paris," Coco had said. For a moment, a flash of that space crowded with Wehrmacht soldiers filled my vision, and I shivered.

I passed the Hotel Le Meurice, less grand than the Ritz but still luxurious. Ania had told me that the top floor of the hotel offered the best view of the Eiffel Tower and the Tuileries Gardens in Paris. Ania knew all sorts of things like that. Maybe that was another quality that had made Charlie love her—that worldliness she wore like an evening gown, casually and with great style.

I missed her, her gayness, her energy and charm. I hadn't seen her since the ball. Where was she? Charlie must be suffering so, I thought.

The next day, when I reported every detail of the time I had spent at the Chanel salon, the cuts, colors, fabrics, accessories, Schiap laughed, winked, thanked me, and added, "But of course I already knew all that. As Coco said, they are already being worn on the street."

"Who was there? In the salon?" Bettina wanted to know.

"No one I recognized," I said, "though there were several women with diamond rings the size of almonds."

"She's useless. Schiap, what were you thinking?" Bettina stormed out of the office, ashes dropping from her cigarette onto the carpet.

"Don't mind her," Schiap said, laughing. "I think she was hoping for Nazi secrets or something."

"Would Coco have those?"

Schiap scowled. "She is friends with Nazi sympathizers and anti-Semitics."

"You already know more than I ever will. What's the point, then?"

"Does there have to be a purpose to everything? I don't know yet. When I think of 'the point,' I'll let you in on it. Maybe it's just a little joke."

Bettina came back in with her arms full of bolts of cloth and a fresh cigarette hanging between her red lips. "Pick one," she said to Schiap. "I need some background drapery. You . . ." She pointed her cigarette in my direction. "I want a seaside scene. Can you paint waves?"

Later that day I went back to Sennelier's for a tube of Prussian blue for Bettina's waves, delighting in the smells of ancient dust and pigments and carefully counting out coins to make sure I'd have enough for my week's rent.

Standing by a display of colored pencils was a girl who seemed familiar, and then, as I studied her from behind the paint rack, I saw who it was. She'd had a baby face when I'd last seen her at the English school, puffy and bland, but Schiap's daughter had grown into a lovely, fashionable young woman.

"Marie!" I touched her shoulder to get her attention, and she turned toward me. She was dressed in Schiaparelli, of course, a summer frock printed with butterflies and a cloche hat, her brown curls carefully arranged around the edges of it. The patrons of the store, mostly men in paint-splattered shirts, gave her appraising sideways glances.

"Mrs. Sutter!"

We looked at each other for a long while, each seeing in the other's face the shared memories of the school, the dreaded therapy room for the "special" students, those still recovering from illness, the bland overcooked food, the cold tap water, the house mistress screaming for lights out. Even the way she had said "Mrs. Sutter," in the formal schoolgirl tone of reverence used for favorite teachers.

"I heard about the accident. Your husband, Mr. Sutter. I'm very sorry." Gogo was shy again, as she had been when she was a student at the school. Even though there was only five years' difference in age between us, out of habit she was deferential.

"Call me Lily, please," I told her, not wanting to talk about Allen. It's difficult to talk about that kind of grief and loss with younger people who have not yet experienced it. "And I'm now working for your mother, painting window displays."

She stood back and gave me that very Parisian glance of assessment. "Well, Lily, then," she agreed.

"And what brought you into Sennelier's? Have you taken up painting?"

Gogo laughed, a full and rich laugh like her mother's. "No. I'm just postponing the reunion with Mummy. Steeling myself. I'm back from a sailing vacation and haven't been home yet. Come with me, let's both go see her."

"You've been here for a day and haven't seen your mother yet?"

"Several days, staying with friends. And we won't tell her, will we?"

In the cab Gogo and I sat politely on either side of the backseat, stealing glances at each other. How pretty she had become, and so very stylish.

"I like the bob," she told me. "The haircut. You don't look as fierce as you did with your hair pulled back so tightly."

Was that how the schoolgirls had seen me? As someone fierce? Allen had sometimes called me his teddy bear, but we are different in the privacy of our bedrooms, aren't we?

"So do I call you Gogo or Marie?" I asked.

"Gogo, in Paris. Mother and all her friends do, so you might as well, too."

Schiap was on the ground floor when we arrived, criticizing a display of gloves in a vitrine, Bettina next to her puffing on the omnipresent cigarette and making faces behind Schiap's back.

"Gogo?" Schiap froze.

"Surprise!"

"I thought you were in Nice!"

"And so I was. But now I'm here."

They stared at each other for a moment, eye to eye exactly, since they were the same height.

There is a photo I saw, later, in a magazine, Elsa Schiaparelli and daughter, dressed alike, eyes locked in a gaze that excluded all others, a gaze full of love and questions and more than a touch of animosity. It is not easy to be the daughter of a very famous woman, a woman who sometimes works twelve and more hours a day, ignoring everything else. It's not easy to be the mother of an extraordinarily beautiful young woman whom one barely knows because of so much time spent apart.

Schiap and Gogo looked at each other, and the room seemed combustible. In one shared look they seemed to express every emotion that can pass between mother and daughter, good and bad.

The mother, though, had only a shadowy existence in the daughter's face. Gogo's eyes were brown but not dark like Schiap's. They were flecked with gold so that when she stood with the sun in her eyes they reflected back as amber. Her brown hair was lighter, her cheekbones more pronounced. Schiap was striking. Gogo was beautiful, and I remembered what Ania had said about Elsa's husband, the fake Polish count, that he had been spectacularly handsome.

Gogo and Schiap, after that long appraisal, ran into each other's arms.

I left mother and daughter to their private reunion, wondering if there was any such thing as a wholehearted relationship, one not tinged with doubt or regret or bitterness. Allen had been out of sorts when we had returned from that London lunch with Elsa Schiaparelli and her daughter, years before. "A waste of time, when you think about it," he had concluded. "So much talk about fashion."

"The yachting party was a bore. All they could talk about was the Duke and Duchess of Windsor, how romantic it was that he gave up his throne to marry the woman he loved," Gogo said the next day, spreading a napkin over her lap. "Ridiculous, I told them. He's a friend of Hitler's. If England goes to war, he probably will side with Germany and so the royal family decided to dump him. But then it turned out that a few people on the yacht also thought Hitler was a splendid fellow. Time for me to leave."

We were at the Dome, sitting at an outside table. The heat was stifling, and every time a car went by it sent dust and grit into the air. We had to constantly shake it off our skirts, wave it away from our plates of omelet and *pommes frites*.

"Chanel seems to approve of Hitler, as well," I said.

"You've met her?"

"Several times. We had lunch a few days ago, and she gave me a hat and some clothing advice."

Gogo gave me an appraising look, seeming more like her mother than she might have wished. "You are dressing better," she said. "Is that one of Mummy's dresses?"

"Yes. An abandoned order from last year. She gives me a discount, and sometimes she just gives me a frock."

"I bet Coco asked you to wear the hat when you were with Mummy."

"Correct."

"They detest each other. When Mummy first came to Paris she invited Chanel to a supper. Chanel came out of curiosity but was rude. She literally held her nose as if she smelled something bad. She made fun of Mummy's furniture."

Gogo put down her fork and took a sip of water that had grown warm and flat with the heat. "It must have been terrible," she said. "Losing your husband. I remember him. How I dreaded that math class. He would get so impatient with us."

"Allen was impatient?"

"Not always. But sometimes, yes, very."

I tried to imagine Allen as impatient.

"I want some more fries, but don't tell Mummy. She's terrified I'll get chubby again." Gogo signaled for the waiter, and he came over at a gallop, eager to wait on the pretty young woman who was making passersby on the Boulevard du Montparnasse do double takes.

"Why Paris?" she asked. "Why not back to New York? That's where you're from, isn't it?"

"My brother was here. And I'm not ready to go back." Every day was a new way of losing Allen, but once I crossed the ocean and left behind all the places we had known, the loss would be complete, and I was not ready to face that.

"Are you still painting? I mean, things other than window displays?" Gogo had left the school the year before Allen's death. She didn't know about the empty canvases sitting in the corner of my studio at the school.

"I stopped painting when my husband died."

"Well, time to start again, I think," she said, sounding very much like Schiap.

"There may be nothing there. Gone."

Gogo looked at me from under her very long eyelashes. "Maybe you just have cold feet. Do you know what Mummy's first creation was? An evening dress, to go to a ball in Paris, the first time she was here. Before I was born, before she married my father. Only she couldn't afford to buy one, so instead she went to the Galeries Lafayette and bought some dark blue crepe de Chine and orange silk. She couldn't sew, not a stitch, so she just draped it around herself and pinned it in place. Off she goes to the ball, and tangoes for the first time and of course she doesn't know how to tango. Does that stop her? What almost stopped her was the dress, because the pins started falling out. Her partner had to scoot her out of the ballroom before she was stark naked. And now look where she is."

"That's an interesting pep talk. But—"

"No *buts*, Mrs. Sutter. I mean, Lily. Do you know how many times she has told me that story? She wants me to become ambitious, like she is."

"And what do you want?"

"A husband. Children. And to be far away from Mummy. I love her, of course, but she is so tiring. She sucks all the air out of the room when she's in it."

I thought of the plans Allen and I had made: a little house, children. When Allen died, I lost the future as well as my husband.

Our desserts came, small chilled cups of chocolate.

"You," she said. "You should paint. What have you got to lose?"

We ate in silence for a few minutes, relishing the food, the company, even the sultry weather.

"So this brother of yours. Is he good-looking?" Gogo smiled at me over her coffee cup.

"Very. And very in love with someone already."

"Too bad.

"More than you know."

· TEN ·

"What are you doing up there, Madame Sutter? The maids are complaining about the mess." The hotel desk clerk glared at me over his eyeglasses. I had planned on leaving my room earlier than usual in an attempt to avoid him, but he seemed to have come on duty early.

"Nothing," I said, smiling in what I hoped was a winning manner.

"Are you painting up there?"

Caught. Perhaps that stain of carmine from a dropped pastel had been the final giveaway. And the rainbow streaks in the washbasin, and one or two splotches on the sheets . . .

"A little," I admitted.

"Not allowed. You have until the end of the week to remove yourself or you will be removed."

"But . . ."

The glare turned into a merciless scowl, with his eyebrows dipping all the way down to the corners of his eyes. "There is no *but*, Madame Sutter."

I slumped into the chair underneath the wall calendar and sighed.

The smile hadn't endeared him, but the sigh helped.

"It will be August soon," he said in a tone that was perhaps one degree friendlier. "People are giving up rooms and apartments and quitting the city. Some will not return. I can give you the names of a few landlords." The scowl turned into a half smile. "If you are painting, Madame, you will require better light than that room offers."

"Thank you."

"You are welcome. And please remember to tip the maids when you leave. It was only when the laundry complained that they reported you to me. Oh, and this came for you. Telegram."

From Boston. I tore it open. *Arrived safely, already in my scrubs. Miss you and the house rosé from Café Magots. Worried about Ania, haven't heard from her. Please look in, report back. Love.*

I hadn't seen Ania since the Durst ball and realized I had no idea of how to find her. She had never mentioned a home, a street, a town or village anywhere in France. I could ask at the Chanel salon, perhaps they had a delivery address, but somehow that didn't seem a wise thing to do. Chanel had set her cap at Ania's lover or protector or whatever von Dincklage was, and even asking an innocent question might start a battle. What if Ania was living with him?

First things first, I reminded myself. I would soon be on the street, and needed to find a room to rent where I could paint without worrying about the floor. I felt a thrill of excitement when I told myself that. And for the first time since Allen's death I wanted to paint, to find an image and get it on canvas with all its colors, shining or muted, reds and blues and yellows, the dominant one sending a vibration of sensation.

I spent all that day, and the next two besides, walking up and down the steep cobbled hills of Montmartre—Rue Lepic, Boulevard de Rochechouart, the Place Saint-Pierre, knocking on doors, spying into attic garrets from bare-lightbulb hallways. The hills of Montmartre are not easy going in the summer heat, even in sandals and a sleeveless shirt. When I could, I stopped into Sacré-Coeur at the very top of all the hills, to let the cool air of its dark interior bring me back to sweating, panting life.

Montmartre, the highest hill of Paris, hadn't become part of the city until about seventy years before, and it still had a renegade air, an untamed quality, and for me, a sense of newness. Allen and I had never visited this part of the city.

On the third day I found my room at the top of a three-story building on rue Ravignan. It was a single large room with two windows facing north. Northern light is the most consistent, staying the same for most of the day, avoiding the dramatic changes that occur in the eastern, western, and southern sky. Northern light, like the North Star, is an anchor; you can put your trust and faith into it.

The two windows took up almost an entire wall and fell exactly between two chestnut trees, so the light was not blocked by them. Best of all, though, the other arrondissements of Paris were spread out beneath me like a crazy quilt. Standing at the opened window was as close to flying as I had ever been, it was so high up.

"You are not melancholy?" the landlady asked suspiciously. "It is a very great fall down from here."

"No," I said. "Not at all. I'll take it. One month in advance for the rent?"

Her eyes glittered. "Two," she said.

"I can't afford that." Soon, my small savings would be gone completely. I'd have to ask Schiap for a better wage, and tell her I couldn't afford any more clothes, even at discount, but if I was careful and ate once a day I could afford the studio.

"One, then. But pay promptly each month, understand?"

I returned to the hotel, packed my bag and my paints, and moved into rue Ravignan, putting Allen's photo on the table and my Schiaparelli gown from the Durst ball, wrapped in tissue, in a drawer of the chipped, wobbling bureau.

And now, I thought, to find Ania. I had coffee at a little café near the Moulin Rouge, sitting in the shade of a chestnut, and tried to re-member all of my conversations with Charlie's lover, to see if I could remember a place she might have mentioned. I couldn't. My knowl-edge of Ania was as blank as a canvas with no paint on it.

"Try the Ritz," Bettina suggested the next day when I reported to the Schiaparelli salon for an assignment. A new window display would be put up soon, in time for the summer showings.

Because Schiap was an artist (not just a designer, not just a seam-stress, she explained), there was a philosophy to her collections, and a theme that demonstrated the philosophy. She was one of the first to do this, and Schiap's themes were more like party announcements than names of dress collections. The February collection for the coming winter, Bettina not-very-patiently explained to me, had been the Cir-cus Collection, inspired by P. T. Barnum, with gowns full of harlequin patterns and brightly colored dresses printed with carousel animals, and buttons shaped like dancing horses. She had shown it the same day that Hitler took control of the German army.

"She pays attention, our Schiap," Bettina said. "Bread and circuses. That's what the Roman emperors gave the working classes to shut them up. Schiap wants to wake them up, to make them pay attention to the fascists and what's going on."

There had been a Music Collection, with gowns printed with mu-sical scales and instruments. My blue-and-white gown, now tucked away in a drawer in Montmartre, had come from this collection. The Pagan Collection had elegant columnar lines, with dresses draped like the tunics on Grecian statues, and embroideries of floral wreaths. This winter she would show the Zodiac Collection, with gold and silver embroideries inspired by the court of Louis XIV, the Sun King, an-other specific reference to power and greed and dictators.

The ensembles also paid homage to Raphael's great painting *The Judgment of Paris*, just as the previous midseason collection, the Pagan Collection, had been inspired by Botticelli. Choose a side, Schiap was saying. And she had added sequined and embroidered images of the constellation Ursa Major, the same constellation on her cheek made by small moles.

The ensembles for that collection, especially the evening jackets, were heavily embroidered with metallic threads and sequins so that they shone like stars in a velvet sky, like the sun and the moon and the swirling lights of the Milky Way. There was a black velvet cape called "Fountain of Neptune" that could only be worn by a woman with some physical strength, so heavy was the gold embroidery. Elsie de Wolfe, who for decades, according to Bettina, had been standing on her head and putting her knees behind her ears and doing other yoga poses, wore it with ease and elegance. I saw a weaker woman bowed under the weight of that cape after the collection had been shown.

Fashion is about color, or the lack of it. Oscar Wilde wore mauve trousers and yellow jackets when most men of his generation were shrugging into the black-and-white suits of the modern man. Color was his badge of honor. He would have approved Schiap's colors for her most flamboyant king of all. Hell, Louis himself, the Sun King of Versailles, would have approved.

When Bettina modeled the shocking pink velvet cape embroidered in gold thread and sequins, it seemed processional trumpets blared to announce the arrival of the Sun King; when she tried on the plum velvet gown and jacket lined in bright yellow, the fitting room filled with the smell of the perfume of Madame de Montespan. Versailles was played out in those fitting rooms, and the other models, caught up in the spirit, tiptoed and flounced and cooed like ladies-in-waiting, all except for Bettina, who stood in her usual hand-on-hip posture, coolly smoking a cigarette.

"Schiap," she argued, "I admit the gowns are lovely, but we all know what Louis XIV did: made an absolute monarchy even more absolute, murdered all his naysayers, and martyred the poor Huguenots into practical nonexistence."

"Exactly," Schiap agreed, speaking around a mouth full of pins, her delicate hands pushing and pulling at the skirt of a mustard-yellow gown.

Après moi le deluge, Schiap was telling us. The flood was coming. Destruction. First the party, then the flames.

"You look awful," Bettina scolded the mannequin that summer afternoon. "You are out too late." Bettina carefully removed the pinned and basted jacket, and the mannequin stood, bare-armed and beautiful, winking and leering to make it quite clear that her evening last night had been, in her terms, a complete success.

"Oh, go away!" Bettina laughed.

Outside the door we heard a slight scuffle, then footsteps tiptoeing down the hall. A board creaked beneath the weight of the eavesdropper.

"I think Yvette is not the only spy among us," Schiap said. "My desk has been gone through. Again." She said it lightly, but I heard something else in her voice, a darker tone of the beginning of fear. Her daughter was in Paris now. Everything had significance.

"My purse was searched yesterday, when I left it on the counter for a minute," Bettina said. "Nothing stolen, but I'm certain it was gone through." The Paris police that summer were going out of their way to search out and arrest communists for any minor offenses—expired business licenses, disorderly conduct, things they might otherwise have turned a blind eye to.

"They are already doing Hitler's work for him," Bettina said bitterly. "Get rid of the communists and no one stands in the way of fascism."

Schiap muttered something under her breath, one of her Italian curses. She left to go meet with a mill owner who had some fabric samples for her.

"I'm certain they are looking for something more than fashion," Bettina said after Schiap was gone. "Could be a spy for Mussolini. You know, after she refused to have tea with Mussolini last year, he had her mother's Rome apartment searched. Plumbers, or so they claimed to be, came at two in the morning, looking for a nonexistent leak. They went through all the rooms, and she had to stand and watch and pretend to believe they were plumbers."

"What were they looking for?"

"Probably propaganda for the Russians. The Germans would want that as well, if it exists." The year before, Schiap had visited the Soviet Union as a guest of Stalin, had designed dresses for the Soviet women. Even communists have to get dressed in the morning. Even communist women would rather have an attractive dress than a sack.

"For a dress designer, she does seem to have the knack of making disastrous enemies and friends on the political level," I said.

Bettina did not like this comment since she herself had married a French communist. A very good-looking one, but a communist just the same. There was a joke around Paris, one based on fact, that you could always tell which woman had flirted with Monsieur Bergery, Bettina's husband, because there would be cigarette holes in her clothes from where Bettina had jabbed her burning Gauloises, for revenge.

Schiap knew about Bettina's bad habit—everyone knew it—and every once in a while she would tell Bettina she really should stop, she might set someone on fire, and Schiap, superstitious, would shiver with fear. And then Coco had done just that, set her on fire.

"You draw little boxes," Bettina said, putting down the pencil she'd been doodling with over my sketch for the new window display. "You think you can close the lid and be safe inside. You are wrong. When the war comes, none of us will be safe. All those little boxes will be crushed, with you inside."

"And Coco? How does she feel about the communists?" I asked.

"Loathes them. Hates unions, workers' rights, the whole kit and caboodle. Anything that might come between her and more profit." Bettina's sneer was so exaggerated it could have been drawn as a cartoon. "Coco and Schiap. You'll never find two women more different in their ideas," she said.

"They seem to also have a lot in common. Talent. Ambition."

"Everyone in Paris, at least those whose names you know and will remember, have all that. Remember, being beautiful is really just another form of talent. Ask your friend, Madame Bouchard. She is full of talent. You want to find her? Try the Ritz. It is where talented women go.

"A constellation. A night sky. Can you do that?" Bettina called to me before she disappeared into a dressing room.

A red sky, I decided. The red just before sunrise, red skies in the morning, sailors take warning. A cautionary sky, and the constellation would be Ursa Major with Schiap's large shadowy eyes staring out at us from behind the stars. In the corner, the eastern corner, would be a pink the color of scorched fingertips, the color of geraniums wilting in the August heat.

That evening I found Ania at the Ritz, sitting alone at a table close to the bar. She was wearing one of her Schiaparelli dresses, the one she had ordered that first day in Paris, when she and Charlie had sat, holding hands under the table in Schiap's showroom.

"You must despise me," she said.

"No, I don't." I meant it. Beneath her beauty, lurking like a pentimento in a painting, a mistake that the artist has tried to cover, Ania had a vulnerability that showed in the way she looked quickly over her shoulder, the way she tapped her feet if there was an argument going on near her, as if she were ready to run.

A waiter came and took my order for a martini.

"Another for you, Madame?" he asked Ania.

"Two more," she said. He smiled knowingly.

"Cheeky bastard," I said, when he had left.

"He knows me, you see," Ania said.

"Charlie says hello. I had a telegram from him. He's worried about you."

"Charlie. Sweet, sweet Charlie." She leaned back in her chair and crossed her legs. "I miss him. So very much. But not as much as I would miss my daughter, if I had to leave her. How could a mother do that?"

Ania crushed out her cigarette and folded her hands onto her lap. "Anton, my husband, will never let me take her. He has a mistress, and he loves her very much, I think. But he wants his daughter, too."

"I'm so sorry."

"Now you want to ask about von Dincklage, but you are too polite to ask." She pushed a strand of hair off her cheek, and her face grew hard. The vulnerable Ania disappeared, and back in her place was the confident, worldly, beautiful woman who strode into Schiap's boutique as if she owned it.

"He has good connections. For me and my husband, and my father, as well. Men aren't like wine, you know. You can't compare vintages. It is possible to enjoy both a Bordeaux and a white Rhine. Oh, well," she said. "That's life, right?"

"You don't love him?"

"Love von Dincklage? That is the most childish thing I've ever heard. I think that a storm is coming, and von Dincklage may be my umbrella."

"Unless you went to Boston with Charlie. Even if France goes to war, the United States won't."

"Boston. Tea with the other medical faculty wives. I can just see it." She laughed, and the strangest thing was that there was no bitterness, no cynicism in her laugh, only wonder, as if I had proposed taking a tiger to the opera. "I am not good for Charlie, am I? He is ambitious, and someday he will be a very great doctor. He needs a good wife, the right wife. Not me."

The bar was full that night, and noisy, but when Coco entered it grew silent. Everyone turned and stared, as if on cue. She was in one of her black sheaths, and with the black garments and her black hair her powdered face seemed captured in a bright spotlight. Von Dincklage was with her, and Otto, his driver.

Coco paused in the doorway, surveying the room, looking for a good table, and she quickly saw Ania and me sitting together. So did von Dincklage. He made that slight bow of acknowledgment, then turned his back on us and followed Coco to a table where a waiter was setting up folded napkins and silverware for them.

"Damn," Ania said, turning her back on them.

"Are you jealous?"

"Not at all. But didn't you see the way she looked at me? I am wearing Schiaparelli. She will complain to him about it. I'll have to go to her salon tomorrow to make it up. I need to be on good terms with her."

"Why?"

"Because I need to be on good terms with him. Don't you see what is happening in the world, Lily? What they are doing to the Jews in Poland? What they will do to the Jews here if the Germans come? Do you know where I grew up in Warsaw? On Zlota Street. The Jewish community."

We finished our drinks in silence. What could be said? Ania could go to Charlie and be safe. But she would have to leave her daughter behind. Heartbreak, either way. I had thought only Allen's death could hurt this much.

When I left, Ania was sipping another martini and Coco and von Dincklage were deep in a private conversation, their heads huddled together over their table. They ignored me, but Otto, sitting off to the side, gave me a cautiously friendly smile.

I nodded a hello and walked out into the Place Vendôme, feeling his eyes on my back, watching, and remembered the touch of his hand on the small of my back as we danced. Evening hadn't brought any coolness, and heat shimmered off the pavement in dusty gusts. I went back to my Montmartre studio, now as hot as an oven, and stood in front of those windows, watching the lights of the city blinking and twinkling below me. From that great height everything seemed distant and detached, even my grief for Allen. Where there had been jagged pain, there was now an emptiness. And fear, for Charlie, for Ania. And the memory of Otto's hand gently pressing me closer.

You could see the August heat in the faces of the shopkeepers, the office workers, the bartenders, the desire to be away, to leave stifling Paris for the coming holidays to the seaside, the ancestral village, the mountains. The women wore plain blouses over light skirts, or dresses that bared their arms and shoulders. The men pulled open their shirt collars and rolled up their sleeves, and sweat glistened over upper lips, on foreheads.

Despite the steamy heat, I was painting in my Montmartre studio, hours every day, beginning at dawn and lasting through the heat of the afternoon, when most of Paris seemed to be asleep. I had painted a wave for Schiap's window, and after that a forest scene with blue trees instead of green. The colors had been jewel-like, intense rather than subdued, the colors that exist in dreams on the verge of becoming nightmares, balanced on a knife edge of yes or no, come or go, together or alone, colors that exist in possibility more than reality. They pleased me. And all the while, I was wondering what my canvas would be. It was there, in the corner, primed, waiting.

I wasn't the only one working through the heat wave. The great couturier houses of Paris were preparing for the next collections, in the middle of summer pinning up and basting the furs and heavy brocade costumes of the winter to come. I went in frequently to see Schiap, and when I was there she was tired, stressed, busy, muttering often and waving me away if I lingered too long.

One day when I went to the boutique to check on a drawing with Bettina, a Mercedes was parked in front of the boutique, motor running, and with a load of girls in the backseat, fanning themselves with their hats and laughing.

Gogo came rushing out the door and almost bumped into me in her hurry. "Have to go," she said, "quick, before Mummy comes out. Oh! Did I step on your foot?" She handed her valise to the driver, who tipped his cap at her and prodded it into the trunk of the automobile.

"Not at all," I lied. "Where are you going?"

"Not certain. Anywhere there is water and a breeze. Mummy is upset, of course."

"It does seem as if you have just arrived."

"Keep your eye on her for me. She does seem to get into trouble. Make sure no one else sets her on fire." Gogo gave me a kiss on the cheek, clambered into the crowded backseat, and was gone.

Schiap came out the door just as the Mercedes was pulling away. She waved frantically and blew a dozen kisses in the direction of the fleeing automobile, gave me an accusing glare, and disappeared back into her boutique.

One Tuesday in the middle of August, I was at the corner café, alone as usual, ready to order my usual six o'clock Pernod, when I was approached by a woman wearing a knockoff of Schiap's little knit madcap. I wasn't absolutely certain, but I thought perhaps her black suit was a Chanel knockoff, and her shoes were supposed to look more expensive than they actually were. Under the tutelage of Schiap and Bettina I was learning to recognize such things.

This well-if-dubiously-dressed stranger sat next to me and ordered a coffee and a roll with butter.

Our waiter thought we were sitting together and jotted both orders together.

"No," I said, "we aren't—"

She interrupted. "It's okay," she said, waving him away. She had a hard voice with a New York accent. "Please, allow me. It would be nice to have someone to talk to."

She wore her summer jacket slipped off her shoulders and draped over her back. Schiap disapproved of the custom since it was so hard on the jacket. "Some women do it just to show off the labels," she had criticized. "And usually they are counterfeit labels, when they do this."

"You are enjoying Paris?" the stranger asked, obviously feeling free to open a conversation because she was treating me to a Pernod. "Not too expensive?"

"No," I said.

"But still, more expensive than one had expected. It is so hard to come by work these days, what you call a 'job'?" Her roll and butter arrived, and she ate greedily, breaking off large chunks and smearing them with butter, then popping the entire piece into her mouth. Her cheeks filled like a chipmunk's, and when she followed the bite with a large swill of coffee she rolled it around her mouth before swallowing.

That last question, I didn't answer. I was unofficially employed by Schiap, paid under the table. I never referred to her as my employer, and when I was in the boutique I acted not as an employee but as a friend of Bettina's. There were strict laws about such things, and while Schiap didn't mind bending the rules in her favor, she didn't want to get caught at it.

"There are ways to earn money. Good money," this woman said, brushing bread crumbs from her fingers. "Can you draw?"

"A little." I grew more wary, sensing what her next words would be.

Sketchers were fashion industry spies with three particular talents. They could observe, memorize, and draw. All the copy houses and the big department store buyers hired them before the new collections were to be shown. Their job was to go to the showings, concentrate on a few select numbers, dresses and gowns certain to sell well, to memorize the details, then, afterward, when no one was looking, sketch them. The copy houses and buyers paid as much as forty francs per sketch, and a good sketcher could earn as much as four hundred francs from a single two-hour showing of a collection. That was more than most seamstresses earned in many months.

Because of the sketchers, each couture house trained one or two salesgirls to do nothing but watch the crowd during the showing, to catch anyone who might be jotting down notes or making drawings on their programs, or even paying a little too much attention to a particular gown.

Sketchers, and their thievery, were why Coco didn't give programs during her showings, only tiny slips of paper on which the viewers could jot down numbers of dresses and suits, and nothing else, Bettina said.

Schiap laughed at them. "There is always something they can't catch," she had told me. "The correct size of the stripes in the lining, the design of the buttons. There is always a giveaway in the copies, and everyone knows it, so it just makes real customers hungrier for the real item, for a true Schiaparelli gown."

"Do you work for a department store or copy house?" I asked the woman, finishing the last drop in my glass and signaling to the waiter.

The woman turned a furious red and wouldn't answer.

"This is for my drink," I said, giving the waiter some coins.

The woman, still beet red, wrote her phone number on a scrap of paper and pushed it toward me. "Our rates are the highest."

The next day, I saw her going into Coco's salon. I was on my way to the Ritz to meet Ania at the bar, and the woman was turning into the rue Cambon. She probably had scissors in her bag and was going to snip fabric samples from the wide seams the couturiers used. This was an unfortunately common occurrence: some garments were so snipped at by thieves they had no seams left, just a few threads parallel to the stitching to hold it in place.

Ania laughed when I told her about the encounter. "Poor Coco," she said, stirring her mint julep. I wondered how she had learned about this quintessentially American drink, but didn't ask. "How Coco hates the copiers. It comes from growing up poor. She resents every penny that should be hers but is taken by someone else."

"Is that why Schiap doesn't mind as much?" Schiap, who had grown up in a great house full of valuable furniture and silver and servants.

"With Schiap, it is not pennies that matter but ego. She thinks that when thieves no longer copy her designs, a couturier is no longer in style. She might as well be dead, or out of business, which might be the same thing to her."

"The only thing worse than having people talk about you, is not having them talk about you. Oscar Wilde," I said.

Ania tilted her brimmed hat a little more over her eye and winked at me. "Me, I'd rather be a penny counter, like Coco, than an egoist like Schiap. And if you ever tell her I said that, I will skin you alive."

"Coco has quite an ego as well. And I think someone is already spying on Schiap."

"Probably. Maybe even the police, since they like to sniff out communists. Schiap should be careful," Ania said. "She has made enemies, and Coco Chanel is not the only one."

"Von Dincklage, too."

"Yes, him, too." She fussed with her hat again. "How is Charlie?" she asked. "He hasn't written to me in weeks. Does he . . ."

"Yes. He still does," I said. "He still loves you. This was more than a fling with him, Ania. You know that, don't you?"

"For me, too. It was so much more, but . . ." She turned away so I couldn't see her face. "My daughter. I can't leave her. I won't."

· ELEVEN ·

The showing of a new couture collection is a rainbow of emotion: red excitement, blue nervousness, yellow optimism, violet regret. For months, Coco and Schiap and the designers had been working on new designs, new concepts and styles, dozens of them, competing not only with their rivals but with their own history. The designers cannot repeat themselves, yet they must stay close to their own brand, they must be identifiable, so that when a customer wears her new dress people can say, "Oh, that's a Chanel," or, "That's a Schiaparelli. Isn't it interesting what she has done this season?" It is a tightrope walk for the imagination.

The great houses of Paris all showed their new collections during the same week, and the scheduling is like designing a battle strategy; the showings are the battles, and there are winners, and there are losers.

That week, collection week in late August, Paris doubled in population. In addition to all the Parisians returning from their summer holiday, buyers and shoppers came from all over the world. You could walk down the rue de la Paix and hear Spanish, Greek, English, Italian, all the different American accents from Texas to the Bronx.

There were duchesses from Bavaria and buying assistants from Macy's, English debutantes getting ready for their first season, Argentinian mistresses hoping to get one last wardrobe from a man growing bored. Wives. Daughters. Any woman who cared how she looked, who could get to Paris, did. The hotels and restaurants filled; the cafés at night overflowed. Paris throbbed with excitement.

Coco and Schiap showed their new collections on the same day, just hours apart, but Coco's was first. I went to the late-afternoon showing and tried to ignore the glance of unpleasant surprise the doorman gave me and my Schiaparelli day dress when I handed him my ticket.

Those tickets were small miracles to come by, reserved for the big buyers, the style editors of the major magazines and newspapers, the other bigwigs in the world of couture as well as the most famous customers: the Duchess of Windsor, Elsie de Wolfe, and others of large fortune and good taste. Janet Flanner, the correspondent for the *New Yorker*, never missed a showing. But Coco had saved one of those precious tickets, one of those chairs in the audience, for me. A kindness? Perhaps.

Her second-floor showroom was filled with rows of silk upholstered chairs and tubs of white orchids. The air was thick with the scent of her most popular perfume, No. 5. The lighting was dim enough to be flattering to faces no longer young but strong enough to show off the clothes. A string quartet played Vivaldi. The buzz of conversation all but drowned out the quartet, and people, mostly women, shifted expectantly in their chairs.

On the showroom floor, shop assistants lurked behind pillars and in corners, ready to confiscate any pencil or pen that lingered too long over the program for the collection. Coco would not let people take notes during the showing, for fear of copyists and sketchers. Journalists and known customers would be invited back later so that they could more closely inspect the collection, but the general audience was not to write during the showing.

I checked the audience to see if the woman who had approached me and asked to sketch for her was there. She was. Hat perched too far back on her head, jacket not well constructed—I was learning some of the tricks of the trade—sitting in the third row. I caught the eye of one of Coco's assistants and carefully, hoping no one else would see, pointed at the woman. The assistant approached her, whispered a few words. The woman shook her head. The assistant insisted. With a shrug of her shoulders, the woman handed over her small pocketed notebook.

She looked over her shoulder, saw me, and gave me a scathing glance, but I was glad I had thwarted her. I hated cheats. Coco had seen this skirmish, and when I looked in her direction again, she smiled a thank-you.

The collections were always shown in a prescribed sequence: first, the day and sport outfits, the casual clothes worn by models who looked ready for the tennis court, a ride in the Bois de Boulogne; then the afternoon and town clothes, sophisticated ensembles for tea and cocktails and matinees; then, the magnificent evening gowns and wedding dresses.

The models paraded out holding the number of their outfit in one hand, the other placed on a hip or stroking a lapel of a jacket. They turned to show the backs, turned to face us once again, and then disappeared, to be replaced by the next model, the next ensemble. The audience sat forward in the chairs, eyes flaming with covetousness as they wrote down the numbers of the outfits they wanted for their own wardrobes.

All through the showing Coco sat at the top of the stairs, half hidden behind a pillar, her face showing exhaustion and worry.

By the end of that showing, though, her pensiveness had given way to satisfaction. The cheering, when she descended the steps, was loud enough to satisfy even the demanding Coco Chanel.

"The lamé dress with the bolero," the woman next to me shouted to her companion, her shrill voice barely audible over the applause.

"The printed lounge pajamas with that huge necklace!" her friend agreed.

Coco's collection was a success.

But the Schiaparelli collection was a grand success.

A crowd of fashion-hungry women raced across the gray cobbles of the Place Vendôme in a loud clattering of heels on pavement, as soon as the Chanel viewing was over, even before the applause had died down. I watched Coco's face grow stormy at how eager they were to see what Schiap had planned. Schiap could have scheduled her showing so that it didn't follow so closely on the heels of Coco's, but when I saw the women, the journalists, the buyers for the stores, racing across the Place Vendôme to Schiap's boutique, I knew this was her revenge for the Durst ball.

I could have stayed behind, talked with Coco, congratulated her. But I, too, didn't want to miss a minute of Schiap's collection. I had already seen the garments, but Schiap didn't just show clothes; she presented theater to her audience, spectacle.

The boutique was all in darkness when we arrived. A doorman solemnly opened the door, and ushers guided us up the stairs to our seats, where we fidgeted like schoolchildren. When we had grown quiet, baroque music began to play, Lully's court music written for Louis XIV. Slowly, imitating a sunrise, the lights came up, just enough so that we could see, but not enough to dim the constellations that glowed from lights carefully arranged on the ceiling of the boutique. The show began.

Schiap's models danced *La Ballet de la Nuit*, slowly twirling, arms extended to invisible partners, and we were all transported to a court ball in seventeenth-century France. We watched with breath held in, not wanting to break the spell of glamour. No one took notes; we were too enthralled with the fantasy.

The collection finished with slender evening gowns in moiré silk that changed color as the models walked, and at the very end they put on the capes meant to be worn over the gowns, all covered in glittering rhinestone embroidery. The models and gowns seemed part of the sky itself, glittering and mutable, full of shooting stars. It was breathtaking.

Gogo, returned from her stay in Nice and brown as a walnut, applauded from beginning to end, never once letting her hands rest in her lap.

"Marvelous," she whispered in my ear. That day Gogo adored her mother, admired her, loved her. We all did.

Schiap was mobbed by journalists and buyers at the end of the showing. The society ladies stayed behind as well, shouting for the attention of Schiap's assistants, who now allowed customers to see the garments up close, to feel the fabrics, see the details of the embroidery, as they made up their minds which outfits they would order. I stayed on the fringe of the crowd, taking it in, but Schiap looked up at me once and winked. *Set me on fire*, her expression said. *Well, I showed her.*

I remembered an old proverb my grandfather had told me once, back in New York when I was fuming over some childish wrong committed against me. *When you plan revenge, you must dig two graves.*

A fter the showings, Paris, that city of changing, dappled light, changed yet again, from sultry summer and frantic collections week to autumn. The tourists and buyers left, and the city seemed like a woman who has grown a little wiser, a bit calmer.

I was anything but calm. I was painting furiously, two, sometimes three new canvases a week, barely letting the paint dry on one before beginning another, trying to capture the light in all its variability, the colors on the trees, the mutable river, the clothing of the women, the cold-pinked cheeks of schoolchildren. There was color everywhere, and I was consumed with the need not to repeat it or try to capture it, but to talk with it, to add my own colors to the silent conversation of hue and tint.

The colors almost mixed themselves on the palette; my skies were bluer than blue, the reds shimmered with passion. The lighting in my landlady's attic was magnificent, and more and more, instead of thinking of scenes, of people walking by the river or a dawn cityscape, the usual paintings made of Paris, I thought only of the colors. I hadn't been able to finish Allen's portrait, and lines, specific subjects, seemed not worth painting. The landscapes I tried, the Seine at late afternoon, the grays of Notre Dame's façade, seemed easy, pretty, no more than souvenirs for tourists. The colors, though, appeared on my canvases in large blocks and ovals.

"But what is it? I see only red and blue," said Solange, the house-maid who swept my floor once a week in exchange for an English lesson.

"That's what it is," I said. "Color."

"But it must be something else," she insisted. "A tree. A swimming pond. Two lovers, there in the corner where the blue and the red swirl around together."

"So you do see more than color."

She thought about that, biting her lip and leaning on her broom handle.

The day that I finished my first canvas without any representational lines at all took me by surprise. I had meant to sketch in two children playing with a beach ball, but they refused to appear. Instead, there was a blur, a spiral brushed into a splotch of yellow. There were brushstrokes of joy, not children feeling joy. It was the memory of joy.

I no longer dreamed of Allen at night. I no longer woke up with my arms formed into an empty searching circle. It wasn't forgetting.

What I felt for Allen is never forgotten, never finished. But it was an acceptance, both of loss and of a need to take a step forward each day, into the unknown future. The future, like some art, is abstract. We must see what we can in it and accept the unknowing of what is not seen.

And as I was accepting the facts of my life, Paris was unwillingly accepting her own changes. By the end of September, Chamberlain, Daladier, Mussolini, and Hitler had redrawn the map of Europe, surrendering Czechoslovakia to Hitler's army. He hadn't stopped after annexing Austria, as many had hoped. I wondered what color Czechoslovakia, now a puppet state of Germany, would be in this new map.

"A mistake," Schiap said. "A big mistake. To make deals with a man like that. He is a monster."

Overnight, it seemed, sandbags multiplied all over Paris, protecting monuments, buildings, bridges. There were sandbags in front of Notre Dame and the Arc de Triomphe, in front of Saint-Michel and Les Halles. The leaves began to fade from green to yellow, the weather turned cooler, and Paris, lovely, gay Paris, began to feel sad.

There was a sense of urgency in the air. People walked a little faster. My landlady began stocking up on flour and sugar and wine, hoarding bags and boxes in the alcove under the stairs.

Ania came and went like a bird, a butterfly. During the summer, her husband had taken her child with him to the South of France, but now they were back and Ania spent weekends with them, in a house somewhere just outside Paris. When she wasn't with her daughter, she was visiting friends in London, going to a spa in Vichy.

One day at the end of November I found her again at the Ritz.

She was tanned and wore huge sunglasses, larger even than Coco's tortoiseshell spectacles, but they still weren't big enough to hide the dark smudge circling Ania's right eye. It was dark in the bar; with those glasses on she must have been all but blinded.

The Ritz bar was getting set up for cocktail hour—candles on the tables, white cloths, aproned men and women straightening chairs and tables. In the darkened room they seemed like attendants from an unpleasant dream, unsmiling, silent, looking sideways at Ania and me at the bar. I had never liked the Ritz bar. Too many came just hoping to find the writer Hemingway drinking there. Too many men still regretted the good old days of just two years before, when women, not allowed in the bar, were required to sit in a small room, separately, on the other side of the hall.

"What happened to you?" I asked, pulling off the glasses and studying the bruise around Ania's eye.

"I walked into a door."

"Looks more like a fist smashed into your face."

"You're wrong," she said. "I walked into a door, and if you say otherwise to anyone else I'll . . . I'll . . ." She couldn't think of a suitable revenge. "Another. And one for my friend." Ania slid her martini glass over the zinc counter to the bartender.

"Is Guido still out there?" she asked, not looking up from her martini glass. Guido was the chauffeur.

"Yes. And not looking happy."

Ania flung coins onto the glistening zinc, and the bartender sullenly fetched them.

"Well, he's not happy. He's lost all his free time because he's been told to keep an eye on me. I'm not allowed to drive myself anymore. Anywhere. My husband doesn't approve of where I've been and what I've been doing."

"Where have you been?" I asked.

"Not with von Dincklage. With a friend, a woman, at Beauville, to get some sun. I turned down an invitation to von Dincklage's house party."

Ania looked beat up and miserable with smeared mascara, untidy masses of blond hair falling out of the chignon she wore in the afternoon. Her dress was a shade of mauve that did not work well with her coloring; she needed vibrant colors. Yet, looking at her, I knew that Charlie would see none of this, would have seen only the love of his life, here on a bar stool, well beyond tipsy. That black eye would have made him fighting furious.

"Strange husband, who prefers his wife to be with her lover rather than a friend."

Ania blanched. "I told you, Lily. Von Dincklage has important connections. We'll need them, and him, in the days to come."

"There's a word for your husband in English," I said. "Do they have it in French, too? Pimp? Procurer?"

"*Merde*, Lily, it's not that simple or sordid, and could you for a moment stop being judgmental? If not, finish your drink and go." She was crying then, so of course I couldn't leave. Instead I put my arm around her and let her sob quietly against me as I finished my martini.

"Better," she said, drying her eyes and wiping away black smears of makeup with a handkerchief. "Let's go see a movie. I need distraction."

She tripped leaving the barroom, and Olivier, the maître d'hôtel of the Ritz who happened to be passing by, caught her by the elbow. "Madame Ania," he said gently. "Are we under the weather?"

"Never," she said, giving him her brilliant smile.

We saw *Algiers* with Hedy Lamarr and Charles Boyer, and Ania made catty, silly remarks all the way through so that the people sitting unfortunately close to us made repeated attempts to hush her. "Look at that dress! A rag! See how she stoops. If she keeps eating and drinking like that she'll have bosoms down to her waist before she's thirty."

At one point, during one of the long kisses between Hedy and Charles, she took my hand. "I really miss him," she said. She stared straight ahead at the screen, where Charles Boyer and Hedy Lamarr fled, their arms around each other, through the labyrinth of the Casbah. "But there is so much I'd have to leave behind."

Ania looked even more devastated than before, when we left the cinema. "I think maybe it wasn't a good idea to see a love story," I told her. "Meet me tomorrow? At the Ritz again?" Something in her face frightened me, the complete lack of expression in her eyes, as if she was about to do something desperate.

"Yes. Tomorrow," she agreed.

I painted all the next morning, but the colors wouldn't mix right, looked flat on the canvas, as if my worry about Ania and Charlie was interfering with the chemistry of pigments. And I was running out of supplies. I had gone through the money Schiap had given me for papers and pastels for her windows.

When I went to the boutique Schiap was upstairs, checking inventory lists with her premier fitter, getting ready to begin order fulfillment for the new collection. It was a chore even the best generals couldn't have achieved with minimum chaos: the Schiaparelli boutique made many thousands of gowns and ensembles a year, hand-sewn, hand-fitted not once but many times—even something as simple as a nightgown could require three fitting sessions. And it was all achieved on a tight schedule so that they could begin work, as soon as possible, on the next collection.

I went into the office and sat in a shadowy corner, waiting, knowing better than to interrupt while Schiap and Bettina and the premier murmured together, flipping through charts and button cards.

When they had finished, a tense half hour later, Bettina gathered up her jacket and purse to leave. "Did you hear?" she asked me. "Schiap's black silk moiré dress with the strip down the side is so popular that six women wore it to the same event." Bettina cackled with delight. She was a beautiful woman who loved fashion, but she also loved to poke at the too-rich.

Schiap closed the door after her and we sat together, each waiting for the other to begin. She could be a mind reader, Schiap. She always knew when something was up, when my appearance was more than a friendly visit.

She eyed me for that usual long, critical appraisal. "You know,

most women overestimate their looks, their charm. You do the opposite. But you have a good sense of color. I like the pale blue blouse with
the gray skirt. Maybe I will have them displayed like that on the sales
floor." She had given me both the skirt and the blouse at separate times,
not intending them, I think, to be worn together. But as she said, the
colors worked.

She lit a cigarette and exhaled a cloud of smoke. "The silk threads
Lesage ordered aren't identical to the ones he used for the models," she
sighed. "He will ruin me. He has to order a whole new shipment, dyed
to order, and it will put that model a week behind the production
schedule."

"Disaster," I agreed, wondering if Churchill in England and Daladier in France paid as much attention to details and schedules as did
the couture women of Paris.

"Well, he'll just have to hire some more embroiderers and make
them work overtime, when the silks arrive. And I think it's time to
stock up on inventory. Soon, it will be difficult to get silk threads in
any color other than khaki."

She pursed her mouth, considering, looking at all the cabinets and
cupboards in her office, worrying that a day would come when she
would open them and find nothing inside.

Schiap looked at me from under glowering black brows. "You want
something," she said.

"An advance. Or to borrow a little."

"Is that all? I thought it was something about Gogo. Do you see
much of her?"

"Yes, when she's in town. But she has so many friends."

"And she likes to travel. We are going skiing in January. Before
that, she'll probably spend a month in London with her circle there."
Mama Schiap gloated with pride. "She's the prettiest girl in London.
How much? The advance?"

I asked for a small sum, the equivalent of a few hours' pay, just enough to settle with Sennelier so that I could keep painting. The cost of linen and cadmium red had doubled in just a few months. Inflation, and fears of shortages, were affecting the price of everything.

"The next time you go to Sennelier's, wear a good suit. One of mine," Schiap advised. "You'll get more credit if they think you are a rich amateur."

It was already midafternoon by then, too late for painting, and time for cocktails with Ania, so I crossed the Place Vendôme to the Ritz. A small crowd had gathered and was watching a bellhop from the Ritz scrub at something on the granite pavement in front of it. I forced my way through to see. *Death to the Jews* had been painted, in red.

"The graffiti is all over Paris," Ania said, coming up behind me and looking over my shoulder. "Some little Nazi-lover has been very busy."

The Ritz was subdued that afternoon. People spoke in whispers and kept their jackets close by, as if they might need to leave suddenly. Monsieur Auzello, the hotel manager, was beside himself, pacing and talking to himself, pulling at the lapels of his suit. He was a muscular, square-faced man who looked like Clark Gable. To see him so distressed, a man usually in control, confident, was unnerving.

His wife, Blanche, a pretty brunette born in New York, whispered something to her husband, then came over and stood next to Ania.

"Are you all right?" she asked, putting her hand on Ania's arm.

"Just fine," Ania said, knocking back her martini. Madame Auzello tilted her head to the side and left.

"She's Jewish," Ania said. "She says she's Catholic, but she's Jewish. So am I."

"But you're married and a French citizen now. Won't that protect you if . . ." I couldn't finish the sentence.

"Maybe," she said. "Maybe not. The rules seem to be written as we go along."

"All the more reason to leave," I said. "I've had five letters from

Charlie this month alone, and every time he asks about you and wonders if you might change your mind."

"I won't leave my daughter. But, oh Lily, I love Charlie so much. Even more, now that he's gone. And yes, I am a little frightened."

We drank a lot, that afternoon. And by the end of it, Ania had decided, finally, firmly, to come to some sort of arrangement with her husband. Maybe he would let her take the child for half the year, or the school year. "Or even for a visit," she said. "A trip to New York. And when we were there, we would stay. Just not come back." She would book passage on the *Île de France*, leaving from Le Havre to New York. First class, of course.

Three days later, I was seeing her off at the train station. Her daughter wasn't with her, but Ania seemed full of hope.

"I did it! I finally talked him into it. He will let me take her."

"How, Ania?"

"I told him we would both come back after a couple of months. I lied. He will send her to me, next month, with her nurse."

I wondered if Ania's lie had been as fully believed by her husband as she hoped, if he might also have been lying to her. "I love Charlie. I really do," she repeated, fussing with the tags on her luggage, and I wondered if she was convincing me or herself. "I know there will be problems." Her voice trailed off.

Understatement. The other medical faculty wives, for a start. And how does one arrange a divorce long distance? How would Ania manage in Boston? I tried to imagine her in a sedate black day dress, her only jewels small pearl earrings, her shoes with sensible one-inch heels. Without that blue Isotta and driver she'd be doing a lot of walking. Did she know how alone the wives of doctors could be, how independent and resourceful they needed to be, just to keep their families together?

And did she really believe her husband's promise?

"Don't cry, Ania. Charlie will make it work," I said, hugging her.

"Do you really think so?" She looked at me with the pleading, open gaze of a child who has been told she can go to the circus after all. "How do the women in Boston dress? I hope I packed the correct clothes."

As if her wardrobe was going to be the most serious problem. "Oh, my dear, Charlie loves everything you wear, you know that. As for the others, they'll adjust. Bring them a touch of Paris."

I helped her find a porter to wheel away her many cases and trunks, helped her choose magazines from the kiosk—*Vogue, Time, Journal de la Semaine.*

It was a gray morning, damp and distracting with the last leaves falling, people huddled into the turned-up collars of their coats. We bought cups of coffee at the train station buffet and took a little table near the window to wait for her train.

Ania knocked back a shot glass of whiskey she had bought to go with her coffee. "Von Dincklage doesn't know I am leaving. Maybe he won't care. I think he and Coco are lovers now; why does he need me? Maybe I'll have a second shot. I feel nervous. Do I look alright? Lily, what will I do in Boston, after I have set up my apartment? I'll get pink curtains for Katya's bedroom. She likes pink. I'll have to find a ballet teacher for her. She has just started studying, and loves to dance." Ania's hands trembled. Outside the window, a train pulled away with a loud grinding of metal on metal, clouds of steam, people shouting their good-byes, the same sounds that had accompanied Charlie's leaving.

"Have you considered taking a class? Studying something?" I knew how my aunt would have answered that question: *Be a good companion to Charlie, improve yourself.* Charlie would be working twelve hours a day. There would be no parties, no cocktail hours, and there was Katya.

"What kind of class?" Fear made her voice small and thin.

"Well, have you ever wanted to paint? To sculpt? To learn German? Dressmaking?"

"German I already know."

"Maybe a night class in the classics? Aristotle and Voltaire?"

She made a face like a bored schoolgirl.

"Can you cook?" I asked. Ania and Charlie would be living not together but in separate small apartments, side by side. Cohabitation before they were able to marry would be more than Boston could cope with, although everyone who knew them would understand the situation immediately.

"Yes!" Ania finally smiled. "I can scramble eggs. I can make escargots and cassoulet. Oh, I make a wonderful tarte tatin."

Snails and duck confit might be a little difficult to find in Boston, but if she said the tarte was an apple pie that would work.

"Then make meals for Charlie. Keep him company, and when you have time visit museums, take long healthy walks with your child." Oh God, it was the advice Allen's mother gave me, when Allen and I married, before I had become the school art mistress.

She looked at me as if she no longer understood my language. "I studied piano when I was a child," she said. "Perhaps . . ."

We finished our coffee just as her train departure was announced.

A doctor's wife should read medical books so that she could follow his conversation when he came home from the clinic. She should entertain his friends, men who spoke only of research and funding, and their wives who talked of their children. I couldn't see beautiful, worldly Ania doing any of that.

I was afraid for Ania and for a moment was angry with Charlie. He, who had criticized Josephine Baker once because she kept a cheetah for a pet and walked it on a jewel-studded leash, was going to try to leash Ania. I loved my brother completely, unconditionally, yet I knew he could be demanding and stern.

We paused for a hug outside her train compartment, and for a moment I thought Ania might change her mind. But she sighed, smiled, tipped her hat bravely forward, went up the steps, opened the door, and disappeared into the great unknown.

When the train had pulled out I realized how very alone I was. I tried to be happy for Charlie, who was getting his wish, but there was a nagging premonition that this was not going to go well for him. Nor for Ania.

The numb hollowness that had replaced my mourning and grief after Allen's death made my stomach lurch.

By instinct, I went to the Louvre. The train station had been so gray, so busy with farewells and the sadness that hangs in the air when people part. I needed color.

TWELVE

There were sandbags piled in front of the entrances to the various wings of the Louvre. There were sandbags all over Paris: at the base of the Eiffel Tower; at the Arc de Triomphe; at la Madeleine, the church built to honor Napoleon and his army; in front of the grand hotels. France wasn't at war. Not yet, those sandbags said. Not yet, but take nothing for granted, not the blue sky or the golds of autumn trees on the Paris boulevards, nor the dying red geraniums in their window boxes.

I entered the museum through the Cour Napoléon. Maybe it was because I had just said good-bye to Ania, but it seemed a day in which I needed to pay particular attention, to memorize the images of Paris I would want to keep for the rest of my life, especially that majestic building, rigorous in its mathematical architecture, the starting point of the ancient axis that runs through Paris, through the Tuileries, the Place de la Concorde, the Champs-Élysées, and the Arc de Triomphe.

"Stand here," Allen had said to me one day, years before. He turned me with my back to the entrance, one wing of the Louvre on each side of me. "Look straight ahead." I did, and saw all the way down to the Place de la Concorde, perhaps a mile or more, straight through the city.

"You are looking at the great axis of Paris," he said. "It follows the sun from east to west, except the axis is off kilter by several degrees."

"Nothing's ever perfect," I said.

"We are," he said. "We are perfect together."

I stood there again, that day, thinking of Allen and departures, of how the red of dawn is echoed in the sunset, how everything runs in a circle.

In the Louvre I made my way through the French painting wing to study the reds in the robes of the angels protecting Fouquet's *St. Martin*. Martin, an ex-soldier turned priest and bishop, was one of the most popular saints of France, famous for having turned the barbarians away from Paris without even lifting a weapon.

Where it had hung on the wall there was now a blank space, a sign saying that it had been removed for cleaning. A small crowd had gathered in front of that empty space, scratching their heads, frowning. "The saint who keeps away invaders has been taken away himself," a woman whispered, and she crossed herself. "St. Martin the protector has been taken into protection," a young man joked. "Shut up," an older man growled at him.

It seemed a bad sign. Numbed, I went up to the second floor to see if another favorite of mine, de La Tour's *The Card-Sharp*, had been removed. No, it was still there, in all its perfect reds and browns and pinks, a painting vibrating with barely controlled passion. And sitting in front of it was Otto, von Dincklage's driver. I started to wave to him, without even thinking about it, and stopped myself. Yet it was good to see him, I thought, remembering the Durst ball, when we had danced together. He was one of the few friends I had left in Paris, except for Schiap and Coco.

He seemed absorbed in the painting and there was something in his face, a sadness, that made me pause. *He's missing someone*, I thought. *Or something.*

"Another day off?" I asked, approaching.

Otto sprang to his feet. "Several days. The baron is making a quick trip to Germany and did not require me."

Ah. So that was why Ania had chosen to leave this week.

Otto glanced at me briefly, then turned back to the painting, and the yearning returned to his eyes. I wondered who he was missing.

"She is surprised but hiding it very well, don't you think? Cheats being cheated. I like this painting. Soon, they will take this away, too. Sometimes I think that if artists knew all that would happen to their work, they might not make it."

"Not so. We can't help ourselves, I'm afraid. It's not about the work, it's about the painting of it. It is when we feel ourselves to be alive. Most alive."

I sat down on the bench next to Otto. We were getting strange looks from the other viewers in the gallery.

"They take them away at night, and if anyone asks, they say they are going to be cleaned," Otto said quietly. "Except they don't come back, the paintings. It is a wise thing to do, I think. The Führer is a great admirer of art."

The Louvre was being emptied of its priceless art, piece by piece. Von Dincklage knew. Yet because France was not yet at war, there was no way for them to stop it.

"Has Madame Bouchard left Paris?" Otto asked.

"Just now, in fact." How had Otto known? Had he been following us?

"I thought perhaps this would be the time, when the baron was away."

"You knew she was going to?"

"I knew she was in love with your brother and had little reason to stay here. Soon, her husband will not protect her. She is Jewish, he is not. Such marriages are illegal now in Germany."

"The racial purity laws. Probably devised by the same mentality that is painting swastikas all over Paris. But this is France, not Germany. Do you believe in those laws?"

"No. But it is the law now, and the Führer is more powerful than any of our beliefs."

"Will Ania's husband send the child over to her?"

"I hope so. Katya would be safer there."

We sat in silence for a long while, long enough for one crowd of viewers to shuffle through the room and be replaced by another. The look I had first seen on Otto's face returned. Sadness.

"Will you go for a walk with me? Have lunch with me?" he asked.

He seemed a different person when he was on his own, not standing stern and unsmiling behind von Dincklage. He seemed as lonely as I felt.

We had omelets and a sweetish white wine at the café on rue de Rivoli, sitting indoors because the day was cold and blustery. We both pretended to ignore the looks the other patrons gave us. Otto was not in uniform, but there was a sense of the military about him, the way he walked, how straight he sat even in a café chair.

"So, you are an artist?" he asked when the plates were taken away and our coffees arrived. He leaned back to smoke a cigarette and offered one to me. He exhaled the smoke in perfect rings and poked his finger through them, laughing at his own trick.

"If you use the term loosely enough, yes, I paint."

"Landscapes? Portraits? Or are you a decadent?"

"More and more I am painting colors, not scenes or people. I guess that makes me a decadent, by your terms."

"Not my terms. The terms of the fatherland. Art must elevate people and glorify our country." He leaned forward, his elbows on the table, and looked very serious again. He was reciting a lesson or something he had learned in a pamphlet.

"No," I said. "Art must simply be art. Its only purpose is to make people look at it and to see something that perhaps they hadn't seen before, or hadn't known they had seen."

"That is an American viewpoint."

"I am an American."

"You are. And I wonder why you are staying so long in Paris."

Was it a warning?

"Come with me, if you wish," I said, standing. "I'm going to show you some good modern work, art that doesn't shout propaganda. Let's go to the Rosenberg Gallery."

"Can you walk in those shoes, or shall I find a taxi?"

I was wearing a pair of heels that Schiap had given me, and they were rough going over cobbled streets, but they were a beautiful shade of crimson. Since I never dressed for evening anymore, I wore them during the day.

"I'm uncomfortable in automobiles," I said. "Let's walk. Perhaps not too quickly."

Otto smiled. "A good German woman would never wear such shoes. But I like them."

We walked for several blocks, holding on to our hats to keep them from blowing off, leaning slightly into the wind. Shriveled leaves rustled down the pavement, and the bare branches of the trees swayed over us. I turned my ankle, not severely but enough to make walking inadvisable. I had been wearing the crimson heels since early morning, and my legs were feeling the effort. We took the metro.

We sat side by side, leaning into each other when the train went around a curve, seeing our faces ghostly reflected in the dark window. Otto's fingers tapped on his knees as if they were a piano keyboard. "I was studying at the Mozarteum in Salzburg," he said. "The best. But now . . . Duty calls."

"What music did you play?"

"The Brandenburg Concertos, certainly. And when no one was listening, Scott Joplin. I like him very much. I like jazz, though it is considered decadent and should not be played."

His voice trailed into nothingness, the pause made when the pianist's fingers leave the keyboard. He took a deep breath. "My professor,

Herr Newton, is gone from the conservatory. All the Jews are gone. Any that were still there at the beginning of the year were told to leave in March, after the Anschluss. They all lost their positions. Jews can no longer have professions in Germany. If only you could have heard him play . . ." Again that trailing off in midsentence, the sound of music that has gone silent.

"Will he return, do you think?"

"He has been sent to a work camp. He was seventy years old."

"Because he was Jewish," I said.

"And Germany must be cleansed of foreigners. The people willed it, the people wanted it. And the Great Leader is giving them what they think they want. I am not supposed to notice that Herr Newton's position at the conservatory has been given to a third-rate pianist who is a nephew of the department's chairman. A member of the party. I would say that only to you. If it were repeated to certain people, I would be sent to a camp."

We rode in silence after that, the train wheels clacking under us with a hard machine rhythm that mimicked a heartbeat. I felt a strange heat on my neck, as if I were being burned by the sun, except we were in a train underground, and the heat was fear rising to the surface.

When the train stopped at Saint-Lazare we climbed up the stairs, back to daylight. Otto took my hand. We walked like that, hand in hand, the way children and lovers do. It was a familiarity, yet it didn't feel rude or even unexpected. His hand holding mine felt friendly and natural.

"Feet okay?" he asked. "Not hurting too much? I could carry you." And to prove his point he put his arm around my waist and lifted me off the ground.

Suddenly, I was weightless. I was held closely, tenderly, by a man smiling into my gaze, both of us slipping into the surprise and delight of the moment. Then, I tensed.

"Put me down. Now."

"Yes." He had stopped smiling, and so had I. There had been a spark between us in that moment. We had both felt it.

Near the Rosenberg Gallery the streets were wider, the cafés less boisterous, and the dogs all on leashes, not running loose. This was the section of the city that artists moved to after they had made their fortunes, where the grand Champs-Élysées led to the Arc de Triomphe.

The gallery had reopened after the midday *dejeuner* break, and a few people, very well dressed, scuffed along the bare wooden floor, moving from painting to painting.

Monsieur Rosenberg had hung a show of Matisse for that month, and the walls were full of color, the exquisite blues and reds and yellows that reminded me of Fra Angelico, except the monk's women were secretive and shy; Matisse's models stared out at us from the canvas, bold and seductive and unafraid.

"Beautiful," I said, moving from painting to painting. "Do you like them, Otto? Do you like Matisse? How can art, any art, be decadent? Especially with colors like these." My fingers ached from the desire to touch the canvases, to feel those brushstrokes, to close my eyes and let the pigment sink into my fingertips.

"In Germany women must be celebrated for their femininity by showing them with their children. These models, they are beautiful and sensual, but I think not that concerned with motherhood."

He leaned closer to me and whispered into my ear, "I approve. They are beautiful. And they look like you. Dark eyes."

"Lovely, no?" Monsieur Rosenberg, the gallery owner, came over, extending his hand to me.

In addition to wearing the crimson heels, I was also dressed in a Schiaparelli day dress, black satin embroidered with bright, monstrous flowers: another unpicked-up special order that Schiap had altered for me. Monsieur Rosenberg, recognizing couture, believed me to be a woman of wealth. *Poor fellow*, I thought. *He thinks he's about to make a sale.*

"Very lovely. Dizzyingly so," I agreed. "The lines seem to move rather than stay still on the canvas." We were standing in front of Matisse's *Purple Robe with Anemones*, a painting of a woman sitting in front of red wallpaper. Matisse's reds were the most vibrant colors in the world, the color of creation itself.

"Most admirers just appreciate the pretty woman that Matisse painted," he said. "Are you are an artist?" Monsieur Rosenberg looked at me with a little more interest, putting his long, slender hands on his hips and tilting his sharp face toward me.

"Yes. That is, I paint. Whether it is artistic or not remains to be seen."

"Well, keep painting till you decide," he recommended. "Don't let others make the decision for you. Stay in the gallery as long as you wish. If you want to see the paintings in storage I'll have an assistant guide you through them as well." He made a slight but very gallant bow and turned to leave. He had ignored Otto completely, except to give him a dagger-sharp look over his shoulder. There was that hint of the military.

"Over here? The Van Gogh?" a man in overalls called to him. Monsieur Rosenberg nodded, and the Van Gogh was taken down.

"Sold?" I asked.

Monsieur Rosenberg hesitated. We were moving into an era when people cautiously weighed their words, how much to say, what to say. Otto walked off to look at a sculpture in an alcove, his hands behind his back.

"No," Rosenberg said in a low voice. One of my blessings in life, Charlie had once told me, was that people felt they could trust me. Something about the earnestness of my gaze, he had gone on to tease. "It is being sent to New York. For safekeeping. Most of these will be crated and shipped. I won't risk having them in Paris when the Germans arrive." Otto was way at the other end of the gallery, his back turned to us.

"You are certain they will invade Paris?"

"Why take chances?"

Monsieur Rosenberg turned to the doorway that led to his private office. One step. He stopped. He looked at me over his shoulder.

"What is your name?"

"Mrs. Sutter. Lily Sutter."

"Well, Mrs. Sutter, when you think you are ready, bring me a canvas or two to look at. No promises. But if they are interesting, I will visit your studio and perhaps choose something for a group exhibit. Just don't wait too long, if you catch my meaning. And choose your friends more carefully." One more dagger-look at Otto, and he disappeared into his office.

One moment can change so much. The moment when Allen and I got into our automobile and drove into the night, not knowing how cold the weather had turned, not seeing the ice on the road. The moment when Charlie offered to buy me a couture dress for my birthday and I said Schiaparelli, not Chanel. That awful moment when I saw Schiap on fire, blue flame turning to red on the finger/branches of her tree costume and realized life sometimes ends that way, Schiap could end that way. But there are beginnings, too, and Monsieur Rosenberg had just offered me one.

"He may show my work," I told Otto, when we were back on the street. "At least, he has offered to look at it."

"That would be good. One should never turn one's back on one's art, if there is a choice. I'm happy for you. But better not to wait too long." He took my hand in both of his and held it, the way one would hold a captive bird, gently, and knowing he must release it. "And now, I leave you. The baron is gone, but there are other matters for me to attend to."

He left me there, on the sidewalk, in high heels and with my sore ankle, staring after him with a sense of disappointment. Just when I thought perhaps I had been confused about what had happened, that spark between us, he turned and waved. He looked sad, but when our eyes met again, he smiled.

Allen, I thought. *I like that young man, that student of music. Do you mind?* People should be happy, he told me once. We aren't supposed to be alone. Life is meant to be shared. And grief must end sometime. Life must begin again.

I spent the rest of the afternoon trying not to think about Otto, trying to forget that pleasant shiver when he had swung me off my feet. The more I tried to forget the moment, the more I thought about it.

W hy did I decide to go see Coco after that? Did my own awakened sense of ambition need to meet on the battleground of another woman's ambition? Or did the "no promise" promise from Paul Rosenberg give me a certain generosity?

Heightened alertness can be the recompense for spending too much time alone with grief keeping you company. When I saw Coco, I saw what the world saw: a beautiful woman, a successful businesswoman, a fabulously wealthy woman, one of the richest in the world. But I had observed the secrets of Coco: her fear of aging, terror of competition, those memories of orphanage meals of soured milk and stale bread, undecorated white walls and black doors.

When you see more than the person wishes you to see, you begin to feel affection, whether you want to or not. It's the same impulse that makes little boys bring home stray dogs, that makes a grown woman dry the tears of a strange child on the street. You feel the humanity underneath it all.

I just knew I couldn't paint that day; I was vibrating with too much urgency. And something drove me to Coco's salon. I owed her a visit, after all. Schiap was paying me for painting backdrops and displays but also for annoying Coco once in a while.

Coco, like the other couturiers, was working on the next season's collection and was in one of the sewing rooms upstairs, the girl who received me at the door said. She must have been new—Coco tended to have a high turnover of workers—and she mistakenly led me up several flights of stairs, past rows of doors that quickly closed as I approached, past clothes hanger racks draped in white canvas to hide their contents, past rooms whirring with the sound of Singer sewing machines, to one of the finishing rooms.

The poor girl had forgotten what had probably been Coco's first rule of her training: no visitors in the workroom unless called for. The girl opened the door of the last room of the hall, and there was Coco, in the middle of a fit of temper.

"No," she yelled. "No and no." She picked up a garment one of the seamstresses had been working on. "The hem is crooked, the seam stitching too loose. And the braid! Did you think it was meant to be worn inside, on the lining? Move it a half inch, an exact half inch, beyond the seam." She flung it in the girl's face. The seamstress lowered her face but not before I saw tears starting.

"Go ahead," Coco said. "Weep. Baptize the gown if you must."

The other girls, some of them no more than fourteen or fifteen, squirmed and stared at the floor. *She is hard on her workers*, Schiap had told me. *They are afraid of her. Hell, her own customers are afraid of her.* Even the formidable Lady Mendl once left a Chanel fitting room close to tears.

I coughed. Coco turned and glared at the intrusion.

"What the hell is she doing in here?" the lioness roared. "Take her back downstairs. Immediately." She recollected herself, and the glare turned into a smile. *That*, I thought, *is how the lioness smiles before the attack.* "Back to work," Coco called to the seamstresses, clapping her hands.

The seamstresses went back to their tables and workstations, and the room filled with the sound of seams ripping, scissors clacking. No one spoke. This, I thought, must have been what the orphanage sewing room was like for her—anger, demands, fear.

We, the greeter and I, fled back to the main floor. She, too, was in tears, having realized her mistake.

"I'll tell her it was my fault," I said, trying to console her.

"Oh, please, Madame!" She fled, wringing her handkerchief. I waited, my hands folded in my lap, trying to look innocent but taking mental notes of what I had seen in that room—purple, in all its various shades: a suit in plum velvet, an evening gown in orchid tulle, a day dress in more demure violet.

When the primary colors of red and blue are combined, purple emerges: purple for royalty, for mourning, for daybreak because it is the color of Archangel Michael's robe, Michael the angel of morning. Purple absorbs light, like blue, and so is seen as a cool color rather than warm, a color of royalty. Chanel's collection, the next season, would offer the color of victory and authority.

"It's the colors of the irises I've planted at my home in the south, La Pausa," Coco said, sitting next to me half an hour later on one of the many beige sofas. "That was the inspiration. Flowers. Beautiful summer flowers. But unlike your friend Schiaparelli, I use only their colors, I don't make giant cut-outs and gaudy embroideries of them. You will tell her, of course, what you saw."

She was right; she knew human nature. "Well, the damage is done. Since you are here, I want your opinion." She leaned deeper into the sofa and lit a cigarette, blowing the smoke gently over her shoulder. "For a very fair blonde, do you think that is a good color?" She waved her cigarette at a bolt leaning in a corner. It was violet satin, shimmering with hints of blue.

"Lovely," I said, "though I'm not fond of violet, myself."

"You're right. It's a difficult color. I've been asked to use it for a dress for Madame Bouchard."

"But . . ." I almost said, *Ania has left Paris*, but closed my mouth in time.

"That's a . . ." I said instead, looking at the tapestry hanging on the wall, a hunting scene rich with flowers and forest animals and a hunter, horn raised to mouth, dogs dancing in and out of his horse's feet.

"Yes. Aubusson. Authentic," Coco said. And that was a giveaway. Schiap, born to a well-off family, would never have said such a thing. It would have been taken for granted. "She'll be back, I suppose," Coco said, and I knew we were still talking about Ania. "Sooner or later. That's why I will go ahead and make the dress she ordered."

Did everyone know Ania had left Paris? Did von Dincklage know?

"He doesn't know. Yet," Coco said, when I asked. "And I don't think he'll mind that much when he finds out. Not anymore. You know, at first, I was furious at you. You were the one who took her to the Schiaparelli showroom, right? Well, now, I think maybe you did me a favor. I lost a little business, perhaps. Very little. But you helped make other people reconsider their opinion of Madame Bouchard. She looks ridiculous in those Schiaparelli monstrosities. It is hard to stay in love with a woman who wears such things."

"She'd look lovely in anything. And a little humor never hurt."

"Do you ride?" Coco asked. On a side table in her sitting room was a photo of Coco on a gleaming chestnut horse. Riding was one of the skills she learned while living in other people's mansions, using other people's stables.

"I ride a little," I said. "And swim. I had dancing lessons when I was seven. In one of Isadora Duncan's studios."

Coco threw her had back and laughed. "Oh God, don't tell Schiap that. Don't you know? It was Isadora Duncan who ran off with her husband. That affair didn't last long. Duncan knew a poseur when she met him. Schiap's husband was very good-looking, I've heard. A little like Boy Capel. Or so people have told me."

An expression flickered in her face, less than a second, you see it and then you don't. Pain. Regret.

Coco lit a cigarette and studied me. Other than that, there was no reaction. She went on with her favorite theme: Elsa Schiaparelli.

"Isadora was attractive, in a pretentious kind of way," she said. "I saw her perform in her salon on avenue de Villiers. It was cheap. She was a muse for the provinces." That, of course, was the greatest insult a Parisian could give an artist, to call her provincial. "Even so, Isadora was much prettier than Schiap. Much better dressed, usually, even in her most pretentious costumes."

"Lunch is served in your office," a white-aproned maid announced, creeping up behind us in the hall.

"Too busy for a leisurely meal today," Coco said. "An omelet will do. I love eggs. When I was a child, I lied and said I hated eggs. Why do I tell you this?"

"Oh, I suppose I'm just a good listener," I said.

"Are you? I will remember that. Well, thank you for your opinion on the violet. And the next time you come, make sure you are announced first."

She walked to the window and stared down into the Place Vendôme. "All those sandbags," she said. "So unnecessary. And give Schiap a message. My next collection will make everyone forget her. She might as well go back to Rome."

"There really is room for both of you in Paris," I said.

"No, there is not. I am the best, and will remain the best."

There was such a fierceness in her words, her posture, with both hands fisted and raised to her waist. Again, I saw the child she had been, raised without love, without joy or pleasure, grabbing for whatever had been put on the table before others could take it away from her.

Her eyes softened when I smiled at her. "Come back and see me again," she said. "I like you. But you shouldn't wear your dress belted that tightly. It makes lumps, and you can't breathe properly. Loosen the belt, like this." She pushed and pulled at me, then turned me around to face a mirror. "See?" she said. "Softer lines. And more comfortable, isn't it?"

· **THIRTEEN** ·

"Purple?" Schiap asked, when I told her I had been to see Coco again. "Well, of course. Coco is thinking in terms of royalty. The empire."

"The Roman Empire?" I asked.

"That, too. What Hitler dreams of, world conquest."

For her next collection, Schiap was using as her inspiration the commedia dell'arte, with gowns as bright and light as a Vivaldi concert, as sexually suggestive as a negligee.

"Classical Italian comedy," Schiap explained. "Columbine, Harlequin's mistress who plays cruel tricks on her employer; Capitano, the military man in his bright diagonal stripes who is silly but very dangerous; Dottore Graziano, the know-it-all who actually knows nothing; Pierrot, the innocent in his baggy white suit; Scaramouche, the boastful clown, dressed all in black."

They all had correlatives in the world around her. Scaramouche was her stand-in for Mussolini. Capitano was Hitler, with his silly mustache. Poor Pierrot represented all the young men who would soon be put into uniform and sent to the front. That season, Schiap made one of the strongest political statements of the year—and everyone just called it fashion.

"Eat, drink, and be merry," she said. One of her mannequins came into the office wearing a muslin mock-up of one of the gowns. "This," Schiap said, pointing out the underside of the jacket, "this will be lined with shocking pink, my color. And you . . ." She turned back to me. "What are you painting for me? A wave? A sunset?"

"Something much better." I was already working on it, back in my studio. "A backdrop from one of the commedia dell'arte plays. The study of Il Dottore." Dottore Graziano, in the commedia dell'arte, is always an old man who misquotes Latin to show off his education, and his study is typically book-lined and full of globes, but with a bit of female lacy clothing sticking out from under a chair.

In the doctor's study I had painted a globe, and in a dark shadow of the upper right-hand corner of the poster I had inserted a little free-floating mustache, instantly identifiable as Hitler's. And on the astronomer's chart I painted in the Great Bear, for Schiap.

"How is Madame Bouchard these days? I haven't seen her in many weeks." Schiap shivered and buttoned her jacket tightly. It was late afternoon, already dark out, and the cold seeped through the walls.

"On her way to Boston," I said. Everyone would know soon enough.

"Is she? Just as well, considering. Though there was a costume I had planned just for her." Schiap sighed. "Chanel must be ecstatic about it. Von Dincklage will be all hers. For a while, at least. He is not a man who values fidelity. They say he has slept with half the beauties of the Riviera."

"What about the other half?"

"Their husbands own pistols, I suppose," Schiap joked.

"I don't know if von Dincklage knows Ania has gone. He's out of town, according to his driver."

"You've seen his driver?"

"Bumped into him at the Louvre." *And then spent much of the afternoon with him,* I didn't say. Schiap gave me a strange look. Not just appraising. Considering. The same way she looked at a wheel of ribbon, wondering how it could be used.

The next day, the next week, the next several weeks, I stayed in my studio, painting, working on a new canvas, reconsidering completed ones, trying to imagine how Rosenberg would see them, what he might think of them.

N either Charlie nor Ania were very good correspondents, so at first I wasn't worried when I received only one brief note from Ania. *I've learned how to cook a pot roast. Charlie says it is very good but I think maybe he hides some in his handkerchief. How is Maurice?* Maurice was her favorite bartender at the Ritz.

Going splendidly, Charlie wrote. *Two more patrons have offered financial backing for my clinic when I'm ready to begin working on it next year. One was at the Durst ball and is now back in New York.* Neither of them said how happy they were, how well things were going or how Katya, Ania's daughter, was.

Time magazine named Hitler as man of the year, that January. Charlie sent me a copy of the issue, with a brief note: "Come home," he wrote.

The cover was chilling: a grimacing, satanic Hitler playing an organ, and on top of the organ a giant Catherine's wheel hung with broken bodies. I took the magazine to the Place Vendôme and showed the cover to Schiap. She shivered. "I need spaghetti," she said, putting away the fabric samples she'd been studying and slamming shut the cabinet door. "Call people. Anyone. Tell them to come over tonight." Schiap hated using the telephone, was even a little afraid of it, so she always had other people make her phone calls.

She had converted the basement of her rue de Berri mansion into a bar and dining room, and the effect was fabulous. The upstairs rooms were filled with flowers, tapestries, leopard-skin-covered chaises, and shocking pink cushions, but this subterranean room was simple with low, vaulted ceilings and almost no decoration, the kind of cell monks would have dined in. The austerity added to the sense of forbidden bacchanal. The room was said to have a secret passage that connected it to the Belgian embassy next door, and Schiap joked once that it would provide a good escape route, if needed. Conspiracies, old and new, hung in the air.

Bettina was there that night, and Elsie de Wolfe and a few other people, including a Frenchman from the fashion syndicate and his wife, both of whom seemed involved in imports, so we had a table of eight. Schiap taught me the ancient Roman formula for a dinner party: you and your partner, your two closest friends, two people you would like to know better, and two people who can be of use. Except we were only seven, since Gogo, who would have had the partner's chair next to Schiap, wasn't there.

Schiap cooked a huge pot of spaghetti for us. She was a good cook, preferring simple ingredients and old Roman recipes. At dinner, we were forbidden to discuss politics, forbidden to discuss that *Time* cover of Hitler playing his unholy organ. There were long silences between bouts of gossip, who was living a little too largely on the Riviera, who was no longer paying bills, often an omen of a bankruptcy to come, which couples were likely to separate in the coming year.

"Happiness," said Elsie, one of Schiap's two closest friends there. Bettina was the other. "How to find it, and keep it? That's the question, isn't it? It is somewhat easier when there isn't already a husband involved, unless one is contented with a string of lovers after marriage. I personally think that is very hard on the complexion and the waistline."

"Eat your spaghetti, Elsie. It won't make you fat, not like bread does." Schiap put a large forkful into her mouth to make the point. She chewed thoughtfully, her huge black eyes solemn, even a little mournful. "I can't say from my own personal experience that husbands are so handy to have around."

It was the most I had ever heard her say about her marriage to Compte William de Wendt de Kerlor so many years ago. It had been Bettina who had filled in the details, including a quick snip that his name had been longer than his capacity for fidelity.

"Girls don't understand marriage, any more than I did," Schiap said. "There was I, barely out of childhood, thoroughly convinced by my mother that I was unlovely, unlovable, and there was this gorgeous man telling me otherwise."

"And so you married the first man who asked," Elsie said. Elsie, who purposely hadn't married till she was on the other side of middle-aged. Elsie, who'd had many women as lovers before setting up home with her Lord Mendl.

"Not quite the first," Schiap said, grinning. "When I was a child, still living in my father's house, I'd had a Russian suitor. My family liked him but oh, he was ugly. He was why I ran away from home, and I thank him every night in my prayers."

"And, of course, there was the sheik," said Elsie, who had heard these stories before.

"Just thirteen," Schiap said, checking her watch once more. "Traveling with my father in Tunisia, and there was this Arab sheik dressed in white floating robes wanting my hand in marriage. Father said no. You should have seen the *fantasia* the sheik performed under my window, those dancing horses and their riders." She sighed. "Lost romance. And who needs a husband? They get in the way. They give orders. Though children are worth everything you have to go through to get them. Oh, the illnesses, though. When Gogo was ill with polio I wanted to die, I thought."

"I hear that Wallis and Edward plan to visit with Herr Hitler. Again." Elsie de Wolfe twirled a modest forkful of spaghetti and jabbed it into her mouth.

"That's not the wisest event to put on your social calendar," said Bettina, lighting a cigarette. Her husband wasn't with her that night—or most nights, for that matter. He was busy with politics, with his meetings with the other communists of Paris, the artists Picasso and Miró among them. I didn't know at the time, but the Resistance was already beginning, already being planned for, even before the invasion.

"No politics," Schiap said.

"Well, the fascists have got the trains running on time." This, from an Englishman I had disliked at first sight, a friend of the Duke and Duchess of Windsor, a rotund and pompous fellow of limited conversational skills, who had been silent most of the evening. He had been pinching Schiap's maid when he thought we weren't looking. I already knew that all the mannequins and *vendeuses* at Schiap's boutique stood clear and made faces behind his back. He was there that evening as one of the people who might be of use to Schiap. A businesswoman must, on occasion, court money and influence, no matter where it came from.

"It will be a high price they pay for those timely trains," Elsie said.

He harrumphed at her, and Schiap hastily passed around the bowl of grated cheese.

"And what will we do when Hitler invades Poland?" Bettina asked, leaning aggressively forward. "Will we let him destroy the country?"

"Poland's problem," the Englishman said. "Should we die for Danzig? What a mistake that would be."

"Experience is the name we give our mistakes," I said, hoping to lead into a different conversation. Schiap was looking angry and unhappy.

"That's an Oscar Wilde–ism." Elsie put down her fork and looked hard at me.

"Our Lily has been educated," Schiap said, and I preened a little at the flattery.

"A knowledge of Oscar Wilde is hardly suitable for a lady's education," grumbled the Englishman.

"I met poor Oscar." Elsie leaned forward, her elbows on the table. "When I was just a girl myself, living in New York. I had an afternoon salon full of freethinkers, some good conversation about art. All the bohemians came, and when Oscar Wilde was in New York he came, too. A charming man." She glared at the Englishman, who had spilled tomato sauce on his tie. "So well dressed and well mannered. And wit. When he spoke, you thought diamonds should fall from his mouth, like in a fairy tale."

The Englishman harrumphed again and murmured something under his breath about sodomy and the Germans knowing better. We all ignored him.

"When I first came to Paris, I stayed at the L'Hotel Paris, hoping I might get his room, the one with the terrible wallpaper," I told Elsie.

"That particular wallpaper is long gone," Schiap said. "You know, he hated the Ritz and all that in-room plumbing. Thought it noisy and unhygienic."

"Well, there's my point, exactly," said the Englishman.

We were having dessert by then. Schiap put down her spoonful of lemon sorbet and rolled her eyes, finally exasperated beyond endurance. "Dear Coco loves the Ritz . . ."

Before she could finish her thought, the door of the dining room was opened and Gogo rushed in, her hat crooked on her head, her cheeks flushed. "Mummy!"

Mother and daughter flung themselves into a tight embrace.

Something was wrong. Gogo had been in and out of town all autumn and often returned to Paris without telling anyone. She was sometimes aloof with her mother, the way children are when they are grown but still haven't quite forgiven all the wrongs of childhood. Schiap hated it when Gogo was away, but sometimes she was too busy to spend time with her when she was in Paris.

That evening, they hugged as if she'd been away for years, not a few days. As if they were frightened. They hugged so tightly that the smart hat Gogo wore fell to the floor and was trampled on. After having her office searched twice, Schiap was worried even more than usual that her daughter might be arrested on a trumped-up charge, or even abducted. Schiap wasn't as wealthy as Coco, but she was still pretty damn rich. Ransom might be asked. They had taken Lindbergh's child; why not hers? We were moving into days when trust would be a very limited commodity. But I had never seen Gogo afraid before. Gogo, who had survived childhood polio and long separations from her mother, years of pain and therapy. She looked fragile, but she was tough, that girl. That evening, she was shivering, and not just from the cold.

"Hi, Lily," Gogo said when Schiap had released her. She inclined her head slightly to the door.

I excused myself and followed Gogo back into the hall, where a maid waited to take her coat. The hat was still on the dining room floor, forgotten, dripping onto the carpet.

"I don't want to tell Mummy. She'd fuss and shout and never let me out of her sight again. But I was followed. I'm certain of it," she said. "A taxi behind mine. He got out at the corner when the taxi stopped here. He walked behind me."

"You must tell your mother. She should know."

Gogo considered for a moment. I was flattered that she had confided in me, but this was too important to keep as a secret between us.

"Right," she agreed. "After dinner. Here we go, into the lion's den." We went back into the dining room, and Gogo had her chair placed next to mine.

"How was London? I missed you." Schiap's voice was full of love and concern.

"Fun," Gogo said. "Is there any more spaghetti? I'm starved." A maid brought in a plate, and Schiap piled it with noodles for her daughter.

"What did you do? Who did you see?"

"Lots of people. Lots of things," Gogo said. From the hall we heard the sounds of servants pulling suitcases, a servant paying off the taxi driver. "What have you been doing?"

"Working. Going to parties. Missing you." Mother and daughter smiled at each other across the littered table. The candles had dribbled wax over the tablecloth; Schiap scraped at a patch and rolled the wax between her fingers, never taking her eyes from her daughter's face.

"What's new in Paris?" Gogo asked the table in general, but it was the Englishman who spoke up in a lecturing tone.

"The Duke and Duchess of Windsor have visited. Stayed at the Ritz, of course. They seem to spend as little time as possible in London now. It was a great mistake, giving up the throne. England will regret his abdication."

"I've heard the duke and duchess prefer Berlin and Berchtesgaden to London," Gogo said, her voice chilly. "Maybe London is glad to be rid of them."

"No politics," Schiap reminded us.

"But, Madame Schiaparelli, as dressmaker to the most influential women in Europe, surely you find yourself interested in their various causes and opinions? You must find yourself praising fascism over communism. One must take a stance." The disapproval in the Englishman's voice stretched it out like a bowstring ready for the arrow.

Schiap had been clear from the start: she was against Hitler, against the Nazis and the fascists, against Mussolini.

"I am more interested in my clients' diet, their exercise habits," Schiap said. "You wouldn't believe how much weight some women put on between fittings, and then after they have dieted it back off they come in, complaining the new gown doesn't fit."

She laughed but there was a harsh glitter in her eyes, and for the rest of the night, whenever the Englishman tried to speak, Schiap cut him short and changed the subject.

"Causes indeed," Schiap muttered, when she and Gogo and I were left alone at the table, well after midnight. "It's men like him that make trouble for me."

He had intentionally set up a predicament for Schiap: to speak against fascism, and alienate many of her wealthy customers and her own native land, or speak against communism and cut herself off from the workers and her own beliefs.

Schiap looked exhausted. Dark circles swallowed her eyes; her skin was sallow, pale. She grew even paler when Gogo told her she had been followed from the train station.

"Would they do that?" Schiap asked, thinking aloud. "Arrest my daughter?"

Bettina was still finishing her coffee. "They wouldn't dare," she said. "The publicity, the protests from the high and powerful, would be terrible."

"You will stay here," Schiap said. "With me. No more traveling alone."

Gogo began to protest, but Schiap gave her a look that quieted her.

"And you," she said to me, "you will pack up your things and move into a guest room. Here."

I knew what she was saying, and that the room would come with strings attached. I was to help keep an eye on Gogo.

"Will I be allowed to bathe alone?" Gogo asked.

Schiap rose and began to snuff out the candles between her thumb and index finger, wetting the tips of her fingers between each snuff.

"I have spoken. And soon, you will both leave Paris. For an extended time. When I make Gogo's arrangements, I'll make yours as well, Lily."

"I don't want to leave. I love Paris," I protested. "I may have a show at Rosenberg's."

She laughed. "Oh, to be so young. To believe you always have the choice."

Schiap joined an antifascist society that winter. I knew only because Gogo let it slip that her mother was spending time in the 11th arrondissement, where the society's headquarters were, and Schiap could have no other reason for traveling to this gray, working-class neighborhood. Certainly, none of her clients lived there. Schiap did not speak of it, even when I asked her directly. "I have no politics," she insisted. "I am an artist. I am not a politician."

Schiap was working even more feverishly than usual, as if she'd had a premonition or a dream of the world to come, a world in which tailors would soon be soldiers and textile mills turned out khaki wool uniforms, not rainbow-colored silks and satins.

That year she created her Cigarette line, a small collection of slim dresses and coats, a collection that used much less fabric than those that had gone before, anticipating rationing and shortages.

Practical, but still whimsical. It was, after all, a Schiaparelli collection. When Schiap, extravagant by nature and desire, tried to be practical, it didn't always work out. There were, for instance, the smoking gloves she designed, with a cuff of little tubes in which matches could be stored, and an attached striking plate.

Unfortunately, the spark of the struck match could easily ignite the gloves. This happened once in the salon, to a customer from the Midwest who shrieked in panic until Bettina put out the tiny flame with her coffee. Schiap went pale and stayed pale for the rest of the day, and I knew she was remembering the Durst ball, when Coco had waltzed her into the flames. The gloves soon disappeared from the boutique.

Schiap was undeterred in her quest to create clothes that were both practical and whimsical, to keep going. Coco, though, was thinking about closing down production entirely.

"If France goes to war, what would be the point of a new collection?" She had sent a note that I was to come to her salon and try on some things. She knew that I was living at Schiap's home then. There were no secrets in Paris. Schiap had sent a maid to do my packing, in case I resisted, and a van to move my canvases, my easel, my paints.

Coco showed me a winter coat, fabulously heavy black-and-white tweed with a sable fur color. "The silly woman forgot to pick it up before she left. I don't think she'll need it now. She lives in Miami." Coco put on her tortoiseshell spectacles as I tried it on, the better to see me with.

The coat was too short and too wide, but there was plenty of fabric in the hem that could be let down and seams could be taken in.

"You can have it at cost," Coco said. "You're going to need something warm this winter." I was still wearing my old wool coat, once a rich indigo blue but now faded to mauve and unraveling on the left cuff.

"I can afford it at cost if you take off the fur collar," I said.

"I'll make a gift of it," Coco decided. "Consider it a late Christmas present."

Schiap laughed when she saw me in it. "You should have told me you needed a new coat! You look like a bourgeois matron," she said. "If you must wear it—"

"It's very warm," I protested.

"—if you must wear it, wear it only with these gloves." Schiap gave me pink leather gloves with circus horses embroidered on them. They looked quite nice with black-and-white tweed. And Coco, of course, would know they were Schiaparelli gloves I was wearing with her coat.

At New Year's, the parties began and continued. We celebrated St. Valentine's Day and those of many other saints I'd never heard of. Any excuse for a party, that winter. Paris and the Parisians partied as if too much wine, too much food, too much laughter, too many costumes, and too many practical jokes could delay what now looked inevitable. All you had to do was look at a map to see where Hitler was heading.

I painted every day in a cleared-out room at Schiap's, thinking, *Monsieur Rosenberg will like this color,* or, *No, he won't care for that but I'll make him see it, make him respond,* planning for when I would take two canvases for him to see. Eventually, all the paintings I made for Monsieur Rosenberg, I destroyed. They were no good, not even to my eyes, especially not to my eyes, and I began painting only for myself, and those paintings worked. Sometimes, I used the tip of the brush to write theorems and formulas, reminders of Allen and his love of mathematics, into the wet paint and smeared them so they showed only as swirls and scratches. But when I thought of Allen, I thought of Otto, too. One love lost; a new one not yet found. I hadn't seen him since the day we went to Rosenberg's gallery.

Each evening Gogo and I met with her friends in nightclubs and we drank too much, ate too much, laughed too loudly. There's supposed to be a calm before the storm. We weren't calm. We were too busy making the memories that would get us through long nights. Remember when Gogo growled, pantherlike, at the snooty Dome waiter? When Schiap painted a clown face on the store mannequin? When Gogo pretended to be a Spanish countess? Schiap dressed for one party as a radish, in red velvet, and we, dressed as birds, pretended to peck at her.

Elsie de Wolfe gave the final ball of the season, the Circus Ball. The marvelous Elsie outdid herself with this one, bringing in Lipizzaner horses in jeweled harnesses, the orchestra of the Cirque Medrano, an all-female Viennese orchestra, a gypsy orchestra, acrobatic performers, and at midnight, a grand parade. Elephants had been hired as well, but they wouldn't cooperate and were left behind at the Versailles train station.

I dream of them sometimes. I am traveling by train and I look out the window at the platform where we have stopped and there, in an early-summer twilight at a Paris train station, are four huge and stubborn elephants waving their trunks in irritation, trumpeting, as their keepers and the other travelers race back and forth in panic.

One of the socialites, that night at Elsie's ball, caused a stir by wearing a Schiaparelli satin cape over a Chanel dress. Both Coco and Schiap were furious. They laughed icily and air-kissed and then, fuming, went their separate ways for the rest of the evening.

And between the balls, Schiap and Gogo traveled. Together.

· FOURTEEN ·

It was during Schiap and Gogo's ski trip in Switzerland that Coco, for reasons of her own, invited me to travel with her. I'd gone to visit her one cold and miserable day in February when solitude and terrible discontent had driven me from my studio.

"You look terrible," she said, looking up from the copy of *Vogue* she'd been reading at her desk and taking off her glasses. She stood and walked a circle around me, appraising. "You need fresh air. Exercise. Pack a bag, enough clothes for a few days. We will drive south."

Just like those two, I thought. *Schiap wants snow, Coco wants sunshine.* They didn't even agree on how they had first met. I'd asked them once, as a test. "We met at one of Elsie de Wolfe's balls," Schiap said. "Coco dressed as a page boy. She likes to show off her legs. Such skinny things."

"We met at Longchamps, after the races," Coco told me. "Schiap was wearing one of those ridiculous hats shaped like a shoe. People were laughing at her, and she didn't even know it."

Two women, so different, with Coco wearing her strands of pearls over her back; Schiap twining her pearls around her wrists. Schiap was fun-loving and her anger passed quickly, like a summer storm. Coco's anger simmered just beneath the surface for months, years. Leftist Schiap; right-wing Coco.

"I'm busy, and I don't like driving in automobiles," I told Coco, leafing through the magazine she had just put down. It was the British edition of *Vogue*, and the cover was of a white dove carrying a friendly greeting card to Mussolini in Italy. England still thought war could be avoided.

"Well, then we will take the blue train," Coco insisted.

Le Train Bleu was second only to the *Orient Express* for luxury, and I knew Coco would travel first class, not in the recently added second-class Pullmans for those who traveled without maids and jewel cases, who wore wool and chenille instead of satin and sable.

"The ticket is on me," she said, reading my thoughts. "Consider it a birthday present for whenever your birthday is, or was."

I waited to hear what the price would be. Not the ticket price.

"When we get to La Pausa, we'll send Schiap a little postcard." Coco grinned. "Let her know what a good time you're having with me."

I considered. Would Schiap feel betrayed, or would she see through this ploy? She herself had asked me to spend time with Coco, to sniff around as it were, though she never explained what exactly I was supposed to be looking for, and I thought perhaps it was truly just to annoy Coco. Both Coco and Schiap were trying to involve me in their rivalry and campaigns for revenge, but I didn't mind. In fact, I enjoyed the company of both of them, as different as they were.

"Okay," I agreed. "Maybe I could give you a painting in exchange for the ticket."

Coco smiled. She didn't collect contemporary work from unknown artists. She was right, though. I needed a change. When I painted, colors were starting to blur, to lose their vibrancy. The canvases were getting dull.

Get out of Paris, away from the leaden sky, the winter days of freezing drizzle, the anxiety, the waiting to see what was going to happen. France and Germany were still at peace. Yet there was a different smell in the air; sometimes the sky seemed a strange color, as if our senses perceived what our minds still denied.

Fresh air, sunshine. Grilled fish right out of the ocean. Yes.

Why did Coco take me to her villa? Perhaps Coco had the same thing on her mind as the curators of the Louvre and the rest of Paris— the coming war—and she wanted to enjoy the freedom of travel while it was still easy, still luxurious. Perhaps she wanted to show me some of her truth, her reality, who she was away from the work, the cutthroat competition.

We arrived in the sunny, rosemary-scented South of France, after a night of wining, dining, and sleeping on the silk sheets of *Le Train Bleu* as the French landscape flew past our windows, to La Pausa, her Riviera home.

Coco's villa on the Riviera had been built expressly for her, from the ground up, on property that had once belonged to the Grimaldis of Monaco. The property and the villa had been subsidized by funds from her then-lover Hugh Grosvenor, the second Duke of Westminster, one of the wealthiest men in England.

The money might have been his, but the atmosphere was all Chanel: vast open spaces, a neutral palette of whites and beiges, an understated garden of olive trees and lavender that blended into the surrounding hillside. And the little touches, those furnishings and additions that make something personal . . . they were a story in themselves.

The large interior stone staircase was a copy of the one at Aubazine. "The orphanage where I grew up," Coco said. "The memory of it never leaves me. The orphanage, the nuns. You can die more than once, you know." Black and white, browns and beiges, the color of habits, of empty walls had become Chanel's favorite colors transposed into a palette of neutrals.

Coco had taken a fine revenge on a world that had made a misery of her childhood, turning on its head the clothing of abstinence and making of it the trappings of beautiful and sensual women who dined at Maxim's, had affairs with princes, bought their jewels from Cartier by the handful.

"When I was at the orphanage, I sometimes daydreamed about setting it ablaze." Coco said it sweetly, the way another woman would have said, *As a child I wanted to be a ballerina.*

"Were you thinking of the orphanage when you danced Schiap into the candles and set her ablaze?"

We were outside, sniffing in the sweet odor of lavender and wild thyme growing on the stony hillside.

"I wasn't thinking of anything," Coco said. "I saw the flames and danced toward them. There was so much glittering, the candles, the mirrors. I was like a moth, I suppose."

"Why do moths fly into candles?" I wondered aloud.

"You make things too complicated," Coco said. "They are attracted by the light and the heat. Have you never been cold, never afraid of the dark? Come. I'll give you the tour." A full staff awaited us indoors: upstairs and downstairs maids, a gardener, a butler, a cook and assistant, standing at attention like soldiers. She greeted each one by name, asked after children, aging parents, and then led me indoors, pride of ownership making her posture even more regal than usual.

The most wonderful aspect of La Pausa was the view from the windows of the three wings: each window framed a glimpse of sea and landscape worthy of an easel and canvas.

"Down there"—she pointed to the coastline far below us, past the hillside *balcones* of the Riviera—"is where the Virgin Mary is said to have landed, with Mary Magdalene, after the crucifixion, before they started traveling north on land. That's why this house is called 'the pause.' Quaint legend."

"Are you a believer?" I asked.

"You don't abandon your faith. It abandons you. But never completely."

Coco led me back up a huge stone staircase. One of the maids, tidy and formal in black and white, swung open the door of one of the upstairs' bedrooms. "This will be your room," Coco said. "I hope you will be comfortable."

Creamy white walls, beige plush carpet, heavy oak furniture, a table with fresh flowers already set on it, a huge bed with a pale blue satin cover. A large carved bookcase, filled with books.

"Mostly history books," Coco said. "Winston's choices. Myself, I prefer novels."

Winston Churchill. I was meant to be impressed, and I was.

"Winston stayed in this room," Coco said. "Now you can say you slept in Churchill's bed. Lunch is at one." She laughed and disappeared to her own suite of rooms.

The maid flung open the window, and the air, even in winter, was soft and smelled of green life, not coal fires and automobiles. She began to unpack my bag, so there was nothing for me to do but wander and stare in awe, as Coco had intended, at the lavish antique oak English furnishings, each piece perfectly situated, the black doors and white walls, the extraordinarily high ceilings, the hillside olive grove. I went for a long walk through the gray-herbed hills, thinking of nothing, soaking up the color, the scents.

By lunchtime I was famished and made my way back to the villa, to the dining room. I wasn't the only guest.

Already gathered on the terrace were Coco, looking chic in white silk pajama pants and a black sweater; another woman; and three men. One of the men was von Dincklage. Otto was with him, in his driver's uniform, stiff and unsmiling. When our eyes met there was a flicker in his face, but then it was blank again. I could tell, though. He was as surprised as I was.

Instinctively, I started walking toward Otto, hoping he would put his arm around me, even lift me off my feet, as he had before. I realized in time, no, I couldn't do that, not with the baron there, not with Coco watching. I did a quarter turn in Coco's direction and headed to her.

They—all except Otto, who stood deferentially to the side—had been talking quickly, passionately, a combination of French, Italian, and English. They stopped midsentence when they saw me approaching. Coco looked at me as if she had never really seen me before, her eyes wide, her mouth slightly open, and I knew that she had seen that flicker between Otto and me. Had seen, and was already wondering how it could be used.

I paused yards away from them, feeling foolish because of the lavender tucked behind my ear.

Coco wore her famous pearls dangling down her back, and they swayed when she turned and beckoned me forward.

"Come meet my friends," she said.

Madame and Monsieur Lombardi were, Coco, explained, old acquaintances. Madame was English with an aristocratic accent that suggested she had been received at court and dined at Westminster. Her husband was Italian, and there was a quality of ramrod posture, hostile hauteur, suggesting he was a fascist, a fact ascertained over lunch, when he frequently referred to his good friend Mussolini.

"And of course, you've met Baron von Dincklage." The head of Nazi propaganda in Paris bowed over my hand, but he did not smile.

"Madame Schiaparelli's protégé," he said coldly. "And Madame Bouchard's friend. I understand you saw her off at the train station. Very kind of you."

I stole a quick look at Otto. He blushed bright red. So he had been following Ania on von Dincklage's orders. Was he supposed to stop Ania from getting on the train? He hadn't. He had let her go to Charlie.

Coco winced at the reference to Ania and led us to the table for lunch, a long trestle set up in the garden with crystal, silver, vases of wildflowers.

"Sit here, next to me, Spatz," Coco said.

Spatz. Sparrow. *They are lovers now*, I thought. *She's being kind to me because I helped remove her rival from Paris.* Spatz—very strange, I thought, to think of one of the highest-ranking men in the Abwehr as a little sparrow—held the chair for Coco and took his place at the head of the table.

"The baron and I have been friends for years," Coco told me. "Haven't we, Spatz?"

"Surely not that long," he said, staring hard at me. "Ania mentioned you. A painter, I believe. A professional woman." His scorn turned up the corners of his mouth into more of a sneer than a smile.

Coco blinked and quickly composed herself, ignoring the condescension of his comment. An adroit hostess, she passed the bread basket and made certain everyone's wineglass was full.

"The Lombardis just dropped in," she said. "Unexpectedly. They won't be staying,"

There was a distinct coolness between Madame Lombardi and Coco; old friends they might have been, but I sensed they weren't any longer. Coco, during the introductions, had visibly stepped away to avoid touching or even coming closer to Madame Lombardi, and never looked directly at her.

Otto stood to the side, waiting. "Fetch the suitcases," von Dincklage finally said to him. Otto's right arm went up in the Nazi salute, and he disappeared. That awful salute. But he was in uniform; it was required of him, I told myself.

We dined on salad and fish with Sicilian oranges for dessert. The conversation was neutral to the point of being boring. Opinions were exchanged on the latest gallery exhibits, the latest films, which restaurants were outdoing the others with their winter menus.

"That fellow, Picasso. How dare he call that stuff he paints art?" Lombardi said. "Decadence. He probably uses drugs." His wife laughed uncomfortably and said, "Now, dear. You know even art must progress and change. Isn't that right, Madame Sutter? What do you paint?"

"Decadent art," I said, but nobody laughed.

"What's wrong with a good landscape, something that looks like something?" Monsieur Lombardi grumbled. "Heh, Madame Sutter, what's wrong with that?"

"Nothing, if you want to stay in the nineteenth century," I said.

His wife, bored by the conversation about art, changed the topic and ended her opinions with attempts at personal reminiscence with Coco. "Remember that night a few years ago when we drank too much champagne on Bendor's yacht and my ring slipped off, into the waves? Oh, I still miss that diamond, so lovely," and, "I loved his previous ballet. I think Diaghilev may be past his prime. Remember? We saw it together, Coco."

But Coco ignored the attempts at intimacy. When Coco was cold, she could outfreeze an iceberg, and she was obviously feeling very cold to Madame and Monsieur Lombardi. Her arched eyebrows arched higher; her thin mouth became even thinner. The Lombardis had dropped in for lunch, but they weren't invited to stay as well for dinner, for the weekend, as they seemed to have hoped.

"I brought my walking shoes," Spatz said when the maid had taken away the cheese plate. "We'll get exercise, yes?"

Coco murmured something unintelligible, but Madame Lombardi sat up straighter. She reminded me of a hound that has caught the scent.

"So you are staying for a day or two?" she asked.

"Most certainly." Spatz helped himself to an orange and, using his fruit knife, cut off the peel in even wedges. Coco studied the sky.

Madame Lombardi and her husband exchanged knowing glances.

Oh Lord, I thought. *I'm here as a decoy, a cover, a chaperone! But Coco's cover has been blown. This is an assignation between Coco and Spatz, and this unctuous woman and her Mussolini-loving husband know it.*

"Delicious fruit," said Madame Lombardi, peeling an orange and still hoping to be invited to stay. She was not.

Coco and Spatz went for a walk, leaving me alone on the terrace with her guests. I pretended to nap and opened a magazine over my face to keep it from sunburn.

When Coco came back and the uninvited guests were still there, her irritation flared into a nervous cough. The sun had moved from directly overhead into the west; the light grew subdued, and the crickets began to announce the coming evening.

"You don't want to be driving these roads after dark," Coco said. The Lombardis rose and, with great reluctance, left.

"Such bores." Coco waved them off as their chauffeured limousine disappeared down the road. Her face was like that of one who has eaten something sour.

"Good. They shouldn't have been here." Von Dincklage finished his brandy and glanced impatiently at his watch. He'd had other plans for the afternoon, and I could guess what they were.

"Well, if you don't mind, I think I'll have a nap. All this fresh air . . ." I left Coco and her Spatz alone so they could speak freely and do what lovers do when the affair is still new, still electric and full of possibility.

I spent the rest of the afternoon reading one of Winston Churchill's history books from Coco's bookshelf, curled on a satin bedcover, the sounds of crickets making the warm air in the room vibrate. Eventually I fell asleep, and when I woke the room was dark and still. Had I slept through dinner?

Hungry, curious, I went downstairs. The villa was completely silent; I couldn't even find a maid. Disoriented, I caught the smell of cigarette smoke and followed it out a side door, into a garden of potted herbs.

The cigarette smoker rose to quick attention when he heard me. It was Otto.

"Lily," he said. "I didn't know you would be here."

"A last-minute plan. How have you been?" I tried to sound casual, friendly. Merely friendly.

"Well," he said. "And you? You are painting?" He remembered, too, I could hear it in his voice. He offered me the chair next to his, and we sat side by side, staring up at the dark velvet sky.

"It is the color of the sky in the hunting scene in the Duke of Berry's *Book of Hours*," I said, "pale blue at the bottom, indigo at the top."

"Ah. So decadent knows of classical art. May I? I have thought of you often, Lily." He reached over and took my hand. It felt natural and logical, that we would sit in the dark night, holding hands.

I thought of Allen, and he seemed both very far away and very near. I thought of how he used to smile at me, his hand over his heart, how the smile had excluded everyone and everything that wasn't me, the secret smile of lovers. In my thoughts, I watched him turn and walk out of the room that had been our shared bedroom at the school, his math books tucked under his arm. He never said good-bye, only *I'll see you later*.

"Where are Coco and the baron?" I asked.

"They have gone into the village. They are dining there tonight."

"And you didn't drive them?"

"No. I have been given the evening off. Mademoiselle Chanel said she wished to drive."

Oh she did, did she? Leaving me here, with Otto, and she had seen that flicker.

"Nice of them," I said.

"Yes," he agreed. "Are you hungry? I can ask the cook for something."

"Maybe some cheese."

"And wine," he agreed. He disappeared into a large arched doorway and came back a few minutes later, carrying the tray himself.

"They are lovers, aren't they? Now. Coco and the baron." From one of the ground-floor windows I could hear a girl's voice, laughing, a man's lower voice. The upstairs maid, the one who had unpacked my suitcase, I recognized her voice. Was she with the butler? A boy from the village? Who would blame them? After frozen Paris, the air in the south felt as warm as a breath on your neck, the afterimage of the afternoon sun still burned red on the back of my eyelids.

"I think so. No, I am certain. He has many women, though." Otto lit another cigarette.

"And you? Do you have many women?"

"You are teasing me, I think." Even in the dark I could see his blush as he lifted the cigarette to his mouth. "There was a girl. At the conservatory. That was long ago, it seems."

"You miss her." I didn't ask what had happened to her. His abrupt silence begged for privacy.

"I miss many things. I miss life before this."

"Then why are you a part of this?"

"You think I had a choice? If I didn't give the salute in school, my father would have lost his job. If I did not join the student party, I would have lost my scholarship. And to be in the army, well, that is compulsory. There is no choice. There are many in Germany who would resist the Führer if they could. But they are afraid, and so they keep silent. I was lucky that my father had enough connections to keep me off the battlefield. I shouldn't even speak of these things. Tell me about your paintings," he said. "What are they?"

"Color. Almost all color. Now reds. Sienna, which is more like brown, like a red that has not yet found its courage; scarlet, crimson. Flame red. Blood red."

"I think blood red will be easy to find in days to come." Otto sighed and crushed out the cigarette.

"If you had a piano, what would you play at this moment?" I asked him.

"Chopin. One of the études, slow and light. Full of questions. Questions I would ask you."

"Now's your chance."

"Now I can't think of them. I think I prefer the silence and holding your hand."

"But it's not silent. Listen. Crickets. An owl." We listened to the countryside sounds of darkness, still holding hands. I leaned farther back in my chair, feeling the warm breeze on my neck, imagining what it would be like to have a kiss placed just there, in the hollow of my throat.

Otto and I finished the wine, the cheese, the plum jam spread on thick slices of brioche, and an hour later, when even the hem of the sky had turned from pale blue to cerulean, I took him by the hand and led him upstairs to my bedroom. The evening required it, demanded it. This desire for Otto, and I did desire him, the way the dry ground desires rain, the way plants desire sun. Zeno's paradox expressed another way: we are always arriving, yet we never arrive, Allen told me once. There are no beginnings, no endings. Each stage of our life, each emotion, swims on the shore where another wave has just eased back out to the sea.

"Are you sure?" Otto asked, kissing me exactly where I had imagined that first kiss, that hollow where the shadow is mauve even in bright sunshine.

"Yes," I said, closing the curtains, shutting out the night, excluding everything that was not just me and Otto.

I thought he would rush, that perhaps it had been as long for him as it had been for me and that impatience would disallow that lovely, slow lingering. He didn't rush. He was slow and careful, his pianist's fingers running trills on my spine, thrilling me, making anything other than a response to him impossible at that moment. I wrapped my legs around him; he arched over me. We slept tangled in each other, slippery with the heat of the night and our own heat, and he murmured in his sleep, German words I didn't understand and didn't need to. In his sleep, he nuzzled his head between my neck and shoulder and cupped a hand over one of my breasts.

I stayed awake long after he had fallen asleep, remembering what it was like to breathe lightly, slowly, so as not to disturb my lover, that hand resting on my breast.

In the morning, he was gone, and so was the baron. But we were still connected. I knew it, just as I was certain I would see him again. And again.

Bettina helped me make some sense of the scene between Coco and the Lombardis later when I returned to Paris. "Politics," she said. "The Lombardis are known spies."

"For whom?"

"Probably anybody who will pay. Her housekeeper is German, the husband is Italian, the wife is English. I've heard their phone bill every month is a thousand francs for all the calls to Munich and London."

"How do you know so much about them?"

"We need to know about them. They hate communists; they are our worst enemies."

"And why does Coco dislike them, if they share political beliefs?"

"They have gotten her in trouble. They are too notorious, too obvious, and they brought her to the attention of the minister of the interior, just because of her friendship with them. Or, perhaps, she just can't be friends with them in public, in the light of day."

Bettina frowned over the sketches I'd been showing her, for a new display. "This," she said. "This might work. The others, I don't think so. You aren't focusing, Lily." She pursed her scarlet lips and studied me. "So, you had a pleasant weekend? I won't ask with whom. I already know. Chanel. That's where you met the Lombardis, I assume. And I do not approve."

"I didn't ask for approval. And besides, you know that Schiap wanted me to spend time with Coco; a little back-and-forth serves her purpose."

"Time, yes. But don't dig yourself in too deeply." She lit a cigarette and glowered. "Not with Chanel, nor with that driver. Ah. She blushes."

How did Bettina know, and so quickly? There are no secrets in Paris, Schiap kept telling me. In the fitting rooms of couturier salons and boutiques, women were more confessional than with their priests, and women, some women, knew everything, about everyone. Chauffeurs tell maids, greengrocers tell cooks, secretaries and receptionists repeat gossip over coffee. Round and round.

FIFTEEN

"No. No, and no again," Bettina shouted at me again, several weeks later. It was spring again, the first day warm enough to throw open the windows and air the rooms of their winter damp. She flung down the sketches I had shown her. She hadn't forgiven me for what she thought was my betrayal of Schiap, when I'd gone south with Coco.

I'd had a particularly rough morning in my attic, when the colors wouldn't come out right and I wasted half a tube of expensive carmine red. Bettina's mood made me wish I'd stayed hidden in my attic.

"Well," I said, gathering up the sketches and jamming them into my purse. "I'll come up with some new ideas." I wanted to shout back at her but didn't dare. I needed the work.

"Do that," Bettina agreed, and when I left I let the door slam behind me.

I ended up at the Ritz bar for an early cocktail. Several of them, to wash down the sourness of loneliness and defeat.

I hadn't seen Otto since my return to Paris. Not a word from him. We had exchanged no promises and I knew his time was not his own. He was a soldier. A German soldier. There was a possibility that my adopted country, France, might soon be at war with his. Even that my native land, America, would join that war against his country. Madness, I told myself. That night in Provence was a onetime affair, not to be repeated. Forget it. But I didn't want to forget it. I wanted to feel his breath on my neck again, his fingers playing a Chopin étude on my back.

Schiap and Gogo returned from Switzerland during my trip south, then left for Tangiers when I was back from La Pausa. When they came back to Paris they were rosy with sunburn, their trunks filled with bead jewelry and exotic fabrics, deep reds embroidered in black and white, orange, blue the color of a late-summer afternoon. "No greens," Schiap pointed out. "It is a sacred color, not to be used with indiscretion. Maybe that's why you don't like green, Lily, because it is meant to remain a mystery. Always," Schiap said. "Always, one must be dreaming of what comes next." She wrapped beaded necklaces around my neck, then stepped back, considering. "I think the fantasy of the clothes must be even stronger now. Clothes you can escape from reality in."

Schiap, that year, traveled frequently and to places that would become important for the war effort: London, North Africa, Portugal. Was Schiap scouting locales, asking questions about loyalties, war preparations? If so, for whom? I guessed that Schiap was talking to people who knew people who could get tickets on steamers and planes, all the required travel papers.

Schiap worked and traveled, and Gogo traveled with her. I was alone much of the time. "Stay out of trouble," Schiap warned before every departure. And then she would wink, and I knew her definition of trouble was a loose one with many allowances. I did stay out of trouble, though, since the only trouble I wanted—Otto—wasn't free to be with me. I was alone and in a sour mood when I slouched into the Ritz bar one afternoon after being shouted at by Bettina.

Ania was sitting at a table, her head drooping like a wilting flower. The dim interior light played across her white-blond hair, her pale face, making shadows under her eyes and plateaus of silver on her cheek-bones.

At first, I shook my head to clear my vision, thinking that too much staring at blurred red and Bettina's shaky lines of what she thought horses should look like had affected my eyes.

No, Ania was still here, huddled into her pale blue silk coat and the famous Schiap madcap hat, that simple jersey tube that one pulled low over the ears and looked like either a fool or a femme fatale, nothing in between. Ania would never be anything less than a femme fatale.

"Join me," she said, looking at me over her shoulder. "Another martini, double," she said to the bartender. "One for my friend, as well."

We didn't speak till our martinis were almost finished. There was so much to say and so much that did not need to be said. I decided to go for the obvious.

"Charlie didn't write to tell me you were coming back to Paris," I said. "You have left him?"

"I only decided just before the ship left. Maybe he didn't have time."

Maybe you broke his heart, I thought.

"How was Charlie, when you left him?"

"I don't know. He was at the hospital. All the time, he was at the hospital."

I disliked her at the moment, because she could break my brother's heart without even looking worse for the wear. I disliked her until I saw the first tear roll down her cheek, smearing a path through mascara and rouge.

"Katya is back, too, then?"

"Katya never left France. Anton changed his mind. I couldn't stay there, not without her. I must be close to her, to see her. Here I am. Back."

I held her as she sobbed into my shoulder.

What a mess. Was it ever simple, was it ever about one man, one woman, happily ever after?

We drank together all afternoon, drank until the official cocktail hour began and dinner companions began arriving and the gleaming bar buzzed with activity and conversation, men eyeing Ania, who somehow was even more beautiful with her smeared mascara and crooked hat, and women eyeing me because I was wearing one of Schiap's famous black-and-white trompe l'oeil sweaters with the bow knitted into it, but it was now stained with Ania's rouge.

The waitress lit candles on the little tables; the bartender dimmed the light behind the bar and gave us disapproving glances. We were lowering the tone of the establishment.

"Where are you staying?" I asked Ania sometime around ten, when it occurred to me that we might actually want to go home, go to bed.

"I have a room here. They will send the bill to my husband. He will pay, no questions. Almost no questions. And on Sunday, I will go and see him, and Katya. The same arrangement as before." Ania sat up straighter, the way people do when they want to pretend they haven't had a little too much to drink.

She had stopped crying by then and was showing interest in the activities in the Ritz bar. Postdinner couples were wandering in; the bar was filling up. It was noisy with the clink of glasses, the murmur of conversations.

"Come with me," she said. "There's something I want to show you." She pulled me off the bar stool and led me out of the bar, exactly the way I'd once seen Josephine Baker lead her pet cheetah. "One of the bellhops told me about it."

She led me through the main hallway of the hotel, down a flight of stairs into one of those passages that great hotels and houses maintain, full of linen closets and mop closets, creeping shadows and flickering lights, then down a narrower flight of stairs into a passageway so far beneath the street, beneath Paris itself, the only thing I could hear was my own breathing and the sound of steam passing through overhead pipes.

Ania pushed on the heavy steel lever of a doorway.

"Are we supposed to go in here?" I paused in the doorway. It was pitch-black inside that room.

"I go where I want," Ania said. *If your husband allows you*, I thought but did not say. She reached up, flicked a switch, and the black hole filled with light.

It was a bomb shelter. I had never seen one before, but those bunk beds, the shelves of canned food and bottles of water, spoke of disaster to come. This was a bomb shelter as only the Ritz Hotel of Paris would devise. The sleeping bags weren't made of coarse khaki and wool stuffing; they were all silk, from Hermès. The rugs were fur. Paintings and tapestries covered the walls; a chess set was already arranged on a marble game table. A Ritz bomb shelter.

We had been a little tipsy before. Now, standing in the deep basement of the Ritz, seeing their belief in a war to come made manifest, we were sobered again.

"I just don't see Coco Chanel down here, wearing the same outfit for several days in a row," Ania finally said, and that lightened our mood a little, but we were silent and thoughtful when we climbed the two flights of stairs and went back into the Ritz bar.

"Ania, you must go back to Boston," I told her after we ordered another round of cocktails. "You won't be safe here, if there is war."

"No," she said. "I can't."

"Steal her. Steal your daughter, and leave."

"Yes. Just put her in my suitcase while Anton and the nurse and the chauffeur are looking the other way. No, Anton wants me to stay, and he is using my daughter to keep me here."

"Does he love you that much?"

Ania laughed. It was not a pleasant laugh. "Love has nothing to do with it. You still haven't learned. It is because I have made connections, I am useful. He wants me to come back to him."

She was wrong, I thought. It wasn't just because she knew people. Some women, as beautiful as they are, as kind as they might be, bring out a fiercer kind of love from men, a love that requires control and ownership, just as a beautiful painting can be owned, possessed, displayed. Anton wanted that kind of control over Ania. Perhaps von Dincklage as well.

Neither of us drank the new round of martinis we had ordered. That bomb shelter in the basement of the hotel had sobered us completely.

"I'm tired," Ania said. "Let's go."

Just as we were leaving the bar, Coco and von Dincklage came in, arm in arm, laughing. They stopped when they saw us. Ania, thankfully, was wearing Chanel under the blue coat, a simple black jersey dress with a costume necklace of green and red glass, and earlier in the evening she had taken off the Schiaparelli madcap. Coco eyed her with approval.

Von Dincklage barely looked at her, gave both of us the briefest, coldest of smiles. Otto stood behind him, the formal, on-duty Otto who looked right through me, then at the ceiling.

Ania gave Coco a kiss on both cheeks. Von Dincklage, blond hair pomaded back so stiffly it looked sculpted, bowed over her hand without actually touching it. His face was a mask.

Coco gave me a hug and whispered something surprising in my ear: "Your friend is in trouble. She needs to make up to him, any way she can." I blinked and nodded.

No one is all bad. No one is all good. Coco had won the rivalry over the baron and could afford to stop short of total destruction of the woman who had been her enemy. Not all women would have been as generous.

My umbrella in a storm, Ania had called the baron. She had lost him and Coco was telling me that Ania very much needed that umbrella.

I saw her up to her room. "I still love Charlie," she said, crumpling on the bed, one high heel slipping off her foot, the other already on the floor. "That's the saddest part." When I left, she was sleeping like that, in her Chanel dress, curled on her side, ladders in her stockings making her legs look mottled in the dim light.

Otto was waiting for me in the small, private lobby downstairs.

"Lily." Just the one word, my name, but I read the look in his eyes. We couldn't speak freely. The desk clerk was watching, Coco and von Dincklage were just down the hall in the bar, people were coming and going.

"I couldn't . . ." he whispered, bending close to my ear.

"I know."

"I wanted . . ."

"I know that, too." The night at La Pausa had been instinctive, casual, impossible to resist. This time, though, required a decision. An important one. Did I want this man? Yes. I did. "How much time do we have?" I asked him.

"An hour, I think. Maybe less."

"Follow me."

I took his hand and he resisted, pulled me back as I tried to pull him forward, indecision making him frown.

"Otto," I said.

"Yes. You're right," he said. I led him down the hall, down the stairs, down the second set of stairs, down the hall with the pipes overhead, the sound of the hotel plumbing gurgling overhead, from faraway kitchen sounds of banging pots and pans, people quarreling.

We made love in the Ritz bomb shelter, on top of a Hermès sleeping bag, both of us almost fully dressed, struggling through our clothes to feel skin against skin, the comfort of his heart beating over mine, and I knew we were bound together, but what remained to be seen was how deeply and for how long.

"This should be all there is," Otto said. "Nothing else. Except maybe music. And your art."

Charlie's letter arrived the next week. *Tell Ania if she comes back, I'll try harder. We'll get a lawyer, we'll find a way to get Katya. You come back with her. I'm worried about both of you.*

I had talked to Schiap about Ania without actually naming Ania, asking her for information about French divorce and custody laws. "If the wife commits adultery and abandons her husband and child, she will not get custody," Schiap said. "I am sorry for Ania, but that is how it is. Of course I knew you were asking about Ania. Who else would you ask for? Do you have the new sketches ready?"

I'm not coming home yet, I wrote back to Charlie. *Getting ready for an exhibit. I hope. I'll keep an eye on Ania.* What I didn't tell Charlie: I was in love.

I questioned it, sometimes. What I felt for Otto had nothing to do with the love I had felt with Allen. Allen and I had had a future, till I had destroyed it. What future could Otto and I have? I couldn't even talk about him with anyone, especially not Schiap, knowing the censure I would receive. I knew our meetings would be rare and brief at best. It was a love based on isolated moments, an emotion as difficult to define as true red, red without pink fading the edges or blue making it electric, or brown dulling it.

Wait seemed to be the word of the season. Wait and see what Hitler does next. Wait and see what will happen to France, if anything. I waited and painted, painted and waited and tried not to think about Otto, whom I loved.

By late summer I had enough canvases to show Monsieur Rosenberg. The thought of him standing before my works, assessing, judging, gave me nights of insomnia. No one had seen them except Schiap's upstairs maid, who swept up once a week. But if I wanted to be a painter, I had to sell my work, and to sell it I had to have a dealer, and to have a dealer, Monsieur Rosenberg would have to judge. Shoulders back, I heard Charlie whispering in my head. *Jump*, Allen would have said. *Take the leap.*

On a clear afternoon when the returned summer heat had driven most of the population of Paris out of the city, I went back to his gallery at 21 rue La Boétie, two small paintings wrapped in brown paper tucked under my arm.

The gallery was quiet that day. Monsieur Rosenberg was in, and two assistants, and one buyer, or at least I thought at first he was a buyer. Dark-haired, young, dressed in tweeds and a bow tie, he prowled through the gallery, glaring, arms behind his back, leaning close into the paintings to see better, standing back, chin in hand, to consider, I supposed, how distance changed the colors, the lines of the painting. He grimaced as if he had just bitten into a lemon when he stood in front of a Matisse; almost growled in front of the row of Picassos.

He left without making a purchase, without discussing even the possibility of a purchase.

"Lucien Rebatet," Monsieur Rosenberg said, after the door jangled shut.

"He doesn't seem to think much of contemporary art." I wondered how anyone in his right mind could find fault with a Matisse.

"He doesn't. He's scouting art for Hitler. The Nazis prefer the old masters, but they aren't above buying a few Picassos just for their market value. He'll be back in a few days to offer me half the purchase price of something here." Monsieur Rosenberg saw the brown parcel under my arm and led me into his office.

"Rebatet writes for the fascist press," he said, closing the door behind us for privacy. "He says the Jews want to start a war in France to overthrow the Third Reich in Germany. That the Jews want to get rid of Hitler. If only we could." He stood in front of a window overlooking the street and for a moment forgot about me.

"Should I come back?" I asked.

"No. No. Stay." His brisk, businesslike manner returned, and with a wave of his hand he gestured for me to untie the package. "You were here before. I remember you. A Schiaparelli outfit. Uncommon, on unknown painters, you know. She is expensive."

"She's a friend."

"I see. She has good politics. A bit too much of a communist for my taste, but at least she hates the fascists as much as I do. Let's see these paintings."

The first painting was a study in blue with circles and triangles of ultramarine overpainted with cobalt, and thin spirals of vermilion in the upper right-hand corner. Rosenberg put the painting on an easel, stood close to the work, and stared hard at it, covering it inch by inch with his eyes; he walked away from it, chin in hand, and studied it from a distance of five feet, of ten feet. He did the same with the second painting, another study in blue but with squares of intense Prussian blue over a solid pale azure canvas.

The two paintings together, for me, were the best of what I remembered of childhood, before my parents died, the blue skies and deeper blue nights, the flashes of the red of skaters' scarves in a winter park. Rather than a pictorial image or an imitation of a remembered vision, they were pure emotion, the unstructured story where there is no beginning or ending. Zeno's paradox. All possibility.

I stood, barely breathing as Rosenberg spent a full fifteen minutes inspecting the two paintings, going back and forth between them.

"Good," he said finally. "Like Nicolette Grey but with bolder colors. Who are your influences?"

"Botticelli and Fra Angelico," I said. "Without the saints and angels. And da Vinci, of course. Sfumato. How to make modeling work when there is no subject."

He looked at the paintings again and frowned. "I might be able to find a buyer. Abstraction is not as hard to move as it was a few years ago. I'll hang two in a group exhibition later. Yes? You will be here?"

"I will be here," I agreed.

When I returned to Schiap's house, the maid had a letter for me, hand-delivered and sealed with old-fashioned red wax.

"Did the appointment go well?" the maid asked. She had been following my progress in the studio upstairs. "Monsieur Rosenberg was agreeable?"

"Very. He will show some of my work. But what is this, Anne-Marie?" She shrugged and went back to her dusting. I broke open the wax seal and read the note.

Come to your old studio. I'll be there this afternoon. O.

My heart raced. Otto. Joy. And then fear. He had something important to tell me, or he would not have risked getting in touch like this, but he had never been to my studio in Montmartre. How did he know where it was? And why was he sending for me? I instinctively thought it was bad news, as bad as any news a telegram might bring. My hands shook when I refolded the note and put it in my pocket.

"I have to go back out," I called to Anne-Marie.

Rue Ravignan in Montmartre felt steeper than it had before. I climbed and climbed, my legs burning with the strain, my blouse growing damp on my back, under my arms, in the late-afternoon stillness. Would he still be there? Had he waited and then left?

"Upstairs," said my old landlady. No other greeting, but her glare was malevolent. People were beginning to leave Paris, and she hadn't been able to rent it out after I left.

He was standing in front of the window, his back to the door, and even when he heard my steps behind him he didn't turn around.

"How did you know about this place, Otto? Did you follow me?" I waited in the doorway.

"Because you were friends with Madame Bouchard. With Madame

Schiaparelli and Mademoiselle Chanel. You were of interest and so, yes, sometimes I was asked to know your whereabouts. Are you angry?"

I wasn't. He had given Ania time to leave, given her that chance that hadn't worked out. And all the women in Paris who wore couture knew I was friends with both Schiap and Coco; it was no secret.

"It is glorious," he said, looking at Paris spread out beneath us like a toy village.

"I used to stand here and imagine I could fly." I crossed the room and put my arms around his waist, pressed my face against his back.

"If only we could. Just fly away. I only have a few minutes. You must listen carefully, Lily."

"You are leaving," I guessed. "I won't see you again."

He turned and faced me, pushing my hands away. "Soon the German army will invade Poland. Then France and Germany will be at war. I will have left Paris by then. And you must, too. Even with your American passport you won't be safe any longer. Foreigners may be interned in a camp. The army won't march immediately into Paris. There will be fighting in the north and west. But France will lose. They are not prepared for what is going to come."

I didn't ask how he knew. Otto was aide to the German head of Nazi propaganda in Paris.

"How long?" I asked.

"There will be some delay, maybe a few months before the army moves south into Paris. But you must be gone before then. I'll find a way to let you know, but you mustn't tell anyone else."

We stood there, staring at each other, memorizing each other's faces. He held my hand, touched my hair, traced his finger along my jawline. I put my hand over his heart, over the coarse wool of his uniform, amazed that the heartbeat vibrated through so much stern cloth.

"I love you," I told him. "Do you love me?"

The sadness of his smile was more than I could bear. "Yes," he said. "But I think we will not meet again."

And then he was gone, his footsteps sounding loud on the creaking wooden floor, the door shutting, loud, rushed steps down the stairs to the street. When I opened my eyes again, he was in the street below me. He turned once and waved up at me, and through all that distance our eyes met. He strode off with that long, lanky stride of his, turned a corner, disappeared. It was like the sun disappearing, knowing I would not see him again. The old grief that began with Allen's death seeped back into me, the blurred edges of loss, the fading of color.

"Good riddance," said the landlady, when I went out her front door a few minutes later. She spat on the ground close to my feet and slammed the door shut.

My feet felt lead-heavy.

When I went to the Louvre again a few days later, at the end of August, it was closed. The custodians had packed up the *Mona Lisa*, the *Venus de Milo*, the Rembrandts and Gaugins, the Delacroixs. A convoy of dozens of trucks had taken four hundred thousand works of art into the countryside, for safe hiding. The great galleries were emptied, and sandbags were piled in front of the priceless ancient windows.

I stood there, in the courtyard, staring at the sandbags that reached almost to the second floor, imagining the darkness inside. Without light, there is no color. That was when the war started, for me, those two days when Otto said good-bye and when the Louvre closed.

Later during the war, after the Wehrmacht marched down the Champs-Élysées, the German officers ordered the museum reopened so that they could view whatever remained. Signs in German describing the rooms and the works were put up. The hungry Parisians, deprived of food as well as art, planted lettuce and radishes and rambling zucchini in the formal gardens of the museum. All of this, I learned later.

That September, after the heavy, hot summer had finished, the German army invaded Poland. France and Britain had no choice, after this latest act of aggression. They declared war. Overnight, France went from a country still enjoying peace to a country at war.

But, as Otto had said it would, the army stayed in the north and made no moves toward Paris.

I tested Otto's name, the various combinations to go with it. Otto, my lover. Otto, the musician turned soldier. Otto, the enemy of France. Otto, my enemy. I had to learn to hate the man I had learned to love. How, though? Love can make you a country of two. Otto, my friend, who had given me information I wasn't supposed to have.

In September, the Parisians who had just returned from their August holiday packed up once again and fled by the thousands, anticipating that the Germans would march in any day. In one day, Paris emptied. Every vehicle capable of carrying people or household items, from limousines to wheelbarrows, fled south, away from the northern front, where Hitler's army was massing for the invasion of France.

Gogo and I walked through the Place Vendôme, marveling at its ghostly stillness. I had thought Schiap would flee as well. I had been wrong. She stayed, working, making preparations for some other event still to come.

"He looks lonely," Gogo said, pointing up at Napoleon.

"And more than a little worried," I added.

The cafés were all shuttered; the stores didn't bother to open. The doorman still guarded the entrance of the Ritz, waiting for a limousine to arrive, a customer waiting for his door to be opened, but no limousines arrived, no customers, and he leaned against a column, smoking.

I hadn't seen Ania in weeks. I missed her and hoped that wherever she was, she was safe.

And then, because no bombs fell after that initial declaration of war, because the German army hesitated at the northern border, the people returned and Paris, on the surface at least, returned to normal. The Phoney War began, those months when France was officially at war yet nothing happened, no bombs fell, no battles were waged, everyone just waited, breath held. We were like insects caught in yellow amber, frozen in a single moment, a single emotion of shared, omnipresent anxiety, as we waited for Hitler to cross the Maginot Line in the north. Sirens were tested, blaring our ears several times each day. Metro stations were outfitted as shelters; gas masks were distributed.

"Needs must," Schiap said one morning at breakfast. "My new collection will have dresses and jackets with pockets so big you don't need a suitcase. You can just grab things on your way out the door. And a military theme, with trims of braid and frogging and colors— torch pink, Maginot Line blue, airplane gray, trench brown. And culottes for bicycle riding," she said. "Soon, there will no petroleum, no cars."

In that collection there were suits with huge pockets outside and tiny secret pockets inside, where small valuables—diamond rings, pearl earrings—could be hidden; frocks with Finnish-style embroidery to celebrate Finland's repulse of the Russians. There was a new print called "daily rations" commenting on the shortages of butter and meat. Schiap's designs weren't just clothes and they weren't just art; they were parts of history, and sometimes they were prophetic.

"And I will make the boutique's cellar into a bomb shelter. Maybe not as luxurious as the Ritz," she said, giving me a sideways glance. "A plane flew so low yesterday it almost decapitated Napoleon."

She spread apricot preserves on her bread. "I will create a new perfume, one that will make people forget all about that No. 5. 'Sleeping,' for people in transit. Lighter than 'Shocking.'" Shocking, her first perfume, in its bottle shaped like Mae West's curvy torso, had sold well, but never as well as Coco's more famous fragrance. "It will be subtle, florals with darker amber, meant to be sprayed on immediately before falling asleep, to help 'light the way to ecstasy.'"

That was exactly how the ads would describe it, once it was ready for market. A light to ecstasy. Pleasure in the midst of panic and fear. The bottle was shaped like a flame-tipped candle, and the color of the package, turquoise, was renamed "Sleeping Blue" that season. Perhaps the candle shape of the bottle was a response to the Durst ball, the nightmare of the flames of her own branch-arms being set alight.

Schiap's other idea was to set up a soup kitchen in her cellar, because Paris, which had been too empty the month before, was now full to bursting with refugees from the north and the east, places where the German army had already invaded. They arrived in a flood of need, carrying their belongings in sacks or in carts, hungry families looking for a doorway to sleep in, a cup of hot soup. From then on, coffee and bread and hot soup would be given out to anyone who asked for it, Schiap decreed.

"Just like Mummy," Gogo said one evening, when we were sitting in the garden of Schiap's house after dinner. Blackout was in effect. The city was dark except for the searchlights sequinning the dark sky, seeking out German planes. It was so dark we could see a million stars in the sky. We wrapped up in blankets and sat on pillows, staring up, each locked in our own thoughts, until we recalled Schiap's announcement at breakfast: "Soup! At all hours. And coffee. Strong. For anyone asking for it."

"She'll probably want to serve lobster bisque or something impossible," Gogo said. "Well, I'll find suitable recipes and give them to the cook. Perhaps beef broth and potatoes. We used to have that in boarding school twice a week."

"Or chicken with dumplings."

Gogo considered. "Rooster with cockscomb."

"Clams with silver dust." We laughed as each suggestion grew more impossible than the one before. Then we grew serious again.

"I've decided I'm going to join the motor transport," Gogo said. By then, the German army had outflanked the Maginot Line. There was fighting in the north.

Gogo was tiny, barely five feet tall, and looked as fragile as a china doll.

"Your mother will never allow it," I said. "Besides, I know she's making plans for you to leave."

"I will leave when I am ready. For this, I do not need permission."

We heard a commotion from the house and knew Schiap had come back from her boutique, where she had been working longer hours than ever. The storm before the calm, she called it. Getting everything in order before departure to safety. She found us in the garden. She looked exhausted, the shadows under her black eyes reaching down, down to the scarlet mouth, new hollows in her cheeks giving her face a sculptured quality.

"What are you two talking about?" she asked.

"I am going to become an ambulance driver," Gogo said.

Schiap paused, cigarette in one hand, already-lit match in the other. She blew out the flame without lighting her cigarette. She was wearing an Oriental tunic over slim trousers, heavy, beautiful silk with a jeweled neckline and cuffs, an outfit that could have come straight out of the volumes of Eastern art her scholar father had in his library.

"Over my dead body," Schiap said. "Don't be ridiculous." That was that, for the moment. Both Schiap and Gogo knew better than to prolong a quarrel because eventually each would do exactly as she pleased. Gogo might have had her father's Slavic good looks, but it was Schiap's determination that formed her character.

Schiap sat and joined us in our stargazing, and we spoke only of small matters, gossip, menus. "Chicken broth with gilded asparagus" was her contribution to the fantasy menu planning. "Remember, Gogo, in India, when they gave us rice pudding with silver leaf on top? I hear silver is good for you, though if you eat too much you turn blue.

Maybe . . ." Her voice grew speculative. "Maybe I'll work that into a collection."

Every once in a while I caught Schiap staring at her daughter, her eyes flaming with worry.

"At least let me take you to the tailors to have the uniforms properly fitted," Schiap tried to joke, knowing this was a battle she wouldn't win.

Uniforms. Plural. She was going to hold me to my promise of keeping my eye on Gogo.

"I'm afraid to drive," I muttered.

"Speak up," Schiap snapped.

"I'm afraid to drive. I don't even like to be in automobiles."

Schiap smiled. "I didn't ask if you wanted to," she said.

PART THREE

YELLOW

• • •

If blue is the color of paradox, and red the color of life and death and the passion between beginnings and endings, then yellow is the color of what is most precious. It is the color of sunshine, of gold, of saints' halos and daisy centers. It is the color of eternity, of autumn leaves and the yellow grasses poking through winter white, new springtime shoots before they turn green.

Yellow reaches the eye faster, and from a greater distance, than most other colors, so it is also the color of warning, and assistance. Amelia Earhart's first plane was canary colored, so that it would be seen on the blue ocean, if it went down. Her favorite evening gown was one designed for her by Schiaparelli, a gown with winglike panels so that Earhart seemed to be flying, even when she walked. Yellow is the color of flight and escape.

Yellow is the color of the badge that Hitler required all Jews to wear.

And yellow is the color of fear.

Elsa Schiaparelli, in love with yellow ever since her childhood, those illuminated books of saints in her father's library, loved to add touches of gold embroidery, thin yellow stripes, to her costumes. We all need a touch of immortality.

· SIXTEEN ·

Three weeks after Gogo announced she was joining the Motor Transport Corps, I was sitting in the driver's seat of a truck, trying not to cry.

"No! Easy on the clutch! Do you want to strip it? This equipment is expensive, and if you can't drive properly you should go somewhere else. Go roll bandages for the Red Cross or something."

The driving instructor was not known for his patience, and he had already explained to me that he had gotten the short straw, which was how he got stuck training me. He was my third instructor that week. The others had turned their backs on me and found other tasks to attend to.

"I have to do this," I insisted. Gogo, already very adept at clutches and gears and oil levels and gas tanks, sat on the grass, laughing. Higher up on the hill of the Bois de Boulogne where we trained, a Spanish family, refugees from the south, sat passing around a baguette and pointing at me, also laughing.

"Have you ever seen the inside of a vehicle before?" the instructor shouted, wiping his brow and blowing a puff of air out of his mouth in exasperation.

I turned off the ignition and glared back at him. He wasn't half as frightening as Bettina. The fitters and salesgirls in Schiap's boutique could have reduced him to a cringing ball of fear in minutes, but I decided not to tell him that. We were, by his terms, the weaker sex, and I didn't think it was my job to enlighten him.

"Look, I had a bad automobile accident. In England," I told him. "I haven't driven since then."

"What caused the accident? Did you try to downshift?" His sarcasm hit the target.

"An icy road. I hit a tree." Now, tears of frustration started in my eyes. Some things you aren't supposed to forget, once you have learned them. Riding a bicycle. Kneading bread. Working a transmission. But I had forgotten how to drive, and every time I tried, my heart pounded in my chest, because I remembered the accident that had been my fault, that had killed my husband.

The instructor sighed. He was a mechanic from Brittany completely at home with all sorts of engines, and his initial joy at being made the instructor of several young Parisian women had soured after he started working with me.

"Try again," he said, a little more gently. "Ease up on the clutch slowly, and don't let the truck slide down the hill."

I tried four more times, each time bouncing halfway down the hill before I got the clutch and shift balanced. But on the fifth, I did it, and the truck, its motor humming, perched exactly where the instructor had left it for me, ready to move forward, like an obedient animal.

Gogo and the Spaniards cheered.

The instructor blew out another puff of air. "Enough for today."

"Well done!" Gogo shouted.

"You learned how to balance a clutch in an hour. It took me three days," I pointed out.

"But you learned. Let's celebrate. Let's have a walk, get the smell of gasoline out of our noses, and then I'll buy you a drink somewhere to thank you. I know you didn't want to do this. I know Mummy forced you. Believe me, I know her methods of persuasion. But we need to do something, we can't just sit around, waiting for the Wehrmacht to arrive. We have to do our part."

"My driving might make me more useful to the enemy," I said.

"You're getting better. You can do it." A quality of her voice made me think she was repeating words she had heard for most of her childhood, during that long recovery from polio.

Gogo was a good walker, with a steady, long stride. It had been part of the strict exercise program for her rehabilitation, and I remembered her at the English school, walking round and round the playing field, rain or shine, sometimes for an hour or longer. That day, we walked from the Bois de Boulogne to the Champ de Mars, all across Paris to the 19th arrondissement. Paris had staged the 1937 World's Fair on this field. Little remained of the buildings except the Palais de Chaillot, and we climbed up its stairs to the terrace.

Before us was spread out most of Paris, with the Eiffel Tower in front of us, the Invalides on the left, and the Panthéon and Notre Dame on our right. It reminded me of the view I'd had from my room in Montmartre, the sense of flying that overcame me just from standing in the window. There, I had begun painting. I had begun recovering from grief, climbing out of the black hole of widowhood. There hadn't been a war, omnipresent fear and anxiety. Perhaps we best recognize joy when it has already faded.

The first smell of autumn reached us, that half-musk, half-dying-flower scent that is the essence of yellow as perceived by the nose, not the eyes. It was the smell of endings.

"This is the most beautiful city," Gogo said. "I hate to think of leaving it."

"I can't leave. I'm going to show my paintings at the Rosenberg Gallery." That, and I still hoped I might see Otto again. Both he and von Dincklage seemed to have left Paris. "They'll be back," Bettina said, always in an ominous tone. "And they won't be alone. The army will be with them."

"If the gallery stays open," Gogo said. "And now you look sad. Like you're missing someone."

"My brother. Ania."

"And Otto. Don't forget Otto," Gogo said. "A German soldier." Her eyes were judgmental. And I didn't blame her.

I hadn't told her about my affair with him, only that he had been at the Ritz the last time I had seen Ania there, and something in my face had given me away. I told no one about our meeting in Montmartre, what Otto had told me.

"He's a musician," I said. "He plays Chopin and ragtime."

"Interesting combination. But he's still a German."

"All the young men were called up in Germany. No choice. In France, too."

"Let's go for that drink," Gogo said.

We walked back by way of the Champs-Élysées and stopped at a café on the corner of rue Marbeuf. Gogo paused in the doorway. It was smoky inside, and only a few tables were occupied, all by men who were middle-aged or older, since the young men had been called up. They turned and stared at us, then quickly looked away, obscuring their faces with their coat collars.

"We shouldn't have stopped here," Gogo said, closing the door. "This is one of the places."

"What places?"

"Where they meet. People who say they will resist. Who will fight the Germans here, in Paris. Who will fight your Otto."

Colors sometimes fade or disappear completely if the pigment used to make the color is too fragile, or its medium is not well prepared. Cadmium yellow, when exposed to sunlight, fades to beige; van Gogh's beautiful flowers will, in time, be faded and pale, not at all vibrant like the flowers he saw and painted in the fields of Provence. Sometimes, the color survives only in our memories.

My life in Paris was falling apart, piece by piece, and I couldn't stop it.

"I think this waiting is the hardest part," Bettina said one evening several weeks later, downstairs in Schiap's twenty-four-hour canteen. She rolled pieces of bread into balls that she lined up on the table like miniature white cannonballs. A cold, heavy rain had been falling for days, an omen of a hard winter to come, the greengrocer who delivered our vegetables said. Even in Schiap's monkish cellar we could hear it pounding down.

"Believe me, it will be worse, much worse, soon," Schiap said. She gave me a knowing glance.

"I know. We must leave soon," I said. I remembered the night that Gogo had been followed from the train station, Schiap's constant fears that something would happen to her. Once the Gestapo was in Paris, arresting communists, anybody who might oppose them, neither Schiap nor her daughter would be safe. "This means no exhibit for me, doesn't it?"

Schiap recognized in me the same hunger that, years before, had compelled her to make her mark in fashion, to change what had been before her.

"We will hope for the best." She crossed her fingers.

"You and those paintings," Bettina said. "Rosenberg will have closed the gallery before you are gone. He is Jewish, remember."

Gogo and I by then had made several trips north for the Motor Transport Corps, driving supplies up, returning with wounded soldiers or crates whose contents we didn't ask about and weren't told. There was so much fear we could taste it, yellow-sour in our mouths and nostrils, the fear of what war could do to tender flesh and, for me, the continuing fear of simply driving, the grinding of the clutch, lurching forward, the possibility of slick roads, trees ahead.

In the morning, we received our orders, drove north and east of Paris, close to borders where the war had already arrived, to villages and farmhouses, to transport the wounded to field hospitals where they could be treated. Sometimes we carried messages as well. Pieces of paper stuck into books with underlined words, a grocery list, a single word we memorized, to be spoken only to a certain person, or not at all.

We drove in silence, dreading the day ahead of us. Some of the people we transported to field hospitals were missing limbs; some were missing parts of their faces. On some, we couldn't see the actual wound, and those were the ones I found most frightening.

The roads, unused to such heavy traffic, were rutted with mud and lined with an unending line of refugees fleeing ahead of the armies, the battles.

A skipping child, her arm full of dolls. An old woman leaning against an even older man, their faces masks of tragedy. A lovely dark-haired woman in a tea gown, carrying a birdcage with two canaries in it. Hollow-eyed adolescents; husbands leading their wives. Thousands of refugees. Sometimes it felt like we were driving to hell.

The trucks and ambulances, noisy green-and-khaki vehicles, were immense. Tiny Gogo had to sit on a pile of pillows to be able to see past the steering wheel. She took a lot of teasing from the doctors and the other drivers, but if the teasing went past her tolerance level she gave her tormentors a glare able to silence even her fearless mother.

And then, after a day in hell, we would return to Paris. That was how close the war was. We could commute to it. Schiap would cook spaghetti for us, try to make jokes, talk about her next collection, talk about anything other than the danger Gogo had faced during the day.

"I would die for my daughter. I would do anything to keep her safe," Schiap hissed at me one night.

Once, we were sent to Crouy-sur-Marne, where the hospital had been set up in a barn staffed with two doctors, eight nurses, a cook, and all the personnel needed to set up an operating room and take it apart again in six hours. This was the nearest to the front we were supposed to go, about ten kilometers or so from the northern fighting.

When we left in a convoy of three trucks, we passed a farmhouse that had been set ablaze. The farmer and his wife and four children stood in a row, watching mutely. The farmer still held a torch in his hands.

"They set the fire themselves. Too close to the border," said Gogo. "They would rather destroy their homes than let them be occupied by the Wehrmacht. They'll probably end up in Paris with the other refugees."

I watched the flames, the red and orange and blue in them, the hint of turquoise at the edges, the black smoke rising into the clear blue sky now receiving its burnt offering.

Gogo and I never discussed these trips in front of her mother, and Schiap seemed to have made peace with Gogo's work. She was so grateful that I was driving with Gogo that to show appreciation, she gave me dozens of pieces from her collections: day dresses, gowns, culottes, even a fur wrap.

"And where am I supposed to wear these?" I asked when she had given me a pair of pink silk satin boots striped with green and gold. "It will be difficult to use the truck brakes when I'm wearing these."

She laughed and pinched my cheek. "Save them for a special day," she said.

And then one day, when the rain had stopped and Schiap and Gogo had taken an automobile trip to the south, they were strafed by a German airplane. They had to abandon the car and take cover in a ditch. Gogo, when the plane had disappeared into the clouds, picked up some of the cartridges and kept them as a kind of talisman, a reminder of how close death had come.

"God, how loud it was. And flying so close to the ground. I could see their faces, and they were laughing. Still, they couldn't hit us," Gogo told me, when they had returned to Paris.

"They tried hard enough." Schiap trembled with outrage and fear. We were having another spaghetti supper in the cellar. None of us had much appetite.

"Well, I'd better get some sleep," Gogo said, rising. "I'm driving tomorrow. Day shift with the Motor Transport Corps. You, too, Lily."

Schiap turned white. "I don't feel well," she said. "Gogo, do I have a fever?" She took her daughter's hand and pressed it to her forehead.

"A little," Gogo admitted. "But it's just the shock. You'll feel better tomorrow."

"No," Schiap said. "No, I won't. I'm certain I won't."

In the morning, she wasn't better. She was coming down with something, she insisted. Worse, she'd had a dream.

"You have to stay home," she told Gogo.

Gogo bit her lip. She studied her mother, the almost supernatural calmness of her gaze, and knew she would not win this battle.

So, I drove without Gogo that next day, with a different woman from the motor corps, one even worse at driving than I was, so I was the driver for the trip. I got into the truck waiting for us at the Champ de Mars staging area, turned the ignition, and jounced into first gear. We were to pick up the wounded at a site the nurse had memorized. No maps allowed. We were especially to try to find Pierre. Only a first name and one shared by more and more Frenchmen, it seemed. It was code for *don't ask questions*. We would be driving into an area where there had been fighting the day before.

"Who is he?" I had asked, and in the office they grew suddenly deaf and dumb, and I realized I shouldn't have even asked. Some of the soldiers in the north were go-betweens for the Free French, led by de Gaulle in England, and the Resistance.

"Well done," said the nurse sarcastically, when I stalled the truck just trying to get out of first.

"Just keep your fingers crossed," I said, turning the ignition again and shifting, first into second, then third, spraying gravel from the spinning wheels.

When wounds are fresh, blood has a touch of blue in it. When the wound is older, the blood dries to a rust color, burnt sienna or hazelnut, or a deep ocher.

Both events are to be dreaded. If the wound is fresh, there is a chance that you won't be able to stop the blood flow; if it is already ocher, and especially if there are streaks issuing from it, infection has set in and possible blood poisoning. Pierre's wounds were fresh when we found him five hours later, just about where the office thought he might be, fainted and crumpled by the side of a road close to the Belgium border.

His wounds were so fresh they were still bleeding, which the nurse said was a good sign in that dead people don't bleed. When she cleaned the clots of mud from his face he opened his eyes and after a moment was able to focus on us. "Friend," he said. "Over there." We were surrounded by open field, and there was nothing in sight but field, mud, road, and, in the distance, an old stone barn.

"We'll have to drive there," the nurse said. "If there's another wounded one, we can't carry him this far."

"Drive through that?" The field was pockmarked from explosions, and a sickly yellow mist hovered over it.

"No choice," she insisted.

Pierre was able to walk, if we supported him on both sides, so we helped him into the back of the truck and wedged him between crates of supplies.

I drove slowly at first, to avoid the ruts and pits and craters, the stone barn coming closer and closer. And so was the noise of battle, the clamor and shouting and a buzz of angry motors not yet seen approaching.

"I think we need to go a little faster," the nurse said.

I went faster, at one moment even closing my eyes so that my foot would have the courage to press down more heavily on the gas pedal.

We reached the barn, and it took an hour before we got the other man into the truck. His wounds were bleeding—a good sign—but they were severe enough that they had to be stanched before he could be moved, and then sewn shut and wrapped in sterile cotton, before we could carry him to the truck.

"Time to go," the nurse said, when the soldier had been wrapped in blankets and made as comfortable as possible, next to Pierre.

"Right." *Turn on the ignition. Shift. Ignore the noise coming at you, the louder engines of tanks coming close to the horizon of the field. Ignore the twilight, the fog. Drive. And hurry, while you're at it.*

The nurse saw the horse before I did, an old gray plow horse released from someone's burning barn, a horse so tired and confused and hopeless that when it saw the truck it stood its ground, waiting, blinking its long-lashed, empty eyes at us.

"Stop!" she screamed.

Instead, I swerved, knowing that a full stop at my current speed would send the wounded men in the back of the truck headlong into a steel partition.

The horse stood and looked at us, watching with calm disinterest, and the truck veered wildly to the left, into a four-foot-deep trench. I hit my head and felt something warm trickle down my forehead.

Before blackness comes, unconsciousness, there is a red-out, when blood rushes to your head. I saw red, flashes of it, all shades, turning darker, darker. I saw Allen again, falling out of the car, his head wound fresh and bleeding, and together, we fell into the red turned black. *Hi, Allen*, I said. *I missed you. You'll be okay*, he promised.

The shrill scream through the black sky was followed by a loud boom and an explosion of color. The muddy French countryside under us shook. Magenta, I decided. Definitely magenta. The one before had been more of a crimson.

"Beautiful colors," I said. "Aren't they?"

"Are you crazy?" asked the nurse huddled next to me. "They're trying to kill us. Maybe your head injury is affecting you."

"All the more reason to focus on the colors. Besides, they're aiming west of us, over the border." In the dark, I could just see her silhouette, the points of an upturned collar reaching for her chin, the bun low on her neck, the wisps catching enough remnant light to reveal the red of her hair.

"You're an artist, aren't you?" she asked, her tone suggesting that the single word explained much about me.

"I like to think so. Cigarette?" I held my packet out to her.

"We aren't supposed to smoke. It's blackout," she said. I quickly withdrew the pack so that she couldn't see how my hand was shaking.

"I think they know we're here." I lit one for myself, the match flickering as if in a strong wind although the night, except for the fireworks overhead, was still and quiet. That's how much I was shaking, and my head was throbbing with pain.

Most people don't like to smoke in the dark because they can't see the smoke itself, which is a large part of the sensual enjoyment of a cigarette. Not me. In the dark, you can see the glowing tip even better, how the orange-red color changes to sienna as the ash at the tip lengthens. You can use the cigarette to scrawl designs in the dark, like we did as children with sparklers on the Fourth of July.

The whistling, exploding bombs lit up the night sky, and I knew that after this I'd never really be able to enjoy a Fourth of July celebration. I'd remember how the Luftwaffe had tried to kill me. Well, not me, personally. They were aiming for the French soldiers farther up the hill, the same hill we had been trying to flee.

After I'd come back to consciousness, the nurse and I had pushed, swearing, pushing again, our feet sucking ever deeper into the muck, for hours and that damn truck wouldn't budge. It had turned from day to night and the fighting was moving closer, and we were stuck.

Another bomb whizzed and exploded. The nurse was shivering; her breath was shallow and quick. Was she going into shock?

"My husband is going to be furious," the nurse said after a long while, after the night had grown dark and quiet again. "I said I'd be home early tonight."

We laughed, and I was glad that she seemed to be getting her nerve back. Except for the pain in my head, I felt surprisingly carefree, as if the worst had happened and soon all would be well again.

We were crouched in the mud, cold and sticky with it. Whenever I moved, there was a plopping sound from under my feet, as if the mud wanted to draw us down into it. I so much wanted to lie down in it, close my eyes.

"Don't sleep," the nurse said, shaking me awake. "You could be going into shock."

"I'm wearing Schiaparelli, you know," I said. "Under my overalls I'm wearing an Elsa Schiaparelli silk jumpsuit." Schiap had insisted that we needed to continue dressing well, even if overalls covered our clothes. "It will help protect you," she said. That theory seemed well disproven.

"Well, a silk jumpsuit will save the day." The nurse laughed.

Another burst of red sparks west of us. I had been timing the shelling the way you time a pregnant woman's contractions, the way children count between lightning and thunder. They were coming faster. They were coming closer. My eardrums ached from the assault.

"We really need to get out of here," I said, as if we both hadn't been thinking that same thought for several hours now.

"Hey!" I shouted as loudly as I could.

"Hey!" Pierre shouted from the back of the truck.

"How goes it?"

"I've had better vacations," he shouted back. "When is the train leaving?"

Was he joking or becoming delirious? I thought he'd only been shot in the arm, but perhaps there were other wounds I hadn't found.

"Soon," I shouted back. *Please, God, make it soon. Soon.* Is there anything worse in the world than being able to do nothing but wait?

Another shell, closer, so close the ground did more than shake; it rose up in tufts and stones, pelting us. Maybe their aim wasn't that good; maybe those bombs were crossing the border!

I forced my eyes open, resisting the urge to sleep. Yellow dots. In the distance.

"I see lights," I said. "Coming this way. Headlights."

The dim, wobbling unmistakable yellow lights of a vehicle came closer, closer, the headlights now blinding us, and the nurse and I leaned against each other for comfort, stuck in one moment when all is possible, when the next breath could decide the rest of our lives and how much time was left to us, where it might be spent.

The vehicle was too far away to tell if it was military or civilian. French or German. Did the Germans take women as prisoners of war? Did truck drivers count as militants? Common sense said to hide till we knew for sure who was coming down the road.

When it stopped just a few yards short of us, I could see that it was a private vehicle, not a military or commercial one. And it was blue. A baby-blue Isotta. Almost all the cars in France had been confiscated for the war effort, but Ania still had hers. Ania had connections; she knew people.

"Lily? Are you there?"

Ania got out of the car and leaned into the darkness, calling through cupped hands, her white-blond hair gleaming like silver under a hat of gauze and feathers. She was in high heels.

I couldn't believe my eyes. The nurse, though, didn't need to hear more. A voice not German was all she had wanted. She stood and waved her arms over her head in greeting.

"Over here! And turn the car headlights off!"

I stood slowly, a little worried that maybe I was as delirious as Pierre. But I wasn't. Ania ran to me and gave me a tight hug.

"How?" was all I could manage.

Ania lit a cigarette and handed it to me. "I went looking for you at Schiap's, and she said you hadn't come back yet. You're very late, aren't you?" She scolded me as if I been late for a dress fitting or a visit to the Louvre. "God, the roads are bad! My little automobile will never be the same."

"Can we all fit in there?" the nurse asked, newly worried. "We'll have to leave the truck until someone can come for it with a chain."

"We'll squeeze in," Ania said.

I'd never been so happy to see anyone. I saw what Charlie had seen in Ania, her courage and loyalty, the strength it had required for her to leave Charlie and come back to France, to her daughter.

Pierre and the nurse squeezed into the backseat, the unconscious man wedged between them. I sat next to Ania in the front, and when I began mumbling about Schiap's autumn collection, the matchbox cuffs that caught on fire, she hushed me and told me to rest.

"You're injured," she said. "Charlie will be so upset."

"Just a little bump and shock," the nurse called from the backseat. "She'll be fine."

"Then I have just the thing." Ania opened the huge purse resting between us and took out a bottle of wine, a Lafite Rothschild, vintage 1932, not the best year but it would suffice, she said.

"Not a great idea for someone with a head injury," the nurse said.

"Sure it is," I shouted back. I opened the bottle, and Ania and I passed it back and forth as she drove through the black night. We sang most of the way back to Paris, on our way back to the city we loved. Ania had a lovely voice and when she sang Josephine Baker's famous song, "I have two loves, my country and Paris," we wept a little, and not just from the wine.

This is war, I thought. Wounded men, burning houses, anxious mothers, young people arriving at their first realization that they were not going to live forever, that they were fragile flesh. And all of this was on its way to Paris.

"But how did you know where we were?" I asked Ania. Our missions weren't secret, but the office did not readily give out specific information.

"Coco told me," she said. "Coco knows everything."

Ania had a cigarette in one hand, the bottle of wine in the other, and was using just the fingertips of her cigarette hand to grip the steering wheel.

"How did Coco know?" But before I could hear Ania's answer I was almost unconscious again, falling asleep from exhaustion. Yellow lights danced on my closed eyelids, and I heard Ania humming to herself. Did I imagine it or did she say, "I do miss Charlie. Maybe I can find a way back to him."

SEVENTEEN

"Ania carries messages sometimes," Schiap explained, fussing over the cut on my forehead with gauze and rubbing alcohol, after Ania left me at Schiap's house. "Sit still. Ania has information. She knew who you were going for and where you might be. They had been looking for him, your Pierre, and Ania knew of the farmhouse where he was hiding. It has been used before. Ask no more. I know no more. That much I have learned from Bettina, who heard it from her husband."

She put down the bloody tissue and frowned at me. "That may scar. Too bad. But it will make a good story for dinner parties, after all this is over."

Ania was a messenger for the Resistance. That was all von Dincklage needed to find out. I cursed her husband, Anton, for the hold he kept over her. But maybe by that time Ania had already decided to stay, to do what she could, like Gogo.

"Sleep," Schiap said. "Tomorrow, you spend the day in bed. And I have work to do, tracking down suppliers. I can't get enough silk to finish the orders we have."

Business for all the couturiers of Paris was beginning to dry up, and supplies—fabrics, buttons, even pins—were becoming difficult or even impossible to get. Schiap was forced to reduce her work staff of six hundred down to one hundred fifty. She wept in her office the day she laid off seamstresses and sweepers and fitters. "Where will they go? What will they do?" Schiap said. She muttered something in Italian, and I couldn't tell if she was praying for her workers or cursing the war.

But Schiap kept the boutique open rather than closing completely. "It is a question of patriotism," she declared at her basement canteen one night, when Gogo and I were testing a new soup recipe.

"Paris is fashion. Fashion is Paris," Schiap said. "We must keep the industry going to show that we will not be defeated, no matter what happens. Without *la couture* the entire French economy would collapse. So, we keep going, however we can, even if we end up selling to Germans. Money is money, and salaries must be paid to those still working."

"It is a question of patriotism," Coco said to me the next evening, when I went to see her. "I will close the business. I will not sell to the Germans."

She poured us both a glass of wine, ruby red, and sat on the sofa with her slender, athletic legs tucked under her.

"I heard of your adventure," she said. "Up north. It was Ania who came for you?"

There was danger in that question. Best not to speak of Ania. I picked up the sketch pad on the low table beside her, and she let me look at it.

"My last collection," she said. Like Schiap, that season was the last season, though I didn't yet know it. She was working with military themes, trim suits in neutral colors, braiding and frogging for trim, practical clothes, not party clothes.

"After I close the business I will live quietly," Coco said. "Rest. Wait. They will take Paris, you know. Eventually. And when they do,

I will not sell to them. To the Germans. They have some good ideas, and they will rid us of the Bolsheviks. But France is my country."

The evening was damp and windy, and an occasional draft at the window rippled the draperies to show strips of the darkness outside. The Ritz hotel suite felt austere, somehow impersonal, despite the dark carved wood screens, sculptures, crystal vases, and other furnishings Coco had installed there. Some rooms embrace you like a friend; other rooms let you know you are completely insignificant, and this room felt like a showcase, not a home. It felt as if Coco was returning to the anonymity of her childhood.

"But what will your workers do?" I asked. "No income, no job."

"Go to the countryside, I suppose. Most people are, anyway."

Two years before, Coco's workers had gone on strike against her, protesting the hours and the pay. Schiap's employees had, as well, and Schiap, that admirer of Lenin in her younger days, had responded with pay increases and handshakes. Coco had not been as amiable and she had never, it was gossiped, really forgiven her employees.

"People may say this is revenge," I warned her. "For the strike. Revenge, not patriotism."

"People always talk. Let them." And like that, two thousand workers, mostly female, were laid off without warning, just as their husbands and fathers and brothers were going off to war.

"Safer, maybe," I argued that evening. "And a little hungry, without an income."

"We will all be a little hungry, I think," she said. "Even those of us living at the Ritz. Have you come to say good-bye? You will go home, now, of course. New York. It is good-bye for now. I am tired." She rose.

"We are friends, aren't we?" She kissed my cheek. I kissed hers. She pushed me gently toward the door, but before she opened it, she said, "It was an accident, you know. That night at the Durst ball."

I didn't believe her, and she knew I didn't.

I got as far as rue du Mont Thabor before the damp wind blowing my hair around my face reminded me that I had left my hat behind. It was a hat Coco had given me at discount, a lovely little white beret trimmed with faux pearls, so I went back for it.

. This time when I knocked a maid didn't open the door, but Coco herself.

"Oh," she said. "I was expecting something from the kitchen."

"I forgot my hat."

"There it is." Coco dropped something small and metallic onto the table and picked up the hat. She arranged it carefully, almost tenderly, avoiding the bandage on my forehead. She was very pale, and in the weaker light the deep shadows around her eyes looked like bruises.

Only then did I see the syringe where she had dropped it.

"Morphine," she said. "It helps me sleep. Oh, don't look like that. It's not as uncommon as you think."

"Isn't it a little dangerous? A habit?"

"Oh, so what?" She sighed. "We have said our good-byes." She pushed me back out the door.

Coco was someone you never really got close to, but sometimes when she looked at me with those black eyes, I saw a different person asking for understanding, someone who, like me, knew more than a little about loss and grief. And then she would blink, and Chanel would be back, stylish, hard, cynical Chanel.

It was an era of good-byes, a reversal of the convergence that had brought me to Paris, to Charlie, to Ania, Schiap, Coco, and Otto. Departure was in the air, so I wasn't even surprised when, the last time I saw Ania, we met at the Ritz bar, as usual, and Django Reinhardt was playing.

"His orchestra was playing at Elsie de Wolfe's party, my first night in Paris," I told Ania. "Remember?"

"Of course I do. Charlie was still sulking a little because we had spent so much time at Schiap's boutique." Ania tried to laugh but couldn't quite do it. She felt it, too. That sense of endings, of departure.

Django waved hello, and I wondered what would happen to him and the other gypsies of France. They were, by Hitler's standards, undesirables.

Ania was wearing Schiaparelli that night, a dress with a fitted blue-and-red jacket over a tiered white skirt suit; it looked like the dress that Manet had painted in *Nana*. The Ritz was doing a thriving business. It was loud with the clatter of glasses and the buzz of conversation, and dark because of the blackout. The windows were covered with thick curtains, and the lights in the bar were as dim as possible. Ania and I sat at a little table and made a running commentary on the outfits the women were wearing.

"Cheap," Ania said of one woman dressed in tight purple silk that glimmered with a vulgar eggplant glow even in dim light. "Not well tailored," she said of a woman in tweeds.

"With all that's going on in the world, why should clothes matter so much?" I asked.

"If looks don't matter, why do we spend so much time and money on them?" Ania countered. "It makes us more desirable, and it makes other women jealous. It is amusing."

"I don't want to be amused," I decided.

"Of course you do. We all do. All except Charlie. He wants to save the world. Charlie has a mission."

I didn't point out that she had acquired one as well. No one spoke of those anonymous nighttime drives, the messages and people carried back and forth. We ordered martinis, and when mine came, I raised it to Django. He remembered the night we had talked at Elsie's party, and he began playing "Dark Eyes" because I had told him I liked his version of it, the upbeat jazz of it.

"I wish I could go to Warsaw," Ania said. "See my father. Anton would let me take Katya, I'm certain. To see her grandfather . . ."

"If you go to Warsaw, I think you'll never leave," I warned her.

General Hans Frank of the occupying German army had already constructed his ten-foot-high wall topped with barbed wire around the Jewish neighborhoods, imprisoning the people who lived there. People who tried to escape were shot on sight.

In Paris, the anti-Semitism was growing stronger, fueled by Hitler's proximity, the graffiti more frequent, more hateful, Jews pushed off the sidewalk, shouted at.

She ordered more martinis for us. "Let's think of the list of people who must be invited to your exhibition at the Rosenberg Gallery," she said.

"There will be no exhibition."

"They will make a treaty," Ania insisted. "France and Germany. God, look at what they are eating." She nodded at a table in the corner where a roast beef had been served, stuffed artichokes, fresh salad. France was at war, yet they were still serving four-course meals in the Ritz dining room, still had their full staff of busboys and bartenders in starched uniforms.

"You'll have to smile at that worm, Rebatet, when he comes to the exhibit," she said. "He covers all the openings, but remember he hates most modern art so don't talk about art with him. Talk about Coco Chanel, I think. Let him know she is a friend. He'll be kinder to you. It helped Picasso. Don't talk about Schiap, though. They detest each other."

Ania lit a cigarette and blew a perfect smoke ring. Charlie had taught her how. "They will house German officers at the Ritz, you know," she said. "If they come here, to Paris."

When I left the Ritz to go back to Schiap's, Monsieur and Madame Auzello were in the small lobby, talking quietly but with obvious agitation. She nodded hello when she saw me and then continued that whispered conversation with her husband. I wondered how she, a famous beauty who had once been courted by F. Scott Fitzgerald, felt about housing German officers at the Ritz. She, a New Yorker by birth, like me, and a Jew like Ania.

Ania and I said good night, and she gave me the two kisses on the cheek common for Parisians. "One for luck," she said. "One for remembrance."

I walked back slowly, making my way cautiously through the dark streets, because the city was in blackout. Life was happening inside, behind closed curtains, shuttered windows, but outside all was darkness and stillness. My footsteps echoed.

The streets were emptied of the chauffeured cars of the wealthy, emptied of cars in general. People walked, or rode bicycles, or stayed off the streets, sheltering in their homes. Color had disappeared. Paris had turned black and gray.

I wanted to make time stand still, to freeze us all into a safe moment when good things might yet happen, when Otto and I could be safe together. The moon made silver ripples on the river, and I paused by the bridge, grateful for those small glitters of light amid all the darkness. I threw in a pebble to make the ripples dance and went back to Schiap's house.

"Monsieur and Madame Auzello won't have a choice," Schiap told me over morning coffee. "If they refuse, the hotel will be closed, and if the hotel is closed, it will be taken over by the Germans anyway. See? No choice."

We were sitting in her bedroom because the rest of the house was filled with Belgian refugees, sleeping in beds, on chairs, some even in the stairwell.

The basement, the private bar and dining room, Schiap had offered as a secret meeting place for British officers and volunteer American ambulance drivers. When I couldn't sleep I would hear doors opening and closing, heavy footsteps, men's deep voices. They were always gone by morning. I knew that for months now Schiap had been putting her affairs in order: packing up papers, diaries, trunks of clothes. Like most Parisians, she hid many of the valuable things that could not be carried away.

The couturiers had closed up their shops, as Coco already had done: Mainbocher, Vionnet, one by one the doors closed, and their windows were painted over for blackout.

"By the way," Schiap said, pouring coffee from a heavy silver pot into her cup. "You had a strange phone call last night, when you were out. A man's voice. He asked for you, and when the maid said you were out, all he said was 'now.' And then he hung up. Who was it? What does it mean?"

It means, I thought, *that Otto hasn't forgotten me. He hasn't.* It was the warning he promised me. Wherever he was, whatever he was doing, he was thinking about me.

Schiap was in a red-and-orange silk robe and had tied a turban around her head and, except for the violet shadows of worry around her eyes, looked as far away from a woman expecting war and invasion as a woman can look. Perhaps that is the point of fashion and couture. It is part of the mainstream of history, yet it can also, to a point, protect us from that history. Dressing well is resistance, revenge, pride, a form of control over forces that try to control us. That's why, when taken prisoner, the first thing your enemy takes is that outer layer of your identity and independence: your clothes. That is why prisoners are put in identical uniforms. They no longer exist as individuals.

"Well?" Schiap asked. "Who was it, and what does it mean?"

"It means it is time to leave."

Schiap sipped her coffee and thought for a moment. "Gogo travels with you. To New York."

"Yes, of course."

And what of Ania? I had promised Charlie I would look after her. How could I do that, an ocean away, thousands of miles away? And what would I tell Paul Rosenberg?

But it was time to leave.

Usually at this time of the day Schiap and I would speak of fabrics and colors and share gossip we had discovered about the seamstresses and fitters, who was seen at the movies with whom, who was cheating on her husband, who was putting on weight and looked to be in the family way.

But that morning, Schiap didn't want to gossip. Her arched black brows pulled together over her nose; her carmine lips jutted forward in anger.

"It begins," she said. "The destruction. The hunger. Oh, my poor Paris. And that woman is ensconced at the Ritz. She will survive, I have no doubt of it."

There is war, invasions and bombs and shrapnel, and there is a different kind of war waged at midnight parties and at dinner tables, fought with glances and whispered comments and underhanded business arrangements. The rivalry between Coco and Schiap would be interrupted by nothing less than a world war, and not even the war would end it.

Schiap spent the rest of the day shouting into her telephone—Schiap, who hated having to make phone calls—and by the end of the day, the plans had been finalized. We had tickets. We had schedules. We had all the paperwork we needed.

Outside, in the deserted streets, the morning drizzle turned to a steady rain, and when I looked out a window one last time before going to pack, it seemed as if Paris was weeping.

That evening, I made one last visit to Ania at the Ritz bar.

"You're leaving," she said. "I see it in your face. All you Americans will. It's what you're good at. Here." She grabbed a piece of paper from her bag and scribbled onto it. "Give this to Charlie. No matter what happens, he can find me here. Or, find out about me. Now go,

Oh God, look at me." She was staring at her reflection in the mirror on the opposite wall. "I have undereye bags all the way down to my chin."

"Lily!" she called when I turned to leave. "Don't forget me, Lily."

"Never." We hugged tightly, and I remembered how beautiful she had been the night of the Durst ball, the night she left without Charlie, how heartbroken he had been, and here was all the heartbreak come back, now tinged black with fear as well as loss.

As I went out the front door, Coco was coming in.

"Foul weather," she said. "That coat doesn't fit you at all. It doesn't hang properly from the shoulders." She reached up and pinched the fabric, showing how it should hang. She pulled a silver case from her purse and tried to light a cigarette, but the drizzle was too thick. Click, flame, and drizzle would douse it. Click, flame, out. Four times till she gave up and threw the damp cigarette to the ground and crushed it under her patent high heel.

"That coat is really awful on you. I'm getting soaked. Good-bye, Lily. Come see me again when this is all over."

I walked the perimeter of the Place Vendôme, trying to see it as I had that first time with Charlie, the grand stone façades of the galleries, the column in the middle of the huge circle, with Napoleon standing on top, oblivious to the omnipresent pigeons that cooed from his hat and the crook of his bent arm, the sandbags surrounding the base, sandbagged against the arrival of the German army.

Thank God for pigeons, I thought. They have nothing to do with change, with history, with good-byes. In that, they were superior to us.

In the emptied streets, my footsteps echoed. And I heard footsteps behind me. When I turned, no one was there. I forced myself to walk at my usual pace, not to panic. They were just watching, I told myself. When I made it to Schiap's door, my hand trembled and dropped the key. When I finally had the door opened I fell into the foyer, so great was my relief. Behind Schiap's door, I was safe.

"Not that coat. This one," Schiap insisted. "That old thing." She took my raincoat and replaced it with one from the most recent collection, a waterproofed silk trench in khaki brown. "Hurry, hurry, the taxi is here!"

"What about you? What will you do without us?" I asked at the train station. It was windy, and we had to hold our hats down with our hands and squint hard to keep grit from blowing into our eyes.

Schiap gave me her comic disbelief look, one she had learned from the commedia dell'arte, with raised eyebrows, mouth dropped open.

"I shall have peace and quiet," she said, but none of us could laugh.

"Mummy," Gogo protested in a low voice. There was often little affection between them. Hugs were infrequent, I'd noticed. But this might be a life-and-death separation, and Gogo was worried, even if Schiap pretended not to be.

"There are some matters I have to take care of. I'll come after. Soon after. Don't worry."

We three stayed like that for a long, thoughtful moment, Schiap with her hand on mine, Gogo hugging her mother, three women facing an uncertain future. Facing a war.

"Don't put it off too long. Please," Gogo said.

"Napoleon," Schiap said.

"And all his little soldiers," Gogo answered.

"Take care of my daughter," Schiap whispered in my ear. "Promise!"

Gogo and Schiap gave hurried instructions to the porter who had our trunks, and in the mayhem of too many people departing at once, I was jostled and elbowed by the crowd. Someone bumped into me, on purpose it seemed because he almost knocked me off my feet.

"Pardon," he said, not meaning it. "Madame is making a journey? Where to?" It was neither a friendly question nor an idle one. He was from the secret police, one of the men who had kept their eye on Schiap, had followed her daughter, had searched through her office. Maybe had followed me the night before.

I didn't answer. Schiap saw him out of the corner of her eye, and she turned to him, furious, slapping her left hand onto her right forearm, the Italian gesture that means "fuck you." A memory forever: tiny Schiap, her face framed by black-and-white fur, her right hand balled into a fist, confronting a man a foot and a half taller than she was, his shoulders twice the width of hers.

He took a step closer to her, and my breath stopped. But then he backed away, smirking but knowing that he had no right to detain us; Schiap had powerful friends, and we hadn't broken any laws.

I dug my hands into my pockets, looking for a tissue, and remembered. Ania had given me a scrap of paper, and it was in the other coat.

"Schiap, that other coat, there's something in it I need," I said. "A paper."

"Yes, yes, I'll send it to you. Hurry, get on the train!"

We boarded, and Schiap waved frantically from the platform, the fur on her coat collar shivering in the steam of the train.

"And my paintings!" I called to her from the train window. "Pack them up for me!"

Gogo pulled down the window, waving and blowing kisses. I sat back against the plush first-class cushions, numb and already grieving for the city I had grown to love.

Good-bye, Paris, good-bye, the train wheels ground out. Good-bye, green linden trees lining the Seine, multicolored rose window of Notre Dame, red striped awnings over bistro doors, cobalt-blue overalls of laborers, black-and-white vestments of nuns and priests, pink cocktails and rosé wines, striped carousel horses in the Luxembourg Gardens, pastel cakes in *boulangerie* windows. Good-bye, my beautiful Paris, and all its lovely colors.

Good-bye to the city where I had fallen in love with Allen and then with a man who was part of the war machine forcing my flight.

Where my brother had fallen in love with Ania.

She'll leave Paris, I thought. *She won't stay. So it doesn't matter about the paper.* Even so, my stomach felt as if someone had kicked it.

· EIGHTEEN ·

The next day we were in a hotel lobby in Genoa, waiting to board the *Manhattan*, the liner that would take us to New York. A couple of thousand other people were sailing with us, away from France and Italy, away from the war, and the lobby was so crowded we couldn't move.

Gogo rolled up the little veil on her hat and looked around, trying to find a place to sit. No point in taking a room; the ship would leave in the evening. But there were no free chairs in the lobby—there was barely standing room—so we forced our way through the mass of men and women and wailing children, and went into the crowded bar for a cocktail. We, along with a hundred other people, tried to get the harried bartender's attention.

The waiters were doing a brave job of it, sprinting from table to table, taking orders, throwing down coasters and drinks. The noise was deafening, especially after the gray silence that had fallen over Paris. The bartender, a middle-aged man who looked as if he hadn't slept in days, kept looking over our shoulders, ignoring us, serving everyone around us. A dangerous crease of anger, very similar to her mother's, appeared between Gogo's brows.

"Can I help?" A good-looking young man had worked his way through the crowd to the bar and stood next to Gogo. He had an American accent and a well-cut suit. More importantly, in the midst of the clamor and panic and shoving, he had wonderful manners, a kind of chivalry; he was the kind of young man you'd want to be near in case of emergency, a women-and-children-first set of circumstances.

"We're trying to get cocktails, but the bartender is pretending we are invisible." The crease disappeared. Gogo smiled at him.

He snapped his fingers at the man. The bar was so noisy we couldn't hear the snap, but the bartender saw the authority in the gesture and responded.

"Champagne cocktails," the young man said. He left money for them on the zinc bar, tipped his hat at us, and worked his way back through the crowd, where he had left his suitcases unattended.

We sipped our drinks and once in a while looked back over our shoulders at him. He smiled every time.

"He's flirting with you," I told Gogo.

"I think that would be nice, if it's true."

The young man turned out to be Robert Berenson, an American shipping executive of Jewish descent, and he courted Gogo all the way across the Atlantic.

The crossing was difficult. The weather wasn't too bad, but there were submarines patrolling the Atlantic, German submarines, and we faced the omnipresent threat of being torpedoed. Under those conditions it's difficult to act normally, to make conversation at dinner and remember to walk around the deck in the morning, for fresh air and exercise, but we did it. Robert Berenson had his dinner seating switched to our table by the third day of the crossing. In the evening, when there was music and dancing in the ballroom, he danced every fourth dance with me, so that I wouldn't feel excluded.

When I danced with other men, strangers, I would sometimes close my eyes and try to pretend that man was Otto, but something always spoiled the illusion: the wrong cologne, a faulty sense of rhythm, a sweaty hand. Only Otto was Otto, and I missed him constantly, deeply. On a personal level, the war was another fatal accident for me. I would never see Otto again, and the grief would have overwhelmed me except this time I could not hide away; I did not have that luxury. *Get on with it*, I could hear Schiap saying. And Ania.

"That's a lovely dress," Robert said to me one night during a fox-trot.

"You find it strange, admit it," I said. I was wearing one of Schiap's, a very tight violet sheath with a yellow bustle.

"A little," he admitted sheepishly. "I don't quite understand it. How are you supposed to sit?"

"Carefully. A suggestion: Gogo's mother designed this dress. I wouldn't express any dislike of it. She may complain about her mother, and she probably will, but she is fiercely loyal to her."

"Now that, I understand," Robert said.

By the time the *Manhattan* sailed, safely, unharmed, untorpedoed, into New York Harbor past the Statue of Liberty, Gogo and Robert Berenson were engaged.

We arrived in New York on June 10, almost two years to the day when I went to Paris to meet Charlie. The excitement of our arrival, the cheers and shouts, the bustle of porters, made it feel like a holiday, even though I could not celebrate. And the feeling was short-lived. The reality of war had reached across the Atlantic. Clearing customs took a very long time. They opened every suitcase, checked every document, but after we'd finally been cleared through, Gogo and Robert and I shared a cab uptown.

The cabbie took us through Times Square, and we saw the news band blinking its way around the Times Tower, news of the Blitzkrieg in Britain. We watched it silently, wondering if and when Paris would be likewise bombed. Beautiful Paris.

They let me out at West 65th Street, at the stoop of the brownstone where Charlie was living, where I would be living as well until . . . Until what? Endings were impossible to guess.

It felt so strange, being back in New York, as much a journey through time as geography. It had been home, before I lived in England with Allen, and then Paris. I stood in front of the door, hesitating, wishing I could magically be whisked back to Paris, before the war. Schiap, even at a distance, gave me courage. *Oh, just knock!* I heard her say. *And straighten your hat.*

Charlie's housekeeper opened the door, an elderly woman from Naples who looked at me suspiciously.

"I'm Lily," I said. "Charlie's sister. Didn't he get my telegram?"

"Ah! Yes. Sister. Come in, come in."

Charlie was still making his rounds, she said, but I should be comfortable, eat something, drink something.

"This is you?" she asked, guiding me through the living room and pointing out an old photograph of me that Charlie had put on the fireplace mantel. Me, years before, my hair still long and wrapped in a braid around my head, my eyebrows thick and wild, my dress shapeless, an off-the-rack thing. Me, before Paris.

"You look different!" she said. "Better now."

Charlie had taken some old family things out of the storage crates in the basement, and I recognized the silver candlesticks on the table, the paintings on the wall, all nineteenth-century landscapes of poplar trees and moonlight and pretty young women in rose gardens. This had been my grandfather's house, and then my father's before my uncle had leased it out, after my parents died. I wondered where that other family had gone, if they'd been happy here. It felt more their home than mine; those scratches on the wall in the hallway had been made by someone else's dog; the living room wallpaper chosen by a different woman. My little room in Schiap's house at rue de Berri seemed more my home than this place, where I had spent a few years of childhood.

I took my suitcase upstairs, and after a quick meal of bread and cold chicken, I sat in the dark living room, waiting.

"Lily?" Charlie came home at midnight. I had fallen asleep on the sofa, and my legs were numb with lingering fatigue when I stood.

We held each other for a long while, and it was like having a little bit of Paris with me, again. Charlie, who had met me at the Café les Deux Magots, taken me to the Durst ball and helped get Schiap out of her burned costume; Charlie, who walked with me through every park in Paris, who sat with me and watched the old men playing *boules*. Paris didn't seem as far away.

"Ania is still in Paris," I said. "She gave me her address, but, Charlie, I left it behind."

He turned white, then shrugged. "Doesn't matter," he said. "It's impossible to get letters back and forth. She knows how to reach me, if she wants to."

He had aged since I had last seen him. His smile was slower, his blond hair was cut very close to his head, his dashing mustache trimmed of its curling tips. There were lines in his forehead that hadn't been there before. His plans to open a new clinic with investors had been put on hold, for the duration of the war.

"Sorry I was so late tonight," he said. "We'll celebrate tomorrow. I'll take you to Delmonico's for a steak."

But we didn't celebrate the next day, either. It was Charlie's afternoon off, and we were sitting in the living room, listening to the radio, when the announcer said that the German army had marched into Paris.

Oh God. Ania.

Charlie put down the glass of sherry he'd been drinking. "You cut it close," he said. "Good thing you left when you did." But he was thinking about Ania, and so was I. Where was she? Was she safe?

I tried to imagine a swastika flag flying from the Eiffel Tower, tried to imagine the shopkeepers who were still in business putting German-language signs in their windows. In Paris, they would be rounding up, arresting Jews, as they had in Warsaw. And communists. Ania and Schiap. Were they still there?

Was Coco still at the Ritz, waiting to welcome the German officers who would be stationed there? Von Dincklage would have returned to Paris. Had he taken Otto with him?

Not knowing was unbearable, but it was impossible to get phone calls or telegrams through. Charlie and I, like thousands and thousands, could only wait and hope that eventually there would be good news of friends and loved ones.

"Charlie, Ania carried messages for the Resistance," I told him.

He put his face in his hands and rubbed at his eyes. "Oh God," he said.

Later that evening I called Gogo and asked her to contact her mother any way she could, to ask if she had found the raincoat and the paper in the pocket.

"Sure," she agreed. But Schiap was traveling, and it was weeks before a message came to me. The old raincoat was gone. She thought the housekeeper had given it away. If we could reach Ania, I didn't know where.

The best part of being home was that Charlie and I were together again. He'd left Boston and was in residence at the New York Presbyterian Hospital, and already earning a reputation as an excellent pediatrician. That had become his specialty: treating young children.

And, as he had suggested after Allen's death, we set up housekeeping together, the hardworking doctor and his widowed sister, sharing the brownstone. Mrs. Taurasi, who was very much like her namesake, a bull who charged around, giving us orders: *feet off the sofa, finish your supper, eat more, sleep more.* She grumbled at me but was, I suspected, happy that Charlie's sister had come to keep him company. "Not good for man to live alone," she confided to me one day. "Men are not good on their own. He needs to be married. I think so. Don't you?"

In fact, he had been seeing a girl, was thinking about asking her to marry him.

"But I just don't seem able to get the words out," he confessed that night, after we learned that Paris had been taken by the Germans and that Ania was in even more danger than he had known. "Patty's a great kid, pretty and smart."

"Perfect doctor's wife?"

He grinned for a half second and looked a little more like his old self. "Absolutely perfect. Maybe that's the problem. And let's face it. I'm still in love with Ania."

We sat down to Mrs. Taurasi's roast chicken and mashed potatoes, bad oil portraits of my grandfather and grandmother staring at us from over the sideboard. We were eating by the light of a single candle, both to save fuel and because New York was already rehearsing blackout, already preparing for the time when Hitler might try an invasion of our shores.

Charlie rose and began to pace over the faded floral carpet with his hands jammed in his pockets.

"Ania is a good woman," Charlie said, sitting back down. "Loving and kind and with her own kind of innocence. I'd take her back in a heartbeat, husband or not. I'd find a way to get Katya here. You know, I sent a telegram to the Ritz but she never answered, and now, with the Germans there . . . I just hope von Dincklage and her husband find a way to keep her safe. They owe her that much."

I didn't have the courage to tell him about Otto. By that time, being in love with a German seemed unspeakable; loving a married woman, as Charlie did, was simply a faux pas. We went and sat in the dark living room and put our feet up, since Mrs. Taurasi was in the kitchen.

"What are you going to do?" he asked. "Sit and knit all through the war?"

"God, I hope not." I held up the sock I'd begun, with its uneven stitches and worried rows where stitches had been dropped. That morning I had registered with Bundles for Britain, an organization of New York women who knitted socks and mufflers and blankets for the people made homeless during the bombings of London.

"Now that is a sorry affair," Charlie said, laughing at the sock.

"I drove a truck in France, Charlie."

He whistled. "You drove again? Glad to hear it. About time."

"And there was an accident. The truck got stuck near the border, close to the shelling. Ania rescued me, Charlie. She found me and brought me back to Paris, in the blue Isotta."

He turned away so that I couldn't see his face because even in the dark the sorrow could be seen there, writ large and clear. Sorrow, the opposite of gold joy and yellow fear.

"We'll find her," he said. "When all this is over."

Sometimes, at home in New York, I would wake up at night and wonder where I was. I felt like I was free-floating through time. Had there really been a ball in the forest? Schiap in flames? I would fall back asleep, and in my dreams I stood in the window of my Montmartre studio and I flew right out of it, over the Place Vendôme, and looked down to see Ania coming out of Schiap's boutique, her arms full of boxes and bags.

I'd see Otto, waving up at me, smiling, one hand over his heart, and then I'd wake up and Otto and Ania would return to the category of what had been lost, along with Allen, my parents.

When I went to the Red Cross office downtown, the lady who signed me up wasn't impressed by my skills. I couldn't type or take dictation, or nurse.

I ended up packing parcels for the Red Cross, to be sent to the European POWs in the German camps. Bandages. Chocolate. Tins of canned meat. Aspirin. A blanket. Fold flaps. Seal. Over and over, all day long, tedious work, but when I thought I couldn't stand it anymore I reminded myself that the package might actually keep someone alive . . . maybe even someone I had once known in Paris.

I worked in a downtown basement with a dozen other women, and during our breaks we would go out to sit in the sun, to people-watch, to gossip. They were impressed that I had spent a couple of years in Paris, that I had clothes from famous designers.

Susan, from Ohio, was the one who told us about the air-raid shelter set up in the Allerton Hotel for Women on 57th Street. "Forty-five feet below ground level," she said. "Filled with bunks and Sanka and kerosene lamps." She expertly folded a khaki wool blanket to take up the smallest space possible in the box she was packing.

"There was an air-raid shelter in the cellars of the Ritz in Paris," I said, trying to imitate her efficient movements and failing. One edge of the blanket stuck out, and I had to tuck it sloppily around the boxes of chocolate. "Tins of foie gras and sleeping bags from Hermès."

"Go on," said Susan. "You're pulling my leg."

"Crystal lampshades for the kerosene lamps."

"Those frogs." She laughed.

I missed Schiap, and sometimes I missed Coco. They were ambitious, sometimes vain, always talented, a new type of women who made their own rules.

Sometimes, I would go to the Schiaparelli perfume shop on Fifth Avenue and sniff the various bottles, remembering which perfume Elsie de Wolfe had preferred, comparing it with the perfume Ania had worn.

Otherwise, fold blankets. Count chocolate bars. Fill boxes to be sent overseas. And in the evening, sit in the dark listening to the radio and missing Otto, a man I'd barely known. How many times had we been together? Three? Yet he had filled the empty places inside me, the hollows left by the earlier loss of Allen, places I had thought would be empty for the rest of my life.

And where was Schiap? She'd been in and out of Paris, traveling almost as freely as she had during peace, using contacts and connections. I read in *Vogue*, now available only by subscription because of paper shortages, that she was planning a new fashion line for young girls to be called Gogo Juniors, for the young miss. Not even a war could keep Elsa Schiaparelli from working.

G ogo, with whom I'd been having monthly lunches, called me one Saturday in the spring of 1941. She was laughing so hard I thought she might drop the telephone.

"You've got to see this," she said. "How soon can you get here? I'm at Bonwit Teller."

"Half an hour," I said.

It was a good day, with birds singing in trees and fresh asparagus for sale at the little grocer's shop on the corner, sun the color of lemons, and chartreuse grass springing up around the brown of tree trunks in their squares of dirt in front of the brownstones. Women had already put away their darker winter clothes and were wearing bright prints and pastels, and slowly color was returning to the wintry black and gray tones of New York. It was the kind of lovely day that made me miss Paris even more, but then the Paris I had loved wasn't really there anymore; she was gray and ravaged.

I met Gogo at the new Bonwit Teller department: Junior Miss, designed by Elsa Schiaparelli, a small partitioned section with racks of clothes designed for younger women.

"This is what Mummy has been up to," Gogo said, irritated and waving at the racks of garments. Her hair was pinned up in soft waves instead of loose on her shoulders, and she wore a neat and subdued suit. Not a Schiaparelli suit, I noticed.

"My God," she sighed, sorting through a section of afternoon clothes and pulling out a girlish white dress printed with puppies. "Puppies!"

A salesgirl saw us and came over. "It's for the young girl," she explained, admonishing us. "Pretty things to wear before she's ready for black silk and the more sophisticated styles for married women."

"Really?" Gogo pretended to be hearing this for the first time and didn't reveal that the designer was her own mother.

"There's also a trousseau collection," the saleslady said. "White lace, for when the junior miss marries. Very tasteful."

Gogo and I bit our lips to keep back the comments and the laughter.

"And I'm to help advertise it," Gogo complained when we were back out on crowded Fifth Avenue. "She's taken out ads, and telling some people I designed it. There will be photographs of me playing canasta at home in my 'gay and cozy' New York apartment."

In the darkening street bustling with honking, swerving traffic, we waited for Gogo's car and driver to arrive, and my bus.

"What news does your mother send?" I asked, wishing I had worn more comfortable shoes. I had a long walk uptown, back home.

"There are swastikas all over Paris and the only people who can afford to buy anything are the German officers. They are emptying the shelves. It's impossible to get supplies or food. She set up a workshop in Biarritz and right now she's in Portugal, planning a trip to New York. But I will be married before she gets here."

"Gogo! I take it it's the young man we met in the Genoa hotel, the one who was so talented at flagging down distracted bartenders, among other things."

"The date is set. Soon. I'm not waiting for Mummy to schedule me into her travel and promotion plans."

Powerful women often have a narcissistic side to them; they suck the air out of the room and, when it comes to daughters, can be even more overbearing than they are with other women. I couldn't blame Gogo for wanting to plan her own wedding, to do things in a quiet and calm manner that would have been foreign to the flamboyant Elsa Schiaparelli.

"Have you heard anything about Ania?" I asked. Gogo's driver had pulled up, and she was climbing into the back.

"Not a word. Not about Otto, either. Was that his name? Lily, if you buy any of those clothes from the junior miss collection I'll never speak to you again."

"I'm too old for them, and I'm on the broke side. I don't think I'll be buying any new clothes for a while." Otto's name hung in the air between us, between Gogo's disapproval and my longing.

G ogo was true to her word and was married before her mother arrived in New York in July. It was a small wedding, as society weddings went. I was not invited and that felt right, somehow. Paris was behind us. We were going separate ways.

New York, too, was become divisive. Bundists marched regularly in Times Square, demanding that all "foreigners" be sent back to their own countries and no more admitted; New York had its own share of Nazi sympathizers and American Aryanists. I couldn't begin to imagine the various strings Schiap had pulled, the contacts she had used.

I heard about her arrival not from Schiap herself or Gogo but from the newspapers announcing the designer's arrival.

Elsa Schiaparelli arrived with four suitcases of her own clothes and a fortune in jewelry—wealthy women during the war traveled with their jewels sewn into the hems of their coats because one never knew when a bank might be closed, a home looted. But she didn't arrive with the new collection she had hoped to show in New York. The boat carrying it had been torpedoed.

After a quick reunion with Gogo and meeting her new son-in-law—I was glad I wasn't there for that quarrel: "You got married without your mother?"—and after a harried flock of seamstresses replicated the collection that had been sunk to the bottom of the Atlantic, Schiap set off on a lecture tour of the country, telling women what they should wear. She showed a new collection of sixteen designs, very conservative coats and suits. Schiap was changing; war does that.

I followed the tour in the fashion magazines and newspapers, reading passages aloud to the Red Cross volunteers as we packed boxes. When the collection was shown in New York I went to the Schiaparelli lecture at Town Hall and watched from afar as the models strutted the stage and a beaming but exhausted-looking Schiap described the outfits, her microphone sometimes giving out piercing squeaks. The stage lights accented the shadows around her eyes. I remembered the first day I had met her, in the boutique in the Place Vendôme, when she had looked like a medieval saint to me, all shadows and glitter, and authority.

When the showing was finished, I went backstage, one of dozens of admirers who had found my way through the wings and backstairs where Schiap held court, surrounded by models and photographers and journalists. Schiap was in midsentence when I forced my way through the circle of store buyers surrounding her, and she threw up her arms, yelled with joy, and rushed at me.

"I was hoping you would come," she said. "Oh, no. What are you wearing? Did I teach you nothing?"

Flashbulbs went off, zing, zing, zing, blinding me.

Schiap wore a simple black dress and a white turban and very little makeup. She looked subdued and uncomfortable. "I'm adapting to the States," she said, "more practical styles for women who don't have time to spend fifteen minutes every morning just tweezing their eyebrows."

She gave me a cool glance. "Those simple skirts and blouses never suited you. You need more sophisticated clothes. Meet me in my suite, in an hour. I'm at the Astor."

An hour later, sitting with Schiap, drinking champagne in the middle of the afternoon and eating pâté on toast points, enjoying the familiar amber and rose of her perfume, the sound of her voice, I thought again how much I missed the distinctive smell of baker's yeast and exhaust fumes and expensive perfumes, the strong smell of Bettina's cigarettes, the eye-rolling of the *vendeuses* and seamstresses when Schiap grumbled at them. Otto.

"Don't worry," Schiap said, reading my thoughts. "Paris will be there when you go back. For me, too. Traveling is becoming too hard. Even for me." She grinned an unspoken admittance that favors had been requested and returned, visas granted when no one else could get them, first-class staterooms and rare airplane seats when even princes were traveling second class if they could travel at all.

We looked out the window at the grimy sky, wondering.

"Elsie is still in Versailles," Schiap said. "She refuses to give up her place, for fear the Germans will occupy it. I have people living in the rue de Berri house for the same reason. If it's empty, the Germans will occupy it. And I have some bad news for you."

I lit a cigarette and braced myself. There were so many possibilities for bad news, that year.

"My house has been safe," Schiap said, shrugging. "It is under diplomatic protection—a friend of a friend helped arrange it—so nothing has been looted, though swastikas have been painted all over rue de Berri. Imagine. The German flag flying on the Arc de Triomphe. I can't stand to think of it. But I couldn't have your paintings shipped over. The paperwork was impossible."

"That's okay," I said. "I'll get them. After the war."

"Yes," she agreed. "After the war. Besides, the Germans wouldn't take them. They don't like abstract work."

We stared out the window some more, the silence becoming a little uncomfortable. I could see that her thoughts were racing in many directions and she was eager to get on to the next item for the day, whatever that was. And soon I would have to do the marketing for Mrs. Taurasi, before the shops closed.

"It's good that you left when you did," Schiap said. "Some of the Americans who stayed in Paris are now interned in Germany. There are rumors about how you knew exactly when to leave. They think I had information."

I couldn't tell her that the warning phone call had been from Otto. I had promised not to, and I knew what he had done could lead to trouble for him. I changed the subject.

"I like your new designs, especially that day dress with the secret hem that can be turned into a full-length gown for evening."

"It is very clever," Schiap agreed with her usual modesty. "Two dresses for the price of one, two dresses with just a little more material than I would have used for one dress. Oh, Lily, it is hard in Paris. So many textile shops doing nothing but turning out woolens for army uniforms. No more handmade buttons, or silk. Silk is for parachutes now." She shook her head and sighed. "So many people out of work. And you should see the way women are dressing. Ridiculous hats, joke hats, and the Germans buy the joke hats because they think they are French. I heard some officer bought a hat with a painted tin can on it."

It was, I thought, diplomatic of me not to point out that she had once made a hat shaped like a telephone, and one like a high heel. "Your boutique is still open. That was a kindness to your workers."

"An artist must do what she was put on this earth to do. I do not give up and go into my little safe cocoon."

"You mean Chanel."

"I do mean Chanel. Closing shop and putting all those poor girls out of work. She's still making a fortune, you know, just selling perfume. The German officers are buying No. 5 by the crate. She says it is just business, but then why did she close her boutique? She is too friendly with the Germans. Did you know that the Germans plan to move the French fashion industry to Berlin? Over my dead body. When this lecture tour is finished, I return once more to Paris. Jeanne Lanvin, Nina Ricci, Marcel Rochas, and Lucien Lelong, we have agreed, we will make sure the fashion industry stays in Paris."

I wondered what Coco had thought of this, if she had known in advance the plans the Germans had made for the relocation of the French fashion houses; if that had been part of her own reason for closing shop.

Schiap lit a cigarette and shrugged. "She's living at the Ritz. With her German, von Dincklage. There are rumors about her, about whether or not she's collaborating vertically as well as horizontally." That was what they were calling Frenchwomen who slept with the invading Germans: horizontal collaborators. And those who collaborated standing up . . . they were spies as well as traitors.

Schiap's face hardened, and her lipstick flamed on her pale skin like a scarlet wound. She was remembering the Durst ball, the night when Coco danced Schiap into the flames.

She poured the last of our reunion champagne into our glasses. "I know you miss it, but it is dismal now, in Paris. All the good hotels are filled with German officers, and the restaurants, too. No one else can afford to eat out; instead they eat potatoes and rutabagas, if they can even find those. Every day the soldiers march down the Champs-Élysées playing that terrible music." Schiap shivered with disgust.

"I will spend more time in New York now," she said. "While the war lasts. Maybe I will become a grandmother soon, who knows. I would like that. And I'm already designing a line of resort wear, for Florida. These American women, so much money!"

"Not all of them." I thought of Susan, who stood next to me in the box-packing line at the Red Cross center, who lived with her mother and four sisters in a two-bedroom walkup in Yorkville, over a polka bar.

"Do you have any news of Ania?" I'd been afraid to ask.

"None. I'm sure Ania had the sense to leave Paris. She was a smart woman, clever, all those languages, and an excellent musician, I heard, though she stopped playing when she got married. Are you ill, Lily? What's wrong?"

Being close to Schiap, to Paris through Schiap, the way we sometimes lapsed into a French phrase, missing Ania . . . it all made the ache inside me for Otto so strong I leaned my forehead into my hand.

There was a tremendous blare outside, a noise so loud that the vase on the table vibrated. Schiap jumped in alarm.

"They are just testing the sirens," I said, already used to the frequent test alarms. "If it were a true air raid they would blast them more than once. And they have put plane spotters on top of the skyscrapers, looking for German fighter planes."

"Ah, well. The war goes everywhere."

She stood, and so did I. We hugged each other and promised to get together again soon. We wouldn't, and we both knew it. Paris was behind us.

The greatest advantage of being home in New York was being with Charlie. He was working terrible hours but I would wait for him to come home and we would sit, talking, remembering, listening to the radio, following the war news from Europe, as summer turned to autumn, and then winter.

"I should enlist soon," he said one night.

"No. We won't enter the war, will we?"

"We should," Charlie said. "I don't know what we're waiting for. Why do we have people checking the East River for German U-boats? It will come to our shores, as well."

The next Sunday, I was at a concert at Carnegie Hall, imagining Otto there next to me, listening to the music, when I heard the announcement. Arthur Rubinstein had just finished Chopin's E minor piano concerto, and after the deafening applause, the announcer came on stage, grim-faced. He had to clear his throat several times before he could get the words out.

The Japanese had bombed Pearl Harbor. America was at war.

Everyone knows where they were, what they were doing, when that announcement was made. Charlie was with Patty, wondering why he felt so numb, so only half alive, when he was with her. I was alone at a concert, wondering if Otto would have enjoyed the music, when I realized Otto was my enemy twice over, a German at war now with both France and America.

Let's fly away, he had said, standing in my Montmartre window. *Away from everything and everyone.*

"I'll be with the medical corps. I'll be completely safe," Charlie said, when he enlisted. "Besides, they'll start calling us up any day. Why wait?"

Concentrate, I ordered myself. *Something important, something terrible, is happening here.* But I didn't want to concentrate, didn't want Charlie to say any more.

Ticking. The grandfather clock in the hall. I realized how much I hated ticking clocks, that reminder of time already lost even when we are trying to measure it. I wanted Charlie to go back ten seconds and unspeak those words. He was all I had left.

Mrs. Taurasi put down the bowl of mashed potatoes she'd been serving and sat heavily in a chair, as if she'd been pushed. "No," she said. She'd grown fond of Charlie—all women did—and as much as she detested Mussolini, she did not want Charlie going over to fight him; that much was clear in her stricken face.

I rose from the table and went to stand by the window. The trees were bare, stripped by the hard season, and snow fell outside the window, white flakes so large you could see the six sides that every flake is supposed to have. The night outside the window was all whites and beiges, grays and browns, a color scheme Coco Chanel would have approved. Underneath our spindly Christmas tree a box of ornaments waited to be strung and hung on the green branches.

"Close the curtain, Lily," Charlie said.

We sat in the darkness of blackout, the air in the room thick with the memories of those we missed, those not with us, the faint smell of green pine coming from the untrimmed Christmas tree.

"If only I knew where Ania is," he said, gulping back two inches of whiskey in one swallow. "She's probably been arrested by now. I bet she never left Paris. They would have found out she's Jewish, they'd have the papers, her birth certificate and passport."

Ania, in a labor camp.

"Maybe not," I said. "Maybe she's in hiding. Safe somewhere. With her daughter."

I sat next to Charlie. I put my arm around his shoulder and felt him turning to stone as he struggled with the grief. I tried to match my own memories of Ania with what might be happening to her, and I could not. Our first afternoon together, at Schiap's boutique, felt a hundred years away, a lifetime away.

The radio was still on, and a pianist was playing Schubert's Unfinished Symphony. Ania had told me once she loved playing Schubert when she was a young girl, when she still lived with her father in Warsaw and they had a baby grand in the sitting room.

"Is that why you enlisted, Charlie? Because of Ania?"

Charlie was sitting bolt upright the way people do when they are afraid they will collapse completely. "No. Not completely. But if I don't enlist I will be drafted, sooner or later. Better to make my own choice. In fact, I'd rather be in the army than marry Patty." He tried to laugh, but it sounded more like he had choked on something.

"Promise me you'll come home. Safe and sound."

"You know I can't do that. But damn if I won't do my best. Oh, Lily, don't cry. I'll be fine."

· NINETEEN ·

New York began to transform itself as Paris had. The city was noisy and bright during the day, but there was a current of desperation behind the laughter. The bars were full; people drank a little too much, too often. Young men in uniform, new to the city, walked four abreast down Fifth Avenue, gawking, catcalling the young salesgirls on their lunch breaks. The nights were dark and quiet. If you went out after dark your footsteps echoed. People bumped into each other, felt their way home by trailing their hands along buildings during the unlit night.

During the day all the colors had a tint of brown or gray to them, yellow turning to ocher, blue to slate, red to chestnut, as if getting ready for the black of mourning. Charlie finished training that winter and was sent overseas. There was a great demand for medical officers; they didn't waste any time getting them into Europe or the Pacific fronts. He didn't want me to go the station with him.

Beloved Charlie, standing in the street below and waving up at me as I watched him from the window. As Otto had done.

I waved back and remembered Charlie in his dashing scarf and driving goggles, driving up to the curb outside the Café les Deux Magots, Charlie looking forward to an afternoon with his sister and his girl, Ania. I wished I had been able to capture that moment in amber.

My brother disappeared into the maw of war, and every time I thought of him, I touched something made of iron, for luck, as Schiap used to do. I had nightmares of Charlie and Otto confronting each other on a battlefield, each trying to kill the other without knowing that they were the two most important people in the world to me. *But he's a medic,* I told myself over and over. *He'll be safe and he's there to heal, not to kill. He'll be fine, he promised me.*

Gogo's husband enlisted, too, and she, just married, couldn't stand the boredom of waiting, the sleepless nights of worry, the fretting and pacing.

"I'm joining the American Red Cross," she told me during one of our Saturday lunches at Horn and Hardart. "I'm going to India, to open a service club and put on little amateur theatricals for the servicemen. Mummy actually suggested it. She thought it might be fun. And safe. I think she's afraid that New York will be bombed next."

Schiap was traveling nonstop all over the United States and the big cities of South America as well, giving lectures on how women should dress during wartime, the importance of maintaining morale through dressing as well as possible. She was still, always, a businesswoman, and clothes must be promoted.

Horn and Hardart was full that day with all women and children, like most of New York, most of the country. When soldiers and sailors on leave did come in, all eyes turned in their direction, hopeful eyes, patient eyes, fearful eyes. And then we looked at our plates, slightly shamed to be so covetous of some other woman's brother, someone else's husband.

"I'll think Mummy will be glad to have me busy, doing something. I can't stand this waiting, this limbo." She was gone two weeks later.

Fold and pack. Pack and fold, knit. My socks never improved, so I stuck with scarves and woolen mufflers. Days of work, dark nights of solitude and darkness, me and the radio. After working all day I spent the evenings pouring coffee and tea at the Soldiers' and Sailors' Club, anything to keep busy. The war seemed like a huge black wolf, trailing me from country to country. I did what we all did in those days: worked and waited. Put everything on hold. I hadn't held a paintbrush since I left Paris. My fingers ached from packing boxes and knitting, packing boxes and knitting.

G ogo was back, two months later. The Red Cross women had been sent to a jungle in Bengal, where Gogo had immediately become ill with dysentery. Tiny Gogo returned thin as a rail, her beautiful long brown hair cropped short and growing in curly and wild.

She came back ill but she came back, and that seemed an omen to me. If Gogo came back, so could Charlie. Otto, too. If Schiap's daughter returned, so could my loved ones.

But they didn't.

In August, I was sitting in the dark, fanning myself in front of the radio, listening to Jack Benny, when the doorbell rang. A boy, too young to fight, stood there, shy and bent under the load of his heavy satchel. His green uniform was neatly pressed, but he had wrapped bands around the ankles so his pants wouldn't get caught in the bicycle chain.

"Telegram, ma'am," he said in a voice not yet out of the higher notes of childhood.

I almost said, *No, I don't want it. Take it back.* But of course you can't do that. You must put out your hand, take the envelope from the boy delivering it. I almost forgot to tip him his nickel.

I sat in the dark with it for a long while, holding it softly, gently, thinking perhaps if I waited long enough the news in it would change. But of course they didn't send telegrams with good news in them.

I sat numb, staring at the gray-and-yellow wallpaper in the corner of the sitting room where Charlie, little Charlie, had once drawn a horse with Mother's nail polish. Most of it had been scraped away, but the outline was still there, a red clumsy horse, rearing up. I opened the telegram an hour after it had arrived, put it off as long as I could, because I knew when I opened it I would be alone, even more alone than I had been after Allen's death, because there was no one to see me through this one.

The Battle of Edson's Ridge. Guadalcanal. Pacific Theater. Words. Just words. All that I understood was that Charlie had been killed.

Charlie with his blue eyes changing from deep sapphire to pale aquamarine depending on his mood, his blond hair white as a halo. Charlie, my little brother, teasing, tormenting. Charlie, who had sent the telegram: *Come to Paris.* Café les Deux Magots. Charlie, leaves pinned to his label at the Bal de la Forêt, Charlie climbing into the baby-blue Isotta, next to Ania. They kiss and stick their hands up in the air, laughing and waving good-bye.

I felt as if there were no ground beneath me, nothing holding me up except my body's own stubborn unwillingness to crumple.

For weeks after getting the telegram I had the same dream. I've been told he's dead, but then one day I'm walking in the Place Vendôme and there he is, with Ania in the baby-blue Isotta, pulling away from the curb, waving.

And when you can no longer deny the reality of the telegram, the bargaining begins. It was a mistake, you tell yourself. They didn't identify the body correctly. You wait for the next telegram, saying it was a mistake. And it doesn't come. Still, you bargain. I won't cry, because that will make it real. When I tell my Red Cross friend Susan about the telegram, I'll tell her, of course, it's a mistake.

B ut it wasn't a mistake. Charlie was dead.

And, what I learned months later, from a headline in the *New York Times* about the Vél d'Hiv disaster in Paris, when all Jews still in

Paris were arrested and deported to camps: Charlie had been killed the same month Ania had been arrested and sent to a camp.

Grief becomes the gesso on the canvas over which other colors must eventually be applied. I began to paint, finding in the familiar movements and smells the absorption and release no other activity brought. When I painted, I felt maybe Charlie was close by. Otto was near, and Ania, too, we all four together, safe for as long as I painted, and when I was exhausted and put the brushes back down, I wept again.

One day, at the Metropolitan Museum where I'd gone to study Correggio's painting of Saint Peter, wondering how the artist had used so much yellow yet kept the glow subdued, a man stood behind me and cleared his throat.

I turned in annoyance, but the irritation at being disturbed turned to pleasure. It was Paul Rosenberg.

"Not quite your style, I think," he said. "As I recall, you had moved into abstraction."

"I study the colors. All the old masters have blue, red, and yellow, don't they? The primaries. Mr. Rosenberg, how good to see you!"

I would have hugged him, except the formality of his three-piece suit, those intimidating black eyebrows, held me back. Instead, we shook hands politely, somewhat stiffly. Paris felt a lifetime ago, but when I looked at him I smelled croissants from the corner bakery, roasting chestnuts, heard the hot jazz playing at Bricktop's.

He looked older, his lean figure even leaner, his face plowed with deep furrows.

"Did you get your collection moved to safety?" I asked.

"Most, not all. Did you get your paintings to safety?"

"They are still in Paris." I shrugged.

He sighed and folded his hands in front of his stomach, the way mourners do. "Too bad. I especially liked the blue one. Are you painting now?"

"I try. It's difficult."

He studied me from under those thick black eyebrows. "I'm sorry," he said, understanding that I wasn't just referring to the difficulty of finding art supplies and time.

"Well, I'll leave you to your musings on Correggio. When you're ready, come see me. I've opened a gallery on Madison." When we shook hands again for parting, he gave me a little pat on the shoulder as well.

"It was hard, wasn't it?" he said. "Leaving Paris. Poor Paris."

This was how I survived the war: I grieved. I painted. I packed unending boxes for the Red Cross, hoping against hope that one might end up wherever Ania had been taken, that she was still alive, and Otto, too. Gogo and I met more and more infrequently; she had her own circle of friends, more stylish people who were named in the society pages, other young wives waiting for their husbands to come home from the war.

When you can do nothing but wait and grieve and fear, colors change. Yellow becomes a mocking thing, a bird cawing annoyingly from a treetop, a false sun that gives neither warmth nor light.

And then, it ended. In April 1945, Hitler committed suicide in his bunker and the German army surrendered.

There were parades everywhere all that week, official ones and spontaneous ones, music blaring from loudspeakers, confetti tossed from windows, and people hugging, kissing, dancing. Times Square was one giant embrace that lasted for days, full of lovers reuniting, strangers bumping into each other, the entire city dancing, celebrating. The war in Europe was over.

Susan's young man came home soon after. We were still packing boxes for the Red Cross because it would be another year or so before all the prisoners were brought home, before the camps would be emptied of those who had somehow survived. Susan shook all over with fear and joy, wondering if he had changed, if she had changed, if the future they had promised each other was still there waiting for them.

"Come with me," she begged. "I don't think I can do this alone. Come with me!"

"Of course!" I stood in front of the cracked mirror in the ladies' room, arranging and rearranging my hat, one of the little summer cloches Coco had given me years before. I pulled it down over one eye, thinking of what Coco had said, that young women didn't need mystery, their faces should be open. But then . . . *You're not that young anymore*, I told myself. *You'll be thirty soon. That's not young, is it?* I pulled the hat even lower over my eye, the way Schiap had instructed.

"You look swell," Susan said, tugging on one of her stockings. They were silk, and she had been saving them just for this day, the one day in her life when she was going to go all out instead of drawing stocking lines up her legs with eyebrow pencil as we had during the war, when silk and even cheap nylon were needed for war materials, not stockings.

I wore a beige jacket from Coco and a black skirt from Schiap, mixing them together in a way that would have infuriated both of them. Susan's eyes darted back and forth between my chic veiled cloche and her own battered felt hat. Impulsively, I pulled my hat off and arranged it over Susan's curly hair.

"No. I couldn't . . ." she protested, already reaching up to touch it in a way that indicated ownership.

"Of course you can," I said, and it was the same words that Coco had used one day when she had given me a pair of kidskin gloves. I hadn't heard from her, or even heard much of her during the war years, except for what Schiap had told me, that she had holed up at the Ritz with her German lover, von Dincklage. *Impossible*, I thought. *I'm actually missing Coco. I hope we're friends*, she had said, at the end.

I gave the cloche one more little tug over Susan's right eye. "There. Keep it low, seductive. A little mysterious."

We went out into the street, humidity making our clothes stick to our backs after five minutes in the subway. The subway car was full, and I tried to read the expressions on people's faces, whether they had had good news or bad. Some people smiled, caught up in the ecstasy of a coming reunion. Others either didn't look up from their newspaper or stared straight ahead, their faces frozen into mourning.

We arrived at the dock just a few minutes after the *Queen Elizabeth*, which had been converted into a troop transport ship for the war, sailed back into the Narrows, with five other troop transport ships following her. The pier was even more crowded than the subway, and we jostled back and forth, a wave of humanity.

"Oh God, Lily, I'm so excited I think I'm going to pee." Susan stood on tiptoe, straining to see. "Oh, Lily. I forgot about Charlie. See, that's how excited I am. I wish he was coming home, too."

"Me, too," I said. "But this is your day. Be happy."

Susan's young man was one of the last to leave the ship, and Susan was almost ready to give up. She was terrified that something had gone wrong, that he had missed the transport call, been wounded at the very last minute. But there he was, coming toward us at last, tall and lanky, smiling from ear to ear. When he swept Susan up into an embrace that lifted her off the ground, I slipped away through the crowd. Otto had lifted me up like that, once. Right off my feet. *Dead or alive, Otto*, I thought. *Where are you?*

Not long after that, I saw Schiap again, on East 55th Street, in front of the St. Regis Hotel. If the Germans had taken over the Ritz in Paris, the French in exile had taken over the Regis in New York, and sometimes I went there and sat alone at the bar, just to hear French being spoken.

Schiap was pacing and puffing angrily on a cigarette, her heels clattering on the sidewalk, her turban hat ever so slightly askew. She was dressed with unusual simplicity in a gray linen suit with a very modest amount of jewelry.

I froze, torn between surprise, joy, and disbelief.

"Schiap?"

"Lily? It is you! A friendly face, just when I need one. But what are you wearing?"

She gave me that old Parisian glance that said, *This simply will not do.* I was wearing an old coat, frayed collar and all, over the painting smock I hadn't bothered to change when I had decided I needed a walk, to clear my head of turpentine fumes.

Schiap was older in more than years. Her face was lined, and her mouth turned down at the corners in a sad little expression of disappointment. There were huge bruise-colored circles around her eyes, exacerbated by slightly smeared mascara.

"You have given up," she said. "You look terrible. Women should not give up, not let themselves go, no matter the circumstances. Do you have time for a drink?"

She seemed nervous, kept looking over her shoulder and then down at the ground, like a child afraid of discovery by an angry parent. That was how I knew something was wrong because Schiap was never afraid.

We went into the Old King Cole bar of the hotel and sat at a table close to Maxfield Parrish's painting of the merry old soul, neither of us feeling particularly merry. It was early in the afternoon, and the bar was almost empty. Schiap had a shot of whiskey. Schiap never drank whiskey.

"What is it?" I was terrified she was going to say she had cancer, or something had happened to Gogo.

She slammed the glass down on our table. "The French Fashion Syndicale wants to question me. At two o'clock, upstairs, I have to appear before them. They want to know what I did during the war. Should I have another drink? This is not good, Lily. Not good at all. I think they want to blacklist me. And if they blacklist me I cannot have showings of my new collection."

"Coffee," I said to the waiting bartender.

Schiap's hands trembled, and as she drank the coffee I dabbed at her eyes with my napkin, wiping away some of the smears.

"There. Now. Tell me, what did you do during the war?" I wasn't surprised they had decided to interview Schiap. She had been trailed by the FBI for years for her communist leanings. After the war, there was much finger pointing, much blaming. Who did what. Who didn't do what.

"My activities. That was the word they used. They want to know about my activities. I trained as a nurse, you know. I learned how to assist at operations. I didn't eat meat for a year. I fed refugees in Paris and carried suitcases of vitamins for children when I traveled. Those were my activities! And now, they send spies to go through my mail, they have men follow me. They stand at the back of the room and stare when I give a lecture."

"No one looks completely innocent, these days," I said, trying to reassure her. But Schiap had somehow traveled freely from country to country and across the ocean when other people couldn't even get a bus to go to the market. She had important connections, and she had used them. She also had some dubious friends, and in New York she had been decidedly friendly with the leftist Vichy crowd.

We sat and talked, and I tried to calm her by talking about the new styles that were beginning to appear, the short skirts and tight jackets and thick-soled shoes.

"It is because of the war, of course. People still have a rationing sensibility. It will pass. I will help it pass. Let me show you something." She opened her bag and took out an envelope of photographs. "Elsie sent me this. You remember Elsie de Wolfe? This is how the women of Paris dressed during the war, to thumb their noses at the Germans."

The clothes were bizarre, far beyond whimsical, with skirts that had dozens of yards of fabric in them, despite the textile restrictions, colors brighter than Schiap's harlequin collection.

"I see my influence in this, don't you? I allowed women to have fun, to laugh, to not always take things so seriously. This helped the women of Paris get through the war." She was proud, and rightfully so, I thought. I was glad, though, I hadn't had to wear any of those hats. They had to be heavy as hell and as difficult to balance as a showgirl's headpiece.

"You know . . ." Her eyes gleamed, and she leaned closer to me. "When I was a little girl I found a trunk of clothes in the attic, beautiful old things made of lace and embroidery, so much you couldn't see the fabric underneath, and with bustles and seaming that turned women into hourglasses. Imagine, a body made of time."

Her fingers twitched as if she wanted to draw what she was remembering. "I used that shape, reworked my grandmother's clothes into my evening gowns. And now . . ." Her mouth turned down.

Two o'clock. Time.

"Will you wait for me?" Schiap grasped my hand.

"In the lobby," I agreed.

I waited almost three hours. When Schiap returned, she was pale but triumphant.

"They wanted to know about Bettina!" she complained. "They said I had Bolshevik tendencies. I told them it wasn't illegal to support workers' rights, or to have friends in the Vichy government. Or to sell to the military. If that were the case, most of France would be in jail. They'd stopped just short of accusing me of spying. Me, who had refused luncheon with Mussolini, who had fought so hard to keep the French industry from being moved to Berlin! Because I had kept my business open and sold to Germans, to Göring's pretty wife, Emmy, to avoid putting even more people out of work."

She lit a cigarette, and her hands trembled with anger. "Men fight the wars, but women, who have no say in them, we suffer, too," she said. "I wept the day that Mussolini sided with Hitler and declared war against France. And this is how they repay me."

"But you are free to go?"

"Yes. Free. But they will not let me be part of any of the parties for the fashion collections."

This was no small thing. Fashion depended on publicity, and publicity depended on being seen. The syndicate was rendering Schiap invisible.

"It could have been worse, I suppose," she said. "One of my friends in Paris refused to sit next to a German officer's wife at one of the fashion showings. And that woman died at Ravensbrück just because she had switched chairs and offended a Nazi officer. Not going to a few parties. It is nothing."

A man and woman entered the lobby, and she sat on a sofa as he went to the desk to register them. Schiap ran her eyes over the woman's outfit, taking in the uncomfortably tight waist, the slightly puffed shoulders of the jacket, the too-high heels.

"Cut all wrong," she whispered to me. "The skirt should be on the bias to give it better drape. I'll show them courage," she said, her eyes burning. "As soon as I have my travel papers, I am returning to Paris. I'll be there before the syndicate returns, and I will have a new collection ready for the fall. Beautiful things. Schiaparelli dresses. A collection that will show Chanel once and for all who is the best designer in Paris. I'll make people forget her. They already have, I think."

So the old rivalry was still on.

"Is she going to reopen?" I asked. "I haven't heard anything about Coco for a long while."

"She is in Switzerland, moving from hotel to hotel. She got out of

Paris as soon as they started arresting collaborators. They wanted to arrest her because she'd spent the war hiding in the Ritz with her Nazi."

Schiap leaned closer. "People are whispering that she spied for the Germans. But her perfume shop is open, and they give away bottles of No. 5 faster than the factory can produce them. Every GI who goes into her shop gets a free bottle. That is how she buys her friends these days, that is how she buys American support." Schiap glowered. "She'll be lucky if she doesn't go to prison. Collaborationist."

On that fine early-summer afternoon, sitting in the lobby of the St. Regis Hotel, Schiap and I fell into a silence that sometimes happens when old friends have been through so much, and yet have also missed so much of each other's lives.

"I still have the blue-and-white gown you gave me when I was first in Paris. Charlie helped pick it out. He died, you know. During the war."

Schiap picked up my hand and held it tightly, in sympathy.

"You wore it to the Durst ball," she said. "It looked very fine on you, even though you had attached those silly wings. And Ania . . . how beautiful she was that night. She and your brother looked so happy until . . ."

Until von Dincklage had arrived. He arrived, and Coco had arrived, and Coco danced Schiap into a flaming candelabra. Schiap on fire, whirling in panic as everyone laughed at the joke, everyone except Coco, who had terrified herself, and Charlie, who knew how to put out flames, and me, who watched, horrified, remembering Allen's death.

"Was Ania arrested, Schiap? Do you know for certain?"

"I heard she was caught up in the Vél d'Hiv mass arrests. That beautiful woman. It doesn't bear thinking about. She and your brother made such a couple. Everyone looked when they walked by." Schiap sighed, gripped my hand a moment longer, then released it. "One must never give up. Here. You might like to look at this. There's an article about me." She paused, considering, the same expression that used to come over her face in her Paris office when she had to choose from those trays of wonderful handmade buttons. She made up her mind and poked the copy of *Today's Woman* magazine toward me. "And some other interesting reading."

When she had left I ordered another drink and thumbed through the magazine. There she was, page 26, dressed in a bizarre party costume, a giant birdcage. It was a good publicity shot, but I didn't think the costume would convert many people to her particular fashion style.

I kept thumbing through as I sipped my drink. The second-to-last page had been folded over and creased. It was a photo page of candid shots, news from across the country, and in the upper right-hand corner was a photo of German prisoners of war kept at a camp in Massachusetts.

The British had taken so many POWs they couldn't intern them all in England, so thousands had been sent to the United States. Now that the war was over the prisoners would eventually be repatriated. *Meanwhile*, the journalist wrote, *life goes on and for some of them much better than it would have for them in Germany. Take this group (photo above) of Germans enjoying an impromptu concert in their recreation room.*

At the keyboard was Otto.

I put down my drink and brought the magazine closer, not believing my eyes. But it was Otto. I put my index finger on his face, remembering the boyish softness of his skin. Otto, alive, in the States.

In classical oil painting technique, wet paint is applied over dry paint. Each layer must ripen, before the next layer of the image can be applied. All the layers of my life beneath this moment were ready for the next moment to come. There was another layer, another color, waiting.

But was Otto waiting for me? Or had the war destroyed us, along with so much else?

· TWENTY ·

"Some questions, first," the guard said. "Papers, please. Relationship to prisoner. Family only allowed."

"That doesn't make sense. He's German, so if he had family here they'd be interned, wouldn't they? How could they ask to see him?"

"How did you even know he was here?" He looked at me suspiciously and turned blank-side-up a folder on his desk, just in case I was a spy particularly good at reading upside-down handwriting.

"There was a photo in a magazine. A women's magazine."

Now he grinned a little. "Not exactly top secret anymore, is it, now that the war is over? Still . . ."

The POW camp at Fort Devens in Massachusetts was surrounded by flat farmland interrupted by official-looking redbrick buildings for the offices and officers' quarters, and behind them stretched rows and rows of wooden barracks, hundreds of them, as far as the eye could see. During the war it had been a training camp for our soldiers. Now, it housed thousands of prisoners of war.

"I'm his friend," I said. "I knew him in Paris. Before the war."

"Paris. Must have been nice."

"It was. May I see him?"

He tapped his pencil on the desk. "I could put down *cousin*," he admitted. "You look like a nice lady, and he's been one of our best prisoners. No trouble. He gave piano lessons to some of the guards. Ragtime. It hasn't been easy for him."

"How so?" I asked, worried all over again.

"Well, he's an anti-Nazi, isn't he? This camp has a special unit of them, Germans against their own government during the war. Some of them deserted and walked right over to the Americans to give themselves up. He refused to give the Nazi salute during roll call. So the Nazi prisoners hate them. They're considered traitors. And the Americans aren't especially fond of them, because they're Germans. The anti-Nazis tend to keep to themselves."

"Can I see him? Please?"

"Sit in there. I'll see what I can do." He pointed to a smaller office, a room with a thick door with a window in the middle of it, and no other windows in the room. No fan, either, so I sat on the hard wooden chair behind the empty desk and fanned myself with the bus schedule I'd brought with me.

Ten minutes later, ten very long minutes, I heard the door open again, heard feet shuffle behind me.

Otto sat on the other side of the desk. He gave me one quick glance, then stared down at his hands, placed flat on the desk.

He was thinner, of course. Older. There was stubble on his cheeks, and he was very pale, as if he hadn't been outside in a long time. Fort Devens, I'd been told, was one of the better POW camps: the prisoners didn't have to work long hours in the fields, as they did in some of the southern camps, and the guards had done what they could to segregate Nazis from anti-Nazis to keep down the violence. Still, there was a ragged scar on Otto's cheek that looked fresh.

His hands, though, looked the same, with the long, slender, slightly spatulated tips of a pianist.

I hadn't seen him in nearly six years. I had tried to forget him, planned

THE LAST COLLECTION   317 •

to forget him. But sitting there, across from him, a longing and a tenderness surged in me that I had tried to bury during the war years. It was more than love. It was history. Our history, our brief hours together in Paris, the night at La Pausa, sitting side by side at the Louvre. He had been forced onto the wrong side of that history and had paid a price.

"Otto," I said.

He looked up. "Lily." His voice was empty of emotion. "You shouldn't have come."

"Yes, I should have. I would have come sooner, if I had known. This is how I found you." I took the magazine out of my purse and showed him the photo. The guard tapped on the window. *No exchange of objects*, he mouthed through the glass. I kept the magazine on my side of the desk and opened it to the photo.

Otto leaned over without touching it. "My eyes have gone off. I need glasses." He wouldn't look at me.

"We'll get them. Soon as you're out."

"Soon as I'm out, I'll be repatriated back to Germany. Imagine how they'll welcome me. I'm listed as a deserter, you know. A coward."

I hadn't thought of that. I thought the war was over for us, that we could go back in time, begin where we had left off. I had thought I would come here, to Fort Devens, throw my arms around Otto, and that would be the beginning of the rest of our story. Easy as that. As soon as I had seen him sit down at the desk between us, I knew that was supposed to be our ending, the resolution of everything that had led us to this moment. But it would not be that easy. Zeno's paradox. If everything is possible, then the opposite may be true. Nothing is possible.

"Otto," I asked him, "do you love me?"

He still wouldn't look at me. But he moved his hands a few inches closer to mine, and I thought of Charlie and Ania, sitting in Schiap's Boutique Fantastique, holding hands under the table where no one could see. I put my hand under the table. So did Otto. His fingers were warm and strong, and they clung to mine.

"I'll think of a way," I said.

"Von Dincklage had me transferred to a penal battalion," he said. "The 999, the German North Africa corps. A penal corps. The worst the army had to offer."

"He found out you gave me that warning, didn't he?"

Otto didn't answer, and that was answer enough.

"If you want me, I'll find a way," I promised. "Come back to me. Please. Come back to me."

We were still holding hands under the desk, leaning toward each other. The guard outside was watching. But he turned his back to the door, and we leaned closer. Closer. Otto looked at me, and I saw in his eyes some of my own feelings. That numbed emptiness in his expression was being replaced by the memory of the time we had together in France, as brief as it had been.

We leaned even closer and pressed our foreheads together for consolation, as a promise, fingers entwined, and it was like the last application of color to the canvas, the moment when you know this is what had been waiting to be completed, this is what had existed somewhere, even if just in your imagination.

You have brought it into the richness of being. Layer upon layer of color, and when the final one is applied, gold bursts upon the back of your closed eyelids.

A quick touch of mouth to mouth and then, *tap, tap*. The guard grinned through the window, shaking his finger at us.

"Time's up," he said. Otto and I pressed our hands together even more tightly, and then let go. But just for the moment. And when I turned to go, giving him a glance over my shoulder, he smiled. I knew my future was in that smile. He would go back to Germany, because he must. And then, I would bring him back. To me.

· TWENTY-ONE ·

Paris, 1954

>*Meet me at Café les Deux Magots. June 9. Two pm.*
>*Charlie.*

Of all the fragile things in life that survive, a scrap of paper is perhaps one of the least likely. More tender even than flesh, paper rips, tears, burns, crumbles. Yet that scrap from Charlie had survived.

After I went home from the gallery I showed Schiap's telegram to Otto. Otto went to the old bureau we used as a desk and took out the telegram from Charlie, saved all those years. I had saved as much of him as I could.

"You should go," Otto said. "You need a vacation. And Charlie would have wanted you to, I think." His sleeves were rolled up, and his hands, those beautiful pianist's hands, were covered with soap suds from the kitchen sink. We had been married six years by then, as soon as Otto's paperwork was cleared and he was allowed to travel again. I was working hard, about to have my first one-woman show in the Rosenberg Gallery. Otto was working long hours teaching piano and playing in jazz clubs in the evening. I had sold the large apartment in the brownstone and Otto and I had moved downtown, to a small apartment on Bleecker Street, where our neighbors were artists and musicians and poets and people who, if they thought anything of Otto's German accent, kept it to themselves.

Our building was short and squat, and when we stood in front of the window, his head resting on top of mine, his arms around me, there was no sense of flight, as there had been at the window in Montmartre, but more of rootedness, like our feet could sink into the floor and we would grow branches and leaves in all the primary colors and the rainbow that forms from them.

We were busy those years after the war, building new lives on top of the older destructions. Every once in a while, in a rare free moment, I would read a fashion magazine, looking for word of Schiap. She was rarely mentioned anymore. Coco was mentioned sometimes, but fashion now was mostly Christian Dior and the New Look, the long, full skirts and pinched waists and jackets so tight that women could barely move their arms. I thought of Schiap's dresses, feminine but whimsical, close to the body but easy to move in.

Schiap, fighting back against the new styles, surrendering to the need for less expensive clothing after the war, had opened a branch of her company on Seventh Avenue in New York, selling mass-produced suits and dresses. The jackets were short and had pockets that looked like camera cases; the fur linings and trimmings were dyed bright colors; the coats were shaped like tents and the lingerie was accented with shocking pink.

The styles were too bizarre for a generation of women who had survived war and loss and deprivation. The Profile hat, black felt cut into the shape of the wearer's own profile and worn like a mask across half the face, was thought a joke, not a work of art. Sunglasses made of straw and dresses with armholes that fell all the way to the waist were openly laughed at. Whimsy had been possible before the war; after, we were all more serious.

Times had changed. Schiap hadn't, at least not enough.

"You go," Otto said. "I don't want to go back to Europe. I'll stay here with Charlie." We had named our son after my brother. Charlie, little Charlie, was five, and as much as I loved Otto, I hadn't known the full force of love, its complete spectrum, until I had held him in my arms.

"Just for a week," I said. "You'll be okay without me?"

"We'll have ice cream every night," Otto said.

"Maybe someone will know what happened to Ania." In all those years, I hadn't heard a word from or about Ania, after the news of her arrest. So many people had been lost in the war. Ania, like Charlie, was one of the people I thought of late at night, when it seemed everyone was sleeping but me.

I flew for the first time, crossing the ocean in hours instead of days, as we had during the steamer ship crossings. In the Paris airport, as in New York, the women of fashion were all dressed in the New Look, with immense skirts that took up the entire sidewalk, and tiny brimmed hats with veils and flowers. White gloves. High heels.

After going through customs at Orly, I took a cab straight to Saint-Germain-des-Prés and the Café les Deux Magots.

It was a cold December day, unlike the lovely June day when I met Charlie in Paris, and I was the only customer sitting outside. I had looked quickly indoors to make sure the two Chinese figures were still there, keeping watch—they were—and then decided to sit outside, remembering the day when Charlie had pulled up to the curb in Ania's blue Isotta.

I ordered a Pernod and closed my eyes, imagining myself as I had been those years before, a young widow not knowing how to move forward, feeling guilty and ecstatic at the same time for being in Paris, waiting for Charlie to arrive. Behind my closed eyelids I saw my brother, the baby-blue automobile, the beautiful Ania.

"Another Pernod, madame?"

Could it be the same waiter, older, heavier but with that same knowing look in his eye?

I still hadn't finished the first. Had I really drunk three of these, the day I waited for Charlie?

"No, thanks," I said. I needed to keep my wits about me, and my head already felt detached from my body; the world was whirling. Desynchronosis, Otto, who had flown back from Germany six years before, had warned me. Caused by traveling too quickly from west to east, or vice versa, a word invented after people began flying rather than traveling by steamship. My body thought it was still in New York, still sound asleep in the middle of the night.

Even with my head spinning, though, even with the changes caused by the war, Paris was Paris. The city of light, of color. There were more cars, newer models, and the pace seemed faster and noisier, just like in New York. No more donkeys pulling vegetable carts.

I left the drink half-finished and walked along the pewter Seine, trying to clear my head, before going to my hotel. At Otto's suggestion, I was splurging on a room at the Ritz this time, not Oscar Wilde's favorite little hotel on the Left Bank. A cold wind blew off the river, and I huddled deeply into my coat, turning up the collar.

As I walked I tried to imagine seeing the Wehrmacht marching down the Champs-Élysées, the swastika flying in the Place de la Concorde, the tanks battling in the Luxembourg Gardens, seeing what I had not been there to see. There was plenty left that didn't have to be imagined about the occupation of Paris, the bullet holes pockmarking the buildings lining the Boulevard Saint-Michel, splotches of paint covering anti-Nazi graffiti on doors.

Paris was still recovering from the war, and would be for a long while. Lights were dimmer, restaurant portions smaller. But it was still Paris, would always be Paris, with bare chestnut and plane trees lining the boulevards, pigeons cooing on the cobbles, the smell of baking bread and coffee filtering out from cafés and bakeries, the Eiffel Tower looming in the distance.

When I crossed the Place Vendôme I almost covered my eyes, the memories were coming so fast. Barely looking, I went through the hotel's purposely small lobby and checked in quickly, thinking that I needed to get to a bed before I collapsed.

"Yes?" the porter asked, unlocking the door for me. "Is the room to your satisfaction?"

"It's fine," I said. "Better than fine. Grand." I tipped him, unbuttoned my coat, and fell onto the bed.

I woke up four hours later, refreshed but my head still feeling as if it were stuffed with cotton. Time, I told myself. Time to go see Schiap.

I dressed carefully in a new suit bought for the trip, a dark blue wool with a semifull gathered skirt and fitted jacket. I wore black shoes, black gloves, black hat. *How boring*, I thought, studying myself in the mirror, longing for the long turquoise gloves, the pink-and-gray-striped high-heeled boots, the jackets heavy with sequined embroidery, that Schiap had shown before the war. *Quoth the raven*, I thought. The world had become a more serious place.

The Boutique Fantastique on the Place Vendôme was doing only lackluster business when I arrived. The doors and windowsills had been newly painted and the shop gleamed, but the customers, women in their huge skirts and tight jackets, with dazed-looking men following close behind, wandered from display to display, case to case, frowning.

"Isn't this too strange?" I heard one woman quip to another as they examined a jacket of shocking pink with black beaded embroidery.

"Is that a bustle?" her friend asked in disbelief.

I went up the stairs, ignoring the salesgirl who offered to help me. "I know my way," I said. "I've been here before."

"My dear." Schiap rose from her desk to greet me, after I had knocked on that familiar wooden door to her office.

We stood and stared at each other for a long time, remembering.

The first time I had seen her, I'd been with Charlie, and Schiap came rushing into her boutique, her arms full of fabric samples. All the *vendeuses* had snapped to attention but Schiap had ignored the other customers and gone straight to Ania. Ania, whose husband promptly paid all her bills, a couturier's delight.

Schiap, now sixty-four, seemed even tinier than she had that day, despite her high-heeled shoes. She didn't slump—no woman of fashion would let her posture dissolve into lazy rounded shoulders or curled spines—but she looked as if time itself were wearing her away, days and years become waves that diminish the shores that are our bodies. Her dark hair had some silver in it; her heavy-lidded black eyes were not as bright. She wore her pearls doubled around her throat, not around her wrist, as she once had. Like me, she was dressed in dark colors.

"You wanted to see me?" I asked. Schiap laughed. It was if I had been away for the weekend, not for years.

"Yes, my dear. You've heard, haven't you, that I'm going out of business. Bankrupt. Retiring."

I thought at first it was one of her jokes. But she had stopped laughing.

"No," I said. "I hadn't heard. I don't follow the fashion news anymore. Why a telegram? I thought something awful had happened. You could have called!"

"You know I hate the phone. And if I called, you would have had a choice. You wouldn't have come, would you?"

"No," I admitted. "I'm busy. I'm having a show. My first one-person exhibit."

"You were about to be in a show when you left Paris, as I recall. Congratulations. But come. You must have first choice before the vultures arrive for the pickings."

"I can't believe you are closing down," I said. "Impossible."

"All too possible. And necessary. I'm bleeding out money and need to close. I thought you might want to take some things back with you."

The great Elsa Schiaparelli, Coco Chanel's most formidable rival, was calling it quits.

I went to the window and looked out at the Place Vendôme, at the huge column with Napoleon standing on top. He had been a kind of patron saint for her. She would share his fate. Exile, not from France or Paris but from the center of the fashion world, the Place Vendôme.

"He looks better without those sandbags all around him, doesn't he?" Schiap asked.

"Much better. How is Gogo?" I asked. "And her babies?" By then, Gogo had two daughters, Marisa and Berry. I didn't see her often in New York anymore . . . the distance between us that started during the war continued. She had her life and I had mine, and we met only three times a year, for a Christmas brunch and on our birthdays.

"Well. And the babies are beautiful, of course. And you are married, with a baby of your own, she tells me."

"A good marriage. To a good man," I said. "You met him. Otto, the driver."

"The German. That can't have been easy. Here, you would have been called a collaborator and had your head shaven, carrying on with him like that."

"He was the one that got me, and Gogo, out of Paris in time."

"Well, give him my regards."

"You know, Elsa . . ." Why had I done that, switched from Schiap to Elsa? Just to remind myself how different things were, as if I didn't live the difference, the change, with every breath. "Elsa, I keep expecting Bettina to come charging in and yell at me for being late with a display painting."

Elsa laughed. "She's still around. We get together once in a while. Did you know her husband was the ambassador of Vichy to the Soviet

Union? After the war he was tried as a collaborator but acquitted." Elsa sighed and lit a cigarette. "So many people were put on trial."

A heavy silence fell around us as we both realized, tried to accustom ourselves to, the fact that now, now she was closing business. Paris without Schiaparelli. Incredible. But bankrupt is bankrupt.

"I loved that little cabinet." I pointed at the built-in storage Schiap had for her buttons and trimmings, dozens of little drawers, all carefully labeled. "It was like a treasure chest."

"Almost as good as a trunk in the attic," Elsa agreed. "But come, I'll show you Elsa Schiaparelli's last collection."

"Truly the last?"

Schiap grinned. "I have built a house in Tunisia with the most comfortable hammock and view of the sea," she said. "I want to catch up on my reading. And I will spend time with Gogo and my grandchildren."

Schiap showed me around the salon as if it were the first time, the downstairs boutique where gloves and sweaters and handbags were sold, the upstairs showing room and fitting rooms. The last collection she had titled "Fluid Line," and it was just that . . . dresses with lines and materials fluid as water, elegant pieces that would be easy to wear, seductive to the viewer, and always with a touch of humor to them.

She gave me one of the dresses, a slender orange gown with a bustle attached. "You won't have time to have it fitted here," she said. "Take it home to your tailor."

"Of course," I said, not admitting that in New York I didn't have a tailor, in New York I only wore ready-to-wear. I would find a tailor, if just for this one dress.

"Do you ever hear from Ania?" I asked, hoping.

"No. Haven't seen her since the war, since before she was arrested."

"I wondered if she'd been released or . . ." I couldn't finish the sentence.

As we passed through the shop, Schiap touched everything with her fingertips, as if saying farewell. She was.

"Have you noticed," she asked, "all the new designers—they're men, aren't they? I think an era is ending."

She grew fierce. "I will pay every penny I owe the creditors," she said. "The perfumes still sell. I will finish with honor. And what else do you do, there in New York? You must have a very busy life, but it can't be all work, all changing nappies."

"I do volunteer work with a new organization called the March of Dimes. We raise money for children with infantile paralysis, and for research. Our fund-raiser this spring will be a fashion show. All the top models have agreed to be there, and many designers . . ." My voice trailed off.

"Not me. I will be in my hammock. But this is a good thing you do. When I think of how little Gogo suffered . . ." Her voice trailed off.

We stood at the window, looking out at the Place Vendôme, and the column with Napoleon posed on top, once again being harassed by pigeons, but there were no sandbags at the base. "When I am in New York, I'll call," Schiap said. I knew she wouldn't.

"Come over for supper," I said, playing the game. "I'll make spaghetti. I remember your recipe."

She took my hand and gripped it tightly. "Courage," she said both to me and herself. "Napoleon . . ."

"And all his little soldiers." It was the best way to tell her I would never forget her. She had been a friend, a good friend, and at moments had filled some of the empty places my mother's death had left.

On the way out the door, she called over her shoulder, as if casually, "Stop in and say hello to Coco. She's back in Paris. Returned, finally, from Switzerland. And somewhat lonely, I imagine. Show her the evening gown I gave you. She'll die of jealousy. Oh, and something else. Wait a minute."

She disappeared back into her office and came out holding a coat.

The raincoat I'd been wearing the last time I had seen Ania. She still had it.

"You asked about this the day you left, remember? I thought it had been given away, but there it was, in the closet. Do you still want it? I don't see why, it's old, very out of fashion."

I took it from Elsa and checked the pocket. The torn corner of paper was still there. An address where I could contact her. The ink had faded with time, and when I unfolded the paper it crumpled where the crease had been. But it was still readable.

From Schiap's Boutique to Coco's reopened showroom on rue Cambon was just a matter of steps. It was growing dark in the way of winter afternoons, the sky turning from pearly gray to blue shot with stars. Electric lights streamed from the windows of 31 rue Cambon, where the seamstresses and fitters were still working. Coco would still be there, too. She worked longer hours than any of them, I remembered. When I sent my name up to her, one of the *vendeuses* showed me up that famous and familiar mirrored staircase to Coco's private apartments.

"Look at how that coat fits!" was the first thing she said to me. "I've told you, a garment must fit perfectly in the shoulders or it won't fit anywhere."

Coco Chanel was seventy-one years old that winter. She had just come out of a fourteen-year retirement; she had survived accusations of treason, the deaths of friends and lovers, a war, exile. It showed in her face but not in her posture or her gestures. She moved like a young girl, stood tall and straight when she rose from her beige sofa to offer me a kiss on both cheeks.

"You have a bag from Schiaparelli," was the second thing Coco said.

"Yes. I have just been to see her."

We sat on the beige sofa, and Coco rang a little bell for her maid to bring us cocktails. Coco's famous coromandel screens were back in place; the walls were lined with books. It could almost have been before the war, the rooms looked so much the same. But it wasn't. The rooms hadn't been occupied or looted during the war years, but there was a sense of desolation anyway, that boot scuff on the door where someone had kicked it, the tarnish on the unpolished silver candle holders.

"How is Schiaparelli? I heard she is closing her business."

I listened hard, listened for gloating and satisfaction, but Coco had trained her voice to a steady neutrality.

"She's fine. Happy in fact, looking forward to time with her grandchildren, time in the hammock."

"Ha!" Coco snorted. There it was. The old competition surfacing, the old hostility.

"Do you ever wish you'd had children, grandchildren?" I asked Coco. It was a rude question to ask a Frenchwoman. They are more private than Americans. But my curiosity got the better of me. I tried to imagine my life without little Charlie, and could not.

"I came from a large family. A large, unhappy family," Coco said. "I don't see that having children would have made me happier. I know that people say that my sister's son was my son. I loved him like one, and that was enough motherhood for me. He almost died, you know. In a Nazi camp. I would never have forgiven myself." She paused to light a cigarette, and her hand was trembling.

She leaned over and rubbed the fabric of my blouse sleeve between her fingers. "Good quality," she said. "It will last. Couture. That was my life, and a good one, too. As for Schiap, you mark my words, she'll be busier than ever, visiting her Hollywood friends, Hepburn and Myrna Loy, vamping it up all over the world. Hammock, my foot."

"What about you?"

"I won't lie. I can't, can I? Schiap will already have told you the gossip. My new collection was not well received. Remember how people used to linger after a showing? Stay behind and meet the designer, gossip, drink champagne. They fled. Nothing to say. I was so furious I wanted to burn the salon."

I remembered then what Coco had told me once, years before, about her childhood, how she had hated the orphanage so much she had wanted to burn it down.

"Surely they couldn't have hated everything in the collection," I said.

"There are still hard feelings from the war, and all of these new young men are climbing up. Dior. Givenchy. They'll never dress women the way we dressed them, never understand how a woman's body is supposed to move. Corsets! They are designing corsets again. There was one suit they liked, though."

Coco brushed back hair that looked a little too black. "Tidy little tweed, with straight skirt and jacket trimmed with braid. I think that will take off. That will restore me. Meanwhile . . ." She stopped and sipped delicately at her martini. "Women will want that suit. I'll give those new designers a run for their money."

I could hear the beginning of a new rivalry. Coco was coming back to life. "I'll be bigger than ever," she said. "Meanwhile, I have sold La Pausa to pay my bills, to keep going. It was necessary. And there were too many memories there, weren't there?"

La Pausa. My first night with Otto, that soft Provençal air, the stars overhead.

"You had von Dincklage as a guest," I said.

"Spatz. Those years are over. No more lovers for me, I think. Time to give up that game. And you had a guest as well, didn't you?"

The silences I had shared with Schiap had been nostalgic, the kind of pause that happens just before a door gently closes. The silence I fell into with Coco was harder and embarrassing. With Schiap there had been too much to say. With Coco, too little. She was a woman who did not easily trust, and without trust friendship is a more fragile thing.

"You were a good-looking couple, you and Otto. Even Spatz thought so." Coco smiled conspiratorially over her martini glass.

"We married, you know. After the war. We have a son."

"No! Well! Congratulations, then. I must give you something to remember me by, before you leave. I bet you named your boy Charlie, didn't you? That brother of yours. One of the most beautiful men I'd ever seen. No wonder Ania fell for him. Poor Ania. Spatz was devastated when they arrested her."

"I thought he was going to keep her safe. Wasn't that the plan, wasn't that the deal?"

Coco flinched. Affairs always have a touch of business arrangement to them, or at least of "understandings," but such arrangements were rarely spoken out loud.

"She herself made that impossible, when she began carrying messages. The Gestapo had her name; there was nothing Spatz could do for her, once she was arrested. After the war, they were going to accuse me of being a collaborator, you know. But Winston made a phone call and kept his old friend out of prison. It pays to have friends in high places."

I remembered the room at La Pausa, filled with Churchill's favorite history books.

A knock on the door, her assistant standing there. "The buyer from the New York perfume branch is on the line," she said. "Can you speak with him?"

I stood. "Thanks for the drink. I won't keep you. I just wanted to say hello. I expect it will be a while before I'm back in Paris."

Coco rose, too. "Thank you for coming. And do have that coat tailored. Before you go, here." She picked up her silver cigarette case from the coffee table. "A little souvenir." She put it in my hands and folded my fingers over it. "Remember me."

A maid had already helped me into my coat and opened the door into the mirrored hallway when Coco said, "It was an accident. That night at the Durst ball."

No, it wasn't, I thought. It had been a prophecy of the war to come, where so many had been hurt or killed. We had all been danced into the flames.

"I run into Schiap once in a while," Coco said. "She looks well, I think. We even had a drink together, the other day. Imagine that."

"I bet that was an interesting conversation."

Coco laughed. "In fact, it was. We are not as different as you might think. We both believe in beauty and elegance. In strong women who know their own minds. No one will look good in her clothes if she doesn't walk as if she owns the world. Remember that, Lily. It's ours, all the beauty we want, if we want it hard enough."

And then she did something totally unexpected. She hugged me, tightly, affectionately. I hugged her back.

The next morning I gave Ania's scrap of paper to a taxi driver and we went out past the Bois de Boulogne, to Neuilly-sur-Seine, to a little street looking onto the river and a stone house with a wooden door and a flower box filled with winter-browned geraniums.

A woman came out the front door to bring in a milk bottle that had been left on the step. When she bent, her white-blond hair fell over her face. My heart stopped. Ania?

I called her name. "Ania!" and she looked up. This girl was too young to be my friend, but she looked so much like her, I already knew what she would say. It was Katya, Ania's daughter.

"Ania was my mother." She frowned. "Do I know you?"

She was aloof in the way the Parisians often are, needing to know a little more before they offer a smile, a handshake. She came to the gate to see me more closely. Ania had been slightly nearsighted as well.

"No. You don't know me. But I knew your mother. Before the war."

"Oh. Well. Did you? You'd better come in, then. It's cold out here."

She made tea for me in the little kitchen of the stone house, and

when she poured, she said, "We don't have a lot of time. I have to begin
my shift at the hospital at noon."

Her voice was Ania's, her movements, her height.

"How did you know my mother?"

"My brother was in love with her. Before the war. And I knew her.
We used to meet for drinks at the Ritz."

Katya made a face, disapproving. "The Ritz. I couldn't afford that
if I gave up eating for a month. But that was *Maman*. Before the war.
I remember the clothes she used to wear. I still have some, packed away
in the attic. Much good they do me. Nurses don't wear sable."

She laughed. Ania's laugh.

"What happened to her?" I asked.

"You don't know? Died in a camp." Silence. The girl—she was
about twenty-one, I estimated—pushed away her teacup. "What happened to your brother?"

"Died. Guadalcanal."

"I'm sorry."

"Me, too."

A door closed in my imagination. Charlie and Ania were on the
other side of it, both gone from me.

The kitchen, with its big tiled stove and bunches of dried herbs
hanging from the rafters, was pleasant but I couldn't imagine Ania in
such a rustic place. Ania of the Ritz.

"Did your mother live here?"

"Only on weekends. I lived here with my father. It was grander,
then. He owned the meadow on the side, too, but I've had to sell it. We
had gardens, a pony. He's dead now. Didn't survive the war."

Katya sighed and folded her arms over her chest. "They didn't get
along, my mother and father. They lived separately, most of the time."
The girl sniffed in a combination of disdain and disappointment, exactly the way Ania had when something upset her.

"*Maman* had lovers, I know. A German officer was one of them.

Von Dincklage. I met him once. He brought me a doll, and Mummy said he would be her umbrella during the storm. I laughed, thinking of that tall, skinny man as an umbrella. Later, I understood what she meant, except he wasn't. He didn't protect her. She was arrested. I came home from school one day and my father told me she was gone. They took her away, and she never came back."

"I'm so very sorry." The words are useless, meaningless. Tragedy sometimes defies our ability to describe it, to respond to it. After VE Day, when the photos of the camps were being published for the first time, I had looked at them and wept for Ania.

The girl plucked at a loose thread on her sleeve. "I've sold the furs, got a good price for them. But the gowns. They still have her perfume on them. Was your brother named Charles or something like that?"

"Charlie."

"She told me about him. She didn't talk that much about her friends, but she talked about him. I was five, and she told me a story about a princess and a prince, named Charlie. I think she was in love with him."

"I'd better let you get ready for work," I said. "Thanks for the tea."

The taxi was still waiting for me, clouds of blue cigarette smoke floating out of the open window as the driver whistled and fumed. Before I got back in, I stood by the river and watched the sun glint silver on it, the tiny ripples of little fish in the shallows turning the muddy green water to miniature circles of pale violet. I threw in the piece of paper with the address Ania had written fourteen years before and let the Seine carry it away.

From the ashes rises the phoenix. The new from the old. Ania was gone, but her daughter was here, safe.

How she must have suffered, that beautiful woman who drank champagne at the Ritz.

The next day I changed my plane ticket for an earlier flight and I was back on the plane, leaving Paris, going home to Otto, to my son, to the future. Paris was my past. I had spent one afternoon at the Louvre, sitting in front of the reinstalled *Mona Lisa* and saying hello to the other artworks that had been in hiding during the war, now returned to their proper places, and there was nothing more for me to do in Paris.

I had an orange bustled Schiaparelli gown in my suitcase and it would be a struggle, but I would find some place, some time, to wear it, in honor of my friends, in remembrance of Charlie and Ania.

I left Coco and Schiap and Ania's daughter, and all the colors of Paris, the reds and yellows and blues, the primaries from which all other colors emerge in grief and joy.

When I was a child, one of my favorite pieces of clothing was a white cotton shirt with French words written all over it. I didn't know it then, but many decades before, an Italian woman living in Paris had designed the prototype for that newsprint fabric.

Later, as I read more about Elsa Schiaparelli, I discovered that she was responsible for some of my most whimsical fashion choices: turbans, roomy skirts with huge pockets, shoulder pads, a leopard-print coat, folk embroidery, funky buttons, a little evening bag of meshed gunmetal as a kind of "make love, not war" statement, even a see-through blouse, though mine had strategic double layers for the pockets. They all originated as Schiaparelli designs that took up permanent residence in the fashion world, filtering all the way down, through the decades, to small-town girls like me who bought their clothing in department stores, off the rack.

The thirties was a golden age of couture, and it was dominated by one city: Paris, and that city was dominated by two women: Coco Chanel and Elsa Schiaparelli. Everyone has heard of Coco; too few have heard of Schiap, as she called herself (pronounced *scape* with a hard *sch*, as in *school*). Unlike Coco, whose rough, deprived childhood is legendary,

Schiap was born into wealth, grew up surrounded by books and art and educated people. Yet as soon as she could, she ran away, first to New York and then to Paris, and chose her own path, her own life, one of hard work, occasional hard knocks, and more than a little heartache.

It was inevitable that she and Coco would become lifelong rivals in that city, in that industry.

One of the central scenes in this novel, that of Coco dancing Schiap into a flaming candelabra, is based on an actual event. That was the passion of their rivalry. The polarity of their political beliefs, as portrayed in my novel, is based on fact. They were both suspected of collaboration with the enemy and spying.

Did they help the Germans? Schiap traveled freely, made and maintained important connections, and, during the war, had many wealthy Germans among her clients. However, in her early years, thanks probably to the influence of the husband she loved, and who had abandoned her, she had been a known Bolshevist and political activist. In Paris she joined an antifascist group and during the war she fought to keep the fashion industry in Paris, though Hitler wanted it moved to Berlin.

Coco Chanel did have an affair with von Dincklage and spent most of the war years holed up with the head of Nazi propaganda and other German officials at the Ritz. Even if she wasn't a spy actively working for the Germans (and there are those who say she was), she was a collaborator or, as they described such women, a "horizontal collaborator." She was far from alone in that category; as soon as the Germans marched out of Paris, thousands of Frenchmen and -women were charged with, or at least accused of, collaborating. There's a good chance that if Winston Churchill hadn't sent a well-timed letter, Coco might have ended up in prison. But he did, and she didn't, and after the war her reputation grew, rather than diminished.

Coco's war years are described in Hal Vaughan's book *Sleeping with the Enemy: Coco Chanel's Secret War*, and there are several excellent biographies about her, including Lisa Chaney's *Coco Chanel: An*

Intimate Life, Rhonda Garelick's *Mademoiselle: Coco Chanel and the Pulse of History*, and Justine Picardie's *Coco Chanel: The Legend and the Life*. I particularly recommend Paul Morand's *The Allure of Chanel* (with illustrations by Karl Lagerfeld), based on his conversations with Coco. It's Coco's life, as told by Coco, and while it may not be completely accurate, it's fascinating reading.

There are, sadly, few biographies of Elsa Schiaparelli, but Meryle Secrest's fabulous *Elsa Schiaparelli* is about as complete as a biography can be, and Palmer White, who was a friend of Elsa's daughter, Gogo, has also written a great, and wonderfully illustrated, biography of Schiaparelli. Elsa's granddaughter Marisa Schiaparelli Berenson published the wonderfully intimate *Elsa Schiaparelli's Private Album*, and Elsa also wrote her own autobiography, *Shocking Life*.

The series *Vogue on* has published *Vogue on Coco Chanel* and *Vogue on Elsa Schiaparelli*, two little volumes that trace both the lives and the artistry of the women.

The Museum of Art in Philadelphia contains several Schiaparelli costumes and put up a show called *Shocking!: The Art and Fashion of Elsa Schiaparelli* some years ago. An important book about the exhibit, by the same name and authored by Dilys E. Blum, is still available. The Metropolitan Museum of Art in New York also includes some Schiaparelli designs and put up their own exhibit and book, *Schiaparelli & Prada*, comparing the two designers and the conversations and parallels in their work.

Other invaluable texts for this story include *My Grandfather's Gallery: A Family Memoir of Art and War*, by Anne Sinclair, granddaughter of Paul Rosenberg; Samuel Marx's *Queen of the Ritz* about Blanche Auzello, who ran the great hotel with her husband during the thirties; *The Hotel on Place Vendôme*, by Tilar J. Mazzeo; *Over Here!: New York City During World War II*, by Lorraine B. Diehl; Charlie Scheips's *Elsie de Wolfe's Paris: Frivolity Before the Storm*; and *Fireworks at Dusk: Paris in the Thirties*, by Olivier Bernier.

I also recommend, for pleasure as well as research, *Théâtre de la Mode: Fashion Dolls: The Survival of Haute Couture*, based on a 1945 traveling exhibit of couture-dressed dolls organized by the Chambre Syndicale de la Couture to jump-start the fashion industry at the end of the war.

I'm sure I've left someone or something out; if so, please accept my apologies. Keeping order and track of five years of reading and research can be like trying to find all the pins on the floor.

Both Coco and Schiap survived the war, but the world changed, grew more serious and less playful. Schiap's couture house went into decline and then bankruptcy. And while Schiap had a pleasant and relaxing time in that hammock in Tunisia, I'm sure she missed the hustle of collection week, the thrill of a new design, a new concept appearing in her imagination. She died in her sleep, in 1973, at age eighty-three. She died not knowing, thankfully, that one of her beloved grandchildren, Gogo's daughter Berry, would die in one of the planes that crashed into the World Trade Center on 9/11.

Coco died in Paris, in 1971, at the grand age of eighty-seven.

I doubt Schiap ever forgot that fashion and politics are inextricably linked. What we wear gives messages about our beliefs, our hopes, our fears, from the everyday blue jeans of rebellious adolescence to the power suits women felt necessary in the 1970s. And when our clothing choices are made for us by others, part of our identity is threatened, some of our freedom removed.

At the end of *Shocking Life* Elsa Schiaparelli lists twelve commandments for women, and number five is my favorite: "Ninety percent [of women] are afraid of being conspicuous and of what people will say. So they buy a grey suit. They should dare to be different." Her last commandment was to the point: "And she should pay her bills."

ACKNOWLEDGMENTS

Many thanks to the people at Berkley who supported *The Last Collection* and guided it from early draft to finished novel and beyond: my great editor, Danielle Perez, who encouraged me to leaps and risks that strengthened the story, Jenn Snyder, Sarah Blumenstock, Michelle Kasper, Jin Yu, Jessica Mangicaro, Lauren Burnstein, Diana Franco, Rita Frangie, Claire Zion, Craig Burke, Jeanne-Marie Hudson, Christine Ball, and Ivan Held. Special thanks to Ellen Edwards, who began this journey with me; my agent, Kevan Lyon; and fellow writer Nancy Holzner, for her support and insights.

THE
LAST COLLECTION

• • •

JEANNE MACKIN

QUESTIONS FOR DISCUSSION

1. At the heart of this novel is this question: how do we continue to live fulfilling private lives in a society that is doing its best to divide us, politically and culturally? Pre–World War II Paris was full of dichotomies, the most obvious being the choice between communism and fascism. What other divisions do you see in this story? Do you see parallels to today?

2. When Lily fell in love with Otto, she realized that she was, in fact, falling in love with a man who would be fighting against her own country, perhaps even her own brother. How did she make her peace with this terrible choice?

3. Coco Chanel and Elsa Schiaparelli disagreed on what patriotism required of them during the German occupation of Paris. Chanel decided to close her couture salon and lay off her workers rather than sell her clothes to the occupying Germans. Schiap chose to keep her salon and to continue to pay as many of her workers as possible, even though it meant welcoming German officers into the shop. Which decision would you have made and why?

4. The narrator, Lily, had strong emotional reactions to different colors. Lilies are often associated with the color white, which is the sum of all color wavelengths, not, as some people think, the absence of all color. (If you shine the primary colors of red, blue, and yellow

on a white paper, you'll see white where the colors overlap.) What influence did the love of color have on Lily?

5. What are your emotional responses to color? Do you have a favorite color that always lightens your mood? Is there a color you try to avoid? What events in your life might have helped form those preferences?

6. There were many differences between Chanel and Schiaparelli, some reinforced by their rivalry and animosity toward each other. Chanel, for instance, insisted that as a couturier she was a craftswoman, while Schiap insisted that couturiers were artists. Do you think couture fashion is art? Have you visited a museum where clothing was being exhibited, and what did you think of the exhibit?

7. Schiap's daughter, Gogo, came down with polio just when Schiap, abandoned by her husband, had to learn how to work and support herself and her daughter. She had to work long hours and spent days, even weeks, away from her child when Gogo needed her the most. How do you think this affected their relationship?

8. Why do you think Chanel invented a story about being educated in a convent rather than admitting to having been raised in an orphanage after her mother died and her father abandoned the family?

9. If you could wear clothing from any time or any place, what would you choose?

10. When Lily was in a period of great grief, she stopped caring about her appearance. What do you think is the relationship between clothes and our emotions?

11. The novel is structured in three sections, one for each primary color. How does the action in each section reflect Lily's emotional response to that particular color?

12. There are several love stories in this novel. Which one affected you the most? Why?

Jeanne Mackin is the author of several historical novels, including *The Beautiful American*. She taught in the MFA program at Goddard College and has worked as a journalist for several publications and as a university research and science writer. She was the recipient of a creative writing fellowship from the American Antiquarian Society, and her journalism has won awards from the Council for Advancement and Support of Education. She lives with her husband in upstate New York and is working on her next novel.

CONNECT ONLINE

JeanneMackin.com

🅕 JeanneMackinAuthor

🐦 JeanneMackin1

📷 JeanneMackinAuthor